Laurent Mauvignier's debut *...om a eux* (*Far from Them*), a poignant monologue about a young man's suicide, was published in 1999. *In the Crowd* was published to huge acclaim in France in 2006, and was his first novel to be translated.

LAURENT MAUVIGNIER

In the Crowd

Translated from the French
by Shaun Whiteside

faber and faber

First published under the title *Dans La Foule*
© 2006 by Les Editions de Minuit
7, rue Bernard Palissy, 75006 Paris
First published in the UK in 2008
by Faber and Faber Limited
Bloomsbury House, 74–77 Great Russell Street,
London WC1B 3DA
This paperback edition first published in 2009

Typeset by Faber and Faber Limited
Printed in England by CPI Bookmarque, Croydon, Surrey

A CIP record for this book is available from the British Library

Liberté • Égalité • Fraternité
RÉPUBLIQUE FRANÇAISE

This book is supported by the French Ministry of Foreign
Affairs as part of the Burgess programme run by the
Cultural Department of the French Embassy in London
(www.frenchbooknews.com)

ISBN 978–0–571–23637–4

2 4 6 8 10 9 7 5 3 1

In the Crowd

I

We could never have imagined, Tonino and me, what was going to happen – Paris above our heads and us with no intention of stopping there. We slipped beneath Paris and the metro carriages headed towards the Gare du Nord. What we didn't say to ourselves, Tonino and me, was hang on, why don't we stop anyway and watch the time and money we haven't got slipping through our fingers? No, we didn't stop, we headed on like that to Belgium, without looking at France and the time we were leaving behind us, without waiting for Tonino to wave his hands around, broad the way you'd imagine the hands of a boxer or a scrapyard bone collector, shovel-shaped, square, strong, promising great times ahead.

Tonino liked to use his hands in mock threat – go fuck your sister! he used to mutter when he'd had a few, before promising whoever it was dawdling too long in front of him to give him a taste of his blade. I can't remember ever hearing him use a word other than that one, *blade* – a threat mimed with a broad and agile motion, never an actual knife, just that movement, supposed to enlighten anyone who happened to pass within range. But we had too much of a laugh in the bars not to see that it would all end drenched in beer rather than blood: ah, yes, Tonino old pal, you're pissed as a parrot again! And more often than not he'd pass right out, snoring sometimes, four or five in the morning, against the fat, white breasts of a redhead whose friend had abandoned her at the bar, or most often in the arms of that old mate of his, that one who was the spit of Lucky Luke.

What was his name again? Hang on, I can't remember what he was called . . . I just know that sometimes those evenings were like rubbing shoulders with the devil. We would end up yelling at each other at the tops of our voices, we gave it all we'd got as long as enough people were watching, and often one of Tonino's big locks of curly hair would get caught between the brown buttons of that mustard-coloured coat that I found one evening on the way home, folded over a dustbin next to the station. It was a shortcut I used to take on nights when we fetched up down the nick, which happened regularly because I'm afraid we had a few bad habits, pissing on the begonias outside the town hall, digging up the flowerbeds with our heels – I can still hear us, Place de la Mairie, no, no, officer, I swear, I promise, I just wanted to dig up some old flowers for my young mother with my heels, that's enough, you can tell me all about it down at the station.

And those U2 and Prince badges that I used to patch up the coat where, on the left-hand side, Tonino had torn it one night when we'd still been vaguely grabbing at each other – I'd yelled, you dirty bugger! and that had made him laugh. He'd hunched his shoulders chuckling, oh, fuck, and there was I, furious, with my ochre-brown coat that I'd found folded nicely, there it was, torn. So I found some badges to fix it up. Why am I talking about that? Why not. At least talking about the winter and those days back then, if it stirs anything it's joy, nostalgia, whatever you like,

I don't give a toss.

But talking about the sun, still talking about that sun and the way we used to slap a hand on our biceps and give it the fuck-off gesture, I have to say it doesn't tempt me. The sun, that day, I think to myself, I'm not sure it's a good idea to talk about it, I'm not sure I really want to.

It would have been better if we hadn't got on the train. But there you go. Rather than staying there, not moving, I got on the train and that day I was one of those who left Liverpool and travelled all the way to Belgium, to Brussels. I lied in my own way, putting on a fake smile and secretly promising myself I would find something in my own lies to console and reassure me. Because to tell the truth I was thinking that I didn't want to leave Liverpool that day. I was thinking that I'd be no worse off at home watching the match with Elsie, rather than taking the train and coming all the way to Brussels. It wasn't as if I was dying to go . . . no. It was just that they wanted me to come with them . . . OK, put it this way, Dad wanted all three of us to go to see the match.

So off we went together.

The three brothers. We met the others at the station. Especially Doug's friends, who laughed to see the three Andrewson boys arriving together, at the same time, each with his bag over his shoulder. Except they didn't really laugh at Doug. Of course. Nobody's ever laughed at Doug, not them, not anybody. But Hughie and me, Geoff, little Geoff Andrewson with his gentle voice, too gentle, they thought, and his long hair that they always laughed at because they thought I was too young, too this and too that, and they don't much care for the way I don't laugh at their jokes. So they didn't talk much to me in the train. They laughed with Doug and Hughie. They laughed among themselves, sometimes they laughed with others. But more importantly they started dreaming of the time they were going to have in Brussels, on the night of the match, a bash to shake the foundations of Marble Arch and Buckingham Palace! The kind of parties they don't have any more, inviting all the demons of hell, that's the sort of thing they were talking about. That was what they promised.

I remember, in the train, the impatience and the girls clamping their hands to the tops of their legs; their tight smiles; the skirts they held pressed against their thighs avoiding the invitations and the loaded sniggers of my brothers and their friends. As if they weren't familiar with those shirts and scarves. As if . . . what? I don't know. I've never liked being a supporter as much as they did. I've never been able to believe in it completely. And yet the Reds is a family thing, a myth far more important in my family than the Beatles are for our neighbours, who are forever heading off to the other side of Sefton or the Wirral in search of records and posters – but in our house the Reds had been the tradition passed down from father to sons since I was born in '66, the year they went to the European Cup Final. Even though it was Dortmund who won, our father always told us that was the year the family felt its heart swell and beat like anything, while I, the baby of the family, was told all about Liverpool's first wins, and why I was called Geoff, like Geoff in the team.

Each time the story came round again, both beautiful and ambiguous, never leaving me in peace – after he told it to me I stayed in my room and waited for sleep that never came. When that happened I blamed the smell of fried onions or mint sauce coming up from the kitchen, the footsteps of Pellet, our half-blind old dog, dragging his dirty, knotted fur around, yawning and making deep, burp-like noises (he was called Pellet because when he was born he was no bigger than a ball of paper and his skin already looked all crumpled).

I had to blame somebody, or something. So I blamed the docks or the statue of Eleanor Rigby. Or me. But when he talked about the exploits of Geoff Strong, it was always with deep admiration. With the same wide eyes that he had when he watched a big match, or sometimes when he enjoyed a piece of good news, he would repeat the exploits of Geoff Strong in the semi-final, against Celtic, when he got his leg injury. And I'll never know if it was because of that injury that something bothered me, or if it was because nobody could ever finish that story without adding that Strong had been nicknamed 'the cripple', or that he was only a reserve, and that he would always be a reserve, because he didn't really have a place on the field either as a defender or a midfielder or an attacker, but instead drifted about the pitch as his team required.

My brothers often talked to my father. But because of the age difference separating us (they were a year apart, as opposed to the six years between me and the younger one) I understood nothing, or practically nothing, of their excitement, and was filled with envy. I watched my father talking about McDermott and Case, and my brothers looking at my father as he sat in the living room, eyes round as marbles. They looked at him, and I looked at them. And then there was that voice of his, warming up as he talked about Clemence's unique goal-keeping style, unmatched by anyone these days. He would pull a face and shake his head, saying, no, no, they invented their own style of play, and now the Reds are the best, maybe not in the world, but not far off, either. That's what our father said.

My brothers: one of them was a carpenter, the other a supermarket warehouseman. My father had stopped working, but I remember when I was little he used to stroke my head with his hand when he passed by, greasing my hair with his oily fingers and getting upbraided by my mother because he was just home from the factory where he did something with joints and pulleys (I don't really remember), which left his fingers black as coal and greasy as cod-liver oil.

It was probably because he said he was too old to go that it would have been cruel to turn down the ticket that Doug had found for him. OK, I reckon that of the three tickets that Doug had got hold of, one was for Dad and not for me. I think he'd have liked his father to show some desire to go to Belgium with the two of them that day. But he didn't. He got up from the table, poking around with his tongue in the back of his mouth, as though chewing on an enormous piece of apple crumble. But we all knew by his gloomy expression that he was only fiddling with his hollow tooth. Frowning, worried, he got up and then said that really, at nineteen years of age, the youngest of his sons should at least have seen one big thing in his life.

That was it. He said he'd be proud to know that all three of us were over there. That he'd watch television to try and spot us in the terraces, to hear his sons' voices cheering on the team. I remember my ticket in my hand. I remember holding that magic thing. And the way he looked at me, too, not just them, but me, too, little Geoff. At least my brothers and I would experience that. Maybe one day we'd even talk about it to our own kids, open-mouthed as we told them, listen, I was there! And it would be the first time that all three of us had done anything without our parents. And for me it would be without Elsie. I told myself that she wouldn't hold it against me. And it's true, she didn't hold it against me, not then. She couldn't. Not because I was going with my brothers, but just because we'd heard so often on the radio that it was going to be the match of the century, and that such an opportunity occurs too rarely in life to be passed up.

The match of the century! they said. And if Michel Platini isn't God it's because la Vecchia Signora is nothing but an old Catholic whore, as they say round our way, that's what Tonino said. And I'm saying (impressed) OK, OK, and he's adding with this look of disgust on his face: for once the French have a player who's God! Not a kid who thinks he's God, no, not some megalomaniac, but an incarnation, a true embodiment of magic, God himself descending to earth to teach all those other tossers how to earn their wages. And the French can't be bothered to go and see him, what a shame . . . Well, too bad for them if they're too thick to see what's going on! God playing for us at Juventus, Juventus . . . striped shirts. Platini. Boniek.

And me and Tonino, quivering with fear and excitement, because right till the end we'd been afraid we wouldn't be able to get a seat. It was such an achievement getting hold of tickets, and we did it so quickly, quick and dirty, given how it was done . . . OK, the way we did it wasn't that great. Not so good. A bit off. A bad script, like in a film: you set off two days early to the city where the match of the century's going to be played somewhere, because Platini's going to be playing and Platini's another name for God, and because he's playing it's going to be one of the games of the century. The Father, the Son and the Holy Spirit was Boniek, Platini's best mate, Tonino said, meaning that Boniek and Platini were like him and me, friends, brothers, like us, he said, adding, we may not be gods, but God, I tell you we're going to make one hell of a racket!

Then, because it was serious he called me Jean-François rather than Jeff, which was what he called me the rest of the year, in our rainy old city where we fooled around vaguely studying art history and – more diligently – vaguely feeling up the girlfriends of mates who didn't pay them enough attention. In the town-centre bars, in muddy cellars or furniture warehouses we ate crisps and drank the most godawful plonk that even a town-square drunk wouldn't have touched. We drank it, though. We went on little outings in 2CVs that we borrowed at night from car parks in the shopping centre or the business development zone up behind the station and the sorting office, from nuns (and how were we supposed to know they were nuns, when it's only after you've committed the crime that you take the time to look at the stickers on the windscreen?) who were doubtless unhappy, the next day, that they couldn't go round giving injections to old men who had been shivering since dawn as they waited for their daily jab. And sometimes the cars belonged to soft-faced, long-haired teachers. Caricatures, you'd have thought they'd all found their vocation by ticking boxes: if you're a lethargic wimp and you like corduroy trousers and your glasses have round frames with a mahogany finish, then please sign here. We were going to travel about and visit the parks of the region's châteaux (and it's a very pretty region), a bit like the way we decided to go to Belgium to see the final. Then there's me, always bringing up the rear: the tickets? what are we going to do about tickets? Mind your own business! Tonino replied, sure that truth would be on our side, God's on our side, I'm sure of it, his name's Michel and the stadium is his altar, Halleluiah, old mate!

My brothers kissed our parents and then their wives, who only just forgave them (or pretended to forgive them) for being forced to stay at home and look after the kids. Doug had two: a little one, Martha, who he dreamt of seeing as a future hairdresser or manicurist. Something like that. Because he thought hairdressing was right for a girl. Jobs with style and elegance, for a woman. As for his son, the job didn't matter much, as long as it was something to do with sport. Doug wanted his child to be sporty. He wanted to get him an electric motorbike when he was little, so that he'd develop a taste for racing and rallying. Then one day, when he was bigger, the two of them would go to the Grand Prix at Silverstone and Goodwood. As he waited, the little boy let his round head droop on his mother's angora sweater, asleep on Madge's big bosom. And he didn't seem particularly bothered about the Reds or the motorbike, or the fact that his father was going away. While Madge was getting agitated and wouldn't stop telling Doug to be careful, or at least not to drink too much. Her eyes, their make-up failing to conceal her anxiety at seeing her husband going away without her, smiling to hide the fear she must have felt, knowing Doug and dreading all the things that might happen when he was around. That, she was surely thinking, must justify her insistence that he call home – repeating it over and over again, looking at me, me, the youngest, when Doug had stopped listening to what she was saying a few minutes ago. Yes, Geoff, you're the serious one, go on, you tell him, promise me, remind him, that's the most important thing. To call home. You promise?

She smiled to make everybody happy, and had no more desire to smile than to stand there like that on the footpath with her in-laws, her arms laden with a child heavy with sleep, a saliva bubble at the corners of his lips. She hated all that football business, and couldn't stand her mother's fatalism when she said: what d'you expect, men are like that! Nothing but football, she added, shrugging her shoulders, as if football were only one more sin amongst all the ones men are saddled with, one more woe to add to the misfortunes of the women of Liverpool: that's just how it is, men like football and there's nothing to be done about it. If you're a man it's unhealthy or a bit peculiar not to like football, to know nothing about the tactics of the game, not to know the name of the coach or how his strategy will or won't benefit the club. Because men love football, they love their team and ours, Liverpool, by a stroke of luck, is one of the best, one of the strongest. That was important for all of us. Even me. It really was important. I remember the shouts you heard in the city. Those shouts that pierced through walls: windows shaking at the most trivial penalty. Impossible not to shiver. Even the women liked to shiver with us and hear the city holding its breath for the whole duration of a match, then falling silent in defeat.

You had to hear the city turning in on itself, in its silence, all pride and arrogance humbled, all shame and fury sated. Then you saw people's stupidity and their lack of constraint, their movements. Letting the Guinness flow in the nearest pub or going back to work with an expression of mourning on their faces and another ten years in their gait all of a sudden – just mumbling incomprehensible words, I'm a bit sick, not feeling so great today. They talked only about their victories, on which everyone threw themselves greedily – not that they were particularly rare, or that opportunities to celebrate were few and far between – drinking and chanting. All of a sudden my father loved my mother, my brothers stopped thinking their wives were flabby as jellies, or that they hadn't the first clue how to enjoy themselves. They even stopped thinking of Elsie as too shy and distant, or thinking that she was that serious, rather snooty girl, disdainful of them, they said, with her nights working as a nurse and her days reading books of poetry in two languages. They felt that victory gave my rather bony frame a strength they didn't know I had. In short, they stopped thinking I wasn't like them, with that quiet way of mine, that way I had of not replying or giving my opinion when they hoped I'd join in with slagging off the Ferwells and their two useless sons as we sat at home eating our shepherd's pie, talking about them because they were both working – finally! – the elder one with his big glasses and the other with his half-witted smile, both working behind the counters at the bank. Because neither of them would ever get his hands dirty doing anything but fiddling with dockets and smart-looking banknotes.

I said nothing, because I knew my mother would have liked me to work at a bank counter. Because she thought it would have been good *for me*. Although given what my family thought about people who did that kind of work, I wondered what my mother really meant when she said it would have been good *for me*. But OK. I said nothing. Because I'd have had to say, yeah, they're exactly as you say, and everything is just as you say. And I'm like you. I like your delight when we win a game. I like seeing Dad tensing in front of the telly, when I hear his breath quicken and when, after the match, as the tension subsides but continues to linger in the air, and the table's covered with tins and the ashtray's full, and there's a layer of cloud above our heads, and Pellet who's regurgitated a few chicken bones and bits of dog-food next to his old brown blanket, that endlessly recurring moment, infallible and repeated at will – is the moment when my father clears his throat and opens a can of beer to phone Doug and Hughie so that one after the other they can comment on the dribbling, the beauty of a counter-attack from Rush, the brilliance of a pass from Dalglish. And I like hearing his voice when he talks to himself, all tensed up, legs pressed together, ready to spring in the air. And those insults with which he swallows back his venom, clutching the edge of the armchair, where the scraps of brown leatherette hang together by a miracle, just under his clenched fist. Then there are the wins when we're all at home, I like the illusion it gives, the feeling it'll never stop. And that's also why I was trembling as I came to say goodbye to my parents, upset for leaving Elsie for two days (she'd said she'd agreed to be on duty for the night of the match, then she said: I'll be able to watch the game in the nurses' room, it won't be the first time I've watched the telly in there, hoping that none of the patients ring and standing pressed up against the door with one ear in the corridor and one eye on the telly, I'll be keeping an eye out for you).

And then there was Hughie.

His three children and his wife. Faith didn't like the games. She thought Hughie spent a lot of time watching the game and not enough fixing the windows and the door-hinges. She worked in a shoe shop over by Clayton Square. She wore perfume and she carried this revolting smell of patchouli around with her. She often used to say she remembered Hughie, coming in to change a pair of shoes at least four or five times before she worked out that he really had something else on his mind. And now they had three children who shouted and fought, and friends they went out drinking beer with. Or rather the men did, while the women sipped soft drinks and smoked menthol cigarettes and talked about television soaps.

And now, from all across Liverpool, thousands of people were going to crowd together in the station. And among them, among the eleven thousand Liverpool supporters, there would be the three Andrewson boys, shivering and suddenly free, carried along by their great joy, by a desire to laugh and run like kids. That was my first surprise. Seeing my two brothers laughing like children and pretending to fight like children. I can hear their laughter. I can see Hughie's rotten teeth and the black where one's missing. Doug's arm stretched out to wave goodbye to his family. And the tattoo on his forearm, a badly-drawn bottle and, rising towards the fist, the drawing of a knife, its blade aimed straight at the middle of the palm.

Otherwise, for Tonino and me the boozing got going really quickly. Because when we got into Brussels-Midi, it was the day before the game and we wondered, how on earth are we going to do this, with backpacks just big enough to serve as pillows, but too empty to be much use – no toothbrushes or toothpaste, not even a bit of soap but what would be the point, because we were only here for the game and Belgium, not to wash and groom ourselves – and short-sighted as we'd been, we couldn't find a place to sleep. I can still see the faces of the hotel clerks and the people in the bed-and-breakfasts and the youth hostels, and their expressions of dismay when they said, but . . . of course not! there's no room here, there won't be any room anywhere! You know there's a game on and we're expecting sixty thousand people from all over Europe, so there won't be places and rooms for everybody!

And adding: there are the ones who booked and then there are the clever ones who try their luck and imagine they'll just be able to turn up on the off-chance and find tickets and beds . . . and why not a couple of girlfriends for the weekend? while we're here? But no, not a chance. You have to plan ahead in life, gentlemen. Tonino nodded at first (yeah, yeah, you'll be lucky), and smiled politely at the man or woman behind the counter. And then in an aside, he would add, shit, the cow's right. It's true, except that we've seen a lot worse, do you remember, in Madrid? Christmas Eve? We'd just got off the train, and Madrid, at Christmas, put it this way, you wouldn't want to be the little match girl, because there's nobody anywhere and everything's shut. And yet there was that one hotel with the drawing room where two men in dinner jackets, bow ties loose around their collars, served us pink champagne. The two gigolos were both as pissed as farts and the two ladies, hardly in the first flush of youth but so filled with listless yearning for them, talked to us for ages about the love of God and the love of men – but of course, madam, I understand. And that evening we could have slept between two gigolos and two lovely fading ladies, in drawing rooms with purple draperies, drinking pink champagne, but no thanks, too tired, we're going to sleep and Happy Christmas.

In Madrid we said long live the decadents, they've saved our skins! And we expected decadents in Brussels, wrongly, not a single one. So we walked through the city, we strolled without worrying about anything but our pleasure at walking in an unfamiliar city, and then evening fell very quickly. Brussels is great, with all those lovely houses, and all those policemen in the city centre. We went and had dinner in a little restaurant, and after that, well, things just sort of happened by themselves, we were in the street and people who were going into a bar asked us: Italian? French? We replied: both! And then a guy said to us: come on, come and join us, I'm celebrating my new job, come on, join us! Come on!

That was how we met Gabriel. How at two or three in the morning we found ourselves in the streets of Brussels, Tonino and me, pissed and happy, thanking the Belgians for their generosity, thanking the shop steps and doorways for acting as an improvised bed – no, not ashamed yet, on the contrary, very happy and proud about what seemed like a miracle: the tickets for the final, stuffed snugly in Tonino's pockets.

As you walk through the rain, hold your head up high, and don't be afraid of the dark. And in the carriage it was like one single body singing: *at the end of the storm there's a golden sky*, one single heavy voice rising in the carriage beneath the amused eye of the policeman who was there to make sure that none of us got drunk quite yet. And I remember hearing my voice singing.

I remember my voice coming out of my mouth and the sound vibrating in my throat and then spreading in the air to mingle with the voices of my brothers and their mates. Their mates: Soapy, the big bloke with a face like an oval balloon, grim-eyed, shaved head and freckles, chin narrow and pointed, disappearing into the thickness and fat of his neck. He had a bass voice that acted as a sort of floor for all the others. As if all the other voices rested on his to rise to the high notes. Soapy, so-called because he stank of sawdust and grease. A mixture both sharp and rancid whose stench spread when he laughed or moved too much. Soapy. With that seedy, stained jacket from an army surplus shop, and those green canvas trousers that he wore all the time, their sheen like a second skin. Few, then, the days when you could have seen him smartly dressed, clean-shaven and odourless to justify the irony of his nickname.

There were the two sets of brothers, the Arrows and the Bennetts. Then the one whose name I didn't know, who didn't say anything and just played with an elastic band. And the others. All the others, in the carriage, who wouldn't stay in one place and kept jumping up and down, taking flasks of whisky from their hiding-places. We started hearing once more the songs that our fathers had sung in '65 against Inter-Milan, to the tune of 'Santa Lucia' we sang, laughing, 'Go Back to Italy'. And the voices rose, making us even prouder, even happier to be there.

This time I wished the voice inside me would fall silent, I didn't want to hear that voice telling me over and over not to trust them, not to walk with them. I didn't want to have those eyes trained on them, or on me. I didn't want to be judged and surprised by my presence among them, my brothers so far off in the very air I shared with them; the world in which they moved, sang, yelled, lived, so strange to the one in which I lost myself trying to dream of joining them and being like them. Still perhaps too slow in getting over the obvious fact that I always had to act *as if*. I was lying. I wanted to lie. And let myself float in this world that they carried, even if I didn't recognise myself in it and had to silence my desire to shout. Yes, my rage against them, sometimes over nothing. Always over trivia that somehow ground away at me, impossible to ignore. But this time I wanted to forget myself completely and be with them, be like them. I wanted to drink the same beers and laugh at the same jokes. I wanted my voice to coarsen and burst into wicked laughter like the others, wanted my glances to revel in the provocations and the girls' flushed cheeks.

But there were also the children that other people brought with them for the big get-together of the final. Some wives, too, who came with their husbands and sang louder than they did, with children on their knees, clutching their little hands, clapping them along. They laughed, and the children in the carriage started running as children do, slipping in and out from one side to the other, laughing loudly, uttering high-pitched squeals and refusing to stay still for a moment, clutching green plastic pistols in their outstretched hands – the Shandy boy aimed his barrel at Doug. Doug didn't move and, when he pulled the trigger, the Shandy boy yelled *bang! bang!* Wearing his Rush shirt, number 9. The child went on yelling throughout the whole train, *bang! bang! you're dead, wop, you're dead!*

Most of all it was the laughter of the true supporters, the ones who had decided to come in T-shirts and face-paint, right away, no waiting, straight from the station. There were the ones who hadn't had time to get ready and wanted to get changed on the train. There were the ones who would be happy to daub themselves with paint once they were inside the stadium. And then the ones whose air horns, stowed away in sports bags, would sound during the game. The ones who wanted to start drinking already, complaining that it was only the Liverpool supporters who were forbidden to drink. As if there had been any trouble in Liverpool. I can still see the two thin young guys, shaven-headed, Walkmans vibrating and hissing through the carriage, one with an earring, the other with a snake tattoo around his neck. They were on the other side of the corridor, facing the engine. We heard them saying that Scousers were great drinkers, far better than those useless Mancs. They didn't laugh when they said that, and they said: at any rate, the guys are on good form, and they're going to be invincible and we'll go on chanting *England! England!* until the end of the night.

Show us! Tonino! Show us, for Christ's sake!

And Tonino showed me the tickets in the pocket of his jacket – he was wearing a bomber jacket with *Chicago* on the back in big white letters whose serpentine shapes imitated the letters of the Coca-Cola logo. His brother had brought it back from the States for him. It was the only time they had seen each other since the older one had gone to make his fortune in Chicago, in IT and not – Tonino made it a point of honour to insist – in pizzas. Tonino himself dreamt only of American movies. Let's just say that all he wanted to hear about was Coppola and Scorsese. Otherwise, he said that Yanks were rubbish at football and anyway who gave a toss about what they could do with a round ball; but if only I could tell my brother about this final we're going to see – because, you realise, Jeff, we're going to see the final! – he'd be so pissed off, my bro, not just knowing that we've got tickets, but also wondering how God could be so blind as to bless guys who didn't deserve such a gift. We'd just have to take care not to bump into Gabriel and Virginie again, because we'd treated them very badly. When we'd worked out that this was probably going to be our only chance to get hold of any tickets, well, too bad, there hadn't been a moment's hesitation.

Tonino's hand darted into Virginie's bag. He took out her wallet and, under the table, maybe while I was telling the story of Michel Miquelon, because it's the funniest joke I know but also – more to the point – because it's the only one I know that has to go on for ages, as if it had been made up with the sole purpose of allowing Tonino's hands and their ten fingers time to commit their crime, and he managed to resolve the problem of the tickets while slipping the wallet into the bag. There we go. Unless he did it at some other time? Could be. And I'd finished telling my story about Michel Miquelon, we'd got to the point when the boss finds himself in St Peter's Square, he sees the Pope on his balcony and Michel Miquelon standing next to him, and this is the punch line, someone in the crowd asks him, hey, who's that guy up there with Michel Miquelon? And as everyone burst out laughing, Tonino laughed harder than anyone else, and to me that meant one more beer and let's get out of here right now. But Gabriel intervened, you guys can't just go like that, you can't sleep outside, come to my place. Because we had actually told him we couldn't find a room because of the game, and more to the point, the issue of the game had only come up when we'd explained that we hadn't been able to find a room in Brussels.

And Gabriel, a tall guy, a bit thin, with that lean, fine-featured face and pink complexion, eyes an almost liquid grey, an anxious expression in a face so calm as to suggest that violence was only being deferred, only waiting. It was there in his smiles, and in that softness of a slightly bent back and in the cut of his brown hair, side-parted, that tense, tremulous voice, ready to break, even when it wanted to laugh, his sky-blue short-sleeved shirt and the creases of his pleated trousers, and then that chain around his neck with his name engraved in italics, *Gabriel* – yes, that face that looked as if it was constantly on the alert, hidden behind the doleful expression of a child trying too hard to be good, he'd immediately made me feel uneasy. For the moment, we'd been invited to have a few drinks with Virginie and Gabriel, and Adrienne and Benoît, in a big bar that was decorated like an ex-pat pub but wasn't. The music was British pop, but there wasn't a Celtic sign anywhere, no hint of a thistle or a shamrock leaf. Still, Gabriel had told us, don't hang around in the streets too much, it's always dangerous the night before a game, and tomorrow's game is going to get pretty rough, especially for Tonino, who doesn't look much like a Celt!

Certainly, Tonino acted the part of an Italian better than a real Italian, his hair was curly and brown like his mother's, he was as keen on football as she was, he was very nervous, as she was, and she was from Roubaix. Nothing Italian there. And Tonino complained and said, my dad's really Italian and he hates football, he hates fighting, it's such a shame, he doesn't live up to a single cliché!

Gabriel talked about his friends, who were all from his 'year', as he put it, and while Tonino was saying to me, ah, yes, she's pretty as a picture, Virginie, don't you think? I answered, yes, she is pretty, but I preferred to look beyond that, towards Gabriel's friends who were coming into the bar, the ones from his 'graduation year'. And that odd term was enough to clear our consciences and erase the unpleasant feeling of doing wrong to someone who'd been generous to us. I know, it's stupid, because of the phrase 'graduation year' and all that it implied in terms of silly chain bracelets and pleats. I imagine Tonino thinking to himself, what sacrilege to leave a pretty girl like Virginie – pretty, despite her stretched jeans and her apple-green polo shirt – with a bloke like Gabriel, a bloke with a 'graduation year' and all that it implied in terms of silly necklaces and side partings. I liked to think of Tonino saying to himself, yeah, yeah, Gabriel's a nice guy, but still, he shouldn't wear a chain around his neck, and short-sleeved shirts should be banned.

So we forgave ourselves our theft, calmly, sipping the last pint that Gabriel had bought us, while words flowed with the foaming beer, saying to ourselves that the tickets for the game might only be a down payment, that we might have been able to – why not? – imagine a little trip with Virginie, away from Gabriel? After all, he's lucky, our young graduate, to have such a pretty girlfriend and all his friends turning up in the bar, blondes and brunettes, all those people congratulating Gabriel for his excellent work. Congratulating Adrienne and Benoît for coming up with their brilliant idea, such great friends re: those two tickets for a final that would be no less excellent and exceptional than they were.

2

If I don't manage to find Tonino and Jeff at the entrance to the stadium I'll wait outside. I'll stroll down the avenue and count the lowered iron shutters one by one, then I'll go into the bar which will still be open on the corner of the avenue and the stadium wall – I'll wait among the few stunted soaks, sitting wizened on the high stools by the counter and, when I can't bear waiting any longer and listening to their comments, after watching the TV for a bit, I'll set off again. And once again I'll walk around the stadium, towards the ticket-desks. I'll look in at Avenue Houba-de-Strooper, I'll do that all afternoon if I have to. I'll even wait after the game, until everyone's gone. And I'll count them one by one, the English and the Italians, stand by stand, block by block. I'll wait patiently, without shivering, without swearing or showing my rage, but with the greatest possible calm and absolute determination. I'll wait until the television channels from all over Europe have packed their equipment away, until there's nothing but a desert. All around, in the shop doorways, bits of chewing-gum crushed against the railings, sweet wrappers, ice-creams trickling on the concrete slabs, all mixed up with hundreds of thousands of crushed cigarette-ends. And also, I imagine, a few rolled-up shirts covered with sweat and beer, left there along with abandoned scarves and petticoats the day after a party when there's nothing left but confetti in the hair and voices hoarse as they tell the story.

There will be sixty thousand tense, taut faces in the stadium, and millions of people sitting in front of their TVs watching the same sixty thousand gripped faces, following the ball, held spellbound by every setback and every tiny surprise, rolling and bouncing with the ball. Millions of prayers across the whole of Europe. And everywhere there will be that silence in which the most furious cries are born: everything expected from the players, a referee to be mistrusted, to be railed at in complete dishonesty. Millions of people in their cars; lorry-drivers in their trucks, and in hospitals, ears will be pressed to transistors, patients in pyjamas and dressing-gowns will wake up keen, panting, over-excited as devils, the old and the dying almost resuscitated as they spit out a blood-clot and shout Long Live the Queen! And the blind, in the blackness in which they live, imagining a yet more beautiful game, perhaps the only ones to be moved and lose their patience as they listen to the radio without trying desperately to find a television. And me. I won't be listening. I won't be watching. I'll be outside, in the crowd, with Virginie, looking patiently on benches and in parks, walking down all the avenues counting face after face, in all the bars in the city, in the minutest detail. I shall stay as calm as possible. My hands against my body; they won't tremble, I won't blush, and I will stay like that for as long as the evening lasts.

And whoever wins – I don't much care now who wins the game and who doesn't, I'll have to concentrate and stay patient to the end, undistracted – I'll go to meet the crowd, legs braced, planted firmly on the ground, chin raised and eyes narrowed not to be blinded by the lights, I shall wait and keep an eye out for bomber jackets, looking for white letters in the shape of an arabesque on the back and also, above the word *Chicago*, long curly hair. Virginie and I will spend all afternoon waiting outside the stadium, watching the coaches spew out the supporters with all their stuff, their flags and pennants, slung over their shoulders and held in their arms, full-throated chants invading the city and, with foghorn blasts and laughter, announcing their readiness for battle. But with them there will be danger and the city's mistrust, gorged on their presence, filled to overflowing with thousands of police and that feeling of impatience, that seething mood that will rise up between the old walls of the city and in the houses, even where the quietest people live, in the dark streets, behind filthy shutters and on the television news in old ladies' kitchens.

And we, meanwhile, will be studying the uneasy faces and the chewed nails in the pavement cafés. We will listen to what the sounds say in the city, and study the migration of the supporters: their way of moving and infiltrating the city, melting into it. And that crowd rippling with the same excitement on either side, separated by a white line and a whistle-blast. Different languages, different-coloured T-shirts, that crowd which, for the time being, looks only like a single body, a single being – hopes, laughter, pennants, dancing, all the same. That split between the two halves will be consummated by shouts of joy louder and more violent on one side than the rage and disappointment on the other. The rupture begun when faces explode with uncontrollable happiness, bodies leaping for joy, and the others are the reverse, suddenly aged and soft, bleak, defeated faces, arms dangling, pennants carried like ropes to hang themselves with. Flags as white as the faces beneath the make-up, bitter tears ready to wash away the face-paint and the last illusions.

But Virginie and I will find Jeff and Tonino. We will ask them why they stole the tickets. Why they drank and laughed with us, as they both did, with the same abandon, the same apparent joy in their smiles and the bonhomie they both exuded, each in his own way. They enjoyed themselves with us and played with us, that's the truth, that's where the evening capsized, and it's there, revisiting each of those smiles and that way they both seemed to be at ease with us, that's what makes me boil with rage. That need to tell them that it's impossible, you can't do things like that. Because I'll tell them I'd taken a liking to them both, sitting on the pavement facing the bar, when I saw them. So they'll have to talk, it'll have to be like a confession, a kind of shame and humiliation for them, their voices will have to be tremulous, their expressions pitiful, just enough for us to put it all behind us, just enough for it to be sincere. They need only say, we repent, and repeat one after the other, in the same tone, voices filled with resignation, that you don't do what they did. And ask to be forgiven, to tell us how they did it and when they made up their minds to do it.

But also they'll have to talk, one or other of them will have to say that that's the only reason they stayed at our table. Or else it was because they were enjoying themselves. That's what they'll have to say. And tell us why they listened when I introduced them to my friends, to Benoît, to Adrienne. Was it just to fill themselves up with the beer and peanuts we gave them? Or did they find out about the tickets, was it all just patience, trickery, pretence? All those smiles just to steal the tickets for the game? But, I know, we'd drunk too much, talked too much.

When I invited them in, I said, come with us, come on, don't worry, drink with us and tell me, guys, who are you? Do you like Belgium? Yeah, how happy I was. I can see myself trying to explain my joy, all that joy because I didn't believe it: first of all this job in the city's most prestigious travel agency! And that meant: no more studies, no more money worries. I so wanted to celebrate that. We really did celebrate it, in the bar. That evening, everyone was welcome. Oh, yes, I'd have liked everyone to come and for me to be able to say to everyone, Virginie, open your bag, your wallet, and look, guys! Look! The tickets my friends gave me for tomorrow, with Virginie, we'll be in the stadium! And I should have reacted and understood the glances they gave each other, the Frenchman and the Italian, when all of a sudden they fell silent and they did exchange that glance I thought I saw, that I refused to see. And yet I've understood. They made their minds up very quickly. And that's why they clinked their glasses together again, despite the fact that we'd clinked glasses two minutes before, all of us together. Why the Italian took his jacket off and settled comfortably into the seat, while the other one, rather than

24

slumping or lolling like him, quite the contrary, brought his chair towards the table and leaned towards me, right, this new job thing's fantastic and just to ice the cake your mates are really nice too.

Then we'll walk round the stadium. We will. Or perhaps I will. Just me. But, even if I have to look on my own, I'll stick at it, I'll be there. Even if Virginie doesn't want to come with me. But I'm sure she will. Turning left we'll go up the Rue du Disque to walk along the side of the stadium. It will be hot and it will be tiring, because of the stench of beer and the exhaustion acquired in the course of the night, all that beer and that wine, the little glass of sake at the end of the Chinese restaurant that we bought as a gesture of thanks for the tickets . . . And I'll curse my vanity and my idiocy for showing them off in the bar, those damned tickets. I see myself all snotty and triumphant, holding them up and brandishing them in my hands like a trophy I'd won myself. As though I had only to click my fingers for tickets to come, great handfuls of dollars, a fist fat and hairy as a Greek shipowner's, emerald and signet ring on each finger and bingo! What a fool I can be sometimes! when all I had was my hands. Their eyes on my fingers waving the tickets above my head, my arms held high so that everyone could see – thinking that the expressions on their faces were envy rather than greed, simply because you don't steal from people who buy you drinks.

And then we'll have to go back up the street on the left of the stadium and along the stadium, see the big wheel turning behind it and the sun shining on the Atomium, imagining Jeff and Tonino as two good tourists stopping to look at the nine iron balls and the cylindrical arms. As tourists, shading their eyes with their hands to see it and wondering what on earth it is, when I'd have been able to tell them and say look it's a molecule enlarged two hundred billion times, and if you want to get into the iron balls – come on! do you want to? If you take the escalator and then the lift you'll get a fantastic view, really, that's right, beneath your feet, you just have to bend down and you've got the whole city spread out below you like a little bunch of wild flowers, and the big wheel right next to you. But it would also be as if you were in the stadium, overlooking everything, you've got an incredible view in that iron thing, I swear. I'll tell them the history of the contraption built to the glory of the atom, telling them how it overlooks the stadium and the entrance, the huge car park, Avenue Houba-de-Strooper and the tiny cars like the matchbox toys they too must have played with when they were kids, turning up to park in their hundreds, just outside, the buses in single file and also, all along the side of stadium, the metal barriers to channel the thousands of people who came to watch the match. The mounted police, the Wilbroek Canal and then the city tightening towards the centre like an old fist closed on its treasures, with parks all around and then, most importantly, the big floodlights facing the stadium turf. They would have seen all that, and the Japanese tower, the Chinese pavilion, if only they hadn't forced us to set off across the city at dawn in search of them.

But we'll have to walk and get our breath back after the Atomium. Go up the Avenue des Athlètes and then back down the other side, along the Avenue du Championnat. After that, we'll have to rest because of the heat. That's when Virginie will want to say, listen, too bad, we can't go on like this. And I know she'll be struggling not to say that it's only a game, because she knows I'll pounce on that and say, glaring at her, that she's refusing to understand, and no, it isn't just a game, it's a – and at that moment I'll see the way Tonino looked at Virginie. But I won't say anything. Certainly not. Because she would say I was wrong. That nothing happened. When I know that smile of hers the one she gave in reply to his. The hidden meanings when he looked at her while his mate Jeff was telling his jokes, and you could see him lighting a cigarette with the butt of the last.

And then that gesture to stub out the butt. The thumb and index finger wiping the saliva from the sides of his mouth; the

26

words he used to talk about the French, which he couldn't control once he started going over the top and said, you know how a Frenchman commits suicide? You don't? He takes his gun and fires it just over his head to kill his superiority complex. And while he reeled off those jokes, checking the attention he was being given out of the corner of his eye, Virginie was still sipping from my glass, just licking the foam really because she didn't want to drink any more, she said, but she couldn't just stay there like that without doing anything.

The wooden table-top was viscous, covered in places with a sticky liquid that clung to your palms and wrists. It was beer mixed with ash, which didn't dry after it had spilled, after it had run the length of the glasses. In spite of the music, Benoît's laughter rose up to us like Adrienne's, contrasting as it did with Tonino's silence. He was sitting on the seat and seemed more remote – or perhaps not that, perhaps just further away, physically withdrawn – because the green banquette was too low in relation to the table, and Tonino was stuck right at the end. He was watching Jeff, on his chair, who sat leaning towards us telling us the stories of the books he was going to write, saying he'd always liked writing stories but never the ones he wrote at home; he'd worked out that writing let you give as good as you got, when he'd been in year six at primary school they'd published his first – and last – poem along the lines of rose oh lovely rose, and the newspaper had been passed around the town although he had never mentioned it at home. And he'd remembered a long time afterwards, with astonishment, such delight, the tears that had flowed down his mother's face when she realised she was the only one who didn't know about her son's talents.

We were listening to that, that story that made us laugh because we didn't believe it. Jeff was sitting upright, looking at us with his startled, glassy eyes, duty-bound to convince us. His arms were two great windmills that flailed in the air to explain and support each of his phrases, as though he might die on the spot and not be taken seriously. But often he folded his hands in front of him in a gesture of distress. He had big bony hands and his attention was focused on the beer mat. I can see his black nails, his long, white fingers trembling and tearing the beer mat into very precise strips, then into even finer strips, just as precise as before, and finally an actual julienne of cardboard, then tearing those tiny strips into little squares, a cone-shaped mound right in front of him: my astonishment at the manic slowness, the precision he demonstrated in tearing each bit of cardboard, and adding it to the little pile with the edge of his hand.

And then his gleaming eye and his anxious expression, that strange bony face – white, the skin almost granular, his forehead slashed with wrinkles. He spoke quickly. He spoke loudly and said he'd drunk too much already and that he'd regret everything the next day, especially having talked about his desire to write. And I think that was true, that he must have regretted talking about it, because he lowered his eyes when anyone looked at him. He attacked cigarettes and beer mats, he drank so much that in the end he laughed and talked only to himself. It looked as if his body would break if he spoke too loudly, if he went on wriggling on his chair when he let out those great nervous laughs about nothing at all, as fake as a TV laughter track.

And there he is, lanky Jeff with his schoolboy jokes, staggering towards the door of the bar, clutching Tonino's shoulder and saying to me, no, no, we'll walk and we'll sleep outside, eh, Tonino, while the other guy was turning down my invitation with the same smile I'd seen on his face all evening, when I was taking orders for drinks, sitting upright on the seat as he drained his glass while you were just blowing on the foam on yours. He looked around and I remember the thick fingers he had, while his face was very delicate, almost feminine, except for his thick eyebrows. His eyes had that suspicious expression of someone who's hard of hearing and has to strain to catch what's being said. But he stayed there like that at the end of the seat, his thighs parted, his hands resting on them and his jacket behind him in the small of his back. I remember that my jacket was next to him, rolled up in a ball, and Virginie's handbag; we'd left the bag next to him. And that way he must have been able to take advantage of our carelessness, or negligence, or stupidity, the moment Benoît and Adrienne came back towards the table – they stayed at the bar for a moment with some friends of theirs – yes, that's it, that's when we got up and I went with Benoît to fetch some more beers from the bar. I don't know, I can't remember all that clearly. So, I imagine that that's how things were. The tickets are flapping around between my fingers, Benoît has his eyes on them and so does a mate of his who's joined us for a drink. And also – perhaps most importantly – Adrienne's smile. She's so proud of herself at that moment, because she was the one who came up with the idea of giving me two tickets for the European Cup Final – yes, exactly! The European Cup, on our doorstep! Right here, in Brussels! She was so pleased with her brilliant idea. She'd thought the opportunity was so right and then, sticking with that idea, she'd told us how hard it was to get hold of the tickets. There were no tickets left, you see, she said, on the radio they said they'd had four hundred thousand requests! It's a very unusual final, in every respect, loads of things have happened since the start, it's incredible, at the semi-final, listen, the Italians thrashed Bordeaux in the first leg, but things quickly turned nasty! They evacuated their hotel when they got back, and even came close to being eliminated, but the Italians are stronger than Bordeaux – because the Bordelais think they've got a *grand-cru* flowing in their veins so they don't like to run too much, that's the problem, and Liverpool, even without Rush as our goalscorer, slaughtered the Greeks. Absolutely! The Reds and Juve, it's going to be amazing! And as far as the tickets go, there are the ones reserved for the team supporters, and then all the rest are for people who aren't English or Italians, who act as buffers between the two tribes, just so the camps are kept well apart.

Except that the tickets had been sold out ages ago – and

Virginie and I hadn't even hoped to see the game anywhere but on television. A game like that. When you knew that all the tickets had gone in an instant, that there were warnings on the radio to beware of fakes sold on the black market, and real ones, too, but the real tickets were being resold at hundreds of times their original price. So Virginie and I both sat there open-mouthed, staggered, in the Chinese restaurant where all four of us had gone to eat before we ended up in that bar, when we'd met there and Adrienne had handed me the little yellowy orange packet with the gold ribbon tied in a cross, tightly curled at the ends, saying, this is from Benoît and me. I can still see the knife-blade cutting the ribbon. The paper tears; I open it up, I look at Virginie and when I understand, when I'm really only starting to understand, Virginie says to me, come on, say something, tell us, then? We were that close to giving up the idea, Adrienne said, but my boss at the office had some tickets, and he even boasted that he'd sold three to some friends who were coming from a village near Milan. He had two left, I couldn't believe it, a miracle, and we bought the tickets without even asking him if he wanted to go to the game.

Oh, yes, thinking back to the dim light in the Chinese restaurant and the three grey fish in the aquarium, beneath the carved wooden dragons on the walls; thinking back to the syrupy Chinese cocktails, pink, each with a stark-naked lychee floating in it, impaled on a pink and blue parasol; and last of all remembering the feeling I had, the joy, the glances we exchanged, Virginie and I, me saying to her, hey, don't leave them on the table, put them in your wallet. And the handbag that I can see on the green seat in the bar, three or four hours later, glancing over with glazed eyes to look at it from time to time, with stunned smiles and flushed cheeks rather than the most basic suspicion.

And when I'd seen them both, sitting outside the bar we were about to go into, I didn't say anything to the others because I was in such a state of euphoria – those moments when everything makes us look happily on the world – that dizziness, that feeling of love for everything and everyone, without a second's hesitation, dripping with goodwill and adding to the sweetness, distributing my largesse, I'd turned to the two of them and when I saw that they looked more Italian than English, and, OK, since I'd decided to support the Italians because of Platini, well, that's why just as I was walking into the bar, I went over to them to ask them where they were from and what they were doing here, sitting waiting on a pavement. And as they said they weren't doing anything, they had no plans that evening and they were happy to join us, I said come on, then, come with us. And, yes, we drank. A lot.

And then we danced. I danced with Viviane, a girl I went out with a long time ago, who was there with some of her friends. I felt her bones under my fingers and smelt the powder on her face; the heavy perfume she wore, whose smell turned my stomach, even more than the stench of ham and pineapple. I was talking to the others over her shoulder, and they were talking to each other although I couldn't hear what it was that was making them roar with laughter like that – either that or I just can't remember. The lights passed in front of my eyes and I saw Virginie at the bar, with Tonino. I think they were alone at the bar for a moment. When I was about to join them, I felt a hand on my shoulder, electric blue because of the fluorescent lights, a bony hand with long, filthy nails and that voice murmuring in my ear things I didn't understand. Jeff's voice whispered rather than spoke. That voice murmured something and finally yelling, talk louder! I can't hear! I can't hear a thing! I had to decide not to understand it, and put all my trust in the hand on my shoulder. And I know he tightened his fingers hard enough to distract my attention from the bar, because he wanted me not to understand, to lean towards him so I had my back to the bar. So I couldn't see Tonino or Virginie. That was it. That way he could confidently talk to me about nothing at all, chuckling, or ask me – why not – with a lustful eye to make his meaning even more explicit, names of clubs, places to score dope or, perhaps, girls as thin and docile as the ones who usually let you buy them a drink when they have nothing more to expect from the evening.

He was drunk. So was I and, when he put his arm around my neck, we laughed like the idiots we doubtless were right at that moment. The music crushed our ears, brutal, binary basses, the people went on dancing. Jeff stood smoking, leaning against a pillar. He stood straight, stiff, his head resting against the wood. He was looking at me, blankly now. His head empty. Nothing in his eyes. Perhaps just the reflections of the spotlights and the reddish glow of the bar? Behind me, I heard Adrienne starting up that scene that she and Benoît always have together when they've had a drink – he kicks in first, manoeuvring, hands dangling, mouth fixed in a moue of regret, yes, I know, it's not good, it won't happen again, and she, lucidly, goadingly replying, you're going to tell me you love me and we'll sleep together, and tomorrow you'll tell me OK, one of these days, and that's it! I've seen it all before, like I do every time, that little piece of play-acting they do for themselves and a little bit for the rest of us, too. I saw Viviane dancing and weaving from one person's arm to another, drenching her partners with the stench of her perfume, Benoît dipping his blond moustache into beer glasses at the bar.

And then I was on my own for a moment. I sat down at our table, where I saw our things, the clothes on the banquette and Virginie's bag, the cigarette packets crushed on the table, the metal ashtray and the mountain of stubs, some with traces of lipstick. I took a cigarette and looked towards the bar, but silhouettes passing in front of my eyes obstructed my vision. And then I did see them, Tonino and Virginie, sitting on stools. A beer in front of each. She, with a cigarette in her hand and that attentive expression she didn't wear very often, that faint smile that I imagined as often as I saw it, and he, leaning against the bar, hands in his hair, talking. So, now he was talking.

Ho hum! Jeff said when he came and sat facing me, blocking my view, it isn't always easy and in fact it's always difficult! And he stubbed out his cigarette as he talked nonsense at me and I talked nonsense back. Late-night ideas, phrases bloated with beer and my laughter because the answers Jeff gave to my questions embarrassed me more than they did him. He knew what he was doing and replied, with a smile, looking slightly numb, do you . . . do you want to talk about it? Is that what you want? No, between ourselves, girls throw themselves at me for my money and my talent . . . they see my rock-star qualities straight away.

And then he sniggered again at his own sarcasm, his own private jokes, turning towards the others and then very quickly coming back to me. He took a deep drag on his cigarette and, leaning close to my ear, he went on. Girls throw themselves at me to find out what my friends want to do to them. Girls hold my hand so that I'll give them cigarettes. They think my face is interesting. The prettier they are, the more they think I must have suffered, and they find that touching, but not much of a turn-on . . . shame, isn't it? And in the evening, in the kitchen at parties, I always end up talking to the girl who's drowning her sorrows, the one who might let me help her forget life's trials. And just as she's about to yield, when she recognises that she wants to save a hopeless case, I start coming out with all these terrible things, how the watch on my wrist is the one my father was wearing the day he died, you're happy, I'm pissed, fuck, no, I don't want to talk about it, but that's what I do with girls, always. They freeze, they're frightened, they think I'm scary and horrible, when I can see that they don't care about me any more than I do, he says, about listening to the story about this gorgeous bloke who dumped them, and they don't see how humiliating it is, pouring their hearts out to some drunk in a kitchen.

But Jeff doesn't get the chance to finish. One of the barmen has struck three blows on a gong: closing time.

Jeff has got to his feet. Paler and gloomier than he was a moment ago, but when the others join us he's the one who spoke first, really, thanks, great evening, we'll be back. A phrase too many, when I think about it. Outside it was a bit chilly. Strangely, I can't remember the moment when we parted – at the same time, when I say strangely, of course it isn't strange, given the amount I'd drunk. We were at the bar, the barman came out to ask us to keep the noise down, and nodded to the house opposite. He apologised and talked about the neighbours and the police who would be swarming all over the place, especially because of the match. Adrienne and Benoît left together. Viviane's tall, bony silhouette clutched the arm of a squat little red-faced guy and my feet were unsteady and tried to stay flat on the pavement; I couldn't hear much apart from my own breathing and Virginie's footsteps next to mine, in the night, when we got back to the Rue Aux-Fleurs. It's ten minutes from where we were, just ten breathless minutes with the taste of beer in your mouth and your head buzzing with unspoken words. We went on smoking as we walked. I slowed down because I didn't dare to speak any more. I said to myself that if I walked slowly either I'd have more time to prepare and find the right words or, if that really showed no signs of happening, Virginie would end up beginning the discussion. But then after a moment, I asked: so what were the two of you talking about, up at the bar?

And Virginie, when she laughed – right after I'd asked the question – it was to say, come on, give me a cigarette, I was just thinking it was taking you a long time to ask . . . She took my hand and, well, she must have told me I was being stupid, that the booze was turning my brain to mush, or something along those lines. And then we talked about Viviane, repeating for the three-thousandth time that she shouldn't put on so much make-up, that by wearing so much slap she'd only attract the kind of guy she wouldn't want to have anything to do with. We both took the piss out of her. Virginie asked me once again how I'd ended up with that girl, even if it was only for a few weeks. We laughed at Benoît's billing and cooing, and Adrienne's pretence at fury. We resumed our usual habits, swapping little observations about the group. We said, tomorrow, yet again, they'll say it's over and Adrienne will call us, you'll see, at two or three o'clock, to say that it was OK, except that he didn't touch her at all, or barely! She'll be outraged because he'll have been asking her to tell him how to get off with his boss's daughter. In a tremulous voice she'll say, what an utter idiot, when you think about it! And then, finally, we'll learn that they actually did sleep together. Adrienne will talk about the moment when Benoît will have said, Christ, I'd better get going and, as he did every time, he'll have jumped into his jeans and cleared off with his shirt still unbuttoned. And as he does every time, Benoît will tell us he had a great evening, a shame his boss's daughter wasn't there.

On the way home we talked about that so that the cobblestones echoed less loudly in our heads, trying to find the quickest way back to the flat. And when we reached the Rue Aux-Fleurs, it was dark, and I didn't know what time it was, or what direction Jeff and Tonino had gone in. We'd given them directions for the city centre, but at that point Virginie and I were still pleased to have met them. We'd given them our address and phone number. I was the one who'd taken the initiative. I'd jotted down the number and the address on the back of a wet beer-mat, and I'd felt the tip of my biro sinking into the soggy cardboard. I told Jeff it was dumb not to want to sleep at our place, and without making a big deal of it he smiled at me and murmured, oh, it doesn't matter, some other time. And if that other time ever does crop up, there's a strong possibility that Jeff isn't going to like it much. Because later on, late this afternoon, I'm going to be standing outside the entry to the stadium, and I'm not going to be feeling the slightest bit kind.

Because they're going to have to give me the tickets, or at least pay for the tickets, if they can't bring themselves to apologise. And if I don't track them down after the match, I'm going to head to the station – why not? – when they're about to leave for home, then, just this once, I'm going to call the cops and I might even hit them, God knows, in spite of Virginie trying to hold me back and my exhaustion discouraging me and at the same time arousing my anger even more – and also my rage against Virginie, too, because I'll tell myself that she wants to calm me down to protect Tonino. Basically, she isn't angry with him. She hasn't been angry with him. Not for a second. And yet she, too, when she searched through her handbag for the keys to open the front door, when I said, no, I haven't got them, they're in your handbag, I put them there, I'm sure I did, she started getting impatient and irritable the way she does. Virginie was looking for her keys in the dark. So I got out my lighter and, when I lit it, she jerked back from the silly little flame, skinny and weak, trembling from the agitated movements that Virginie was making near the lock. And her voice going on, thinking out loud, take that bloody flame away, I can see well enough by the moon, fuck, where are my keys, where can they be, hang on, my wallet's open, the change has fallen to the bottom of the bag. She grabbed the keys and held them out to me, because I like to open the flat door and go in first to make sure there's nothing dangerous in there. We got our breath back and I walked over to her, very close, right up to her. I hugged her. I ran my hand through her hair, telling her she was beautiful. I must have told her I loved her – I remember her smile and her amused, almost surprised expression to see me so tender.

And then we laughed when she said, Christ, I'm pissed. Me too. We talked about the tickets. Oh, yes, but really, all the same, that Adrienne, she's the only one who could come up with an idea like that. Can you believe it! Seeing the final! When I think that last year we abandoned the idea of going to Rome at the last minute saying we'd probably see the European Cup Final some day! I'd never have imagined it would be on our doorstep. We went into the kitchen and poured ourselves big glasses of mineral water. Then Virginie went and changed in the shower room. And it was then, alone in the sitting room, that I looked in the bag on the coffee table. The ecru strap, Virginie's handbag. I heard the shower running, and sat down on the sofa in the sitting room. I opened the handbag, there was small change on the bottom of the bag. There were the car keys, various papers and Virginie's wallet. I picked it up and opened the side pocket – and my heart suddenly started thumping when my fingers felt nothing but some metro tickets, bank receipts and restaurant bills, yes, a dry-cleaning ticket and nothing else; then I opened the bag wide to turn it completely upside down. I emptied it completely and got up; I pushed the halogen switch with the tip of my toe; I turned the light up as bright as it would go, I scattered everything on the coffee table and the noise of the glass table-top rang out when the keys clattered down on it. I emptied the wallet, shook it, pulled it apart, but fuck, Virginie what have you done with the tickets? And she, in her dressing-gown, wet hair on her shoulders, telling me how much good a shower does you – that's when I start yelling in the flat, Christ alive, Virginie! what have you done with the tickets? She didn't understand, not yet. She didn't say anything. Suddenly so pale. That's it. We both worked it out simultaneously, and we saw two silhouettes wandering towards the Quai aux Briques, a big gangling guy and another, smaller one, with the word Chicago in big white letters on the back of his jacket. Their silhouettes disappeared past the docks. They turned right, after Sainte-Catherine, towards the Rue du Chien Marin. They disappeared like that, off they went into the night. I remember their voices, their laughter. Yes, they laughed and their laughter in the night echoes weirdly, it spreads into the city, far off across the whole of the city, even to the north, in the direction of the stadium; where the whole of Europe is due to meet up tomorrow.

3

I was thinking about Elsie and Liverpool. The docks and the fog. Water Street. Because it was a beautiful spring day in Brussels. I was thinking that I'd send a postcard home and one to Elsie's parents. And one to her, of course, I wanted to send her a card to tell her how sorry I was that she wasn't with me, imagining what we'd have done, how we'd have given everyone the slip, my two brothers and the rest. We'd have gone for a walk on our own as we've never done in a continental city. And we'd have been won over by the strangeness of an unfamiliar language, two languages, even, because everything here is written in French and Flemish.

Yes, a card to tell her that it would like a foretaste of our future, because we will leave one day, the two of us, further than the docks and the estuary. I wanted to write and tell her I'd have loved to have her beside me. But by the time she got the card, I would be beside her. She would be lying on the green sofa, one arm climbing up the back, her hand falling on the edge, while in the other hand she'd be holding her bilingual paperback of Arthur Rimbaud – with him, pinch-lipped, wearing his nervous good-boy expression, on the royal-blue cover. At the window, I would hear the sounds of the docks and the rain. There would be a smell of burnt rubber and smoke from the factories, and that pewter grey in the sky. Soon the postcard from Belgium would be Sellotaped to the fridge, and whenever anyone wanted a glass of milk or a beer, an egg or a tomato, they'd have to take a detour via the Grand-Place and find themselves in the heart of Brussels every time they felt peckish.

But no. The truth is that I knew I wouldn't be sending any postcards. I said to myself, no, Elsie, not even you will be getting that card I promised you. Because first I'd have to find a card, and then I'd have to go to a counter to pay for it and ask for a stamp. I know I'd never do that. And maybe she, too, knew that I wouldn't dare, that I wouldn't be able to slow my brothers down for that, one simple promise, one further example of my childishness. At first, things went slowly. People had gone off in little groups to spend the afternoon in town, and we bumped into loads of them, recognising them straight away, even the ones who weren't wearing red scarves and T-shirts, even the ones who weren't singing. But the look of people travelling together and waiting for the fateful hour was betrayed in each face. Some had opted to go straight to the stadium, to gauge the atmosphere and sample the evening to come. Not far off, we knew there was an exhibition park. Maybe some of them would go up in the big wheel and others were just going to eat sandwiches and hot dogs as they waited, drinking beer among the cars or outside the stadium entrance, on the esplanade or in the bars? We'd opted to go for a walk in the city. Doug. Hughie. Soapy and another bloke I didn't know and my brothers didn't seem to know very well either. A big guy with curly red hair, good mates with Soapy, with a fat, round face and an unusually turned-up nose. He laughed all the time, his eyes were very lively. He was the first one to stop at a grocer's shop, like a corner shop back home. When he came out he was carrying a big bottle of beer in his hand and two more whose necks stuck out of the khaki canvas bag that he carried on his back. The foam flowed down the neck of the bottle, and the cap rolled on the ground. He drank from the bottle and his Adam's apple bobbed, his glugging as noisy as the belch of satisfaction that he let out when it was over and he passed the bottle – already half empty – to Doug.

Doug drank in his turn, as we would all drink, one after the other. It was already hot and soon the beer would be luke-warm, and then completely flat. Soon we'd throw restraint to the winds and then the laughter and the yells that my brothers had let out in the train would be able to swell and expand even more, as they did when everybody talked about getting the hell out of our place, saying over and over maybe we should use this opportunity to leave for ever? On the other hand . . . it's not so bad being a bunch of blokes all together . . . without any women. It's true, at least you can talk, you can say any sort of old bollocks. You can live. Get a load of that one, the one in front of you – no, not the thin one, the other one. The way she moves! Hughie said. Look, that gorgeous girl, did you see her? I'd shag her any day, wouldn't you? Come on, Geoff, loosen up, you'd cop a feel at least, you dirty sod, wouldn't you, you're not a poof at least? We won't say a word to that little nurse of yours, go on, it'll be a laugh, don't you fancy a bit of a laugh? I can still see the girl walking in front of us. She didn't dare turn round when she heard the laughter and felt our eyes on her. And my problem was that she really was gorgeous. People heard us, the beer ran between my fingers and around my mouth, which I wiped with the back of my sleeve. Come on, said Doug, give us that bottle. You saw that canal. It's really nice around here. They've got some nice stuff, the Belgians do. They look dumb, but they've got some nice stuff. Doug chucked the empty bottle into the tepid, sleeping water of the canal, not even bothering to look at how it floated on a little wave that still wrinkled the surface of the water.

Yes, indeed! The pleasures of spring and waking up in the street at daybreak! Your back aching and gravel stuck in your palms because the shop doorways where we found a corner to sleep (badly), with our hangovers and the stench of beer quietly preparing to ambush us in the morning, were never quite clean, or quite free of rubbish. But, hey, who's complaining? We've woken up like this plenty of times, Tonino and me. We got up pretty early, meaning quickly enough to avoid being chucked out by the cops or the shopkeepers. That morning in Brussels was as beautiful as a spring morning can be, like that one a year before when we were awoken by a volley of tennis balls practically right over our heads – do you remember, Tonino? And we talked of that night when we slept somewhere on the banks of the Vonne, on an open tennis court, facing the railway line – what on earth were we thinking of, what got into us, do you remember?

No.

Me neither.

And we laughed again as we talked about that night when we decided to go to the sea and touch the sand on the beach; we had to touch the sand and the lichen and the rotten logs by the sea, we had to do it, just as we had to dip our feet into the seawater up to the ankles and, because you shouldn't put off till tomorrow what you, blah blah, we'd set off hitch-hiking straight away, at about one in the morning. We'd got lifts as far as Vivonne, and that was it. In the end we'd chosen to sleep on a tennis court set back a bit from the road. The people had started their game early in the morning, and we'd been able to enjoy it, the sky still milky and those delightful legs, the white skirts, the spring freshness. Because it's true, spring is always beautiful. And at night, the stars, the slightly chilly wind, the smell of the flowers and the first bees. The smell of flowers, even in the cities, and surprising how long it takes for your coffee to go cold in the cup, outside, when we go first to a pavement café, as we did that morning. We'd sat down, and all around the square there were splendid houses, white petunias and cascades of red geraniums. We heard water for the flowerpots trickling along the façade of a building, we heard bells, and cars in the distance. I remember how tired we both were. That hangover and the big black coffee we drank in the pavement café, watching, heavy-eyed, through swollen lids, the people passing – few at first, what time was it, eight o'clock perhaps? I don't know. We saw people on bicycles and all the commotion of a city gently beginning its day, its movements still imbued with the slowness and delicacy that it will gradually have to abandon, until evening.

We each went to the toilet in turn. I plucked up the courage to take off my shirt and my T-shirt: the water from the tap was icy but I splashed my chest with it, taking care, the way you do when you're getting into a cold pool, to rub and damp the nape of my neck the better to bear the cold. Except that it really was very cold. Almost painful. I caught my breath and quickly washed my face, paying particular attention to my eyes; and then I rinsed my mouth and said to myself, fine, that's me good and washed, so I went back to Tonino who was reading the paper. And it was at that moment, when I hoped the heat of the sun would warm my cheeks – and dreaming that my hands and my lips would be warmed by the warm contact with the cup – there I was, sitting on the left of Tonino, when I saw a phone number written in black biro on the back of his hand. Hang on, there's something you haven't told me. So, spill the beans? Little Gabriel was worried when you were up at the bar with Virginie. Tonino looked down from the paper and closed it before getting up – without saying a word, theatrically – to put it on the table next to him. Wait, he said to me. Give us a fag. It's her work number. She wanted to give me a number other than her home number because he's jealous, is our friend Gabriel. You see, Tonino said to me, we were all together but, I don't know . . . There was the way she was looking at me and I couldn't always take it, it was difficult. Tonino explained to me that getting off with a girl whose handbag you're busy emptying isn't, well, frankly, admit it, it's not that easy, is it?

OK, I admit it.

He said, you know, that girl's amazing. First of all, if she dressed properly she'd be really beautiful, not just pretty, but really, properly beautiful. I realised that when the two of us were up at the bar. And he talked about her hazel eyes, almost yellow, and her rather high cheekbones, the hair that she should cut or put up or at least stop scorching with cheap dyes. I know Tonino was troubled, I felt that he was sorry for taking the tickets, because it meant the two of them wouldn't be able to see each other again, he wouldn't dare call. And yet, even if he hadn't asked for a pen to jot down the number on a piece of paper, he hadn't washed his hands, either. He chose not to erase the number, not to wet or rub or rinse the back of his hand. And he said to me, you know, when we were at the bar this weird thing happened: our hands touched, and she was completely terrified. Yes, terrified, really. She looked around to make sure no one had seen what had just happened, because she had a ring and it slipped off her finger before falling into her palm. Nothing serious, but there was a real moment of panic in her eyes.

Then Tonino talked to me about that ring. He said, it's a ring from some country or other and it's made of three interlocking rings, they say that they can't separate, unless, unless it's because the woman wearing the ring chose to take it off, you understand, the old adulterer's trick, and, click, it undoes itself, it falls apart and it's very hard to get the three rings to interlock again. When I brushed her hand, Tonino said, the ring fell off all by itself. Virginie sat staring at it saying that the rings had never separated, not once since Gabriel had given them to her.

Those faces seen in the train and on the platforms, all those bodies crammed on the seats, which I barely noticed as I boarded the carriage, all the ones clutching fanned cards or throwing those dice with rounded corners that rolled across the plastic tables – I have images of them in my head as sharp and intact as everything else is vague. Everything else. This story, getting darker and darker as I've worked to forget it and rid myself of it so as not to bring it back to Liverpool, or live with it, shrugging away everything that has happened, but which will return in those sharp-focused features, the youngest ones in jeans and T-shirts, sitting on the floor in the aisles, others in the luggage racks, spilling out and threatening to fall on the seats and the other passengers. And I don't think I've forgotten a single thing about all those people and the faces I saw again in the bus that came to drop us off at our hotel, those faces and those voices, the warmth against the glass and the words that were said. Not even those pasty faces and the worried, suspicious expression of the man at reception. That thin nose of his, its tip stretching practically down to his mouth. Nor the rather sad, doubtful or merely bored pout on his wife's face.

That room, with the three beds and the little window overlooking a courtyard dark and narrow as a stairwell, and, on wallpaper with a beige background, the repeated image of dozens of wild ducks flying over a blue puddle that was supposed to represent a pond. Or am I making it all up? Perhaps it wasn't ducks on the wallpaper, but some other sort of bird. Wild geese. Ash-coloured cranes. What do I know? Maybe there weren't any birds but just a pack of hounds, and trees rather than rushes. It doesn't matter. That's how things come back to me. So real that my memory may play tricks with me and my imagination distorts the world on a whim. But it doesn't matter. Not from my point of view, which is the only one I've got. Yes. Make do. With the memory of those voices we heard through the partition, cackling and mucking about in English, because the entire hotel had been booked for the English, the ones who weren't going to leave till the day after the match.

And it was from there, from the hotel, that lots of them went out into the city for the afternoon, free of the luggage and the clothes they'd brought with them. And it was there, too, that the whole thing started. That tacit agreement between all the ones with Union Jacks on their T-shirts or tattooed on their arms or their backs. All the ones who looked like Brits from Liverpool, their faces so red and round, most of them, unless they were thin and broken, as if the wind and rain had grafted old Indian totem-pole faces on to them, carved from the bare wood with scythes or billhooks, red and straw-coloured hair wandering all through the city.

Except that of course the differences weren't quite so clear, and I recognised faces I knew, the ones I would run into at the turning of a street or on the banks of a canal, by a set of traffic lights or the entrance to a shopping arcade, by their way of appearing different and impatient, in spite of their brown or chestnut hair, their height, their clothes, all the things about them that might equally have come from Brussels or Berlin, Paris or London. That's it. Because lots of them got really confused by everything. And they were easily spotted because they had that special way of walking and recognising each other. Of huddling in little groups that you would wave at when you recognised them even from a distance. They were seen as strange and dangerous. And these were people just like us. We saw the surprise and suspicion that froze the eyes and the hushed voices of the shopkeepers. It was said that the Italians got a better reception than we did, because people didn't imagine terrible things about them. People are scared of us. It's because of the television. They think we're Man United supporters and that's the advance publicity we get. They mistake us for something we aren't.

And yet I can remember seeing Hughie having fun with that fear, over by a fountain where some kids were playing football. Without a hint of a smile, he'd started running at them to grab their ball off them. And the kids didn't dare move. Because they hadn't seen him coming, that big bloke with his soft legs running and hogging the ball so that none of them could get it back. Then Hughie laughed a big loud laugh that scared the children out of playing with him. He sent the ball rolling far on the other side of the fountain. Then he took the bottle from Doug's hands. And, walking on with the others, he started talking so loudly that people came to their front doors. Cops stopped to look at us; they waited at the other end of the street, but we'd gone on walking and they didn't follow. And I know what intoxication there was, beyond the alcohol, in seeing a whole city mesmerised, waiting to be devastated so that it would no longer have anyone to fear. That was what was going through our heads when we bumped by chance into fat Gordon. People in Liverpool said that Gordon never spoke until he'd downed his tenth pint and he couldn't keep his trousers done up because of the belly spilling out over it. He was there. Already chortling when he saw us – and already garrulous. Gordon came charging towards us and it was as if his belly and his body were being tossed by a huge storm. His left hand held up the top of his trousers, because a belt would have been useless.

He came at us like that, heavy and ridiculous, with his eyes swollen and his hair cut short across his forehead in a sharp fringe, while a thin streak of hair like a rat's tail or a spider's leg fell between his shoulders. He talked about the sunshine and the spring. He said that if it was up to him he'd never set foot in a factory ever again, in Liverpool or anywhere else. He might stay right here, he said, scratching the bristles of his moustache. Because here even the cops stayed silent when they saw us. Even the passers-by were surprised to hear us yelling. Right now, he said, we could just go on walking and no one would get in our way to tell us what to do or where to go.

So it's like a fairy tale, a revelation, an epiphany! Halleluiah, Tonino! I said – peppering my tirade with the most mocking laughter I could muster, about this business of rings falling into a palm. I had a smile in the corner of my mouth to show how little I was taken in by that soppy story, so, my old mate, the man Virginie was waiting for has finally arrived, isn't that lovely? And then the two of us, having woken up a little on the terrace, exploded with laughter to hide the fact that we weren't really too unhappy about the idea because, under the gruff exterior that he affected, I knew that Tonino liked soft-hearted girls and the kind of nonsense we spout for them.

He liked the idea of that encounter because he liked the idea of the irreversible nature of all encounters. I said and said again as I tied my laces, yeah, whatever, what I think is . . . that the awkwardness of the dropped ring has more to do with beer than revelation. And him telling me that what I was saying was probably true, immediately adding, never mind, what matters is that we were both troubled by it, there was that glance we exchanged.

We had another coffee and stayed outside for age heads heavy from last night's beer and all the cigar smoked. And we stayed on that terrace looking at the sc reading notes written in purple ink on sheets of squared We looked at them and we looked at the people greetin other; we looked out for the ones who knew each other because we would have liked to do as they did and pretend to be used to the place, here, this city, this square, as though we could forget our ties and imagine we were someone else. We wished we could always have lived in Brussels, wished we had known the yearning to flee from Brussels, its history and the people who made it, that history and all the proofs of its presence – monuments, streets, all the invaders' architecture, with its hints of conquests and mas- sacres – and then seen ourselves in turn as a passing Baudelaire, and hated the faces of this place, just as the faces back home could torment us, taking us into the very depths of all that annoyed us and roused our fury. We didn't often talk about such things, Tonino and me, and it was a long time, yes, a long time, after that spring, after that particular day, before the two of us worked out that our lungs were ready to burst in the city we lived in, that we were suffocating under the watchful eye of the cathe- dral and the Loire. It took that spring day in Brussels, and a ring falling into Virginie's palm, it took that bar, when Gabriel was about to walk in, and Tonino and still talking about the match, oh, yes, that match we discussed again when we looked at the tickets, sitting outside after finishing our coffee, when, after a brief moment of shame and regret – swept swiftly aside – the excitement returned, even more intense than it had been the pre- vious day, probably revitalised and reinforced because the time of the game was approaching, because we were tired and conse- quently, perhaps, more vulnerable.

We walked the cobbled streets; we looked everywhere and there was still that freshness you only ever feel in the spring, that slowness in the movements of the shopkeepers opening their shops, putting out their displays or sweeping outside their front doors. It's going to be nice. It's really going to be a lovely day. We

.ought about the extra two or three degrees of warmth we'd have needed to be justified in hoping for summer sun and the heavy heat of July – oh, yes, walking with my back straight, not bent as if beneath the pressure of winter cold, when you've got your nose buried in your scarf, your head bent over your shoes, your forehead beating against the wind, and the winter still standing firm, because in the shade nothing has changed: winter is on its guard, it has pockets of resistance, it sets ambushes, it leaps out at you from the corners of the buildings, it surprises you violently beneath the damp stone porches. But I remember the lightness in our feet, that holiday feeling, when we saw the first Juve supporters. Yes, Tonino's smile, ear to ear. We quickened our pace, looking for the metro to head for the stadium. And we said nothing and we didn't suspect a thing when, from a distance, from somewhere in the city, voices reached us with their bogus threats, repeated on a loop, in the air, *England! England!* high above the streets, above the rooftops.

Fuchsia-coloured geranium petals and black chewing-gum blotches on the cobbles. The fine yellow pollen dust marbling even the water in the gutters with coloured veins like the covers of exercise books. Images to drown out yet older images, from what we thought of as our childhood and our memory. Mine alone, those memories of robins pecking at the snow. Pictures from my own little story. Inalienable, dirt-proof. Perfect little icons of a stable, fantasised world that won't survive even in images, since we had to understand that each one of them was reproduced for each and all of us, for no one and nothing. On the other hand, there was that image of the knife. That tattoo on Doug's forearm and his big veiny hands marked with little scars, white or pink, on those palms of his that applauded as soon as we saw some guys from Liverpool sitting in the shade of a church near the canals. Some blokes my brothers knew. And had to admit they knew. I said nothing, in spite of their shaven heads. In spite of the death's-head on the backs of their sleeveless denim jackets. In spite of their khaki bomber jackets.

Nothing. Just surprised to see my brothers knew them.

And we headed up towards the stadium, all together, clutching cans and bottles of beer, because we stopped at every corner shop to stock up and quench our thirst and that need for noise, shouting, Soapy and Gordon mopping their brows. There were about fifteen of us at the most, maybe less. I can't remember. There was the heckling and that surging movement that whips people up when they're in a crowd and they've had a few drinks. We'd go to the stadium like that. On foot. Raising our voices so the drivers would let us past and we didn't have to wait at the lights. Because there were loads of us and nothing to stop us from laughing and saying in a language we thought no one else understood all the things that ran through our heads, provided those things were neither serious nor placid. Because with the heat and the beer, with the walking, the voices we heard in the distance – *England! England!* – we felt quite at home, better than at home. Unconstrained. Shedding our old skins and hurling laughter and abuse. The first threats barely concealed beneath the refrains of the old songs. The first insults, this time actually shouted in the faces of the people we bumped into on the pavements, insults that hit home in an instant, giving no ground, walking side by side to force anyone we met to leave the pavement or staring them in the eye so that they had to look down first. Threats, and jokes that we didn't just mutter slyly, as we had done until now, when the alcohol hadn't yet loosened tongues or stirred up mischief, but merely caused our hearts to soar: the Belgians are a bunch of poofs and poofs break like twigs! But it was all in English, and we assumed no one could understand what we were saying. I no longer knew what I was hearing when my voice merged with theirs, yelling insults at some Belgians, angry and suspicious, who were forced to give way, when they had to brake to avoid an accident and let us pass, at the last moment, because one of us suddenly stepped right in front of the car staring at the driver and threatening him with a fist, bellowing at him and all the Belgians, who wanted to crush the English.

And I said nothing. And I even remember I had that smile

49

tugging on the skin of my face. All the time I was thinking about that smile I was wearing, tearing at my muscles, so conscious was I of smiling and not wanting that smile, being ashamed of it but unable to wipe it off my face or even admit that I should have done. Because I liked what was happening and I knew I did, the part of me that always surprised me when I encountered it, or because I had to act as if I could bear it, as you do with a physical defect. But no. It wasn't a defect. It didn't matter. It was just the opposite of what I was. Something that appeared on my face to turn me away from all my certainties, turning me into what the others dreamed I was. It was broad daylight, on the three- or four-lane road leading to the stadium. The sound of car horns. Headlights flashing to warn us of the presence of the cars. And on a pathetic, trampled patch of grass, we sat passing beer from hand to hand, trying to throw cigarette butts to the other side of the road – and we saw the car wheels throwing them up as they passed, in whirls that rose five or six feet before the glowing tips of the butts, revived by the motion, finally settled further off, in an explosion of sparks like sparklers on a birthday cake. Everyone was scared of us, and rightly so. Because we weren't like the supporters who had brought their families, and because what held us upright, what held me upright like the others, was the sense of power that you sometimes get from being drunk in the eyes of others, and being far from home, so far that I suddenly started imagining I had nothing to explain to anyone, not to my parents or even to Elsie. Suddenly believing that everything was easy. Believing that with a snap of my fingers I could shape the world's destiny, just like that, click! make it bend and roll beneath my fingers, make it explode like the exploding empty bottles we threw into the road. And saying to myself that it was funny to see Gordon laughing and walking at the head of the procession, barely able to walk and staggering over the cobbles, the great mass of him rolling, as a thoughtless animal walks, indifferently, with the same stupid bonhomie, to slaughter or stud.

Gale and Peter Farns, the two moustachioed brothers who looked completely run-of-the-mill when they weren't speaking, the elder one with his chewing-gum and his hands in the pockets of his torn red imitation-leather jacket repaired at the elbows with red sticky tape, the other one chain-smoking and clearing his throat every other minute and scratching his neck. They were the ones who chanted *England! England!* the loudest with big cavernous voices dragged up from who knows where, both of them normally so shy, so calm in the factory where they worked. My brothers have known them since childhood and today, very soon, they will see them in the stadium, shaggy-haired and leaping on the spot as they wave the Union Jack.

Did I fall asleep in the metro, despite the rocking of the train and my neck, my head bouncing against the metal bar? Or was I just dozing, suspended between two sensations, one fed by the other, dreaming of a stroll beneath the lime trees and a child's hand, I still don't know whose (just fingers and an open palm, held towards me, a tiny hand stained with redcurrant)? Was it because of those voices I heard around me, was it because of them that I dreamt those images of cool air under the lime trees? Or just because it was cold in the metro? I don't know. Anyway, I'm sure that what woke me up was recognising Tonino's voice and the special intonations it assumed when he was speaking Italian, because while a person's laugh doesn't change with the language he is speaking, his voice takes on different inflections and different rhythms. It takes the ear a bit of time to adjust to this new and unfamiliar tempo, which makes the voice at first unrecognisable (a voice accustomed only, you are forced to acknowledge, to one tone, one range of possibilities and not, as you had thought till then, the voice as such, because it wasn't stretching either its capacities or its range). It's a little like the surprise you feel when you think you know someone perfectly and one day they astonish you by doing something you thought they, of all people, could never have done. I didn't recognise his voice at once, as though it were that alteration, that unfamiliarity, that had woken me and roused me from my drowsiness. The fact of recognising Tonino's voice and then saying to myself, hang on, who's he talking to? He's talking in Italian. And then that slight discrepancy, the voice that wasn't quite Tonino's as I knew it – it seemed faster, lighter, too, and when I opened my eyes to look, Tonino was standing with his back to the door, the metro was heading north-west, towards the stadium, and next to him there was this girl, facing me. She was holding on to the bar and smiling as she looked at me, while the guy she seemed to be with – I could see him in profile – stood with his neck bent and his back leaning forward to hear what Tonino was saying.

He was the one I could hear most clearly. When I say he, I mean the guy, not Tonino; I mean that it was that guy's voice that I could hear most clearly, and Tonino's only in answers and laughter. Hearing their voices I said to myself, Italian isn't a singing language as they say, no, it's got nothing to do with song – it didn't sing, it leapt, it rippled in the ear, lighter and swifter than the jolts of the metro darting along the rails. I saw Tonino, his hands behind his back against the ochre door, no, cream-coloured, café au lait, a rather sad colour, like the seats, which were orange, but covered with drab plastic. I remember that cream or beige colour that drew the eye and made me feel sick like the abrupt jolts of the train, that long, strident screech that began before each stop and died away as the train came to a standstill. And then, all around us, there were other Italians and people who weren't Italian but who were going to the stadium as well.

When I opened my eyes and straightened my head, she was the one I saw first. Standing, she smiled at me as if she knew me already, as you do, I should imagine, to the person you wake up next to in the morning. Yes, like a smile of welcome. As I slowly woke, still unable to emerge from the images of my dream and the smell of lime trees that existed only in my head, I got up (but slowly, with the desire to put things off and avoid confronting the moment when I would have to look her in the eye and really smile at her) to return her smile, more shyly, almost a smile of thanks. But I must have blushed – of course I blushed, I must have done, how could I not have blushed or lowered my eyes? Eh? Knowing me, when she appeared in front of me, blonde, such a smiling face, delicate fingers clutching the bar, almost curling around it, because they were very long or very thin, her face almost milky apart from a few freckles at the top of her cheeks and on her forehead, but also the very faint white scar above her lip, her eyes an indefinable colour, almost the colour of brandy. She was wearing a black leather jacket, a Perfecto; her skirt was red with white polka dots and she wore a red scarf around her neck and her hair was held in a ponytail by a big elastic band.

I remember hearing her voice telling Tonino I'd woken up. And Tonino when he'd finished his conversation with the boy and looked at me, smiling and happy as he introduced the couple saying, they're going to the match, and guess what, they're from a village close to mine, one of those four villages clustered together, which we'll see when we go there, come on Jeff, wake up, meet Francesco and Tana. And he told me about how he had met them in the metro (and I imagined the first words – Are you here for the match? – Yes – Where are you from? – Near Genoa – Yeah? – Montoggio – Really? That's where you're from? No way, my family has a house just near there, in Casella). I can see Francesco, with his black hair even curlier than Tonino's. His eyebrows were very thick and close together, the skin on his cheeks almost blue, quite a big chin; he was wearing bottle-green jeans and smiling at everything Tonino said. There was that movement of doors opening and a big crash when they closed again before the train set off again, and the movements and the voices of the people boarding and leaving and jostling, a quick glance and then ignoring each other. Still no English, but uniforms – policemen? – No. Firemen.

But for me the most violent image was the slight movement, from left to right, of the ponytail sweeping Tana's shoulders.

My eyes focused on the swing of it; the movement quickly lifted my heart and I said to myself, Christ, that'll teach me to drink that much; I saw the previous evening's beers and cigarettes passing before my eyes, I heard the sounds of clinking glasses and I saw the foam of the beer trickling down to the beer-mat. Oh, honestly, why would anyone drink so much and make themselves sick, how stupid is that, and really, dozing on the metro, what a rubbish way to sleep!

After spending a long time working side by side in a tyre factory (somewhere near Stoke, I think), Gale and Peter Farns now worked in the docks. We knew the Farnses pretty well. And that day we laughed to see them as no one had ever seen them before, both so excited, so noisy. I reflected that I didn't know them, and it's true that my brothers' childhood friends had never been anything to me but shadows and voices murmuring their lives more than living them, and it's also true that I knew them only from our house. We had bumped into each other and watched each other grow up, but that was all we knew of one another. Because for them, too, my life was summed up by my presence where my brothers lived, when they came to see them at our house.

I was just there, like my mother in front of the television or Pellet bringing up his dog biscuits or dragging himself on to his brown blanket; there, when I was very young, and I watched them sprawled on the sofa, listening to music and drinking, smoking a lot. I remember it was Doug who opened the pack of cigarettes that he nicked from our dad, from a carton that my mother hid in the bedroom, in the bedside table drawer. I, Geoff, was that wide-eyed shadow that my brothers' two friends looked at with irritation, one clearing his throat rather than talking, the other moving his head to ask Doug and Hughie to get me out of the room when they wanted to talk about things I was too young to hear. But I would hear them even better through the partition wall. I looked forward to the moment when Doug told me to leave. I would disappear and listen from the other side of the wall to the big boys talking about fights and pop music, and games that I didn't understand. I just had to press my ear to the wall. Hold my hand flat over my other ear. And the voices came in bursts to tell me what it meant to be an adolescent and dream about half-naked girls in sports cars. In the end I knew far more about them than they will ever know about me. And for Gale and Peter, that day, in Brussels, and even – or perhaps because of that – even if I didn't yell as my brothers did, and I drank less than them, and tended to bring up the rear, I was still there, always, like that idiotic shadow who didn't irritate them quite as much as I had when I was a child. They didn't know me, either, but, for some years, they had learned to recognise me in the street and hold out a hand in greeting. Because as far as they were concerned, at least my face bore the features and expressions of my brothers.

Now I felt as if I was swaying in the wind, legs wobbly from the rising heat and the beer rising in my head, too, and blurring my vision, more and more quickly, beer and revolting images seething in my brain. They were playing with the sway of my legs. A step. A word. I love you, I'm falling. I was almost enjoying myself chanting and, looking at the loops of my laces, my trainers on the tarmac and the cobbles, I could see Elsie in her starched white uniform. Who would she have to talk to at this time of day, when I was already shaky on my feet, hearing her footsteps echoing down the corridor of the hospital, resounding in my brain, when she might have been talking about me to a colleague, and about the match she would be watching this evening? My heart was already thumping so hard. It was the momentum of the beer and the wind. Our walk, our bearing. As if even our steps and our shadows were swaggering and loud.

So at that precise moment, for the first time what I felt for Elsie wasn't love or gentleness, imagining her, seeing the sweetness in her eyes, that melting look she always had, as if she were going to heal all the things in the world and protect them with her rather soft tenderness. Yes, at that precise moment, what I had going for me was the fact that I was the beating heart, that I was elsewhere, that I believed in freedom and the strength you get from beer and other people when they're with you in the street, when the wind carries them and rage and laughter carry them too, there's that great surge demanding that we lose ourselves, whispering in our ear that this time it's possible, that everything is possible, and that the world is a drop of water sliding down the palm of our hand, saying, come on, enjoy yourself, your heart is beating, your skin is vibrating, I felt no love for her. There's something unpleasant that sticks to the skin. The alcohol that may have gone to your head too quickly, that furry feeling in your mouth.

Then the heat, and the noise, too. The smells of car exhaust. The hubbub as we approached the stadium, Avenue Houba-de-Strooper. The fear rising in me, yes, that apprehension about what was going to happen when we met the crowd that would have to be confronted and elbowed away, bodily shoved aside, perhaps, so that we didn't get lost. I suggested that Doug give us our tickets so that we could find our way to our seats if we did get lost. He said, get lost? We're not going to get lost, no danger of that. But for now it wasn't the crowd. We still had some way to go before that. It was only the early afternoon. We'd have to wait and we were still going to wait for hours, outside, in the sun, by the stadium façade. And then in front of the barriers that channelled the crowd, Turks and Pakistanis running chip stalls. There were policemen. Like the ones who stopped us then, the four policemen who'd seen us jaywalking, or throwing bottles. They merely asked if we were here for the match, greeting us with a very quick, barely noticeable nod of the head. Then the biggest of the four had told us several times to be careful and not to go throwing bottles around the place. The one who had spoken had stayed in front of us for quite a long time, discreetly clicking his fingertips to calm his impatience and irritation. The gesture hadn't escaped anyone, and when the policemen left we all looked at each other, unsure whether to laugh or spit. While Doug, pale, biting his lip, had clenched his fist and, with the toe of his shoe, had started to crush a cigarette lit only a moment before with a particular determination, as if he were fighting it and had decided to reduce it to mush.

Tonino and Tana were the only ones who could speak both Italian and French. As we talked, we wiped our lips and chins with paper napkins; the tubs buckled and jiggled in our hands with the laughter that shook our bodies, our chips were crushed by the tips of our greasy fingers as we held our tubs tight to keep from dropping them, as they threatened to spill out and fall. I remember wanting to lick the salt on my fingers, with greed frustrated by the thought that it's better not to act like a pig when there are people around, and you should instead look with fake indifference at the mustard and ketchup spilling over the rims of the tubs.

And every time laughter rang out – not quite every time, in fact, because sometimes Francesco didn't get what the others were laughing at, or the glances and shrugs and hand gestures that followed, as long as the allusion had been made in French rather than Italian – I had a sense that I was the one left by the wayside. Perhaps because Tonino got a lot of pleasure out of speaking Italian, which he couldn't do with any of his French friends, not with me, at any rate. With every word that was spoken, I had to wait for other words before I could join in. So I looked at them, round-eyed, starting a smile that would soon grow in confidence once I knew what was being talked about, all accompanied by a nod of the head and a glance at Francesco and Tana. I said to Tonino and Tana, Christ, it's humiliating to be so crap. And then, five minutes after everyone else, I was given the translated version of the facts that had prompted the laughter that I had heard and seen without being able to react. After the translation and explanation, I would start laughing, a more reserved, less open laugh, a bit forced, because laughing all on your own or when other people are watching is never terribly funny. But my delayed laughter in turn brought on the laughter of the others. And Tonino patiently passed on everything to me, as the couple told him about themselves. I heard Tonino gulping down his chips, I watched the bulging movement of his jaws as they crushed the white, floury chunks of potato, and lifting his greasy fingers to tell me that Francesco and Tana had got married very recently, without inviting any members of their respective families, goodness, what a carry-on, he said, but OK, that's what they did, they got married without their families but with just a few friends, because as Francesco says, marriage is too serious a business to involve your family in.

Tonino explained, commented, reprised, and we walked towards the stadium in the sunlight; I saw that Tana had red highlights in her hair. I really liked her smile. And the faint line of mascara and the almond shape of her eyes, her lips not full but very red, hardly any lipstick, perhaps none at all. And then there was Francesco, something very earthy about his gestures, his movements rapid, almost violent – no, not that, he emanated a kind of power, something like the expression of a desire and the power to achieve it – in spite of his smile and the gentle way he had of looking around him, which gave him a shy look, the surprised eyes of a stray child. Francesco talked, and although I didn't understand his words, I heard in his voice his emotion at being there, rather than driving a truckload of washing-machine drums across the whole of Italy or even the whole of Europe, but being here, with us, holding the hand of the woman he loved and who loved him.

Because their love was blindingly obvious to us, to Tonino and me, in the way they looked at each other. Yes, it was blindingly clear. We could see this way they had of being together without saying a word, just looking at each other for a few seconds, sometimes seriously, but so discreetly that we said to ourselves that they were so accustomed to their complicity that they couldn't have been aware of it. And I remember that in the shadow of the chips stall awning, the smells of beer and frying mingled with a scent of mimosa and pepper. That was when we found out how they'd got married, only telling their families two days before, causing choking and irritation. But they still pointed out that the worst was yet to come: not only had their families been told at the very last minute, but their only consolation was the relief of remembering that there was no need to get flustered about preparations, or the dress, or the presents. No, no need to worry on that score: no one was invited.

But, Francesco and Tana said, fine, it's true, we didn't observe the ritual of the wedding, but equally we could have avoided getting married at all, and wouldn't that have been even worse for the family? They told us the story of the wedding, each one adding details that they were particularly fond of, and then they talked about the few friends who had been invited, the indispensable friends, four or five, including Tana's sister and Francesco's brother – the only two people for whom the anti-family law could be circumvented – barely ten close friends at the most, sun, wine and a picnic. But the family hadn't had its final say. A month later, on the second-last Sunday in March, the couple had gone to Francesco's parents' for lunch, and when they had arrived in the courtyard they hadn't noticed the strange, too perfect silence. And one after another, their voices sometimes overlapping to tell the story of that Sunday, when they went into the courtyard and then into the house, where all of a sudden cries and laughter came raining down on us, they said, streamers flying all over the place and handfuls of rice, flashes and Polaroids and all those hands in the air clapping to cover the tears of the mothers and the cries of the children – running through everyone's legs shouting Long live the married couple! Long live the married couple! – the men, wearing ties and grey or dark blue suits, stood upright and proud as if for a funeral. The women shivered in silk dresses, wearing pearl necklaces, jewellery and make-up, their hair blow-dried and permed. The whole brood of Francesco's uncles and aunts stomped around the bouquets of jasmine and roses, the lace cloth on the big drawing-room table, beneath the eyes of that Cupid the size of a five-year-old, suspended above the table with his cardboard arrows and his quiver, supported by twisted wires and crêpe-paper flowers, and garlands to camouflage anything that still protruded – I wouldn't wish it on anyone! Francesco concluded with a laugh, revealing his gappy white teeth. Tana and he had laughed and they were still laughing as they remembered how their mothers' tears and cries went to their heads with the champagne bubbles, and then those voices that still echoed with the reproaches they claimed were forgotten. But why didn't you get married in church! In church, at least . . . Don't you love God, when he loves you with infinite love? So you don't understand – yes, yes, calm down, Mother, calm down Mother-in-law, and off goes Mother-in-law, too, wailing long and loud.

And both of them, Francesco and Tana, overwhelmed and overpowered by the members of their family, still wanting to laugh and telling us how, a month after their wedding, they had had to go through the very thing they wanted to avoid. And there, to top it all, was grandfather Gianni at the end of the table, all his old bones atremble, bewailing the passing of time, before helping himself to a slice of Parma ham and mumbling sagely, ah yes, the turning wheel which will turn for you, too, children, and then the presents brought by the really little ones, the nieces and nephews who had suddenly appeared out of nowhere. Then they had had to hear the rebukes and the bitterness underneath the jokes – ah, yes, you understand, we hope you'll like it, since there was no wedding list . . . it was really hard to know what you needed. Crockery. Tools. We did the best we could. A vacuum cleaner. And flowers to plant on your balcony and bed-linen, of course, and a magnificent white tablecloth, finely embroidered, and also, that bit of madness of which they were particularly proud: a honeymoon in Amsterdam with, as if that weren't enough, a stop in Brussels from 28 to 30 May at the Bellevue Hotel, and two tickets for the European Cup Final no less!

4

All afternoon with this fucking corn on my foot, in these fuck-ing new shoes and thick socks. All that time spent tightening and loosening the laces. And then walking all the way round the stadium, looking at the main ticket desks and wondering which one they're going to go through – will I have time to find them, to catch them and get the tickets back, to demand that they give me the tickets? And all afternoon here I am with the rough stubble of the beginnings of a beard scratching the palm of my hand when I want to rub my nose or my mouth, and my tongue moistening my dry lips. Talking-drums and tom-toms; cigarette smoke and the smells of burnt meat and fat. Then the coaches lined up in single file with their sheets of paper on the windscreen with the name of the cities and countries the coaches came from written up in felt-tip pen.

I'm still furious, Tonino's face is stuck in my head, only leav-ing it to make way for the arabesque letters of his jacket. They only disappear to make way for the curls of his hair, then Tonino's face again. The idea that he's going to be there, with that other one, that guy Jeff you'd only ever notice because he makes just enough noise not to be plunged back into the silence and darkness from which he seems to have emerged, so pale, so white that you sense immediately that he's pretending to exist, while that other one, Tonino, has this terrific presence whether he's surrounded by objects or people, as though every-thing were there just to do his bidding.

I feel that presence so powerfully that when Virginie and I worked out what must have happened, it wasn't Tonino that I accused first of all, but her, Virginie. I said, shit what were you talking about? I saw you laughing with him – my shame when I said those words, when I heard my voice coming out with them. And then there's the ludicrous situation of confessing that you're jealous and weak, having slyly spied on what was happening in the bar, making believe I didn't care and that she could talk to whoever she liked. But rather than saying nothing and asking forgiveness, rather than lowering my head, closing my eyes, rather than being able to blush at my weakness and my lack of trust, as ever, that flaw, that crappy suspicion that I drag around with me, and that hatred, too, that won't let me love anyone or let them get close to me and say, trust me. Instead, I had to,

yet again I had to,

And Virginie, whom I suspect of loving me for the delight she will take in destroying me on the day she decides to leave me, just like that, just to see what happens. She says I'm mad. She says I'm violent. And yes, it's true, rather than doing what I should have done, I charged over to her and yelled again, what were you saying? You didn't want to drink and yet, with him, at the bar, you had another glass, you didn't want any more and yet you stayed at the bar with him, the guy who didn't bore you.

She didn't let me finish. She shrank back, very quickly, and now I'm alone in the crowd, in the heat of the afternoon. Alone and peering towards the main entrances in search of two silhouettes, a tall, skeletal-looking one straight out of a Vincent Price nightmare, and the other one, the Italian one, smaller and curly-haired, with *Chicago* in curving letters on his back. And how, looking for the two of them, I think of Virginie and at the end of last night, when she got up and lit a cigarette, sitting on the edge of the bed, in the dark, with the light of dawn just beginning to peep through and then the glow of the cigarette.

I wasn't sleeping and I looked at how her hand was shaking. How hard she drew on her cigarette. I saw the glowing orange light, the shades of sunrise on her shirt and her hair. I remember her breathing. She knew I was watching her. She knew I wanted to tell her to go back to bed, it doesn't matter, we'll see tomorrow, I've had too much to drink, I'm jealous, it's stupid, I know, I know. And she said: no, what's stupid about being jealous, eh? Tell me, I might want you to be jealous – except that here are two types of jealous guy – the ones who are scared of losing what they love, and the others, of which you are one, she said. They're so scared of being abandoned that they forget the very thing they love. She told me she couldn't cope with my jealousy any more, and my fear of being alone.

And I thought about all the things she had said while she was shouting. I thought about that, in bed, in the early hours, when she was sitting smoking on the edge of the bed and the daylight was already illuminating her outline clearly enough for me to see her shirt and her hair, the hand that she put to her brow. And then I find myself thinking about that time in the street, early afternoon when, unable to wait any longer, I'd said, I'm going now, hoping that she would come, that she would react. But no. She was wearing the long collarless shirt that reaches her knees, the one she wears every Sunday when we decide not to leave the flat all day. And she stayed like that. She refused to shower, refused to go out with me when I went to buy cigarettes. I went out and had a coffee, not far from the flat. I heard some old people saying the English had broken shop windows over by the Grand-Place, that there had been some fighting. But at that moment my first thought was for the tickets and that evening; I conjured up images: Virginie and me in the stadium. Virginie holding hands with me and watching the game. Virginie drinking a Coca-Cola through a straw at half-time. And then I saw the irony of supporting the Italians when it was an Italian that had stolen our tickets.

And I'm alone when I go and see if I can find them outside the stadium entrance. Alone with this fucking corn on my foot in these fucking new shoes. I don't feel like smoking, and yet I'm smoking. I bought some cigarettes, dark tobacco, Gauloises. I like Gauloises when I need to forget, to get a move on, when I need to console myself and not start thinking the way I'm thinking now as I head back towards the growing crowd outside the stadium while I wait for the noise, as they say, that noise, in the air, voices and the wind mixed together and confused, the noise that distils and carries its tide of lies and gossip, I go towards it, I hear the first Italian and English voices. They're laughing. They're talking loudly. Shouts are coming from all directions. I hear the hoofs of the police horses, the engines of the vehicles still running in the car park, outside the main entrance. Some guys playing music. I can hear laughter, tom-toms getting louder and louder and Africans selling sunglasses and belts, scarves, posters of Bob Marley and Michael Jackson. People looking for each other beneath red and gold or yellow pennants, black and white checks, it doesn't matter. The football community is a single nation and the whole of Europe is waiting to the sound of car radios, rattles, air horns that have started to ring out in the middle of the afternoon, under the sun, which is already burning the bare torsos of some supporters. Many have been waiting since the morning. More are still flooding in. They're wearing striped hats, like jesters' hats, with bells on the end, and you can hear them jangling along with the laughter. And then there are people sitting cross-legged, the youngest sitting on the cars. They're waiting for the ticket-desks to open behind the barriers. It can't be long now.

Looking at the giant floodlights that you can see from outside – they jut beyond the top of the stadium, and soon they will cast their kilowatts over the match – that's it, rage is taking control of me again, I have to get a move on. Where are they? I'll have to start walking again. I slip among the crowd and I go on looking, in spite of my foot which is getting more and more painful. I'm hot. I get blasts of cigarette smoke and laughter full in the face. That fucking corn on my foot. My socks, too hot for today's heat, the dust rising from the ground, suffocating me. I draw on my cigarette. I try not to put any pressure on the top of my left foot. People get in my way. The closer I get to the entrance, the better my chances of seeing them. That's what I say to myself. People pass in front of me, Italians, all Italians, no, there are Belgians and French, a few Germans, too. So, I'll have to wait; get squashed in the crowd and put up with the voices of the cops and stewards, the big ginger-haired guy yelling at us to come in one at a time. And I'm waiting. I'm looking. I stand up slightly on tiptoe. Even worse for my corn, my foot too tight in its shoe. I pull a face; no, not because of that, because of the stench of beer, my dry lips and the scorching sun. Eyes narrowed, I look, but what am I looking for? I know they aren't the ones I'm looking for, I wish they were, I try to make my eyes focus and search for them, the two guys from last night, recognise their silhouettes because I'd recognise them out of a thousand, both of them, with that youthful almost exuberant air they have from standing the way they do, awkwardly for Jeff, a bit slow, hands in his pockets, the other one lean, nervous, shoes with platform sole, a Hawaiian shirt and a jacket with *Chicago* on the back. So I should see them. I'm going to see them. That's why I'm here, for the tickets. But it's not true any more. I know that deep down, now, it doesn't matter to me. I don't care. I don't want to see them. I don't want to hear any more about those two, or their big mouths, or about this evening's match, or anything. I just want to find myself saying, here she is, she's come to get me. Yes, that's all I want.

Because here I can see that it's for Virginie that my eyes are searching and plunging into the crowd, among all these people. I say to myself she's going to join me, perhaps she'll come. She'll appear in her saffron dress with the crumpled flounces, her yellow sandals, and she'll tell me it doesn't matter if we haven't got the tickets, we'll go to the cinema or to a smart restaurant where we'll both eat lobster risotto which is so good and so expensive that even the price will make us burst out laughing. We'll talk very quietly in the restaurant, I'll stroke her hand under the table. We'll gaze at each other and forget everyone else, we'll forget what happened last night, my stupidity when we worked out that we didn't have the tickets, that they'd stolen the tickets, those two guys, Tonino and Jeff.

Yes, perhaps she'll come, she's sure to come. In the end she took a shower and then she had something to eat. She took some aspirin, she put on some make-up to disguise her tiredness and in a little while I'll smell the powder on her face and the scent of her perfume. That's it. She'll come. She's on her way. She's looking for me to tell me that once again it doesn't matter, she isn't cross with me even if I did scare her, last night, when we'd both worked out what had happened at the same time and stood there in silence, shocked, facing one another, her in her dressing-gown, wet hair falling to her shoulders, like stalks, and me looking into her eyes for explanations that she couldn't give. As if at that moment I had imagined that at the bar she had sold Tonino the tickets, or just taken it into her head to give them to him, as a token, a smile, just to show that she could, and,

She had worked it out before I did. Even before I dared to say what I had been thinking, before the words had formed. She was the one who had spoken and yelled to say, you don't believe . . .? You can't possibly imagine . . .?

And at the time I didn't see that rage coming or that looming, leaping lump in my throat that yelled so loud and so far that I needed to cling to Virginie, I needed her to understand, to listen to something beyond the tickets and beyond Tonino, further than that evening and the beer and the moment they both went up to the bar (and I can hear her saying ironically: what do you mean the bar? Who stopped you coming and joining us? Did I? Did I say that? I dare you to say it wasn't you who chose to watch from your corner all the better to shout and yell and torment yourself like a fool?)

There was nothing I could say to that. Unless it's that like all men I imagine that the hurt I want to inflict is being done to

66

me. Because even here, all of a sudden, without really intending to, almost out of habit, I'm looking for girls in the crowd. It's a beautiful day. I love the sun. I love the skin girls have, I love their shape. And I'd like them all, just for me, to leave their lovers, their lives, everything, for me alone. Now I'm here, standing up, and it's hot. I'd like her to come, but all around me I hear people talking in French, three men. They're right next to me, and straight away I want to tell them they're wrong when they say that if Juve won in January it was because Liverpool were playing without Dalglish and Lawrenson. And that one there, the little fat guy insisting that the Italians haven't a chance, laughing his head off because UEFA refused to allow Juve's manager to have his team blue or yellow jerseys! He laughs, he says, it's stupid, yellow would suit them so well! They'll settle for black and white, and too bad for the chairman of Juve! Guys! Black and white brings bad luck! That's what the Italians are saying! Because they've lost two finals in black and white! And this other guy adding in a loud voice, yeah, the Reds are going to have new jerseys. I hear that. I look behind me. Well, no, not exactly; I don't look, I see, I hear. Beneath the voices and amidst the crush of slowly shuffling feet, laughter, bottles falling on the ground, I've recognised a laugh and a voice, Jeff's. And all of a sudden I see the two of them, a few metres away from me, a bit further on, the diagonal path that heads up towards the avenue. So quickly. Forget everything. The heat. The corn on my foot. The people shouting, not understanding why I've done an about-turn, why I'm leaving my place and wanting to turn back against the current of the queue that has formed behind me, the queue for the ticket desks. But now that I've seen them, now that I've seen Jeff at least, I know, yes, they're here, Virginie, are you listening, I'm going to get the tickets back!

And then I'll go into a bar, or a phone box, and, and I'll phone Virginie to tell her it's all sorted, I've done it, Virginie! I've got the tickets! You've got to come; you see, all I had to do was go along and have a bit of patience but, come on, let's go!

Make an effort! Why aren't you talking to me? Come on, Virginie, let's go and see the match! And Virginie and I will go and see the match. We'll bring the house down when we see Platini and Boniek. And we'll hold hands until she tells me to let go, because it's too hot and her palm is damp. And then at half-time I'll go and get a Coca-Cola and Virginie will drink it with a straw, making the last bubbles rattle and blowing down the straw when the bottle's empty. And then we'll laugh and smoke until the match resumes.

But for the moment I have to turn back. Head in their direction, even if they're walking quickly. People are getting in my way. I have to jostle my way through a group of people who are pretending they can't see or hear me, even though I'm shouting. Sorry. Scusi. Pardon. No, no use, no one moves. Then I get agitated, I start losing my patience because I know they're getting away. Even now I can hardly see them; I spot their heads, their hair, soon hardly anything, just fits and starts. They're behind some people trying to make their way to the ticket desks. And Jeff and Tonino are further away now, they've almost reached the entrance to the metro. I can't get to them or think what I could yell to attract their attention. Should I call them or do I have to follow them, stick as closely as possible to them and wait until I've reached them before yelling? They're with some other people, a couple. Tonino's doing most of the talking. And then they disappear again, behind a group gathered laughing around . . . what? I can't see. I can't see a thing. Someone blows into a trumpet, pulls a face, a flash of sunlight gleams on the brass. I look further off, higher up, beyond the human tide. Beyond it cars are driving very slowly. A few glances towards the stadium, faces behind the open car windows. Arms dangling from the doors, waving at a crowd that isn't looking in that direction, back turned to the avenue, to the policemen keeping watch on the crowd, keeping it under control. On the other side of the Avenue de l'Impératrice Charlotte, an old man with a cap is walking a greyhound, bony and muscular as a skinned rabbit;

Jeff, Tonino.

I'm going to follow them. I'm not going to say anything. I'm just going to follow them. Right now I can see the letters on Tonino's jacket, and his hair, too. I can't hear what they're saying, but I see hands and arms being waved around. He's talking and the others are replying. Except maybe Jeff, standing a little way back. Apparently distracted, he looks at his shoes and smokes, scratches his ear, looks to right and left, what's he thinking about? Does he have regrets? No, no, he has no regrets. Why would he? I'm going to pass in front of the church, too, and I'll stop so as not to approach them too quickly, when what I should really do is head towards them firmly, resolutely, why wait? Why? What am I going to say?

Now I need my anger back.

It's always the same, you discharge your anger on the wrong people, the ones who happen to be there, your relatives, your friends, your brothers. Always on the girl who listens to you and consoles you, telling her off for being like this rather than that, when you loved her precisely because she was like this and not that. But she's the one who gets it, always, that revolting law, I feel my footsteps slowing now, I feel myself slowing down. Braking

I have to get my breath back.

What if it wasn't them? What if the bag had fallen open and the tickets had dropped on to the seat, on to the ground, in the bar? What if it was someone else? Someone we don't know? Why did we immediately think of them? Because he's Italian and all Italians are thieves? Could that have been it? Maybe even Virginie thought it was Tonino . . . because he was Italian? Maybe all that nonsense we've had our heads filled with since childhood, you know, never trust anyone from the South, that kind of thing. But no, it was the two of them, Jeff and Tonino. Not just the Italian. Not because he's Italian, but because he was wearing a Hawaiian shirt and looked like a thug. And clearly she didn't see things the way I did. She might even have found that look a bit sexy. She won't admit it, but

69

she can't have seen him the way I saw him, with my obsessive mistrust of everything and everyone.

And the other thing Virginie said to me, in her fury, as she stood in the sitting room, fists clenched and held in front of her, then sometimes opening them right out and spreading her fingers as far as possible, swinging her forearms, shrieking, tell me, do you think you're a suspicious sort of person? And her rage rising, her voice breaking to say, Gabriel, it's always me that you suspect, me, never anyone else; no, you're not suspicious, you weren't suspicious this evening when you invited them to join us. And now it's all my fault – she cried and I wanted her to let me comfort her and take her in my arms.

But whenever I tried to, because I've always tried to, every time I did, she would push me away. I know that look: the look that Virginie displays when she wants to bite, or kill, or insult, or whatever, I don't know, I've never seen anything worse, anything harsher, than the expression that comes into her eyes at times like that. When it takes only a second for them to be sweet and tender, indifferent or even loving, affectionate, yielding, no, not exactly yielding. And that reproach that I'm thinking about again now, because, yes, it's true, she was right, I was the one who invited them over. Why am I trying to accuse Virginie when I'm the one who invited them to join us? And if that's the case, what's to be done? Speed up and cross the avenue? Follow them past the church and then do what they do? Go on? Head towards the exhibition park and try to catch up with them, at a walk first of all, just behind them, nearly catching up with them, just to hear what they're saying? Staying far enough away that they don't see me while I listen to them talking and laughing, and – why not – boasting to this couple about what happened last night, how they laid eyes on some tickets, how those two other morons must be bewailing their fate?

And to hear them say: serves them right. They shouldn't have been so naïve, especially him, with his son-in-law looks and his shopping-channel manners or something even worse,

70

something pallid and utterly grotesque. So no, I'd like to say to them, wait for me. I beg you, wait for me, I'm not so stupid or drab or pallid or pathetic, give me the tickets, give them to me, if only you knew, with that confident smile that I've lost or never had, I've always been scared, I look at life from a distance, because that's how it has to be and there's no other way, and I want to stop, I want to be in the world, create the world and live and have Virginie on my arm, to be there, I'm not going to lose her, I don't want to lose her. But suddenly there's this movement, shouts, some England fans have thrown bottles of beer at a group of Italians. And suddenly it's as if I'm waking up. I hear, I see eyes turning to look, then, nothing, the tension subsides again. The cops are only there to filter the people towards the barriers, to check the tickets. It's hot. People are on edge. A funny atmosphere, sticky, suddenly electric. The queue is barely moving. And I'm barely getting anywhere. I can't see Tonino or Jeff any more. I stop, they must be with that couple. There are people taking pictures of each other as they wait for the queue to move. They've opened the ticket desks, I've forgotten my watch, I've no idea what time it is, maybe half-past five or six, but when I look up, this time there's nothing to be done, I can't see Jeff or Tonino.

I'd like to see Virginie coming and then we'd drop everything, the game, the city, we'd go to the sea and stay there, all night and right through until tomorrow. But no, she isn't there. I hear an English cop, I remember they said on television that the English police were coming to control the supporters. But right now, as I approach the fences, trying to see what's happening, I understand why I can hear the *tifosi* yelling, two agitated guys calling the cops as witness. They're shouting, pointing at something over there, behind the barriers. But the cops are too busy checking tickets. There are so many people there for the game, it's the game of the century, and Christ almighty I was nearly one of them and I won't be because of those two bastards. But the Italians are insistent and the cops aren't listening to them, they can't see, back there, that just after they check the bags and jackets, to see if there's anything, they don't see – do they? They see? Do they see? It's happening right under the eyes of the policemen, in spite of the methodical searches – bags checked, pennants, stiff plastic flagpoles, weapons, knuckledusters all confiscated. The few Italians at the front are still calling to the cops: the English are chucking poles and iron bars over the wire mesh; the ones who have got through the control bare-handed are getting their stuff back, taking advantage of the chaos, the cries of the few Italians who are fed up not being heard. And meanwhile I'm still looking for Tonino and Jeff. Another second and I thought I recognised the arabesques on Tonino's back, his hair. No, it wasn't him. But that girl over there, with her black jacket, her ponytail and her red skirt with the white polka dots, I think she's the one who was with them.

She's smiling and talking to someone. They must still be together. I've got to find them. Soon it'll be too late, there are too many people, I'm being jostled, everyone's trampling. Now everyone wants to find their place in the stadium. It isn't rage that's overwhelming me now, it's surprise and amazement: a bottle has exploded at my feet, beer has splashed my shoes and the hems of my trousers. I don't move and I stay there, I wait, I lift my head and hear voices coming from the top of the terraces, where you can see faces, young men running along the tops of the terraces, they've been there for how long? Up there, facing outside the ground, towards us, looking at the people still waiting to get in? And they're getting whipped up into a frenzy up there, getting excited and stamping their feet, making obscene gestures at us. They're yelling, throwing half-empty bottles that explode on the ground. The people down below, next to me, aren't afraid, they're waving their fists and yelling. I've seen some of them, in turn, beginning to throw stones and empty bottles that smash against the perimeter wall.

And the shouts, the sudden jolting movements of the flood of people as they pour inside. There's nothing I can do, I'm being dragged towards the entrance, towards the double-door where the police and the ground security men are checking tickets. But I have no ticket. I have nothing but my body which is being carried along and my feet refusing and braking in the dust, in the heat. I can't do this, I stiffen and resist. My muscles tense and then, for a moment, there's a sort of gap behind me. I take a big step back. Then another one. I don't want to go in there now, not like that, not without her. Where is she? Virginie. Without whom the final is nothing. Without whom nothing is anything. My anger subsides, I need to rest, I need time to get my breath back, gulping deep breaths of that luke-warm air that stinks with the smell of merguez and exhaust fumes, saturated with dust, spitting it back out in short, quick pants. My chest swells above the rising smell. And when yesterday evening I felt like the king of the world, utter-ly preoccupied with getting my first job and tickets for the cup final, here I am with a sense of having nothing now but the sun above my head. And suddenly this hand on me, clutching me. Turning round, I see them, those friendly faces, astonished, even more surprised than me – Adrienne, Benoît, what are you doing here?

They've told me everything. They've told me how Adrienne rang the flat (as planned), Virginie's voice, a whisper, answer-ing and telling her how the night had deteriorated. And how, in the morning, she hadn't wanted to talk to me. She said I'd left in the early afternoon, furious with her, because of what I'd called her *fatalism*. But she also talked about the morning, very early, when I'd finally got up and in the kitchen I was looking at the boiling water soaking into the filter, and then the black drip-drip that the coffee made when it fell, that tiny deflagra-tion, *plop*, *plop*, that comes back to me with the sound of the gas-ring sparking, the crackle of stale bread on the end of a knife, above the blue flame and, behind me, Virginie – drag-ging her feet and waiting, hovering around me, her slippers sliding on the lino. And me staring at the bits of bread burning on the ring, which I turn off. I hold the knife vertically, blade in the air, so that the skewered bread doesn't fall off. I'm pretending. I'm still listening to the water boiling in the pan before it drips into the filter, on the teapot we use as a cafetière. But all of a sudden I can't do it any more, I say to Virginie, stop hovering. What are you going to do all day if you won't come with me? We've got to see if we can find them, don't we? And she didn't reply, she just stood there limply against the fridge, waiting for me to say something, but what? For her, for us? No, I don't know. Adrienne and Benoît told me she wasn't crying on the phone: she was waiting for me to come back. She didn't dare join me. So that was why they decided to come, to help me find the other two or tell me to go home.

But there aren't that many people outside now. The mounted police, the stadium security men. You have to stand a little further back to see, above the terraces the cameras and the guys in shirtsleeves, headphones over their ears, already bent over their camera viewfinders. And then those flags and the sound of a stadium full to bursting. Voices spilling over towards the city, piercing us through; the impatience of the England supporters, the incomprehensible words of their songs. But we hear the rage that lifts the stadium like a soap-bubble and makes the ground shake, and the walls, as though the air were vibrating to the sounds of voices and air horns.

And now I'm thinking that it's too late, that we'll never see Tonino and Jeff outside again. Or perhaps later on, after the game, if we're lucky enough to find them in the crowd, then head in their direction, following the movement of the people, then going against the current, just to be told that it was a magnificent match. And say what, without being left looking like idiots? What would we say? Just frighten them, threaten them, but with what? Beating them up? Us? With those flabby muscles of ours? Yeah, right! Great idea! Deliver a grand speech about good and evil and betrayal? And I can already see them exploding with laughter and laughing openly just as we begin to consider calling the police. As if the police would be interested in us on an evening like this. That's what I'm thinking when Adrienne and Benoît say, no, we've got to try, they mightn't have got in yet. There are so many people.

Of course they've got in.

So there we are, all three of us, and Adrienne and Benoît want each of us to take one side of the stadium. To walk along one part of the stadium and wait. OK, if you like. I'm going to walk a little way, but not too far. I'm going to wait. I'm going to have another cigarette. In spite of my dry throat and the shame I feel for yelling at Virginie and losing my temper with her, as I always do. And I'm going to smoke to choke down my self-disgust as I watch Adrienne setting off to the left, while Benoît has headed to the right. Yes, self-disgust when I say to myself, you dumb twat . . . you just had to sleep with Adrienne one night when Benoît wasn't there, didn't you. And why did you do that? When you didn't even fancy her? Perhaps I didn't feel like it and that's why I had to do it, doing the thing you think is forbidden, to let yourself go beyond what you take for granted? And that shame, at the sight of those big, soft buttocks, those fat thighs, my disgust for that body and having wanted that body, for having made love to that body, when Virginie's is so beautiful and,

come on,

shut up. Listen. Look. A cameraman dressed in yellow, in a cradle at the end of an articulated jib. You can see him next to a green and red flag and, now, overhead, in the blue of the sky, that white piece of moon, keeping an eye on the stadium and listening to the voice coming from a loudspeaker, barely aware of the pain in my foot, barely noticing how I'm curling my toes in my shoe, I'm staying here, like someone who's forgotten what he wanted, completely empty. I want to leave but I have to wait for Adrienne and Benoît. They'll be back soon. When they've worked out that everyone has gone in and the cops who are here aren't waiting for anything, that's when they'll come back and we'll be able to go home. They'll have dinner at our place, and we'll watch the game together. It won't be so bad. And like that, all four of us, nicely, calmly, we'll snuggle up on the sofa. I'll take Virginie's hand and she'll smile at me because after the meal and before the game she'll have wanted to clear the table and do the washing-up and I'll have said, leave it, we'll do it later. That's what will happen. But someone's looking at me. He's right in front of me, face to face with me, and he's holding tickets, waving them practically under my nose and murmuring,

'Liverpool tickets? Tickets?'

The bastard holds the tickets out to me while another guy next to him keeps watch. The one holding the tickets wants to demonstrate his impatience, he repeats, getting more and more annoyed, tickets, tickets, yes or no, he's worried, it's now or never, and all my thoughts are jostling one another. These two sniffed me out ages ago. They must spot people who are just waiting about, like I am, people who look as if they're searching for something. They spotted me as instinctively as those other guys that you can still see by the entrance walking up and down in black and white check suits, two-tone shoes, with the nervous, greedy look of touts. So all of a sudden I have this craving to ask him, how much are they? I say to myself that he'll tell me an exorbitant price because the game is starting in less than two hours and I say to myself, so? Shut your eyes, take the tickets, pay! pay! That's the price of tickets these days. Get out your money, go on, get it all out, give them everything you've got! Quick! and after that you'll call Virginie and you'll tell her, I've got the tickets, hurry up! Virginie, come on, forgive me for last night, it's all sorted, you've got to come. I'll tell the two others, Adrienne and Benoît. So that they can go away and leave us on our own, Virginie and me, and everything will be peaceful. But the guy doesn't ask, he's waiting for me to talk. He chews on a match, wooden fibres sticking out at the corner of his lips.

So that'll be no. I say no. At least . . . I don't say: no. The word doesn't come out of my mouth, no words come out of my mouth. I stay there, my eyes wide open staring at the tickets and the guy's fingers, the hands that he's waving about, faster and faster – hurry up! hurry up! come on, get a move on! He's waving the tickets around in front of me, and no, I shake my head, no. But no sooner have I made this gesture than he's already turned around. He's two metres away from me and he's joined his friend. I take a step towards him, I hesitate and I . . . then no. I haven't the strength. I'm hot, but my sweat is cold on my shoulders and my back. I'm ashamed not to be able to blow all my money on a whim, preferring cowardice to the glamour of a pointless gesture.

And the two guys have disappeared.

I look at the coach drivers who have stayed in their cabins, leaning on their big steering-wheels and listening to the radio. Outside the car park they'll wait for the end of the match, smoking and eating sandwiches, their radios turned up full to hear the game. And in the background they'll hear the shouts, the waiting, the whistles that will reach the coach door, open because it's still so hot. What time is it? How strangely still all of a sudden. The noises now are coming out of the stadium or the avenue, the sound of passing cars. But here, now, it's silence, or rather the emptiness of a deserted place where there's nothing left but cigarette-butts and rubbish, the dust in the air, before it has settled, and then this space, now vast again, when a moment ago it seemed too small, so confined that now, by contrast, it seems pointlessly huge. A few people glancing towards the stadium and, on this side, the mingled sounds of birds and leaves in the trees. A few passers-by, curious onlookers glancing over and continuing on their way. Then that voice, from the coach, behind me, yelling with the metallic tone of the radio, as though the speaker wanted to climb out of the car radio and the coach:

. . . *the whole of Europe is holding its breath . . . fifty-eight thousand spectators! The whole of Europe is in suspense for tonight's match!*

I realise that I'm tired. I hear the voice on the microphone, inside the stadium. I think it's Italian, but the sound is blurred when it reaches me, it has trouble climbing the perimeter walls and passing over the stadium, over the chants of the supporters. So, it's hard to make it out; the chants get louder; we can't hear the words; they don't drown out the radio in the coach, or the metallic voice that continues:

Rossi will be playing for AC Milan next season, and Tardelli is thought to be about to move to La Fiorentina.

I stay in the car park, and while waiting, I've sat down on the bonnet of a car. On the perimeter wall, facing me, there are the letters Y and Z, written in black capitals. From behind me, I hear the hoofs of perhaps ten horses. I turn round and see the police on their mounts. They're advancing in single file, very slowly, indifferent to the chants, which are now getting even louder. Inside the stadium, hands are clapping and the applause swells with an incredible echo rising from the cauldron – that's what they call stadiums, because of the heat and the madness that prevail on evenings when ardour seems to inflame both hearts and earth, impatience, feet drumming against the concrete slabs and the stands, from which whistles and shouts are rising,

yells white-hot like the bonnets of the cars,

grass, sand, tarmac, all trampled and deserted,

And then suddenly the voice on the radio going mad. The guy on the bus has craned forward to turn up the sound. It's coming from very close by. I don't know where it's coming from, but those whistles reach me like a flock of swallows when they skim the streets and pavements – I say towards me because they're in the tunnel, just behind the barriers. And they're shouting. They're coming.

... the capital is on a war footing, yes, security measures ... the police spokesman has announced that measures would be even more draconian than those put in place for the Pope's visit last year.

I'm going to get up, I'm going to walk towards the barriers. I don't understand. No time to think, I reach a food stand, look at the two women making hot dogs, they look worried.

It's true that around them there are about ten other people, all noisy, visibly drunk, and they all look small under their parasols, behind their table. I still have time to imagine the two others, Jeff and Tonino, in what were our seats in the stadium, Virginie's and mine, and the two of them rubbing their hands as they wait for the match. The bastards. They will have the shouts and the surge of joy when the players come into the stadium, to the applause of the standing crowd. Boniek! Platini! And the national anthems picked up by thousands of people. The crowd drunk with itself and the sound of the whistle to announce the start of the match. And the match will start and at the kick-off there will be such powerful, such intense emotion, that expectation and tension in people's faces and in the necks craned, shoulders tensed to follow the ball – and meanwhile I'm outside; I'm going to sit down further away on the bonnet of a filthy Renault 5 covered with pollen and dust, fuck, no, I can feel my heart beating harder now, my fists clenching again. Some people have kicked down bits of the perimeter wall and suddenly, at the foot of some unattended turnstiles, I see some tickets; they look as if they haven't been torn, but I say to myself that that can't be true, it mustn't be true, so I come back towards the hot dog stand; a guy who looks as if he's on the prowl, he looks at the two women and then finally he looks as if he's leaving. There's the sound of birds in the trees. Conversations in the distance. A bicycle bell. The police horses whinny and stamp. We listen, and on the coach radios we hear the reporters' commentaries, all the languages of Europe in the same tone, the same surprise,

some spectators are trying to invade the pitch

Outside the barriers, the stadium security guards look at each other in disbelief, vaguely worried. Some policemen, soldiers they look like, walking around and waiting for instructions on their walkie-talkies; red and grey uniforms. In front of me, I see Red Cross men running. They're carrying big cases, I just about have time to tell myself that someone must have fainted or fallen ill when the guy who was looking at the women selling hot dogs comes back. But this time he's not alone, there about ten others with him, and they look as if they want something. I can see that the two women are worried, the younger one is clutching her handbag to her chest, they've closed their till.

And we've seen the first stones being thrown and there have been scuffles but apparently the police haven't said anything

all of a sudden, the ten boys have encircled the stand, the two women are forced closer together, they all stay like that for a moment and then one of the guys throws himself under the table, he must have leapt in a single bound; the others join him, shouting and yelling, I can see the hand and the arm of the guy on the other side of the stand, he's grabbed some banknotes, maybe from the till, yes, he's plunged his hand into the till and he's grabbed a fistful of notes, the women are starting to scream, but the other blokes are there, grabbing at one of the women's apron pockets, they're snatching banknotes, no one comes, no one does anything, something's happening next to the entrance: from behind the black mouth of the tunnel, from behind the barriers. The few security men who are still here, outside, have stopped looking towards the coaches and the avenue. This time they're turned to face the stadium.

No one hears the voices of the women shouting for help. Nothing. A man threatens them, the handbag slips from the hands of the younger woman and finally slides on to the ground, the other guys dash to steal it from her, she's shouting, she won't let go, she grips the strap,

a dozen Belgian Special Reserve policemen have warned their officers of a breakthrough by the England supporters, and no – they're saying, but it's not official, that thirty people have been injured . . . people are saying there are

I barely have time to turn round, some men are standing next to me drinking bottles of Coca-Cola.

The woman holds on hard to the strap of her bag, rolls and sandwiches fall to the ground, and the thieves trample the bits of bread; it's crushed under their shoes, the woman is on the ground and now she's screaming, but the police arrive, first two, then more. The men have disappeared just as they arrived, like a cloud, vague, blurred, they've dispersed and meanwhile wild-eyed faces, men, spectators are appearing from the back of Block Z; you can see spectators jumping into the void, they look terrified, they are terrified, men throwing themselves into nothingness – get back, get back, the foot of the wall, the south end of Block Z, you can only escape on to the athletics track, get through the two little gates, but they're closed, the fence has collapsed for a length of several metres, they'll be able to escape through the opening, hundreds of people are trying to get away.

Francesco,
  Francesco whatever you do don't let go of my hand and don't listen to the screams, hold my hand, don't protect me, why protect me and get yourself beaten up; I don't want to, why, why should you take the blows, listen – they ran towards us. They ran or rather they've charged and you said to me.
  Run! Run, Tana!
  We've got to run, but you've stayed behind me to protect me, I know it, because they've been throwing stones and bottles, bits of glass and I can hear you, your voice barely covering the roaring around us, stones being hurled, whistles, the voice in the loudspeakers and your voice in my ear, forcing its way through and trying to tell me something, yes, that's it, you want me to take your hand and we'll run as fast as possible, but everyone's running already and we're being dragged along,
  Run! Run, Tana! we've got to get down to the field, we've got to get away,
  they're saying the wall has collapsed, that people have been crushed and this time they're talking about ten fatalities, most of them Italian.
  Outside the stadium, the security men have stopped talking. They're just exchanging quizzical glances, as though they can't believe what they're hearing on their walkie-talkies. But they

listen and reply. And then they look at each other again and they look indecisive as if they can't believe what they've just been told. Then their faces freeze with disbelief for a moment, before changing completely. And now they have their backs to us and we can smell the dry smell of dust and concrete; there are silhouettes in the shade of the tunnel, I've followed the running policemen, no one said a word to me, no one saw me and I heard the man who had been shouting, get back, get back, the spectators were still jumping, the wall moved, definitely, the wall is shaking, I take a step back, the wall collapses and with it you see eyes, mouths, shoulders and whole bodies and the first faces, the blood and the terror on the faces, but, are they still faces or scraps of terrified, beaten flesh,

what's happening here, it's war, it's war, we're seeing apocalyptic scenes in here

those images crushed against faces and screams, weeping, the crowd suddenly emerging from the dust, shadows in flux, dozens of people, hundreds, spreading and running now to find a way out, and the faces – that sheer terror and the aggression from all that shouting and yelling, there they are, invading the pitch in their hundreds,

Francesco,

Francesco, please, give me your hand, hold my hand, really hard, hold me tight, don't let me go. You aren't going to leave me no you haven't given me a child, we haven't seen the game and we haven't made love in this city and we haven't seen Amsterdam and its black canals, the frozen water of the Venice of the North with its coffee shops and dope-smokers – we haven't seen the red bricks, the yellow sandstone, or the towers, the narrow houses, so high that their gables graze the sky,
what,

what do you want to do, there's nothing we can do but roll and run, breathe, can't go on, you're behind me, your hand is in mine and my arm is behind me, you froze when you saw the spurting blood. And that woman whose hair had been set on fire by a rocket. That noise. The whistle of the rocket. The spit of flame. The pressure of fire, smoke and the woman's screams, her hands in the air waving over her head. You stayed like that and then that empty bottle splitting the forehead of the grey-faced man,

Run! Run, Tana!

And you don't want us to head back up to the top of the stand because the English are here already. They are there, now, just a few metres away, and we can't see their faces, because what we see is their hands, their fists clenched, striking fists, knives dancing in their hands and tearing the air thick with the smell of beer and sweat, the air and the dust shredded by knife-blade blows. I'm scared. They're closing in; we're going down, we're going down even further, we have to follow the movement that drags us down, your voice behind me,

Your hand! Tana, your hand!

give me your hand!

And as soon as they arrive in the light from outside it's as though they were running after their voices, their cries far ahead of them, in front of their swollen bodies, I say to myself, me, trembling, legs soft, ears roaring when I hear these words in my head, saying they've gone mad and, what, on the other side where are they coming from, and, fuck, fuck! stop! stop! stop! what's going on? Hundreds of them tumbling down, on top of each other. I want to speak and say stop, tell me, but now it's still ahead of us, growing – all of a sudden I understand I haven't seen a thing. The worst is still to come, impossible, unthinkable. And still that violence destroying even the possibility of finding words to express it,

those foreheads, those hands held in the air, a woman running and running and me wanting to help her – that guy with his red tracksuit top, its red merging with the red on his hair because it's the same red as half of his face, the trickling blood and that open mouth, his hand in his hair – he's coming towards me – I don't want to – I can't. And the voices of women and children, those cries that only children make but most of all it's men who come yelling as they haven't screamed or yelled since they were born, and it's as if the stands were spewing them out one after the other, then they walk mad-eyed and in their eyes their gaze has come from a place more remote than fear, their eyes drained of colour – some of the England supporters think the match is being unnecessarily delayed,

We want football! We want football!

Chants like war-cries from where, from what wars – what carnage – no, not even that. They haven't understood. There are too many people in there. Nobody's seen anything. Nobody knows anything. The people in the stadium don't know. They haven't understood. Not yet. They're delighted and the Italians' delight is sinking into tears and terror, finger-nails hooked to the icy metal rims of the stretchers. Shouting, no,

no,

hardly any shouting now.

voices groaning and over there, all alone, an old man moaning because he can't find his wife. And another leaning against a woman and her looking at him and stroking his forehead, handing him a handkerchief; that smell of sweat and dust; the stench of piss and blood with the brown blankets being unrolled; men coming in with stretchers, metallic clanks and groaning voices while on the other side of the stadium,

and me looking for Francesco, I can't see Francesco. I've seen Tonino and Jeff a bit further back, because they ran and they were a bit higher up: Jeff's face, downturned mouth and thick heavy lips falling like soft flesh between his ashen cheeks. And Tonino, quite different, eyebrow gushing bright red shining liquid, eyes full of fury and hands clenched to fists, face tense, muscles taut but lips bellowing, threatening, his fury explod-ing, he can't see me, he's looking at the English, they're look-ing for the English; and this time he says he's going to kill them.

84

We want football! We want football!

And then from the back you hear the hubbub of an army. Dogs barking, there's a young woman with an Alsatian. Horses stamping. The cops want to come in, cops, soldiers, they're appearing from all directions and circling the stadium amidst the cries and confusion, move! clear a space! room, we need room! Dozens of stretchers, helicopters lifting up sand and clothes and hair. In front of the main stand they're setting up tents, three white tents, the sign of the Red Cross,

the European delegation, I've seen them, all of them, that's right, all the officials, the President of the Commission came out first, it wasn't even eight o'clock, and I was still standing by one of the doors and I saw the black-suited men, they came out, I recognised the face of the European President, and around him there were people in black, in grey, they left, the President was at the front and the bodyguards were trying to follow him and then some journalists, I heard, fatalities, they're saying, they're now putting out the terrifying figure of twenty-four dead – at least, that is, they're saying at least twenty-four dead, and the President was so shocked that it was as if he hadn't heard a thing

Blankets being stretched out and the first casualties being laid out on them. Ambulances and crew. And the first comings and goings that will last for hours. The helicopters and the fury of the blades tugging furiously at the supporters' hair and scarves. Even the skin of their cheeks is moving and flapping like the red and gold pennants, and white, and black, and behind those lost faces you can hear someone saying

There are at least ten dead, apparently

No, I heard – it's twenty they're saying, twenty,

But your voice,

you can't die, Francesco, not *now*, not here you don't die on your honeymoon like that, you don't die at the stadium, not like that, crushed, your muscles tensed in an effort that you can't sustain. And holding your head raised high enough to breathe and keep from being crushed against the bodies, all those bodies, all those weights crushing one another no longer men and women and children but tension, cries, breath; behind me I can feel your breath – is it really you, is it? Your weight, your body, is it your cry, your voice,

Run, run Tana! You've got to get away!

You've got

Your voice, you've got to hang in there, Francesco, not now, why are you here trying to protect me? Forget your stupid manliness, stop, you've got to come with me and think of the honeymoon they gave us and the smell of orange-blossom and rose-petals outside the door; your face, your smile and your promises; think of your promises and all the vows you made and the things we're going to do together, all the things that make your life and mine impossible because we've never lied to each other, have we? Since we made our promises, our life doesn't have to be the way it is in poems, I told you, in novels, a life of love, you promised me that life of love, you,

Protect yourself! Bend down,

Tana, run,

Tana

Is that my voice chanting along? Is that me I can hear with my brothers, running and yelling *Here we go! Here we go!* Am I really doing *that*?

So don't die, Francesco, keep at it, Francesco, we're still going down, me at the front, you're behind me, just behind, I've let go of your hand but you're very close to me, I know, I can hear you, I can hear everything, your breath, your body, your heart beating so fast and the muscles under your skin, blood and your heartbeat thumping, the veins hammering in your head, ideas jostling and destroying one another in their terror, what are you thinking about? Are you thinking about anything apart from saving me? I'm just in front of you, my body arched, forwards, hands clasped over my ears.

I don't want to hear the screams, but there are too many people in front of us, not getting anywhere, not moving, they've stopped and turned round – trapped by a wall, a fence and on the other side, towards the top, there's the pack, the mob tumbling down on top of us; the English; faces hidden behind bandanas, they're clutching iron bars, and knives; cries almost as piercing as the knives and feet thrown out in front of them to keep the crowd from climbing back up towards the top of the stand and your voice yelling at me,

Run, don't stop! Don't stop!

All of a sudden hope is the stadium's pitch,

Francesco,

the grains of rice flying and the red tulips on the glossy paper of the tourist guide, fields near Amsterdam, come back, we're going to see them, soon, do you remember the fly-specks that dimmed the light-bulb at your mother's house, above the sink? And Gavino and Roberta and Leandra and all your nieces at Christmas, squabbling and playing with the old set of wooden jacks that you keep so preciously? Tell me, do you really not want to see this life again? Not the rabbit hutches or the little carnations embroidered on the curtains by the window; and your mother's apron, her hands and her nails stained with blackberries; your mother's tiramisu,

that bit of pitch spread out in front of us, too far, so far, inaccessible behind the barriers and the crowd clustering in front of them and then behind them always the same pressure from the English, while in front of us the stadium is a giant anthill and flags, yellow, red, gold pennants, black and white checks, the chants strangely slow and calm, serious, threatening, so sure of themselves, of their strength, the power of war-chants before a battle – as if the chants knew that after death we have all the time in the world to think ourselves immortal, simply for having survived. And it goes on. These voices and these chants behind our breath, in spite of our cries, in spite of our bulging eyes and the madness screaming at the back of our skulls with its furious little voice: live, live at all costs and you,

I can't hear you now – I can't see you – you're not behind me – you're not behind me now – where are you? Where are you, Francesco?

Did I do it too? Did I threaten people with a concrete paving-stone or block – picked up where? some slab pulled away from somewhere, who by, what for, is it possible, am I too running with Soapy and Doug, charging, am I running with them, my mouth dry, no, Doug, you mustn't – Doug thumping once, twice, that man shielding himself against the blows with his newspaper, I can't,

And the others, back home, in Liverpool, can they see this? Can they see us in all that, the sated look, the victory signs brandished by the ultras, the Italians hiding behind their scarves to strike, will Elsie see, back in Liverpool see that photographer getting a rock on the head as he runs to get away from who, from what,

Behind me, Francesco, there are bodies rolling and climbing on top of one another, my head still outside, but for how long – how long can I hold out? – bending, falling, weeping; I'll have to die, I'll have to accept that I will never see you again in your striped jersey or with that look you had, so touching and so ill at ease in the suit that was slightly too big for you, the loose hems of your trousers, it's unthinkable, never seeing you again as you were in the photograph,

Run! Run, Tana!

And all of a sudden I lean, I bend, the ground rushes towards my head, it's as dark as it is in a hole and there are feet, hands, newspapers and also that face and the colourless eyes, red cheeks, teeth, tongue and slobber and foam as in the photograph near the Comacchio Lagoon with the red paint of the boat, the nets and the baskets, the clouds and your smile, Francesco, your skin, nearly brown, and the blue and white stripes of your jersey – but here, the foam is the sticky saliva dangling and dribbling from a mouth, a face that has rolled close to my head. Wretched saliva to stifle screams, while all around there's the disaster of bodies being crushed and voices wrenched, jettisoned in the hope of an exit:

The pitch!

Telling yourself – no, not daring to tell yourself that the real stroke of luck was having your tickets stolen. And for a moment I wanted to call home, to tell Virginie that I can't leave, not like that, without helping, staying rooted to the spot when I should at least offer help, comfort, but there it is, I'm staying where I am, motionless and fixed to the ground, as if my feet couldn't walk, as if,

those sounds of bones and creaking and those voices getting exasperated, and my forehead splintered with tiny bits of gravel – I can't see anything, I shut my eyes. Oh, Francesco, hold my hand, hold me tight and don't let yourself be crushed or bent in two by the bodies falling and covering us up. I can hear breathing. It's like being in a hole. What is it that's shrinking around us? Where are you? I can't hear your voice now. And do you hear that roaring noise? It's like a roaring in your ears, but this time no, I can't put my hands over my ears to keep from hearing or smelling the smell of soap and lotions mixed with grime and sweat, you have to fight to hold out. Hang in there. Hold on. Don't break in two. Twist your spine round. It bends, it bows, act like reeds in the wind, I remember the rod my grandfather took with him when he went fishing for monstrous fish and reeds that my grandmother painted on the bottoms of the plates that she kept for antipasti, but also the reeds you make pan-pipes from; don't break, don't yield, round your back and leave enough space between yourself and the ground, look down, bend your head down and whatever you do, stay like that; be the opposite of a reed because your arms mustn't bend, your elbows must stay straight, your arms tensed, palms out flat. With all the strength in my body I have to protect this bubble of air beneath me and shout to find the strength to stay tensed in spite of the weight of a body breaking my back, but if only it was you, is it your body? Is it you, Francesco?

Tell me it's you,

Adrienne and Benoît join me, bringing their numbness, that expression I've never seen on their faces before, the speaker says something, it sounds like a list, a list of names, Italian names and personal messages,

it sounds like names left behind in the stadium,

Someone's suffocating, someone's pleading, someone's pushing down on my head. My ponytail has come undone, and I've seen the band that tied my hair a few centimetres away and that's when I understand that my face is so close to the concrete slab; I have to hold myself upright on my hands, on my elbows, and press harder against the movement trying to crush me against the concrete, my knees hurt, the concrete burning against my bare kneecaps, even if my strength comes back – because it always comes back when I hear your voice,

Don't bend

Tana! Tana! Tense your arms!

as if your voice could reach me to tell me what to do. And you, Francesco: don't give up! You're not going to die here, you can't, you know, nothing that's happening to us here is real and it's impossible – it can't be happening – because it's all made up for the television or some stupid film, but it isn't real, that shouting, that madness isn't real and soon we'll laugh about it, I promise, on the sofa back at our flat when we look at the photographs, soon – but too bad, there won't be any photographs, the camera smashed to pieces when I was pushed and fell – I saw the little Kodak rolling and exploding into a thousand tiny pieces like dust and fragments of glass, they glittered on the concrete steps, the film like a long streamer, so we won't sit on the sofa looking at the photographs, but for now what we've got to do is stay alive, and to do that, think, imagine the Van Gogh Museum, think of the Rembrandt Museum, of our Leandra and her postcard collection and the foreign ones you promised her; and then remember our reservation in the houseboat hotel; the yellow sandstone and the tulip fields, the idea of finally going on holiday, just the two of us; a week without thinking of your truck or the rainy days where you've practically got to scream into the phone box so that I can hear what you're saying, because of the gales and the splashing trucks and their honking horns; think of the canary, who's going to feed the canary? And just to conjure up some stupid, dreamed-up happy-family magazine pictures – who's going to give me children and hold me by the waist when we go up the street to see my mother, among the oleanders and the scents of marjoram and mace? Why can't I hear your voice saying,

    Tana

But now I'm here, with Adrienne and Benoît. With voices coming at us from everywhere, ahead of us, behind us, the stretcher-bearers and the policemen who want room to get in and out of the stadium,

    and the voices of that woman, that man, and the sobbing and the murmuring, heads lowered, faces dazed, staring into the void, all those voices and laments can't cover the chants now rising into the air and hanging over us, *England! England!* The deep and serious chant engulfing faces as it passes; now it's night; night is falling and time expanding to fill it, the helicopter blades, the soldiers' rhythmical steps, we want to help too but it's all going too fast and my body feels so heavy that my lips are sealed shut when I try to tell Benoît to be quiet he's talking so much,

Your voice,

    Tana! Tana!

    Nor your breath behind me, Francesco, where are you? I can't hear anything it's all a blur.

    If you bend your head will be crushed,

    They're going to crush your head.

So I won't bend. So I'll hang on and too bad if they walk on my hands and if that pressing hand crushes my head, if they kick me; I'll hold out because you're asking me to, because you know what has to be done and you've always known what had to be done – why are we here? Why am I going to die here? Like this? Crushed, pounded? No, I'll hold on. And you'll have to hold on too, Francesco,

Tana! Tana!

You're not going to die, you can't die here,

Tana!

And your voice and mine parting and seeking one another; your hand and mine parting, seeking one another and finding only grains of concrete dust under their nails.

Tana, I'm going to die,

No, Francesco, you're not going to die, look, no, don't look; they've trampled on my hands and my hands are covered with blood, I feel terrible, I feel suddenly cold, so cold between my thighs oh Francesco don't look, I couldn't help myself, it's as if my bladder couldn't hold out with the pressure, and nor could I with the fear, it's because of the fear, I'm crying, Francesco, there I am with bouquets of jasmine and roses, the white table-cloth, you remember, don't let me be cluttered with all those images, Francesco, I feel warm, salt tears like the ones my mother used to lick from my cheeks when I was a little girl to make me laugh and the laughter came, it flowed like tears that are running calmly down my cheeks, no panic, and there's that smell on me and that cold between my thighs,

Tana! Tana! I can't breathe, I

lift your head, Francesco, you've got to lift your head, lift yourself up, it doesn't matter, come on, lean on something, anything, any shoulder no matter how much it begs you to leave it alone and no, don't listen to anything but yourself and your furious, vicious desire to live like a madman whispering in your ear that you need air at any price, Francesco, come on, grab the air where you find it, crush the others if they stop you, crush me if I stop you, you've got to live, you've got to, but you can't leave me, not now, not here, I'm getting up again, I feel the pressure on me easing and there's this bubble under me, under the curve of my belly – this bubble, and you're not there any more, I can't hear anything at all, there's a droning noise,

Francesco,

Your voice doesn't reach me now, nothing, there's nothing but a body trembling and muscles in my shoulders, that muscle pulling in my left arm – that body is mine, hemmed in and crushed, is it possible, out there in the street, to imagine that all these people, all these bodies, these arms you can't see, these people you laugh with and bump into and ignore, is it possible to imagine that by hemming each other in and pressing down on each other, they form this cage, this hole, this thing,

we're outside, I mean, outside the stadium, the orange reflections in the stainless steel of the stretchers, and then behind some hastily erected barriers, Virginie is there. She looks at me without saying anything, without so much as a wave, her image is orange, alternating with blue. It merges with the colours of the cars. There's nothing we can do. I should go towards her, but she's the one who comes to me, she's there, I take her in my arms and she tells me that she's heard on the radio, that she's seen the pictures on television; I run my hand through her hair, I recognise the apple smell of her shampoo.

And the injured are still pouring out of the tunnel, tottering, dragging bent, frail carcasses. They lift their eyes towards us but their eyes see nothing.

Oh now, Francesco, all those lights, those bright patches in my eyes, blood on my hands, pain in my chest and the cold, the stain on my skirt and between my thighs and yet I did as you said, I stayed tense and I don't know how I managed to get out of that thing and that shape and those faces rising up and falling back – arms outstretched, photographers, men coming and pulling on an arm and prompting screams, pleading, wail-

93

ing, weeping, weeping, blood, eyes so lost and fixed so far back in the skull and you, Francesco, you, I can't see you now, I see only the crowd collapsing again, down as far as the field, at last. Something collapsed as if it was making a signal, and the crowd followed the movement and was engulfed. There was something like a cry. A frozen breath. And the policemen, down at the front, didn't understand, they didn't see the crushed, rolled bodies coming towards them,

walk on through the wind, walk on through the rain, though your dreams be tossed and blown,

They say it's because they're beating up some England fans that we've got to get to the other side, that we've got to rip down the fence separating us from the Italians, they say the Italians are beating people up, Doug says we've got to go and defend the English,

Francesco, great balloons in a blue sky calm as wallpaper. And they're flying, dancing and falling on to the pitch. Francesco, I see the dance they're doing in the air but I can't see you now, I'm looking for you everywhere, Francesco, in the crowd; but above the people's heads you see the shadow of the balloons floating over the stadium; and the balloons, do you remember, the pop of the rifles you fired at the holiday fairground?

Francesco, where are you?

The section cordoned off by policemen holding back the English and the Italians as best they can, on either side of this big hole, right there in the middle. And my hands hurt and my back hurts but I'm looking for you, to find you in the middle of all these people. And just think of the ridiculous things I'm being forced to look at: the black ties and white shirts of the mounted police. But I can't see you, Francesco, Francesco, I'm scared and I'm so cold and I've been walking since, what time is it now? how long? walking, I saw handrails along the whole height of the stand, the flags still floating on the other side with the image of the cup on a flag, a death's-head with its pirate bandanna over its eye and death no I'm not going to think about death. You're somewhere. You're going to come back. And now I'm going to run and find you, and go back down, and walk on to the pitch; and too bad if I've worked out that part of the railings where we were standing has collapsed under the pressure – there are no stretchers left, loudspeakers at ground level are asking us in Italian to return to our places, but my place is with you.

It's him! Him! He's over there – Benoît's voice that stops shouting as soon as he catches up with me, resting his hand on my shoulder to whisper in my ear: over there, look, on the other side of the railing, at the entrance to the tunnel, do you recognise him?

But I don't recognise anyone. How could he still be thinking of that? And Adrienne who's joined the crowd and I see her crouching by a plump man wiping his glasses and crying, striking his thighs with the palms of his hands, he's talking and his mouth trembles like an old man's while she rubs his back; she holds his arm and looks all around, as if she wanted to help everybody all at the same time. But we stay where we are. Virginie and me. Because Benoît has decided to help the ambulance men as well. And my ears are tensed just to recognise the strange sound of the match beginning, because they're starting the match and outside there are voices and screams, and then the whistle and the crowd rising to its feet with a great shout and bursts of applause inside the stadium. Yes. Outside the stadium we hear the match. In the street we hear the match. Applause. The cries and hurrahs lashing and caressing the Avenue Houba-de-Strooper, the exhibition park, all the way to the city centre, perhaps, as far as the depths of the eyes of the people who are there waiting to be delivered from the nightmare they're going through, their bones vibrating to the echoes of the chants, the voices, the stadium loudspeakers. And now it's the sound of a match over the city while outside all those people don't yet dare admit that they're going to play the game, *that game*, in spite of what's happened, the game of the century, that they're going to miss it, the people who were in there, right by the field, they'd come only for that, they never imagined they'd see anything like this,

my place is next to you.

My place, I'm married, I'm your wife. A woman's place is next to her husband so I'm looking, I'm starting to look among the people being evacuated, we have to get out, maybe you've got out? Someone pushed you outside? And you, Francesco, if you were there you'd be saying, what's the name of that player, the number three who's coming towards us to tell us what? To explain what? And all the players are coming out. I recognise Platini and Boniek. The crowd haven't understood a thing, they're applauding because they've seen the players coming out and they're raising their arms to greet them and I want to shout, no one can see anything, it's as if no one can see a thing! The players are applauded as they shout, get back to your places! Get back to your places! but the crowd don't understand and yell with joy, their arms raised higher and higher, they want to hug the players, they want to touch them. They don't hear the loudspeaker asking the people to get back to their seats, or the players who have arrived, they're here, back to your places! back to your places! and I'm here. No one sees that I'm there. I'm looking for you, Francesco, and my eyes wandering, oh yes Francesco, where are you? Back to your places! those voices saying: your places! and I would so much like to get back to my place, to be beside you and get back to my place – is it me screaming like that, Francesco, by this makeshift camp with all those people weeping?

And this policeman holding me by the arm, trying to support me because I'm staggering and the people walking and running around me; and those women, that child, those bodies lying on blankets – in my head I hear my voice murmuring, I could die here, in Brussels, tonight, during a football match.

Francesco, you realise, it is possible to die as young as you are, to come as you did for your honeymoon,

  and die, *now*,

Benoît shakes my arm, his voice finally rises all the way up to me, Gabriel, look, there, at the back, on the right, it's him, it's him, come on, we're going, although we're not going to leave you all on your own, I say to myself that it's impossible, and yet, Virginie's hand takes mine, come on, don't stay here, she says to me. Virginie walks ahead of me. We walk among the people there, as if we were in a dense forest in the middle of the night. Virginie holds my hand and guides me, she passes on my left, she steps forward, and behind her I hear the sounds and the falling night fills me with its blackness, and what can I do if the stars above me shine only to mark their distance from us, what can I do,

  But I don't want to go.

  To do what, who for, why play the mean trick now, when on the contrary what we want to do is help, do something, but I no longer know what to do, I don't know anything now, and then, suddenly, that voice, that stifled scream beside me, she's there, that girl, I stay close to the girl who I don't recognise straight away. Like an idiot I can't do anything when she looks at me with pleading eyes, that's it, I recognise her, the red skirt, the polka dots. She speaks, a few words in Italian, and I don't understand what she's saying. She's looking at me but she doesn't see anything, her tears drown her eyes, she laughs, she blushes, she weeps. And tears on her ravaged face carry her make-up with them, the black streaks it leaves on her pale cheeks, on her freckles. Her blonde hair has come loose, it isn't in a ponytail but I recognise her as the girl who was with Tonino and Jeff, I'm sure of it, her black jacket, the red skirt with the white polka dots on it.

The white tablecloth, the jasmine, the strong smell of mud from the canals waiting for us, you can't die, and knees trembling I screamed, I know I screamed so loudly that I bit my lip and because of my fat, heavy tears my eyes thought the world in front of me was being erased. And all that lasted was the ridiculous business of not being able to put my elastic back on and do up my ponytail while I saw the inscriptions on the concrete barriers.

Adrienne helping someone. Benoît and Virginie, both of them, surrounding that big clumsy body resting upright against the wall of the tunnel. He's still there, eyes open, staring straight ahead. And I can see those male nurses wrapping the other guy in a blanket, I go over. I ask how he is, they tell me he's fainted but he'll be OK. I've seen the blood on his eyebrow, bruises on his neck, his Hawaiian shirt torn and bloody. I look towards Virginie and the others.

I see the hand that's been laid on his chest, the other dangling on the edge of the stretcher, they'll come and get him at any moment, he's waiting to go to hospital. Oh, yes, my sadness and that rage when I pull back the sleeve of his jacket and wet my thumb with my tongue – looking at Virginie as I do so. She's talking to the others, I press very hard on the back of his hand and I wet my thumb again and then I start over, on the back of the hand, harder, until this time, once and for all, the black ink of the phone number is completely erased.

Francesco, there were flags so big you'd have thought they were blankets or even sails like the washing hanging up between our windows at home. And the slogans like banners under the balloons that still danced above the advertisements for brands of cigarettes and hi-fi chains, posters for Sony and Canon, all brands and all kinds of things that you'd like to have at home. And I'm there, I can see those names and all around there are screams, men in white and others in pale green. They're carrying these huge cases, and the police are carrying transparent shields with white stripes. I can see that. The balloons in the team colours. The night falling slowly, very slowly; a man comes towards me, a policeman. He wants to help me and speaks to me slowly, in French. I can hardly understand him, he's asking me if I'm OK, and what I want. Then I look at the advertisements, I think for a little while, I'd like a cigarette to burst the dancing balloons and see night fall and then, yes, Francesco, excuse me, sir, I don't know where Francesco is.

5

Did I run with them? Is it me? The third son of Susan and Ray Andrewson? Back in Liverpool, my father is sitting in his brown imitation leather armchair. He's sucking on his hollow tooth and getting worried, unable to believe it, he delivers a great kick to the filthy dog, who goes rolling over and can't understand why, when he usually enjoys serene indifference, he's been kicked in his old ribs. Pellet rolls his pale grey eyes towards my mother, who barely looks at him, then crawls towards his blanket, which stinks of dust and dog-hair. And my mother stands frozen in the corner by the door, not even taking the time to rest her shoulder against the frame.

And then she steps forward. She puts her damp hand, just wiped with the tea-towel that she's still holding in the other, against the back of the armchair. There are still some very fine bubbles of washing-up liquid and the smell of lemon on her whitened fingers. She watches the television with him and they both see, in silence, faces that sit uneasily with what the reporter's voice is saying. And then they wonder, where are our sons? Are they involved? What are they doing? I hear my father shouting through the house, alternately getting up and sitting down, champing impatiently and dragging on his old cigarette-butt, lighting it again every few seconds without noticing that it hasn't gone out once since he's been seeing these pictures.

And both leaping to their sons' defence. Even though it's he who says the first words. Straight away. He's the one who has to say that it was the Italians who started it. The filthy wops.

Like all foreigners, they're all the same, they're all the same shit (and my mother perhaps trying to mumble a few words to temper my father's outburst, just because she thinks there are things you shouldn't say, words that would make her blush a little rather than shocking her). And this time I see the two of them glued to the screen as if he found it easier to contain his rage when he was closer to the picture. He hasn't seen Doug or the two others. But they are parents. They know their boys. They know their shortcomings better than anyone. Probably even better than their wives do, because they didn't see them as children and they've never heard how those voices have changed over the years, or witnessed them becoming the men they are today. They don't know anything about how the three of them spent their teenage years, with Doug as the eldest, the gang-leader – yes, that's him: that spotty boy, bare-chested and violent, who spends afternoons with a jar in one hand and an old fly-swat stained with mush from the heads and bellies of squashed flies in the other. He's the boy who squashes the flies and throws them into his jar. He does that. He laughs. He shouts. You can see his teeth, the black stumps of the stupid old man who's already yelling through him, through that body. The bare chest of an adolescent with long, dirty hair.

No doubt about it. He's one of the ones running. He's one of the ones throwing his fists around. Even if he's no longer the adolescent who used to wipe his Doc Martens on the sitting-room carpet, his mother having given up shouting and resigned herself to seeing the sea-blue of her wool carpet disappearing under the mud of the great boots of her sons and their friends . . . How long has it being going on? And where did it start? Doesn't matter. She knows as she sees the pictures that her children are there, and that they are among the roaring ones. She thinks she can hear their voices.

Did I run with them? Is that me running with them?

She rubs her hands with the tea-towel again and again. She goes to get my father a beer and he knows too. He doesn't see his sons in the pictures. He doesn't really need to. He doesn't understand that they're talking about shame brought on the country. Or perhaps he is ashamed. Perhaps he doesn't know what to think and he can't think because of the beer and it's our fault too, because he can't help imagining that we're part of the pack, that we are the pack. And then he sees these pictures and bandannas over the faces, arms in the air, tattoos, Union Jacks. Chants. Screams. The television doesn't show everything. It didn't show the charge and yet when my father suddenly sees it, the bodies, the rubble, the newspapers and the devastated stadium, his first idea is to think, what a bunch of idiots, there'll be no match now and it's their fault. And my mother standing there, rooted to the spot, worrying and hoping that none of the English have been wounded and especially none of her sons, none of the neighbours. None of the Scousers. Nobody. No, none of the people she knows.

And she shakes her head when it occurs to her that quite to the contrary, they're on good form, great form. They're still shouting, she knows. She pretends not to believe it and to get worried for them, when she knows she should be worried about them, because of them, I mean because of them, worried by them, by her sons. Because she knows the tattoos and the knife on Doug's forearm, which stretches all the way to the palm of his hand, and his taste for booze and scrapping. When he was younger, there were the joints and the girls, too. The attacks on Pakis that he used to organise with his mates, and when they used to go queer-bashing, as they boastingly called it, when the clubs closed; and also sometimes picking up lone girls in the streets at night. For a laugh, they said, they'd slip a beer-bottle down their trousers to make it look like they had a huge cock, and they'd stroke it and make the girls watch. She knows all about that. She's never said anything. She thinks boys are like that. That's why she spends all day looking after the porcelain figurines on the shelf in her bedroom. That's why she likes their lace dresses and the Venetian masks on the walls. Their faces so white they look like cream or milk. Their eyes rimmed with make-up so pink it's as if the masks are moonstruck – and that's why, at night, my mother watches the street corner through the window, without hearing the night train or, behind her, the snores shaking my father's paunch and swelling his cheeks, making him look like an old trumpet-player.

Corridors and corridors, orange chairs and milky coffee in a polystyrene cup, waiting to see Tonino's face again. The plastic spoon that I turn and turn at the bottom of the cup, so as not to stare at Gabriel's eyes. And yet there's no rage in his face. Gabriel's there – he didn't even think of pretending to despise me or play at being someone who's waiting and can't forget why he has come. No. I watched him first of all in spite of all the time it took to react to his presence, when I saw that he was close to Tonino before Tonino was taken to hospital. I don't know why I'd reacted to his presence when he was a long way away from me and I didn't react to Virginie and Benoît who were so close to me. He was the one I'd seen, from where I was standing, doing that thing it's impossible to think about, bent over Tonino's hand (and it was that gesture that told me it was Tonino lying there), that soft hand, his torn shirt, the recurring image of Gabriel moistening his thumb with his tongue and then, with infinite slowness – it seemed to me – slowness and precision, he had gone over to Tonino and rubbed his hand to erase the phone number – when around him there were all those noises, the rotating lights of the ambulance, the screams of a woman looking for her son and the stretchers and the gurneys and all that hubbub with the casters of the stretchers with the crackling of the walkie-talkies and the voices spitting orders and a jumble of apparently meaningless words. I saw that thumb and that gesture, and all around us the numbers pinned on the photographers accredited for the match, leaning over the people on the ground, clicking madly away, just as inside the stadium a moment before they'd gone on taking their pictures right under the eyes of the people stretching out their hands to be pulled out of there.

And in this waiting room where now I have to stay and look at the cup I've been given, with that freeze-dried milky coffee and the plastic spoon, that coffee and the faint warmth through the soft cup, on my hands, is it real, that heat that's barely warmed my fingers? Is it true that I'm here, in this waiting room, and that it was Virginie who handed me this coffee? My voice saying thanks. My hand taking the cup, and my voice asking how I got here, who brought me here, what are they doing here too, so pale beneath the hospital lights? And all those voices jostling and echoing, the clanking of the trolleys. The metallic sounds and the lift chimes when the door opens and closes. We're there waiting for Tonino to come back out with someone to tell us it's going to be OK, because we've been told that everything is going to be fine, nothing serious, a few bruises, a few bumps, they'll do some X-rays and then everything should be fine. We'll be going very soon.

The voice above my head, Virginie's voice speaking gently and saying, come for a walk, don't worry, come and have a cigarette with me, we'll go into the courtyard just out here, get some air, won't you come? And I'm so incapable of doing anything, I follow her without answering. I know it's quite cold outside, and that cold will help me out of my torpor. It'll soon be night-time, with that moon like a nail right in the middle of the sky since the afternoon.

No one has spoken. But there was that moment when we could have done, after the astonishment of meeting up outside the stadium by the makeshift sick-bay. First of all they could have said to me, Jeff, you stole our tickets, you cheated us. And I could have said, what the hell are you doing here and then instead we looked at each other; they looked at me and around us there was this impossible world, those impossible pictures, and that powerful desire to escape the fury of the helicopters over our heads, the ambulance engines and the smoke from the exhaust pipes, the smell of the exhaust and that smell of alcohol and disinfectant. And then those gaunt faces, what is there to say, nothing to say given the smell of dust from the brown blankets, the flashes from the rotating lights. Suddenly there's nothing. Just seeing that we're there and that we have to go with Tonino to the hospital. Not a word about the tickets. As if it were better to forget about that now, and that it was all in the past and not something to be mentioned.

I was asked how I was, what had happened. I was shaking as I talked, as if it were a memory of another life. As if I were being asked to tell them what it was like to have a bath in the iron tub in the courtyard when my mother drenched us with the hose in the summer, or stomach-ache from eating too much rhubarb, or describing the jam that drips from our sandwiches and sticks to the tiles like the fake scars that we put on our wrists with a strip of liquid glue and the skin folded on both sides, holding very hard until it sticks. That's how I talked. That's what I was able to do. A bit. Just a bit. Because then as the words came out I forced myself to dispel the images, images are the worst of all because they steal your imagination. Then I spoke as I've always spoken, when I'm given the floor as ever, it's as if I've been asked, how come you're still alive? Eh, Jeff, my old mate, tell us? How did you do that? How come you're still talking and how dare you, you're managing very well, oh, yeah, very well, hiding your hands under that lukewarm cup, and looking at the bottom of the milky coffee that you're still stirring to see if the whirlpool in the middle mightn't just swallow you up, as you listen to your hoarse little voice telling the story, choking and breathless with all the effort, as though if she spoke it would bring the nightmares back to life so no, come on, tell us, because that's what makes you so amazed that you're still alive.

Did I run with them? Is that me running with them? Is it the same beer turning my stomach and making my breath stink? Elsie's grief and her hands clutching a paper tissue, in rags since the early afternoon. My mother with her make-up on. The Chinese restaurant on the corner, Madame Kyon, which had put up its colours up in the window. God Save the Queen.

My father in the sitting room must be threatening the plaster amphora on the TV, and even the picture of the grandchildren in the frame of pink and yellow shells. My mother must be sitting there in silence, her fingers twisted in the tea-towel. But she's going to have to talk, because the phone's going to ring and my father won't move to reply. So she'll pick it up. It'll be Doug's wife. No. Hughie's wife; it'll be Hughie's wife first. Because as to the question of whether the three Andrewson boys are part of the pack, Faith will know the answer has to be yes, because Doug's there, because Hughie doesn't know how to do anything except follow Doug, and the little one will do what he can, meaning not much.

I imagine her, hiding her children and forbidding them to leave their room while she discovers and devours the pictures on television. Hunting down the faces. Looking closely among the crowd, behind the bandannas and the wide-shots sweeping a stand where in places all that remains is the wind swirling between two sheets of newspaper; a shoe, a lighter, jeans and trainers beneath the chants still shaking the stadium, with the terrifying calm of slogans and refrains.

Is that my voice chanting with them? Am I chanting with them too?

Hughie's wife, with her blonde curls and her orange lipstick to make her look like Kim Wilde, as savage and seductive as that, her carefully dishevelled hair behind the counter as she sees the men and women coming into the shop in search of shoes, always shoes, all day long – and Faith is surprised that anyone might not want to do what she does, just because she doesn't think that you could dream of anything better in life than this ideal: a job that doesn't mean getting your hands dirty. So I can imagine her on the phone, giving off a fog of patchouli and mimosa, furiously crushing out a menthol cigarette beside the phone, looking furiously towards the corridor, where, behind their bedroom doors, the children must be killing themselves as they whoop like Red Indians or roar like furious extraterrestrials buying the earth for three bits of chewing-gum. And then she looks behind the slightly blurred picture on the screen. And she listens to the commentaries and my mother's breathing on the phone, not saying a word. Or saying that she should get off the line, perhaps they'll call. Perhaps. Surely they'll phone to tell us they're out of danger? Faith must let my mother talk and then interrupt her, saying, anyway I expected as much,

No.

anyway with Doug, what do you expect?

No.

I'm telling you that anyway when you know his mates,

No, no, no, it's not true. It just can't be. My mother's voice trying to defend some ideas that she no longer believes in. But she knows how to be a mother as she's been taught to be a mother and a wife: to defend her children like a she-wolf, fuck like a bitch, work like an ox and stay silent as a goldfish, all that for so little, so that there's nothing left for her but the pitiful consolation of rebelling by being neither a bitch in the bedroom nor a goldfish in the kitchen. Rebelling and being gentle at the same time. Like when she tries to make herself look nice and on the days when she sweats and drips, drying her face with a brush and powder. Today she must have put on some blue eye-shadow. She has a wart on the left-hand side of her nose. She must have arranged the cardboard boxes in the hall. Then she must have looked at her husband all afternoon, and programmes about clouds of locusts and blue coral reefs, the depths. And now desperately trying to defend her sons saying no, they're not there. They can't be there. Desperately, frowning. And replying to Hughie's wife who's already attacking Doug and defending her husband saying, you know, Hughie isn't capable of changing a window-pane, he spends the whole weekend on the sofa watching the football, I can't imagine him running like a madman, not like that madman Doug, his brother.

And she keeps on about Doug. If anything happens, it's Doug who's to blame. She studies the television as she talks on the telephone. They both bite their nails, each at the end of their phone line. They peer through the pictures and the game when it starts. Nothing. There's nothing. They've seen very clearly that the Italian players have come on to the pitch to calm the *tifosi*. Yes, they saw that. Everyone saw that. My dad saw the *tifosi*. He saw Boniek and the rest on the pitch, coming out to talk to the Italians. The whole of England saw that, the whole of Europe. And Doug's wife saw it too. Perhaps she wept with fear? Perhaps she told her children to tidy their rooms and go and play outside? Perhaps she thought her husband had no part in it and all three of us were at the other end of the stadium? Is that what she thought?

Perhaps Elsie thought that too? Or did she choose instead to arrange the bunch of plastic carnations on the counter and tighten the belt of her white uniform? Perhaps when she saw the Italian players on the pitch she thought I couldn't get involved in all that and she hadn't got involved in all that either, that she wasn't living out the same story as me, hundreds of miles away.

Corridors and corridors, voices surrounding me with superfluous concern. What I do want is to be allowed to see Tonino and understand what's happened. To be told what really happened just before, rather than hearing yet again the four others telling me in the same faint voice that everything's OK, that Tonino's coming back. They tell me that as if we hadn't stolen their tickets. As if they were pretending not to know. And I'm there in front of them, and I want to act as if I hadn't seen Gabriel outside the stadium, repeatedly glancing round to see if anyone was noticing this gesture that he made when, pretending to comfort Tonino, he was just desperately trying to erase the digits of a phone number.

And I knew what was going on. I had to do the same as Gabriel did, pretend to have seen nothing, to have nothing to say. But perhaps I hadn't seen anything, and now I have nothing left to say, just as he had nothing to say at the moment when, stunned by the surprise of reading that phone number which he must have seen by chance, and reading it without paying any attention, almost as a reflex, and then being surprised to recognise the digits and the number they made, he must have settled for being surprised rather than flying into a rage, just making that mending gesture, calm, definitive, by way of reprisal: erasing the mark of betrayal to forget it straight away. Starting over, pretending. And now he must be as surprised as me that we find ourselves reunited here, in the waiting room of a hospital in the city centre, so late in the evening.

But all of a sudden that door swings open.

And all eyes – but no silence here, no impact, no John Wayne and no returning hero, nothing but Tonino, pale, a few bloodstains around his eyebrow and that thin bandage over his eyebrow, the sloppy Hawaiian shirt under the open jacket, stained and torn lengthways from the belly, showing a triangle of skin that he doesn't even try to cover up by zipping up his jacket, quite the contrary, already parading the tear and the blood mixed with the orange and yellow flowers of the shirt as proof of his resistance. Tonino comes towards us, towards me, he doesn't react. And it's Gabriel who moves first. Who steps forward and then, all of a sudden, that sense that nothing more can happen, that it's all happened and we've won, Tonino and me, a kind of weird respect, a silence around us. No mention of the tickets. And no mention, in fact, of anything. Nothing. There's nothing, just Tonino and me. We hug and say, all right? You all right? Repeating the same words and surprised to see ourselves face to face, checking it with hands and arms, his hands on the back of my neck. And looking at each other for a long time, dumbstruck, without understanding Tonino's torn shirt, or the bandage on his eyebrow where the blood had flowed, finally drying and leaving only a faint brownish crust.

And then his furious expression when he speaks, Tonino, the

same look he had the moment when the English charged, when there were four of us, with the Italian couple. At the top of the stand, and what we saw first was the spectacle, right before our eyes, of a stadium filled to the brim. The strength you feel at that moment, the miracle of knowing that there, in that stadium, beneath the sixty thousand pairs of eyes turning towards a bit of pitch, they're going to be playing the cup final of the century. Those chants returning and the voices of the Italians, the wheel in the exhibition park, right opposite the stand, on the other side of the stadium; I see it turning and turning in my head, that image and the screen with the giant letters running by, orange or green, I can't remember. A shiver, something because of the slow, heavy chants which, lifting air and space, make the pennants dance, the colours, that red, that gold mixing with the blue of the sky and the moon up above. Just behind the stadium, in the exhibition park, the big wheel turns slowly, and facing it we speak of it and its movement in the sky; we aren't moving, and it's as if the first screams behind us had nothing to do with us.

Furious people. Everyone was furious. And the horses on the athletics track, the lanes marked off with white lines – did they see the horses pawing and stamping the red ground and the hoofs erasing the white lines? The uniformed cops and the calm of the soldiers when they entered the stadium, slowly, in single file. They took up position between the pitch and the stands, facing the crowd, helmets lowered, truncheons in their hands and shields held in front of them. No, it's not a matter of knowing whether they've seen all that in Liverpool, or even if they've watched to the end. That's not what worries me. Or even knowing if they managed to react without shame and without a desire to scream, without crying when they saw, in their sitting rooms, surrounded by their wallpaper and the trinkets in the glass case, the empty stands and the rubble, abandoned shoes, their laces ripped out, and chewing-gum wrappers, newspapers, thousands of metro tickets like confetti;

did they see all that at home? No, that's not what's worrying me.

Not really. It's thinking of that confusion that Elsie must have wanted to banish or deny, or simply cancel out by averting her head and carefully replacing the plastic carnations in their glass jar. Then blowing her nose again, hands soft and trembling, finally tightening the belt of her white uniform; yes, I can see her. She's got up again because she can't stay sitting down and see that violence without moving or doing something, there must be someone who needs her. Someone must need her. Let the bell squeak like a dog's toy. Let the little orange bulb above her desk start to flash. Let a room number appear to get her out of there. That's what she wants with all her heart, the moment Elsie begins to see the pictures of that place where she imagines me.

Elsie's pain and her hands clutching her paper handkerchief in rags since the afternoon because in the end, that's it, unlike me she's never been so naïve as to imagine that things will work themselves out. She says to me: you want to think they'll like you if you do what they do. But they'll never like you for yourself. Because you're their brother, they even make themselves believe they love you; it's what they've been taught, the duty of loving your family. It's simple, she says to me. Because you look like them. Your nose. Your eyes. And that means something to them. You're like a crumb of themselves and that makes you endearing in their eyes. But for you, clinging since childhood to your desperate hope that soon you wouldn't hear the walls shake when Doug squashed a fly and scraped the bloody wall, afterwards, with that wicked laugh of his that's driven you mad since childhood, scared you witless. That's what she says to me. And your dad with his beer, in the brown armchair, you're scared of him too, don't lie, you always have been; even when you were a child, when he was out of work that time and drowned his misery with beer from Madame Kyon, bought with money he stole from your mother. And your mother yelling. Dare to tell me that you weren't scared of your mum too, and her shouting, and her tears even more. And Hughie, even more of a moron perhaps because he wasn't even clever enough to be wicked. So soft. So slow behind his brother and his heavy metal posters, his pictures of sports cars, and his indifference to everything, because the only thing that interested him was following your brother. So you, Geoff, why would you want them to love you the way you love a brother or a friend, the way you love someone just because he's nice? You could do what you want. You'll never be anything to them but a copy, a ghost, the same nose and the same skin. You have their white skin, that's not so bad, that grey complexion that men get when they're scared.

So why, Tonino said to me, is the first picture that came into my head when I woke up in hospital that yellow flag floating with the words *mamma sono qui* in big black letters? I didn't reply. Then we went outside to smoke, followed first by Gabriel, the three others bringing up the rear.

In the courtyard of the hospital, Tonino's fingers tremble, clutching that cigarette that he has to draw on as hard as he can, with all his might. And I can see the others around him, all four of them, uneasy, ears pricked for what he might say, as though they were personally threatened by the words he might come out with: and then his voice trembles and says nothing, his eyes look at his hands clutching his cigarette, while his voice starts up. And he stares at me as he speaks, things that I saw too, things that I too could have said, what a stupid feeling that is, the realisation that it's utterly pathetic to notice the advertisements around the pitch; the luminous panel with the words UEFA WELCOMES YOU, when you could see a cop and three guys in plain clothes, knees and backs bent, each at one corner of a blanket now serving as a stretcher, because there were no stretchers left, carrying a body like a heavy round ball, mute and incredibly heavy; all those people that had to be carried that way, haphazardly, like objects, dead dogs on the side of the road; always with that image of joyful supporters who can't see and can't begin to guess what's happening, the importance of the dust and the violence, while down below you can see a couple of cavalry battalions on the athletics track, and the photographers on the pitch, with arms and hands holding their cameras above the people's heads, above their cries.

The English appearing from nowhere. And then we have to tell the story of how Tonino didn't want to run and how he stood to face them, how he wanted to get a punch in when he saw a big guy charging at him with an iron bar. No. It was a broken flagpole. He was sweeping it in front of him and around him there were two or three blokes pulling up their bandannas to hide their faces. They knew what they were doing as they pulled their scarves up to their eyes so they wouldn't be recognised while the blades of the knives they were holding sliced the air and the space in an arc in front of them, with just enough time to run and take a step back to keep from being cut. And yet, Tonino said, this blood on my shirt isn't mine. First of all they injure someone, a man beside me who yells and holds his ground ready to fight, not to be defeated and he tries to lash out but the blade slashes his wrist and the blood's his blood that's spurting, and Tonino taking another cigarette, he talks and looks at his feet. Now his hands are making arabesques, miming the movements of the men with the knives. He tells the whole story. How it's quite simple, as he sees it, impossible not to go apeshit.

So he throws himself in front of a group of four or five Englishmen and he tells us how, eyes half-closed, he throws himself screaming and hurling out a volley of the filthiest words he knows, fists clenched and nails plunged so deeply into his palm that he tears the skin. He throws punches into the void. Soon he feels faces beneath his fists, bodies beneath the kicks he's throwing as they're throwing stones, iron bars, bottles all around him. It's here that a fist gashes his eyebrow. He doesn't notice straight away, no. First he has to conquer his rage. First he has to lose his desire to strike out with fists and feet at the bodies that come within his range. Now what he wants to do is leave the hospital and have a drink, have done with it. Yeah, let's go. I want to get out of here, I need a drink, a brandy, something strong. That's what you need to forget and talk about what you've seen – and then he says, we have to get back down there for Francesco and Tana. Where are they? They were with us. I hope that

And Liverpool watching me running with them.

Not to see myself, running, panting and charging with them, head lowered. Not to hear my own cries in that crowd that I see in front of me. Tonight in Brussels. That strange, black, silent night in the hotel room. And in this bed with its blankets too white for me, too smooth, no roughness, I didn't sleep, while my brothers slept, their heavy, calm breathing smashing through the silence and the sirens in the city that made me start and tremble. Because for me that doesn't change anything about what remains: the image and the sounds. The roar of voices and returning images. That cup that the Italians held up at the end of the game. And we hadn't understood. I saw the blood and I said nothing. I saw Soapy and Gordon getting insanely furious, both of them, how mad and furious those eyes, those faces – did I really see the blood? And that girl, afterwards, on the pitch, all alone and I could see that she was waiting. That she didn't understand. She was there, wild-eyed. She was trying to put an elastic band in her hair. She was trying to make a ponytail and she couldn't do it. She smiled back at the people who talked to her. She couldn't see them, she couldn't see anyone. And then the police took care of her.

As clouds of locusts fall on cornfields; the blue coral that my mother watches on television in the afternoon. As if we were animals, a nature documentary? Did I really run with them? Did I run, too, like that, yelling those chants?

During the night, I tried to pass the evening and the previous day before my eyes as a way of understanding. The voices and the images that cried out at me, conveying an impossible truth (why the cigarette-butts that we threw in the wake of the cars as we were crossing the four-lane highway in the afternoon? Why the beer bottles and the noise they made on the cobbles? The people's eyes and the red-faced laughter with which we answered them? The careless air and the knife-blade in Doug's palm?). I felt I was colliding with her. Elsie's face turning slightly away so as not to see the television. I shouted and sang the same songs as I watched the Farns, Doug, Hughie. And Gordon too.

I didn't call home. I didn't call Elsie. What's going to happen now when I'll have to say that I didn't want to call her to repeat yet again, was that me, was it really me, the one who ran with them? Was it me who chanted and drank with them, and who are they? Is it true that my face is as white as theirs and my face is only a copy of theirs? Tell me, Elsie, you told me one day, yes, that I wanted to be like them because I wasn't like them, and that if I did want to it was a lie. You're going to have to help me to be quiet if you don't want everything to explode. As long as you don't ask me any questions. And I looked at the ceiling of the hotel room, pleading that tomorrow, when you're standing in front of me, you'll have the courage not to ask. Elsie, if you knew how much I want to cry and believe that I'm about to wake up. That I didn't yell. That I didn't run. I saw people falling and they say people died. They say the fence ripped people's throats out. They say that people were suffocated to death. They say that people,

and my brothers sleeping in the night and the night coming anyway as if nothing was wrong. And those eyes, tomorrow, that will rest on us, and we'll have to try not to see the questions that trouble them. My mother and Hughie's wife who'll be screaming, God almighty, why didn't you phone last night, we were scared, so scared! And I'll be disgusted to hear them saying – as if it was true only for them – back here, we didn't get a wink of sleep last night.

II

6

All night I'll listen to Tonino and Jeff, I'll stay with them. I'll watch as Tonino, having washed his face with a simple jet of cold water from the toilet tap, becomes himself again. How it's up to him now if he wants to open his eyes and look at Virginie and talk to her, perhaps, but only if he decides to, because looking at her without having anything to say is enough. And also staring at her and leaving me alone with the awkwardness of bearing that indirect, oblique look, that breach the two of them have been digging in my life since we arrived in the bar – not the one last night, no, in the city centre this time, in the old, yellowed *bruincafé* I used to go to when I was younger, before I met Virginie. We came here because Tonino wanted to drink, because he said: I need something strong, a brandy, and afterwards we'll think; let's go to Tana and Francesco's hotel and see how they are, what they're doing.

Jeff is there, his arms spread and his elbows far apart, his back so bent that his chin is only a few centimetres away from the bar. He has that disdainful, almost haughty way of holding his beer glass, hooking his dry, white fingers around it, his black nails, without looking around him. I'm going to go to the toilet to think and stop feeling either the effects of the sweet beer or the burning in my stomach. The corn on my foot is still hurting but, sitting on the toilet seat, I can finally take off my shoe and rub my foot; I put it back on and tie the lace, feeling the new leather, still hard, as though by stroking it I could soften it. When I get back to the bar, there they are, all five of them in the middle of the few remaining beer drinkers.

People are talking about what they've heard and what their plans are. They're talking about the victims and the heads that will fall in the ministries, but also about the fact that the match was played anyway. Who knows what would have happened if the match hadn't taken place? They probably had to play it (and I find myself suddenly thinking about the people I'd heard outside the entrance to the stadium, talking about the Italians' superstition that the black and white jerseys would bring them bad luck), yes, no doubt, or else everything could have been worse. And the six of us wouldn't be here, but all around the city there would be the same fear of skinheads, that anxiety that the city is going to tip into definitive and irreversible violence. But the English have gone. The police and the army have filled up the buses and now calm is going to return. In the bar I see faces swapping questions, wordless, no movement but that lingering surprise on people's faces. And then, finally the words ring out; attacks, indictments being hurled around between two mouthfuls of beer. We're talking about the shame of experiencing that here, in Brussels. We hear people saying, no, no, it can't happen here, it can't happen now, it's impossible; just as it's impossible for me to say to myself that these two guys here were in *my* place; Tonino breathing so hard as he drinks his brandy – yes, I need another one, he says. He tries to concentrate to think. And Jeff beside him, having refused to sit down, sometimes rubbing his stiff neck and leaning his head back; he too has taken another glass, and he barely dares to look at us, barely sees Adrienne and Benoît chatting on the left of the bar, with a guy who's just come in. Virginie joins them, and the barman does, too, a glass in one hand and a bottle of Perrier in the other.

I can hear the hubbub and the voices mingling with the music from the jukebox at the back. The television has been switched off because that's enough, the barman says, what happened is too harsh, he says, hesitant and stressing the word, clearly too weak, as they all are. Then, at that moment, what could I have said? or rather, when I saw Tonino and

Virginie looking at each other in silence and that it seemed to me that something was passing between them, something obvious, yet as impalpable and persistent as a smell, with the stubbornness of certainty: they were talking amongst themselves and there was nothing I could do about it. I told myself that what I feared most wasn't so much the danger of losing Virginie, but that I couldn't bear my fear of being incapable of keeping her, having no response but hatred and resentment, or perhaps the vague hope that what I was seeing was nothing, an idea, a hallucination. But you should be wary of hallucinations and ideas. And it was as if Tonino's voice was coming in search of me from so far away that I had trouble hearing it, calling to mind the image of his face. And yet he's there. In front of me. The movement of his lips, like footsteps. No. They aren't footsteps.

What? What are you saying?

My voice rising to shake off this torpor into which alcohol and exhaustion – and fear, too – have dragged my legs and arms, perhaps even my whole body, when only my head is trying to stay upright, and, with words it doesn't even hear itself beginning to utter, trying to fend off, all the things that have happened since yesterday.

What? what's that you say?

Oh, of course. Avenue de la Toison d'Or. Yes, behind the Saint-Hubert Galleries. A stone's throw from here, well, not exactly, it's a stone's throw from the Grand-Place. What's that, which hotel? I make him repeat it once, twice. He drains his glass, and as I see him slamming it down on the bar, I have a sense of extraordinary strength, as though an explosion of rage had allowed him to come back among us. Tonino wants to leave now, he says he's worried. I give a nod, but so uncertainly, with such restraint that I'm not even sure anyone could have seen it. Jeff finishes his glass with a great gulp. He coughs, his face turns red. Tonino looks at me, and I don't even know what to say to him, or how to improvise. So I just say we've got to go now. That we just have to go to the hotel, which isn't all that far; I ask for confirmation from the people around me, without asking the name of the hotel, because I know that locals are usually the worst informed about hotels that they don't have to use. But everyone knows about the Saint-Hubert Galleries. So we leave, all of us together, because Adrienne and Benoît wanted to stay with us.

And off we go, amidst the freshness of the night as it turns to cold, with that silence falling and the two black dogs we meet on the corner of Rue Grétry as we head down towards the Grand-Place. The two dogs are sniffing at each other on the pavement, barely disturbed by our footsteps and the sirens in the night – ambulances, police, the sense that nothing really comes to an end and the echo of the evening, its shockwave is still reverberating in the streets. And we say to ourselves that the hatred of the English will go on chasing the hatred of the Italians all night, even without the Italians or the English, in spite of the silence of the tables that the restaurants and flats will camouflage beneath a background of songs by Jacques Brel and operatic arias.

We walk up towards the Saint-Hubert Galleries and towards the Avenue de la Toison d'Or, because that's what the Italian couple had told Tonino, the Hotel Bellevue, specifying that it was an Art Nouveau hotel. They'd told him that, but most of all they'd talked about the two amusingly incongruous desk clerks: twins with a very priestly air, one seated, the other standing behind him. Like two great Russian-accented mastiffs, with the chubby faces of two big kids never parted since childhood. Was that the name they'd given, Hotel Bellevue? Behind the Saint-Hubert Galleries, could that be? Is there such a thing as the Saint-Hubert Galleries? Tonino asked again. And yeah, I know the Galleries, but the name of the hotel doesn't mean a thing. It doesn't matter.

Tonino and I are ahead of the others, we walk and he talks, he talks, he starts talking so loudly and so incoherently, phrases fading away and re-emerging from unexpected directions, he comes back to the name of the hotel, he says that the name doesn't matter much because the important thing is that it's an Art Nouveau hotel, that it was the wedding present they were given, a trip they didn't ask for but were given anyway. He thinks it'll be easy to find and I tell him yes, I'm sure we'll have no trouble finding it. We have to find a wooden counter with two big sleepy-looking blokes, each the spit of the other. And then, in the hall, weighty mouldings, voluptuous shapes and lithe, serpentine lines like seaweed rising to the ankles, the thighs of nymphs in the undergrowth, interlacing and spirals and iridescent floral fabric wallpaper, delicately coloured, pastels of pale blue and faded pink, the whole box of Art Nouveau tricks.

The two desk clerks are just as we expected, strangely smiling, a little dazed, the first sitting behind the massive, shining wooden counter, the second behind him, standing, a hand on his hip, watching a television off to the side – we hear the gasps of a voice talking of the reaction of the English and saying that the thirtieth European Cup will be the last. I come in first, followed by Tonino and Jeff. The others stay outside and when they see us coming back towards them they understand straight away.

Nobody? Virginie asks me. And I don't reply, just pulling a face to say no. We decide to go to a bar where we'll be able to get something to eat as we wait, and then we'll come back here. Now I look at Tonino standing in front of me, waiting to see whether in the street, on the other side, he can see the couple coming towards the hotel. He says that if they don't come, if they still haven't come back to the hotel soon, we'll have to go round the hospitals and ask where they could be. I say we need their names. Their names. Tonino says yes, that's true, and then returns to his plate and starts eating slowly, as if he were chewing glass rather than meatballs in tomato sauce. Some voices reach us from a back room. We hear some Dutch voices and a man shouting because his rollmops haven't arrived even though the mussels are there. And as we hear that we say nothing, and we're surprised both at being together and at hearing this man calling for rollmops when we've come here because a young couple must be alone somewhere in the city, and also because this thing has happened, this thing that the whole of Europe has seen, unable to believe its eyes.

While as for us, with our translucent blue plates and damp, soft, burnt bread that we've been served with the tired *ballekes* and *choesels* in Madeira that don't even look all that appetising, we'd just like to have finished. We'd like to understand, in spite of the certainty that even with all the time in the world we'll never grasp the event or even why all six of us are here together, an unlikely collection and useless as a fridge on an ice floe with our mouths chewing and behind the voices the glasses chinking in the back room, amidst laughter and swearing; not even spying on each other any more, as we still could as recently as last night. Tonino struggles to eat, the bits of beef rolling round in his mouth, giving him a stupid and sad expression. We drink beer, surprised by the thick, white foam. Adrienne asks Virginie the time. Benoît has gone to the toilet and I'm facing them: Jeff eats without looking at me and, suddenly, Tonino looks at the back of his left hand. He immediately looks at me. And then he tries to smile, he looks deep within himself, behind the exhaustion and the alcohol, behind the burden of the day, for the hint of a smile that won't come – and it's his voice that comes instead, gently, with unexpected caution and delicacy.

Gabriel, he says. I think we ought to talk.

Francesco,

I can't even hear my heart beating or my pulse or my blood or the sobs in my throat, those sobs that I want to silence and calm to hear my voice telling me, don't be stupid, stop sniffing like that and blow your nose. Then wash your hands. Go on washing your hands. Again. Rub. They're filthy. The water hurts my hands; the blood has stopped flowing; the skin and little scratches like crumbs of blood-reddened skin. My hands hurt, I'll have to wash them again and then blow my nose – it'll be OK, it'll be OK, calm down, what did they say? What did the doctor say?

No, he wasn't a doctor, that guy in the white coat, that young curly-haired guy with the melancholy face and the bulging eyes. He disinfected the marks on my hands with cotton-wool soaked in alcohol. He did it slowly. We were sitting facing one another, and as he threw away the soiled bits of cotton wool and took another one and then yet another to clean the bloodstains from my hands, and the soil, the scratches from the concrete, he repeated the same words two or three times, forced to repeat them because I said I couldn't hear him. In the end I pretended I'd heard and nodded my head, but the truth is I hadn't heard anything. He tried to articulate and he spoke slowly, that's true, and his movements were slow; he held my hands and each time he had to start explaining all over again.

I watched his movements and saw nothing else. I heard only the cotton wool slipping over the backs of my hands, catching on the scratches, I tried to understand and feel my hands again and the movement of my wrists, my fingers, except that everything was going too quickly. Everything. Too quickly. Those screams, that night, the blue lights and the police dogs barking and the coaches outside the stadium. Even the trees frighten me. The sound of the wind in the trees, I'm frightened, what did he say? I can't remember. The papers. What have I signed? I signed some things, some papers, they told me to go to the embassy as early as possible tomorrow morning and someone – I think it was a woman – gave me an address that she wrote on some very thin, almost transparent paper. Then I folded it in two and then in four, and then in eight, and finally I stopped listening to anything she said to me about the office hours, perhaps, I don't know. After that, the young man with the bulging blue eyes gave some water, too cold, in a plastic cup. He gave me a little bottle of tranquillisers, saying they would help me sleep a bit tonight, and that they would relax me for the time being. I let a tablet melt under my tongue to calm me down. I can't remember very clearly, I know that after a few minutes I realised that my fingernails were no longer plunging stubbornly into my palm, and that my hand had finally agreed to open. It was at that moment that they gave me the papers to sign – no, no, that was before, when I'd just told the young man I had to call Italy. He walked me to a cabin in the corridor, but all the cabins were taken, so I waited. He stayed with me for a while, and it was then I said I wanted to go to the toilet. He walked me to the door, supporting me by the arm,

Francesco,

And now words, all words and gobbledygook and I'm in a cold sweat, quick, water on my mouth, my lips are chapped from murmuring your name, my skin scratched to pieces from thinking it wasn't possible to see you, to see the shape of your body under the brown blanket and the straps so that you wouldn't fall out, and me walking behind with my neck craned and my knees broken, my body leaning forward and eyes that wanted to, that tried to, while you wouldn't answer my cries. And what's going to happen? You've got to come back. I'm going to finish washing my hands. I'm going to run water through my hair and then take off the elastic band that I've put around my wrist. I'm going to put my hair in a ponytail again and after that I'm going to wipe my hands, arrange my collar, I'm not going to cry any more. I'll regret not having any make-up (this time I'd like to smell that woman smell, powder on the cheeks and lipstick grease, eye-shadow on the lids to hide the darkness in the eyes and the rings beneath them). And then the door will open, you'll be standing in front of me and I'll throw myself into your arms, exploding with laughter. Tears that will smudge my make-up. Your hands will crease my neatly straightened collar and your fingers in my hair will pull out the elastic band that will fall at my feet and then, yes, I'll have something to drink, the way the cat used to drink when I was a child. I'll do as he did, lapping at the stream of water falling gently from the tap. And I will listen to my heart beating till it calms, till it sees reason and stops intoxicating itself with its own fear; until it thinks about the rhythm it's giving my blood because it's all swirling in my head. I feel a fire in my cheeks and my fingers, and in my legs, too. And yet I'm so pale. That's when I realise that the black I had around my eyes has flowed with my tears and that the red of my lipstick has fled with my screams – hang on, I've lost the bandanna I was wearing around my neck.

That's it, then, I'd have to put my make-up on and then you'd come and we'd leave here, I'd come out of the toilet, we'd leave the hospital and I'd say goodbye to the young man with the bulging eyes and that sad expression on his face. We'd breathe in the cold night air and take the taxi to head for the hotel, and it would all end up with us in bed, you and me, drunk on the peppery smell of your after-shave and the slightly rancid smell of the wallpaper in the room, beneath the eyes of the glass paste flowers of the green and yellow bedside lamps. Now I'm mad, I'm completely insane yes completely crazy so much so that I could scream with laughter and laugh at my hideous, pathetic image, haggard and wretched, in this mirror, too clean, no streaks, no toothpaste splashes like real mirrors have in real bathrooms. Now I've got to calm down. I've got to get my wits back. I've got to understand and retrace that whole path, I've got to hear your voice and understand what has brought me here, to the toilet of a big hospital in Brussels, how it was that I ended up here. I'm Tana. I'm your wife. I'm twenty-three years old. Blonde, with red highlights in my hair, a new bride. And you are Francesco and you were holding my hand. We left home by train and arrived in Brussels where we saw our hotel and the big red flowers in the bedroom, the wooden mouldings and the arabesques on the feet of the bed. And then on the metro we met Tonino and that other guy, what's his name, Jeff, who was asleep and his head danced and bobbed like one of the balloons I saw dancing in the stadium later on: the stands, the people jostling each other and then the nightmare, everything's going too fast, too loud, your hand, your voice, I'm suffocating under the others, I'm being pushed and I can't see you any more, Francesco, that's what happened. I'll be told that that's what happened.

But I know it isn't so. Do I have to believe that we were outside afterwards? I mean, will I have to believe that after all those cries and all that panic we were outside the stadium and then a few hours afterwards in that room in the hospital morgue where you were laid out like a corpse, beside other people laid out like corpses too, as though they had really been abandoned by life and dead like in the pictures shown over and over again on television, like the corpses in the television news, so good at imitating Hollywood corpses in their corpse postures, with their white faces, corpse-pale or black and swollen. The night, and the shouts from a game we will never see. Do I have to believe what I see, what I've seen? No. No. Absolutely not. No. Sooner believe that the Russians have dropped the bomb, or that the Martians have landed, or that Reagan is playing his finest part, sooner believe that I was never born and that you don't exist either; my mother is a girl who reads magazines for girls and dreams one day that she too will have a daughter.

I'm just a dream, I don't exist, I'm not in these toilets, in Brussels, I haven't finished drying my hands with those paper towels which I throw away and which accumulate in the bin under the basin. And my reflection in the mirror, the footsteps and announcements I can hear, it's outside, in the corridor, all those people and that endless tension. You're going to come. You have to come. It's incredible, I'm still in pain, my back hurts, my hands, you can't be dead, it's impossible,

Were you there?

What? There? Me? Yes, we were there and now, I'm waiting, I don't know.

Francesco,

This girl standing by the basin, next to the one I'm clinging to, bent-backed, my arms and legs trembling. She says nothing. She looks at herself in the window and performs the same gestures as me – that is to say, the movements I've been performing mechanically, without noticing: leaning over to drink water, breathing heavily and splashing her face with water and spreading it on her cheeks, on her forehead and then washing her hands and waiting for the shaking all the way down her legs to stop. I look at her and ask her if she was there too. She says no, I have a friend who was there, but it's OK, just a few blows to the head, a lot of blood, but nothing much, a few stitches, I was terrified. And what about you?

About us.

Francesco, we were there and now I'm waiting for them to tell me something about you. While here, I'm waiting to crush within myself whatever it is that's keeping me straight and stiff. And as I see the girl taking make-up from her bag, I ask her to lend me her powder, her lipstick, something to blacken my eyes. Eyes first. Take time over the eyes. Lean towards the mirror and stay firm, don't breathe. I've never been very good at putting on my make-up, but I think it's because I don't really like it; I wear skirts and ponytails and hardly any make-up, hardly ever. Today I put on some lipstick and a bit of mascara, because we're on honeymoon, so it's unusual, but otherwise I wear very little make-up, only every now and again. I wear a Perfecto jacket, I don't like being in a crowd of girls and I hate being given flowers, irises and roses but fuck shit fuck what am I on about, my hand's shaking, the girl's talking and I don't reply. I hear her voice coming towards me, from a distance, she's talking too quickly. I don't understand French when it's spoken too quickly, I tell her. She says she'll speak more slowly, then, but she goes on talking just as fast.

And I go on blackening my eyelashes with her mascara, my hand shaking more and more. The tranquilliser tasted like flour, or the Host, and by now it's dissolved under my tongue – and I feel as if it was all long ago, it leaves a furry taste in my mouth, a heaviness that clings to my tongue and saliva but doesn't calm the agitation of my hands or the feeling of panic that surges along with waves of nausea that make me totter on my feet. So I've got to stop putting on make-up, cling to the edge of the basin and then wait for a moment, panting. No. My heart is beating so hard now, Francesco. And then, when I hold the mascara out to the girl, she looks at me and with a smile, probably to comfort me, she tells me I look much better now. She rummages in her big handbag and while she tells me she can never find anything, never! she repeats, she takes out a brush for her hair (which is very long, very thick) and then finally that ochre-coloured compact that she immediately holds out to me. Now I open the compact and, with the round sponge between my fingers, I start moving it around over my cheeks. I want to take my time. The movement has to be like a caress so that the sponge, stained with almost orange powder, reveals my face, drawing it as though it were inventing it, drawing it out from some improbable magma that waited only for this gesture, this gentleness, to know its own design. And on my face the colour awakens my skin, it invents a non-existent freshness. But the important thing is for the pallor to disappear and everything to be possible, everything to be erased, for you to come, for you to look at my skin and the vanishing pallor. Fear fades, the expression of grief disappears, Francesco, Francesco, my skin, I feel my skin beneath my touch, and my blood, and my eyes following the movement. I hear the girl talking again and murmuring words that I don't understand, because she's pulling a face, applying lipstick as she speaks.

Now she's lent me her lipstick. And I too want to put some on and watch my gestures in the mirror, paying no heed to the harsh, blinding light above my head, without listening to what she says, this girl who stays by the mirror waiting for me to finish. But I don't want to do it quickly. I don't know how to do it quickly. The urge to cry sometimes rises in me so fast that I have to lean very close to the mirror and gently make the gesture of following the outline of my lips; first the V shape under my nose, careful with the red grease that too violent a motion, too heavy and clumsy a pressure might crush and spread over my mouth, in compact little lumps. I have to pay close attention and think only of this task. Listen to nothing that reaches me, neither the noises outside, in the corridor, nor those of the people coming in and out of the toilets, or the voice of the girl next to me telling me how scared she was, and starting to talk about the madness of the times and all the usual nonsense; although I mustn't listen, my hands are shaking. I'm going to have to leave the hospital and go back to the hotel, alone, and understand that you won't be coming back. I'll have to call your parents and my mother.

But no, no, not too quickly,

not straight away.

First thank the girl as I give her back her lipstick. Then breathe deeply. Take a paper towel and slip it between my lips to get rid of the surplus make-up. Look in the mirror and then at the few traces of red on the white towel that's going slightly fluffy; then crumple and throw the bit of paper. Yes, I have to follow the girl – I heard the zip of her bag, her heels when she headed towards the door and this time the door opens and I too have to leave and go back to the hospital hall. The girl is in front of me. All of a sudden she stops and turns round.

Can I help you?

I want to smile again, but smiling hurts.

Maybe I could drop you off somewhere?

And I'm lifeless, I have to hear what's being said to me. I have to say yes, take me away from here, I've got to get back to the hotel and then I'll sleep. And tomorrow . . . but no, no, I'm not leaving here tomorrow. I'm not going to leave just like that, not without him, where is he? What did they make me sign, that declaration, what declaration, a declaration of loss, I've lost the man who loves me like when you lose a keyring and you can't get back into your house, as ridiculous and impossible as that, or is it for my own treatment, my bleeding hands? And the police there, in the hall. And all those wild-eyed people there, all speaking Italian, I could almost forget I'm not in Italy. The man in a tracksuit, sitting on a chair with his face in his hands. A young woman playing with a rubber band around her wrist, and the one chewing gum as if it were a piece of overcooked meat. And me waiting for the young man to come back. He said he'd come back. In front of me the girl has joined the man she was telling me about. He has a bandage on his head, with a safety-pin holding the gauze around his head.

But . . . you,

Francesco,

And the young man in a white coat,

I don't want to leave like that, I don't want to leave without you. So I'm going to prepare myself for a long wait. I'm already searching in my pockets and I'm going to take out my cigarettes to smoke them and go on smoking until you come back. I'll have to stand right by the door to the hospital, outside the entrance, like that, and smoke cigarette after cigarette until you join me outside. Until they tell me you're not dead. That this is a hospital and not a morgue. And not listen to that voice telling me that hospitals have their own morgues, that this is a military hospital – there's that urge to throw up again, my cheeks and veins exploding, I have pins and needles all over my cheeks, I want to scream, I feel I'm going to scream again, but no, it subsides. I've managed to bite my lip and the grease of the lipstick, that texture that I don't like. From now on the tears fall and I don't even have to cry. And with them I drain myself of all the things I've seen, of your body, your name, those screams, and I'm being jostled again, people meeting one another, outside, by the entrance, unable to understand why they're here. There are firemen, people from the Red Cross.

I'm here, stupid and empty. I look into the hall and know I'm waiting for your silhouette to appear at the end of the corridor, saying to myself: you're going to come back. You're going to come back with the blue-eyed young man and we'll thank him, because we'll really have to thank him for his kindness, his attentiveness towards you. And then we'll leave, the two of us, you with your arm around my neck. Then I won't have sore jaws as I do now, from keeping my teeth clenched for so long. My saliva won't be thick and sticky like flour, and at long last we'll be able to go.

I know it's ridiculous, but I want to be careful, everything matters, you have to be precise, that's what I tell myself: you mustn't cry, so that you don't get your face dirty. I'm going to take care to hold back my tears, however hard it might be, they fall like curls that get in your eyes, sticking to your damp fore-head with greasy sweat. I stamp out my cigarette-end. I have to get back to the hall, I'll phone Italy. I have to call my mother. I have to call Francesco's parents. Back at his house I expect they'll still be finding grains of rice between the steps. And I'm going to let them know in the clearest voice possible that it's over now. The wrapping paper from the presents must have been folded away in the sideboard, to be re-used at Christmas. I think of Francesco's mother, I hear her yelling in my ears that we should have got married in church and no, you should go to church whether you like it or not. That we didn't want to go to church for the wedding, for God, and now God wanted to reclaim what we'd tried to keep from him. And my desire to laugh, thinking that she would be saying that to her husband, because in the end she mightn't dare say it to my face. And him not listening to her, I imagine him lifting his head to check if he's finished polishing the oak or maple plank with which he's busy making a toy-box for the grandchildren he will never have, at least not with us, ever, and he won't be listening to his wife, I know, he'll be looking at the wood-shavings on the concrete floor. The uselessness of objects, I know that, too. And of the seeds to be planted in our little garden. New things. Photographs only just taken of a marriage already old, dead, ruined.

And in the boxroom I imagine the blue and pink crepe paper of the cupid, the size of a five-year-old child, wilting quietly, standing rickety on the wardrobe among things that have been there since the dawn of time. They will take out the suits and ties again. They will burst into tears when, as they sweep up, they come upon grains of rice and they'll regret not having boiled the white tablecloth straight away to get rid of the wine-stains. And the empty bottles that they will have left for too long in the garage, beside the bins and the bicycles. Why am I thinking of that? Why can I already see the things waiting for me at the hotel, and why should a toothbrush and a pair of shoes suddenly scare me so? I don't want to find myself alone there. I don't want to leave you alone here. No. I don't want any of that. Those people, that noise, and the girl coming towards me,

Don't stay outside, you're frozen, you've got to come back in.

And her hands, her arms around my shoulders guiding me towards the hall, where the young man has joined us. He looks at me and he too has to lower his eyes to speak. Then he looks at the girl and tells her that it's very kind of her. She replies that it's perfectly normal. The young man goes away, he tried to smile at me. Then the girl and the man with the bandage take me by the arm, they say nothing at first – we leave the hospital and each step that takes me away from you forces me to make the considerable effort to approach you through the images in my head. They take me by the shoulders and the arms. They try to tell me gentle things that I don't understand, your absence makes a noise, the metallic clank of a stretcher, a belt-buckle around the stretcher, a brown blanket, that racket. And suddenly the door and these people asking me where I have to get to.

I don't know.

Yes, I do. To the centre, the Hotel Bellevue. I'm scared. I want to say I'm scared. I force myself to say it, it's an incredible effort, I never thought I would have to make such an effort, but still no one can hear me. It's like someone stamping on my heart when I hear the name of that hotel, something terrifying, the red flowers on the walls and the sponge-bag unpacked in the bathroom – as if nothing more insurmountable had ever been created than the existence of two toothbrushes and a plastic cup, nothing crueller than the fluorescent lighting and the taps in a hotel bathroom.

Again the sense of exasperation and the cigarette-lighter slaloming between Tonino's short, stubby fingers. The lighter that Tonino stares at when his nails and fingertips stop tapping the table, or counting, yet again, the seconds of impatient silence. Soon whole minutes pass without a word uttered. Where once he would have thrown random notions across the table, now he's silent. His head rocks back and forth, now resting on the fingers where his lighter dances, and then suddenly upright, alert, as soon as a sound comes in from outside, gazing at the other side of the room, beyond Gabriel's shoulders, towards the street.

And I say nothing. I look at Tonino and Gabriel, facing one another. Tonino looks at the picture of the Tahitian girl on the lighter between his fingers. On one side you see the girl from behind, but mostly her swaying hips and her orange monokini, and then, incidentally, the fact that she's looking at the atoll in the shade of the palm trees, arms spread and held high, her hands in her thick black hair while on the other side she shows her naked breasts, face raised, mouth half-open and eyes half-closed. Tonino looks at the two pictures in turn, perhaps amused, certainly surprised, as though the lighter were the girl's body. Then he probably imagines her dancing around him, but as he waits it's his own fingers that pass over and under the Tahitian girl and the palm trees, like a majorette's baton, while Gabriel walks back over to the table. Stainless-steel feet scrape against the dirty grey tiles, when with a sharp and violent motion he drags the chair towards the table, noisily getting up and sitting down again, nearly knocking over the glass in front of him, catching it without looking, a nervous, ungentle motion performed purely as a reflex. And that way he has of putting his hands on the table as though about to pull a knife or speak his mind, or say to Tonino, like a good poker player, OK, let's go, time to put our cards on the table.

But there's nothing on the table but the debris of a finished meal, leftover crumbs and torn paper napkins, stains of wine and beer. And still that laughter coming from the other room, the one at the back. Voices as heavy and cheerful as ours are pale and faint, almost insignificant; perhaps as if we have nothing to say: Virginie, Adrienne, Benoît and me sitting there, chattering about nothing, as a way of coping and enduring the sound of what's happening around us, the silence that's crashing down on our table but also that fear of the moment when the first word will come, one of those words that aren't vulgar smokescreens like the ones we're using so cravenly, here, to endure the sense of expectation that's hovering around us, or above us, not far away, in the cigarette smoke and beneath the yellow eye of the neon lights. But it's bound to come, that much is certain, sooner or later, because something, a word, a few phrases – insults? – has been on the cards since Tonino told Gabriel they ought to speak.

The waiter clears the table. And as he takes away our plates and the wicker bread-basket, as his arms fill with dirty plates and cutlery and he goes on with his work like that, indifferent to our hands holding our cigarettes or our eyes following the swirls of smoke that rise above our heads, it's Gabriel we see and hear, because he's the one who starts talking and saying how they'd got back home last night, he and Virginie, and how they'd discovered the tickets were missing.

In the midst of it all, that sudden void; that silence and the waiter's hands dancing between us again. That sound of plates, indifferent to Gabriel's voice, which starts rising and assuming a confidence that it didn't have at first, quite the contrary, because it was almost hushed when Tonino had said they needed to talk, although he didn't give any idea of what it was that he wanted to talk about. And sitting next to Tonino, I looked at his hands and the game they'd begun with the lighter, as soon as Gabriel said the first words. And now I see that Tonino can't bear that look, he lowers his head over the lighter and goes on playing with it, passing it between his fingers.

Sometimes he breaks off, long enough to light a cigarette, or to do nothing at all, with tense little motions, when he turns the striker wheel, sliding his finger over it and rubbing it slowly, then speeding up until a flame is produced. I watch that and what I see first of all is the back of his hand turning and turning again while he fiddles with that lighter that doesn't seem to belong to anyone, perhaps it was left on the table by someone who was there before us. And Gabriel facing him, thinking that Tonino must have noticed that the phone number was no longer written on his hand. But does Tonino perhaps imagine that it's perfectly normal for the ink to be rubbed away after all that's happened? Or on the contrary, perhaps he was aware of everything, perhaps he saw, perhaps he hadn't fainted when Gabriel had taken the opportunity to rub the ink from his skin?

I pretend to laugh at pointless little jokes I've made up. Just like last night. Jokes to break the tension we all feel, no, we can't, we can't stay like this. We have to say something. We can't go on with Adrienne and Benoît looking at Tonino as though he were the one who would burst the boil, the business with the tickets. Virginie blushed as she stared at Gabriel when he started talking about how they'd got back – she's beside me, on my left, I can feel her getting agitated; she's getting impatient and dragging so desperately on her cigarette, her breathing quick and loud, she's drinking a lot, too, little mouthfuls, an undistinguished red wine whose dark colour, almost garnet, stains tongues and teeth, the edges of the lips. And I see the image of Gabriel outside the stadium – persevering until he comes up with a way of carrying out that gesture, patient, meticulous, persevering till he gets to the back of Tonino's hand, as though the earth had somehow slipped beneath his feet. As though the only thing to do was to rub away that number, rather than panicking about what had just happened around him. His voice speaks of getting back to the bar and mentions nothing but his alarm at discovering that the tickets were gone. He talks quickly. He describes Virginie's wet hair hanging like stalks over her shoulders, the sound of the keys on the glass of the coffee table, nothing, no tickets, just imagine, he says, all the things that ran through our heads, and the rage that gripped us and everything else, make an effort, just try to imagine God almighty imagine yes imagine the hands opening the pockets of the wallet, the papers, the metro tickets and the orange cinema tickets, the dry-cleaning tickets, the rage, Gabriel says, into our silence, Tonino and me first but also the silence of the others, of Adrienne and Benoît. And most of all Virginie's silence; her eyes lowered.

So would you rather have been there? Is that what you're saying?

Virginie's voice suddenly yelling that she's had enough. We hear the sounds of glasses, the next round of beers. Benoît has ordered them, and wants us to clink glasses, he says, come on, to make peace, all calm down, we have to. And Gabriel sits up on his chair, he's the first to pick up his beer, quickly, eyes staring into Virginie's. He says, yes, I know, I'm tired, I was so scared. And he's the first to say, shit, what's happened is incredible.

Incredible.

Unthinkable. Unimaginable.

Terrifying. Hideous. Disgusting and then after that it'll be the turn of atrocious, abominable and tears in Tonino's eyes, like that, because of all the adjectives that anyone can drag up which will never express a thing, because words are like hollow tin billy-cans that ring out only when they're empty. Nothing to temper the terror that lingers on our faces and inside our heads. Tonino tried to speak, and had nothing to say. And what was he thinking about when he told Gabriel he wanted to talk? The tickets, the phone number? I don't know. I know that Virginie looked at Gabriel at that moment.

On the lighter, the picture of the girl is a sheet of plastic. Tonino starts tearing at the top of it, gently. He watches his fingers working away as they tear the top of the plastic and meanwhile Gabriel goes on talking – this time his voice is gentle and

Virginie's neck is craned, her face turned towards him and towards what he's going to say. Virginie doesn't move and it's like in the detective novels that my mother reads in the evening, in her worn green armchair, a Gitane burning away in the terracotta ashtray; I know there's a whole arsenal of words in there for saying things: stony faces, dark glances, lips bitten to say what I see there when Virginie seems capable of prohibiting or censoring anything that Gabriel could or might want to say or give vent to, like that barely suppressed rage, that simmering desire to scream his jealousy when it's crying out from everything about him, his way of blushing, his well-ironed shirt and collar, his gold necklace and the bracelet around his skinny wrist.

How could it all have happened? Eh? Didn't you see it coming? How come the fences didn't hold, and what about the police? There weren't enough police? When they said on the radio that there would be more than three thousand police in the city, would they have forgotten to put any in the stadium? Is that it? How could it all have happened, how did we lose the tickets, and you, yes, both of you, how come you ended up in there and got out alive? And now being here, how is it possible that we're all here, how can it be? Tell me? How is it possible, Tonino, because it's true, isn't it, that we have to talk about it, as you say, the two of us?

Now the words he's speaking aren't words of rage. He says he looked for us all afternoon, around the perimeter of the stadium. That he spotted us when we were walking near the church, on Avenue Houba-de-Strooper, with a young couple. That's it. That girl. The Italian. Blonde, with a red elastic band in her hair. Perhaps – certainly – the same girl as the one he saw afterwards, he too, a few hours later, in the confusion of the stadium car park, when he was joined by Virginie and he saw us. Or rather he saw me, standing lifelessly in the tunnel entrance, my shoulder against the concrete wall while they'd already laid Tonino unconscious on a stretcher. And Gabriel says, as if he'd finally dashed towards Tonino thinking nothing, imagining nothing, but also not telling the others, not telling Virginie, that it was Tonino he had recognised on the stretcher, by his Hawaiian shirt and its loud, bright floral motifs. He hadn't mentioned the back of his hand. Nor the number, that thing he did straight away, without thinking. He didn't mention that and he stops talking while Tonino goes on, slowly, with the tips of his nails, tearing at the plastic picture on the lighter.

The top is already bare, white. It's as if Tonino is peeling an orange, the plastic skin forming a bracelet or a garland around his hand. That's it. The girl is headless now, the picture no longer has a sky or an atoll on the horizon, it has shrunk to the amputated figure of the girl.

How are you?

Hmph . . . *borracho.*

Yes, like the Spaniards we saw in the bar on the Rue de Lille, spilling on to the pavement, since the bar was always packed. And I wanted to say to Tonino, come on, let's go, let's get out of here, I've had enough, let's go. Let's get home. At Brussels-Midi station there was that smell of hot chocolate, you know, that almost nauseating smell, when you leave the station, of cocoa and pastries. And then most importantly we'll be able to sleep on the train. It'll be hot, we'll forget everything. The pain in the back of my neck, from my shoulder all the way down my back, now, as if the muscle were already twisted and maybe it's all the things that I refuse to shout myself as I look at them all, one after the other, and guess at the menacingly hovering words.

Not like the ones I read on the toilet walls (there's also that poster of the family tree of the Belgian kings), after I decide to go there just to stretch my legs and not let my legs go numb with alcohol and exhaustion. I look at my hands and I'm trembling. I try to see it all again, the bodies, the helicopters, all those people. I try to see them again because I'm saying to myself that it's all wrong, that I didn't see all that, that it isn't possible. And I look at myself in the mirror and I look for a long time at the image of my face. That face; that exhaustion, my exhaustion. And then I reflect that silence is a good thing for trying to recapture fragments of reality when it goes too quickly. Yes, that sense of respite that silence brings. But I have to get out of that damp toilet where the tap-water is too cold, the towel drenched and too heavy with the water that it can no longer absorb.

There, I leave, hands still wet, wiping them like that, carelessly, on the back pockets of my trousers. And I hear the nearby laughter of the people in the back room, with that Flemish accent that reminds me where I am tonight. I step forward. When I get there, the table is empty, there's no one. The chairs have been pulled out, the jackets are all there, on the grey-blue Formica backs of the chairs. The half-filled glasses of beer, the glasses of wine, too, and the bottle, and the cigarettes on the table. By Tonino's seat, the lighter is white, completely, and beside it the plastic is torn and ragged – I can see the saturated blue of a postcard sky, and the orange skin of the girl, but crumpled, wrinkled. And then I look ahead of me at the boys behind the bar; they're looking outside. Then I in turn see what's happening, first tears, then voices, and finally, at the door, Benoît and Adrienne, Virginie and Gabriel. Further off, towards the middle of the street, when they're about to come back in one after the other and they're already opening the door and coming back inside, they let the space open up behind them for a moment and then I can see the street very clearly and, in the middle of it, like a ragged, crumpled ball: Tana's body in Tonino's arms.

7

So imagine what the silence will be like at Victoria Station, early in the morning in London, with the bowed heads of the first supporters when they get back from Brussels with their folded flags and banners, no songs on their lips, just the desire to disperse as quickly as possible into the big hall of the station, opening their aching, ringed eyes to try and avoid the journalists' microphones and cameras.

And this train for Liverpool in which every compartment will hold only the thick, cotton-wool silence of difficult awakenings. The hangover and halitosis in the mouth to accompany the rocking of the train on the rails. But also that soothing motion that we will have to inflict on ourselves again, rocking motions to lull us and keep us from fearing the hubbub to come, with the bright, chalky light, too white, above indolent sheep that stand like Christmas figurines, invading the space of the window. The fields. The cottages torn from calendars and brochures, before the red-brick factories of the working-class cities that will appear almost in counterpoint to make everything look unreal.

So imagine Gordon, with that way that he has of disappearing and dissolving into silence, his lips sealed as they were before all the pints he had to drink to recover the use of words. Imagine Gale and Peter Farns coming shyly back towards the docks, perhaps crestfallen, without turning around or talking to anyone. Imagine the two of them. And then all the others in the station, trying to merge into the grey background, falling into the arms of wives or friends, of parents who will come to wait on the platforms, and then running quickly to shut themselves away in the shade of grandmother's curtains and posters of old commercial ships. Because what awaits us are words written in black and white: *the brutes of Liverpool, the bloodbath*. And at home, stuck up in bold letters on the newsagents' walls, that page of the *Liverpool Echo* that will ask us, as soon as we've got off the train, *How many deaths is a football match worth?* Not to mention all the faces we will have to confront when the city as a whole refuses to shoulder all the blame.

And the city will sway in the wind, to oppress us with its silence and shame. From the very depths of the city we'll hear the sea lashing the port. And from the tops of their domes, the Liver Birds will be ready to swoop down on us to evoke that pain, palpable even in the water of the Mersey. This city, our city. We will have nothing to say in our defence. Because we will have to try to defend ourselves. And I, Geoff, will look at my friends, I will listen to Doug and Hughie's voices saying fuck, obviously, we always get the blame when everybody knows that there weren't many people involved, they said on the radio.

We heard that, we heard that too, Madge and Faith will agree. Madge and Faith, standing more firmly together than ever before to say the scandal isn't as great as they say it is, everybody always wants to blame the Scousers. And Faith, with her persistent smell of patchouli and her lips painted with big layers of gloss, her eyes drowning in the thick lines of her blue eye-shadow, her voice too confident as she asserts what she says she's heard on the radio, that you just had to reach down to pick up stones from the terraces. That's what the stadium was like, she will say. And she will firmly take Hughie's hand to show her support and that way of resolving the difficult issues that may have fallen, almost innocently, from my mother's lips, or my father's, after we start talking, all together in the sitting room and around the table, our bags dumped in the hall just a moment before. Doubts, worry perhaps – and especially – of which they want to rid themselves, just as you can spend all day trying to shake off the sickening impression left by a bad dream.

Tell us you weren't involved.

That's what everyone will want to know and no one will take it upon themselves to ask. As if there could be any doubt. Of course they weren't involved. You aren't involved. We saw it on telly, on the BBC news, they'll say, the young blokes with the shaved heads, it's always them. Unemployed thugs. But you're not like that, you don't know any of them. That's what we'll have to hear. And I won't say a word. I'll look exhaustedly at that poor dog forced to drag his old bones and his old flea-ridden fur around the place, with the soft grey skin underneath it, waiting yet again to choke up one of his ill-digested splinters of bone. I'll watch him, trying to think as he does; to be with him; to be a dog, old and wizened and flabby, watching the others all around the table, from as far away as possible, from the blanket, with a bestiary of ticks and fleas for company. From down below, on that turquoise carpet, as worn-out as my carcass and my good humour, I'll see their legs and their feet. I'll hear their voices and watch their feet to guess when they're lying, when they scratch one leg with the other, when they make one foot dance frantically as they claim they weren't involved, mumbling that besides they weren't even that close to where it all happened.

I will be calm. Sometimes it will stick in my craw. And then I'll be forced to bring up my dog-biscuits, in spite of the dusty, chemical taste of fish that I'll have got used to, which I'll have ended up liking. I'll have to shut my eyes so as not to be forced to see or hear my parents reaching an accord, just to keep from being afraid of their children. Yes. I'll be able to watch and hear without feeling myself blanch, without having to lie to myself. I will feel free and happy, calm at the level of my bowl and my parents' gnarled toes. My blanket, the size of Europe, and my universe peopled with dog-biscuits and boneless meat – because I'll hate bones – I'll be able to watch the world without having to leave my territory or my silence. I will be constantly forced to regret seeing Doug and Hughie getting worked up and lying, when one after the other they will claim to have nothing to do with this whole affair, saying they've never known any of the shaven-headed blokes.

I will watch my parents and my heart will be overwhelmed. Him sucking on his hollow tooth and running his hands over his head every five seconds, trying to say between two puffs on a cigarette, yes, I saw it on telly, they were talking about that wop in a green shirt who was threatening the English with a gun. And he will insist on this image, maintaining that the Italians are easily a match for the English where violence is concerned, eh, isn't that right? And his little round eyes, shining with a gaslight-blue flame, searching the faces of his three sons for some sort of reassurance while his wife, her voice as frail as his will be soft and unconvinced, will try to accuse the Belgian police, repeating details she's heard and read in the press, only stressing certain aspects. For once she will see her two daughters-in-law supporting her with a nod of the head like perfectly-behaved little girls.

My parents will be like children who don't understand the rituals and conversations of a group of teenagers, or, perhaps like old people, slightly breathless and trembling, puny little things on rattan chairs that creak like their bodies, making up ideas to endure a world that they no longer understand. And I will watch them, sharing their grief over an era that is proud of its stupidity and sense of spectacle. I will have the calm commiseration felt by those who see the cogs of some terrible machine dragging in people who can't or won't fight, people naked as butterflies pinned to a picture above a scientific name that it is their sole purpose to illustrate, with their flesh-and-blood hearts, their whole bodies, from their moist eyes down to their clenched fists, and the expressions of alarm behind which they harp on about the few ideas from which they cobble together their lives.

The smoke from Faith's mentholated cigarettes, the aerosol

smells throughout the whole room (mixed perfumes of lily-of-the-valley, rose and lilac), will all turn my stomach. Less than Hughie's children who will run charging after each other, and to whom no one will say anything – certainly not their parents. I should say especially not Hughie, who will just roar in his big manly voice to tell Faith to sort the kids out. She'll look at him contemptuously and act as if he hadn't said anything, and he'll take a swig of beer and clear his throat.

You realise they actually played the match? They displayed the cup! You realise that the stands were full of all these *tifosi* with iron bars running on to the pitch and threatening people; we saw them on telly, the pictures of those *tifosi*, you know? And so on all around the table with everyone adding his own little line or two, with Ray, my father, more stubborn than the others acting as if nothing had happened, first of all, then bringing the whole thing down to a lost match. And badly lost, he'll say, everything hung on a free kick and a penalty that should never have been, never! – eh, Doug? Isn't that right?

And his eldest son will flare up, in turn, followed by Hughie, all so happy that the conversation is returning to football, to Juventus's imaginary penalty. And they'll all talk at the same time. Voices will mingle together, the men's voices dominating and crushing down Madge and Faith's, although they're no laggards when it comes to shouting at my mother, who won't reply because she'll just sit there listening, dazed and lost. But right up until the end she will listen to the two girls who will speak to her and go on without worrying about the fact that everybody talking at the same time will produce a hubbub in which no one will be able to hear anyone else; without worrying that the men will talk to each other, my two elder brothers and my father, yes, about another scandal, that penalty whistle in the fifty-sixth minute because they'd decided that the Italians had to win . . . That's the truth! they'll say. The truth is that Gillespie didn't foul Boniek in the penalty area, he was outside it! . . . and so there should have been an indirect free kick, not that sodding penalty! And their voices will get heated. Their confidence will return and suddenly rise to say that it was all a fix, maybe one decided in advance against the English. Always the same, we're never involved. And my two sisters-in-laws' solidarity will be more intense than it has ever been before, than it ever will be again, saying over and over that what happened was done by about ten skinheads but as ever, because of them and all the ones who never lift a finger, it's the working men, the ones who have to get up every morning who suffer and get the blame . . . while the bone-idle and the unemployed . . .

And for me it will be time to tell myself once again, for a fraction of a second, that I don't understand why Hughie married Faith. I'll look at him almost impassively, surprised to see and understand that I'm going to spend my whole life trying to come to terms with the fact that my brother is this bloke who I don't know. Who is called Hughie Andrewson and whose surname I share, after our lives ran side by side for so long. Yes, that one, so terrorised in childhood by his elder brother. Despite the noisy, unsophisticated manifestations of his eagerness to please him, out of proportion even to his own weakness and his admiration for Doug. And seeing today how he will reply with the same submissiveness, accepting of his lot and his powerlessness to escape it, almost jubilant when Faith, as a worthy successor to Doug, humiliates and mocks him in front of his own family.

But OK, maybe that's how he likes it. Because no one's shocked. Because that's how it is. It's normal for Doug to have a wife so proud of him that she'd follow him to hell with a smile on her lips. No questions. Nothing. Not even love, I'm sure of it. But with the absolute certainty that it's better to keep on acting like silly women to avoid having to confront their own submissiveness head-on one day. Poor Madge, she reminds me of Mum. The same stubborn silence, the same shifty eyes, the same desire to escape and the same obstinacy in sticking by a man who frightens them. At least that's what I think. Because there's also the fact that she'll always leap to

Doug's defence, and even if she lies, soon, in a minute, because everyone has seen the tickets. None of us could claim not to know that our seats were right in the bend in the stadium where it all happened. The events, because soon that's how we're going to have to talk about them. But right now it's time to convince ourselves that no one remembers – that no one will have read that our places were in Block Y: no one will ask where our places were because everyone knew.

And soon Madge will lie, accusing the skinheads again, saying they're all from London, or even if they are from here they aren't the kind of people you see in the pubs, the people Doug might have met up with on Saturday night when he goes out with his mates and comes home so late at night. No. She won't say it. Just as she won't mention the gallons of tears she shed on the first few Saturdays when she realised that he'd be going out without her, and that from now on every Saturday night would be like that. She'd reflect that his job was difficult – up there, for any length of time, on the scaffolding and the roofs, with all those splinters in his hands. Then she'll have ended up saying to herself that it's completely normal for her husband to go out without her and see his mates on a Saturday evening. Normal for him to come home drunk and wake everybody up at five o'clock in the morning. And it also makes a sort of sense that when he comes home stinking of beer and stale tobacco, he needs to make love – so quickly, so badly – before sleeping on his side like a slaughtered beast. She won't want to speak ill of her husband. Or of those evenings on his own with his mates that he'll never introduce to her because you mustn't mix different areas of your life. She won't say what's happening. The stuff we imagine when he's been drinking. And of course she won't mention those strange marks on Doug's body.

Except when she should really have admitted to herself, if she was brave enough, that on that first night when they ended up naked in bed together, and the next morning she'd made a cup of tea or coffee and Doug had sat smoking by the window, in jeans but no T-shirt, that while she had actually been able to remember finding him handsome, his belly still flat in spite of the beer that he consumed in such great quantities, and his skin quite tanned from afternoons up on the roofs, she should also have remembered the knife tattoo on his forearm, and the one of a bottle, that was true; but did he already have those injuries, those scars and slash-marks inherited from street battles, broken bottles, blades, knuckledusters? I remember them, because I remember I'd already seen Doug naked to the waist, sometimes at the site. And at the start of his marriage. So I too have to confess my surprise when I saw him naked to the waist in the hotel, unexpectedly – I'd seen him just as he was coming out of the shower: and he just shooed me out of the bathroom saying: oy! you little poof! out you get! And then he'd laughed, flicking me with a towel the way you do to shoo away mosquitoes or flies. Those flies of his. Before, I'd been left with that image of cuts on his torso, bruises, too, which he might have got that very evening, but not so many scars, not gashes as deep as that, not so bulging, making him look almost a flayed man.

So imagine what it'll be like to run through those images and hear exactly the opposite, there, at table, as a family. Imagine how they'll each go home, my brothers, having got their smiles back and regretting that things turned out as they did – because now English supporters will be banned from attending matches. The English teams will be banned everywhere in Europe because of something that went wrong, my brothers will say, because I won't say a word, I will just sit there frozen, stunned, rooted to the spot as I hear Hughie talking about the Italians who went and stood on the pitch and provoked them; and then the Belgian police and horses and that madness and then finally the match, the match again and the Italians and the children squabbling over a plastic toy to be shared between the three of them.

Everyone will stay like that in the corridor, long enough to say goodbye beneath the porch light. Doug will take his jacket from where it's hanging up on the top of the sitting-room door, since he always puts it there, and then I'll watch him hugging his father and mother – and, as I do every time, I'll wonder how they could be so different in size, how Doug has to lean down towards them, my parents, so small, both of them, next to him. How could he ever have got out of her belly? And then, immediately afterwards, I will wonder: and what about them, isn't that even more incredible, the effort they have to make without saying a word to each other, both of them, to resist the truth? – the truth: that thing that they have to keep silent, that they have to erase; the thing they have to pretend to forget if they're going to go on living without too many worries or complications. They'll do it very well. They have plenty of experience. Yes, they will know, I'm sure, because they've known since the start who their children are and who Doug is. Doug, who once threw stones at a drunken tramp until he fell down on the pavement. It was my father who witnessed the scene and told my mother. And after getting out of bed because I couldn't sleep, I'd approached the wall dividing my parents' room from mine, and spying, as I sometimes did, on an intimacy that worried and troubled me, I'd pressed my ear against the wall – my good old Sioux method! – and I'd heard, even when I was still a little boy, one of those discussions that I tried to hear because I knew that for my parents bed was the place for words and stories forbidden to the rest of us. The words my father murmured to my mother that night terrified me because my father had been struck and bewildered by what he had seen. As though his concern had reached me through the partition wall. That it had been palpable in my father's voice, and in the wrinkled corners of his whispered words. He was talking about what happened when the tramp was on the ground. Doug had gone over to him, he said, and he had stood in silence over the old man, just getting closer and closer and leaning down over him, until his face was right up against the tramp's. My father saying he'd thought it was to listen to what the old man had to say, but no, because my father, when he too had gone over and been able to see and hear exactly what was happening, he'd seen this: my brother using his sweetest voice to insult the tramp, telling him he stank. He had said that when you stink like the old man stank, you had to block your nose, and with his thumb and his middle finger he'd pinched the old man's nose, and the man had struggled to get to his feet and couldn't. While the old man's eyes rolled in their blackish sockets. Doug had added in the same sickly voice that you have to wash yourself when you smell as bad as that – and then my father confessing that he'd left when he'd seen what was going on, that he'd headed back to town and that he hadn't lingered around the pubs and warehouses where the scene had been played out, peacefully, without anyone else but the eyes and cries of a seagull or two, that he hadn't had the strength to run over, to hit his son, to stop him, but had instead, just for a second, felt as if he didn't have a son, not that one, that it was better for him not to see him, not to say anything – but keep his trap shut, he hadn't been able to do that completely, he'd poured out his pain to his wife. And so: he'd seen Doug bending over the old man. The old man's hands as he tried to get to his feet, flailing around above the damp pavement, deserted after rain. In the late afternoon he'd seen Doug pinching the old man's grimy nostrils, while the tramp, forced to open his mouth to breathe and expel the air that lifted his chest, opening his mouth wider and wider and the other man, standing over him, parting his lips to let a long, thick packet of foaming, snow-white spittle gush from them until the old man was in tears.

But now, no, everything's OK. Bye, loves. Safe home. Why am I thinking of that? What would call to mind that old story, which has always seemed so strange to me, because of what it told me about how Doug didn't treat his parents the way a child should. The discovery. The discovery I had been forced to make about my father's fear – yes, from that day onwards I understood that fear was everywhere in our house, and that Doug enjoyed it without really knowing it, but with a kind of intuitive knowledge that gave him full rights, even if he never had to lay claim to them. I understood my parents and Hughie. I had understood them since that discovery. But now there's something else I'll have to understand. I'll have to go further in my acceptance, and repress that desire to vomit and leave the house yelling that I'm not the kind of person who can just sit and watch his two brothers leaving with their wives and children like that – will I be forced to hear the doors slamming and see Hughie's children squabbling in the background while Doug and Madge leave after them, Madge with little Bill sleeping in her arms, with his little pink mouth moistening the hair of her angora jumper? Will I have to hold my breath as I hear Pellet choking on his blanket, or yawning at the sight of the table with the chairs pulled out in a smoky room? And then what? Finally watching my parents shutting themselves away in separate rooms on either side of the landing so they didn't have to look at each other or talk to me, to ask me the truth?

And am I supposed to wait here, in the middle, in the corridor? Step forward and say to my mother, Mum, you know there's a stain on your polka-dot blouse? And ask my father if he wants some cinnamon with his bananas on toast? No, he'll want butter, not cinnamon. I know that already. I'll hear the signature tune of the programme on African animals, and the voice of the commentator, the cries of the jungle animals, and my mother lighting a cigarette. My father will go to the bedroom and lie down on his bed, legs crossed, hands in his pockets. He'll look at my mother's Venetian masks and he's bound to find them ridiculous. And I'll have to go to my room and think about Elsie, very quickly, very hard, to imagine how we can get away from here.

8

That red and black slicing through Tana's face, giving it a roughness, a hardness as if it had been carved with a knife. And Tonino's face, just before Tana arrived, when I understood that he'd stopped looking at me and started looking outside, over my shoulder. He'd frozen, waiting to be certain that it really was she that he saw in the street. And the expression on his face at that moment, when his features hardened to register concentration and doubt. As if he had to plunge his gaze far beyond my shoulder, behind the glass door, in the street, staying silent when I asked him what was wrong, so that he wouldn't have to separate himself off from what he saw.

I stopped talking and turned round on my chair, because there was nothing to wait for now. And that was when I saw how Virginie, after glancing outside, had turned towards him, barely, in a very brief movement, perhaps as swift as her glance at me, just afterwards (to check what? that I hadn't seen?), yes, that's it, just one or two seconds? Her face, hiding from me. And that pain, that burning rage that was quickly stifled in me – no, it's nothing, nothing at all, I haven't seen anything, I thought I did but no. And when I turned round to see what Tonino was looking at outside, she was the one I saw: Tana. The image of Tana and the couple with her. A jeweller's shop sign behind them, the interlacing letters missing the first S in the word Osiris.

Tana was walking between a man and a woman. All three were walking not as one might have expected to see them, heavy or bent, but straight and alert. And in the middle, I recognised her immediately, even though in fact I'd barely noticed her, with the black blouse, the red skirt and white polka-dots, the long hair in a ponytail. Then came the sound of Tonino's chair as he leapt up in a single movement, unthinking, with that sound of rubber on the tiles, that sound of vibrating feet and him leaping up and not waiting for anyone, not even Jeff who was in the toilet. And then we all got to our feet, hesitantly at first, wondering why we were leaving – and I was thinking, why, who for, what did I expect of this? Adrienne looked at me but it wasn't me she was telling to wait before getting up, no, it was Benoît she told to wait, saying, hey! can't you leave them for two minutes? They're not going to fly away! It's got nothing to do with you. Or something along those lines, addressed to me.

Outside, the image of them, in the middle of the street lit by the light from the bar-restaurant; and the two others with her, the couple, the man with a bandage on his head. Now they're shaking hands with her. They leave and she turns slightly towards them, as though she doesn't quite understand what they were doing there. And coming back, as we came back inside, it's Jeff I see coming towards me. He looks outside and doesn't move, waiting for me to tell him that she's there, outside, that Tonino is with her and that they're both talking as they do, in Italian. Perhaps she's crying, at any rate she's agitated and you can clearly hear the hiccups in her breaking voice, even from inside the bar. From here you can see the scene and Tana's hands waving around in front of her. Because now she's no longer in Tonino's arms. She took refuge there when, surprised and incredulous, she saw him charging out of the bar and calling out that name – hers – which she seemed at first not to recognise, trying to dredge it up from deep within herself like the forgotten face of someone you've seen again after many years and whose name only comes into your mind gradually, in fragments.

Jeff wants to go out and join them, but I tell him to wait,

154

perhaps it's better. Jeff's expression, as if he's seeing me for the first time. As if it had taken till now for him to let me speak. But we go on sitting there. Adrienne and Benoît are there too, and I saw him take Adrienne by the waist even though he always hides their relationship because he's ashamed of it. And every time he denies it to his friends Adrienne rings them up to tell them all about how hypocritical he is and how she has to put up with her humiliation because, she says, there's no alternative. I saw what he did. That hand around Adrienne's waist and her face as she looked up at him, the moment when she smiled, her eyes delighted and surprised.

And immediately after I see them, they're there, in front of us: Tana, Tonino. And the girl's voice when they come in through the door to the bar. She speaks without seeing us. She doesn't see Jeff, either, even though he's right in front of her. We let her past and then we all step aside as we turn back towards the table. I take another cigarette, and from her expression I can tell that she doesn't recognise Jeff. He stands there for a moment, feet fixed to the ground. And it's as if she can't see him even as he approaches her and kisses her, as if she can't hear Tonino introducing us one after the other, and her gaze is straight and steady, somehow stubbornly set in the back of her head, trying unsuccessfully to settle on something, and we wish she would sit down, calm down – we see her trembling, her make-up too heavy, that pallor beneath the powder – because her hands, her face, everything about her is trembling. Tana looks at Tonino because she can't help looking at him, as though she were kept alive solely by looking at Tonino. And his hand shakes, the cigarette in his fingertips, like stalks that might break they're twisted so tightly around the cigarette, is she hungry, thirsty? What can we do for her? Tana, who, not even noticing what she's doing, pulls the elastic from her hair and lets it fall over her shoulders, then sends her hands running frantically over her face again, over her forehead, pushing back the tendrils that have spilled on to her forehead, sticky with sweat.

And that nervous movement she goes on making even when there is no hair on her forehead and it's all been pushed back. But she goes on making the gesture with one hand, and smoking with the other, she draws on her cigarette and then sobs with a series of little gasps – no, she doesn't want anything to eat, she doesn't want to stay here, she wants to go. Yes, she'll have a drink, perhaps, some wine. The waiter rushes to serve her a glass of wine and she drinks it down in one, not quite aware of what she's doing or what she's saying, speaking French but sobbing and swearing in Italian, when her voice breaks and she says she wants to go back to the hospital, that she's got to try her best to understand and retrace her steps, the reverse chronology of all that's happened. And she struggles like that in the void, not seeing anyone when she speaks with her eyes fixed on the table. She's lying when she says she isn't scared. She says she can't imagine going back to the hotel on her own, that it's impossible to imagine taking the key and climbing to the third floor before turning right to go to the end of the corridor, putting the key in the lock, opening the door and finding herself back in that room where she'll find her suitcase, barely unpacked, and on the shelf at the side a bottle of water and her pink strip of pills. Then, in the bathroom, there will be the sponge-bag, the toothbrushes, the shaving foam and a used razor. She laughs convulsively, and her laugh rises to a shriek when she says it's impossible to imagine that the things at the hotel haven't moved, that they have stayed exactly in the same place, that they haven't moved one iota, not a millimetre, that they've scarcely been touched by the dust in the air of the bedroom.

And her laughter is even worse than the weeping it tries to mask. The conversation and the laughter from the back room barely reach us – as if they could spread calmly into infinity, as if one of those sounds would bring us out of our isolation and into their orbit. But she laughs. Yes, that's it, she's laughing now, because she's here, alone with us. It makes her laugh, she says, to think that she still hasn't called Italy. She imagines the faces the family will make, but mostly the outraged, furious face of Francesco's mother, oh, yes! especially Francesco's mother when she learns that,

because she'll have to be told that,

acknowledge that,

but no, she says it's impossible for her to call now, because first of all she had to begin by collecting her ideas and concentrating but it was impossible because of the tranquilliser she'd been given at the hospital. And she says, exploding with laughter and weeping, waving her hands in front of her eyes that are blinking too fast, that there, right now, if she were told to tell the story, it wouldn't be all that interesting; she'd say she remembers some balloons floating above the stadium, the moon in the middle of the afternoon and the black ties of the mounted police and the whinnying of their horses and the bits of newspaper flying over their heads and the screams. But also she'd have to talk about the image of the red elastic band that she saw on the ground. And the ground very close to her. The feeling of the bodies. But otherwise she can't remember anything, she says, laughing so loudly, almost apologising, shrugging her shoulders to say she's sorry; but really, there's nothing but black ties and helmets, maybe the numbers on the backs of the photographers. And then remembering the loudspeakers telling the people to return to their places and remembering being told to go back to her place. Because, she says, yeah, my place. I can't remember. How I found myself back at the hospital, it's very vague. And then Francesco's bruised body. Not his face. Not that. Just that brown blanket, that iron clank of the stretchers, that's all.

And the smile, the kindness of the people who brought her here, that's what she can still talk about. The words get jumbled, and if she looks at everyone, if it seems that she's looking at us one at a time, we know she can't see us, she can only see our outlines. If Tonino's voice reaches her it's just because Tonino is speaking to her in Italian; and his laughter mingles with hers, impervious to reality. She repeats that she remembers

Jeff, standing down below (at that moment she finally does seem to recognise him, she looks at him), perhaps the English, and Tonino yelling that he's going to kill them. And then nothing, she says. This time she has trouble breathing, she's still pale, short of breath, she's panting, the tip of her tongue on her lips tries to moisten her mouth and it's between her lips as she talks about the English and the hooligans, the dogs sniffing nearby, police dogs, the trip they have to take, Francesco and she, and the Rembrandts that she's been dreaming of seeing for years, perhaps even more than the Van Goghs, the trams, the canals and the pewter skies, but also seeing Ostende, she says. It's just a murmur coming out of her mouth: yes, what I'd like to do is go and see Ostende.

And we stay there, not knowing what to do, whether to sit there and wait. Then I start talking about Ostende and the colour of the sea. I talk about that, but I'm not listening to what I'm saying. I look at her and she looks at Tonino. She has this gesture of stretching her hand towards Tonino's eyebrow, to the place where his wound is only a crust of blood, a little reddish mark, nearly brown now, not covered by his little white bandage. No, Tonino is almost fully recovered. He says he's going to have a bruise, that it's nothing, the pain like when he was a child and they put a five-franc coin on the bump he'd given himself on his forehead, and then a bandage to hold the coin in place. He laughs as he says this, the memory of fingers holding the coin on his forehead, with the secret hope of keeping it when the time comes to take it off. She laughed with him, then as she looks at him she sees his torn, stained shirt. Her faces freezes even more. All that remains of the laugh that she had on her face, too hard, too white, is this mask on a milky face. And that silence that Virginie wants to break by calling to me: Gabriel, we're not far from the flat, why don't we go back and you find Tonino a clean shirt, what do you think? And I say yeah, of course, and then you'll be able to shower if you like, and perhaps relax a bit.

In the night, perhaps it's the cold that makes us walk quickly, I don't know. Virginie is up ahead, she's the one who's leading the way. She's put her arm around Tana's shoulders, and I look at that hand with which she strokes and rubs her back and her hair. They don't speak. They walk. There's the sound of footsteps and heels echoing on the cobbles. Night all around, with its pale grey or bluish pallor. Perhaps none of it's possible. Perhaps it's the exhaustion and nothing has happened for the past two days – but then there's that pain in my shoe and that welling violence, when I see Virginie in front of me, supporting Tana and sometimes turning round and looking behind her, very quickly, a glance. It isn't my eyes that Virginie seeks, no, it's Tonino's. And I can hear Jeff talking to Benoît and Adrienne. All three of them are walking at the back, behind Tonino. And there's still that glance of Virginie's that I catch sometimes, which sends a jolt all the way to my heart.

Francesco, all that space and these people around me. It seems too vast, Francesco, because you're not there to be the horizon I reach out for with all my being, even with all of them here, talking to them about things I don't understand. All the things they're saying to me, which I can't hear and which seem so distant that the effort to hear and see dissolves in the grey of night – faces, voices, even that pain I had in my back and my hands. Even that is over now. And the exhaustion fades, too, leaving me empty, numb.

That journey that was like the beginning of our life together, that was the beginning of my life with you and this time I need to understand that it's all over because some people charged at us and there was that fence and all the shattered bodies, I need to tell myself that it was all down to a fence and a concrete wall and our crushed life, our burst lungs, and with our bodies all our hopes and expectations; tell myself that everything's aborted now, that I won't have a child by you, never, that we won't live together ever again and my life, still, my life, when we got married, it was as if it was only beginning.

I no longer hurt as I did just now, I see everything, I feel everything. The girl's hand stroking my back and my neck to relax and comfort me, she thinks, relax that tension that keeps me stiff and porous in the chilly air. But perhaps it isn't chilly? It's as though my bones were turning hollow, the wind blowing through them, as though I were made of bamboo. What do I look like when the very fact of breathing strikes me as extraordinary and so horrible, knowing that you aren't there and that for me everything works as it did before and that the air is going in and out of my lungs and my mouth, I'm breathing as before, hardly any faster, choking, no, not even that, barely, perhaps I'll suddenly find myself breathless and liberated. It's as though I were deceiving you, here, just by breathing and opening my eyes to stare in front of me; the street spreads out ahead; I breathe and I'm with the people in the street; people are talking to me; I reply and yet the truth is, the thing I can't get over is that you,

you're not there.

I left you somewhere in the city and you left me somewhere, there, in the night. We're so far apart, how is it possible to stay so far apart on a honeymoon, tell me, what am I supposed to be thinking about? What am I supposed to say to that voice that I hear inside me, weeping as it hears my breath hesitant and tentative before it resumes, again, still, without the courage or the decency to grant me a silence, yes, a minute's silence. My breath that hasn't even the decency to choke, stubbornly going on breathing in, breathing out, breathing in, breathing out, heedless of who I might choke and sob for. And furiously wanting to silence that machine, breathing in, breathing out, and the jolts, the trembling muscles and nerves, and me inside, all of a sudden, breathing in, breathing out, this body that's mine, becoming alien to me, yes, I see it as if it weren't mine, or else I feel like a drowning woman inside it, lost and drowned,

inhaled,

if my chest hurts it's because the pain of waiting for you is stronger than the air I breathe, oh yes, Francesco, so bad that the pain dissolves in the impossibility of telling you, when they ask me if anything hurts, because it looks as if my shoulders are bending, my torso crumpling. From outside, it must be plain that my body is growing stunted, that I'm shrinking or ageing, or that I'm wearing away so quickly in this air so empty of you. But no. I can see everything very clearly. So clearly that I can hardly believe I see the door the girl's opening with the key she took from her handbag. I see everything, I hear absolutely everything: the sound of fingers rummaging in the bag, the keys, the movement towards the lock.

And then there's this other couple, the girl saying that they're not going to come up with us. They're going to leave us, she says, because they have to get back to work tomorrow – and I'm flabbergasted by what I'm hearing, I'd forgotten it was possible to go on working when I was on holiday here. And even, on the way here, you remember, Francesco, our astonishment on the train when we saw that some people were taking the train to go to work and not like us to go on holiday, smiling and with our eyes wide open and so far away, both of us, as we climbed aboard the compartment we'd been led to – I can see in my hand the tickets and the list of changes to Amsterdam. The hotel brochures. The tourist guides and the pencilled crosses by the things we absolutely had to see. The schedules we'd drawn up together, with advice from various people. And that idea we thought was impossible we had of being the only people to experience the happiness of a honeymoon at a time of year when nobody's holidays had started back at home.

Not thinking that that moment when we climbed aboard the train had been not only the honeymoon that we hadn't hoped for, but something else, let's say, for me, something like the beginning of this life I had dreamed of a hundred times, as I had always dreamed of the day that would come when I would leave with the man I had chosen to marry. Yes, why not say it, even if it's ridiculous, grotesque, the man of my dreams. My white dress. The lace. Starfish and sequins in my long curly hair. The man in a dinner jacket, like Ken, and me like a precious powdered Barbie: all the things I had dreamed about as I sucked my thumb as a little girl, at night, in that dark, damp room in the corner of the tiny house we lived in at the time. So dingy, our house, in spite of its apple-green shutters above the garage of the uncle who made his Alfa Romeo and Jaguar engines roar to shock the Catalina girls, who spent hours on the wall opposite, cigarettes in their lips, hair dishevelled, scarlet varnish on their fingernails, who impressed me so much, not to mention the radio on which they listened to love songs and pop songs on a tape-loop; my uncle sent the engines of his beautiful cars roaring, but also the engines of the silly little cars he used to fix, as grey as my bedroom, even with the posters of singers on the walls, their brilliant colours damp and blackened by the exhaust fumes that rose up the stairs, clucking and rumbling. Then we had trouble breathing and our clothes were oily, often drenched in a kind of soot and a disgusting smell of sump oil. And here I am breathing, thinking of the little idiot I was, dreaming of her Prince Charming when she was given mini-housewife sets for Christmas, with a fuchsia-coloured plastic iron and an ironing board and an apron; and all that crap that made me dream of submitting as my mother had done and now no,

Francesco,

Francesco, I'm raging against the way fate has treated us, the violence we have to do to ourselves just to stay standing. All that business about the right kind of wedding and your mother who's going to scream and say I'm a slut or a whore because we refused to have the wedding and God and all the cherubs. That's what's happening, she'll think, too happy to scream rather than take me in her arms as if I were her daughter. But no, she won't even do that. She'll just harangue your father in his garage, because he'll be fiddling with planks of wood or sweeping up the shavings or the iron filings on the workbench. But you, Francesco, you won't be there, and now I'm alone on this staircase that I have to climb, and see that girl in front of me, hear what they're saying, Gabriel and the girl, about the couple who have just left.

And when I walk into the flat, just behind the girl, there it is, right within reach, completely available: the telephone. It's by the door, beside the big coat-stand, on a little table covered with notebooks and directories. I'd rather keep my Perfecto on. I don't want to take it off, because I want to be ready to leave. And I don't want to relax or take off my jacket or why not take some time and settle calmly on the sofa while someone else puts on some music, before asking me if it's my first time in Belgium. Is that it?

Not that, no,

I won't relax because I'm not relaxed, I don't want to relax. But I'm thinking about the phone. I say to myself that I'm not going to ask if I can call, when that's what I should really do, call Italy. Call and tell them all what's happened. They must be worried, Mamma is always worried, and now, I can imagine what she must be saying, they'll be thinking that in the end out of sixty thousand people there isn't much of a risk that you'll be the one, isn't that right, Francesco?

Francesco,

so few risks, oh yes, so few out of sixty thousand people and it has to happen to us – it couldn't happen to us, not us, not here, not tonight. You leaving me alone and me looking at this couple's flat; the sofa-bed I'm sitting on, the white painted parquet floor and the halogen lamp that hums and smokes as if flies were roasting on the guard. And the pale blue walls, the dark-coloured sideboard and the round table in the middle of the room. And then the low coffee-table facing me, with its smoked glass top. And this couple getting agitated. There's an old oil heater that looks like the one we used to have in the sitting room, over my uncle's place, which must take up a third of the room, that huge pipe sticking into the wall that must make a hell of a racket when it gets going. But now it's fine, no need of heating. No need of music, no need of coffee, no, just a glass of water. But, yes, a coffee, because the others want a coffee. Virginie goes into the kitchen opposite the front door, behind the partition wall I'm sitting with my back up against. I can hear her moving things about, and the things vibrate against the wall and now it's the wall reverberating against the sofa. The three boys have gone into the next room, on the left. The door won't stay open, it's closed itself, resting half-shut against the frame. And through the chink I can hear Gabriel's voice as he hands out towels and a shirt for Tonino. Then I can barely hear the voices, probably they're coming from the bath-room now. Jeff comes back with Gabriel. In a few seconds we'll hear the sound of the shower in the distance, and it will be as if it's to drown out the hum of the halogen and the water heating in the pan, because Gabriel's started explaining that they haven't got a coffee-pot, but they have to boil water first, and then pour it gently, very slowly, on to the filter over an aquamarine teapot with a spout shaped like an elephant's trunk. But it's OK, he says, it's still coffee. He's trying to light-en the atmosphere, and instead our smiles stiffen, so thin, so fake. And the surprise of our bodies feeling bigger and more real, heavier than in the street because the ceiling here is quite low and the room isn't very big. Yes, it's like being in a box. And your absence crashing into me because the word box caught me by the throat, Francesco,

Francesco,

I have no business being here, with these people who don't know how to talk to me or what to say to each other. They're looking at each other. Virginie is sitting opposite me, on the other side of the table, with her back to the heater. She smiles at me and invites me to join them and sit on a chair around the table. We stay there, like that. In the middle, there's sugar in the tin with pictures of biscuits and then there's the teapot steaming next to an ashtray that's going to fill up very quickly. Jeff smokes in silence, he looks at his cigarette. The couple don't dare to look at each other. That's obvious straight away, that she's avoiding his eye and they're each waiting for some-one to react, for something to happen. Gabriel says that things like that shouldn't be possible. That people should come down harder. And the hooligans, the terror that's spreading, that old fascist terror that will poison Europe until the end of time because the Nazis are gaining ground everywhere, he says, we have to prepare for difficult times and see them destroying stadiums like that and killing people all over again . . . And her saying we're still in shock, we have to take our time and try to calm down a bit, not to think about all the images we've seen, we'll see them more clearly tomorrow. Yes, tomorrow, tomorrow Francesco,

Francesco,

tomorrow's another day, another world, another life; my death starting tomorrow because I'll have to take charge of everything and have the courage to organise it all: going home, our families, the papers. No, it's impossible. I say to myself that the night is driving me mad and I refuse to let it be real and everything to spread and stretch and swell over me and over everything and the noise of the shower that's stopped now while the door squeaks as it opens, revealing Tonino, his hair wet and combed back, tendrils falling across his damp forehead, the gash above his eye, still red. And that sky-blue shirt so well-ironed that the folds on his arms are like stripes dividing them in two, a recto and a verso, back and front, all to simplify the world.

And now Gabriel has taken out a new pack of Gauloises. I ask him for one, because I like dark tobacco. He hurries to offer me one, shaking a cigarette from the pack but not taking it out. Then he holds the pack out to me in a trembling hand. The coffee is too hot in these goblets. But the image of the goblets has passed in front of my eyes, and I can see the same stemmed thick porcelain cups still in their boxes on the big trestle-table with flowers on the white tablecloth; the boxes of those presents that we didn't want anyone to give us. And now my hand is trembling because the goblet is heavy, I feel weak, the coffee won't go down, no, it's the taste of the wine coming back up into my mouth – that glass I had without thinking,

Francesco,

the heat of the boiling coffee passes through the walls of the goblets and the images of the presents we got pass through my mind, the vacuum cleaner and the sheets and pillow-cases, the bouquets, the cotton flowers and the peonies on that table with the white paper tablecloth, the cameras. And what's your brother Gavino going to say if I call him? And Grazia, at my place, she'll be there, she won't say a word and I'll hear her breath in the receiver, and behind it my mother's voice will chokingly say what, Francesco? Stay calm, I've got to, but what will I have to do, what, call them up and tell them not to cry, tell them it's got nothing to do with them? Or leave them like that, don't tell them anything, leave them to reflect, each on his own, bit by bit, that without them we'd be in Italy today, and that without the presents they wanted to give us, even though we didn't want anything, without that wedding they organised without our knowledge when we'd done every-thing we could to get away from all that, that control, we didn't ask for anything, that's it: they'll say we're responsible for, that we're guilty of the,

of your,

No,

none of it's true. We'll see tomorrow; tomorrow is another day, Francesco. Mamma. Mamma, come, together we'll go to my uncle's, both of us, and Grazia, too, like when I was little, and you'll cry in my uncle's little office, among the invoices on the desk collapsing under piles of greasy papers and the calendar-girls on the walls. And then my uncle will tell you that not all men are bad, and that crying won't bring them back – and you'll tell me again, you see, darling, men aren't like that, they promise things and then off they go, they vanish, they go to get some cigarettes and a truck full of gas cylinders knocks them down when they're coming out of the shop, and the phone rings; madam, I regret to announce that your husband,

Francesco,

why Francesco do you agree with Mamma when she tells me

that men work and suffer and die with an idiotic expression on their faces, like newborn babies? They're stupid to expect any answers from women, because there are no answers and because they die before they've heard the women talking to them, and they're stupid and malicious as well, because the men leave them alone carrying children and wanting to die till they can hardly bear it. I'm too hot. My legs feel weak all of a sudden. Virginie looks at me and tells me a shower would do me good. Yes, perhaps. I tell her I'd like to take off my make-up.

In the bathroom, the cotton pads are black beneath my fingers, and red with that thick red lipstick smeared from mouth to cheek. Incapable of tears, I'm still trembling. I'm waiting to stop hearing their voices, which reach all the way to the shower room. But they don't cover the noise of the extractor fan spinning like a bicycle wheel. I look at the towel. I'm not going to take a shower. I'm not going to undress: where are you? Francesco? What do I care about their voices and their conversations, eh? Francesco, I'm alone in this shower room barely wider than a corridor, and there's the torn and bloody Hawaiian shirt, rolled up on the floor, beside the scales. And how much weight do I carry in all this, amidst those voices, those discussions I can hear, nothing, I'm weightless, and what about you? How can you leave me like that, how can you have slipped out of our plans, out of our life? It's as if you'd planned it all, yeah, that's it, like a sort of deceit, that random violence that rained down upon us and the conversations to forget – but what do I care about any of that, with my legs trembling and that smell of piss that I can still smell, yes, Francesco, I have to take a shower, I have to wash, I have to, I'm going to take a shower even if I don't want to, for fear of finding myself naked and walking barefoot on the tiles, it's cold, my body naked in a place I don't know. A shower, then; this shower and the water running from the shower-head, white and dirty with lime and mould. But my clothes are already dropping on the tiles and my body is naked, trembling, so soft, so weak. And the water. The sound of the shower, the heat. And this time those few minutes are for me, to forget the terror and the taste of wine in my mouth – I take some water in my mouth and spit it out immediately. Thinking about nothing. Saying nothing. And letting the tears flow now they've come back, brand-new, to flood the water from the shower and flood my skin, so soft and asking only to soften still further and relax.

I want to sleep. And yet my breathing is agitated, I can't understand where I am, under the heat and the steam from the hot, hot water, on the enamel, yes, the heat and the water splashing on to the tiles when it falls on my shoulders and my hair. I'm going to leave. I want to be outside, walking through the night to forget and forget that it's you betraying me and letting me down by leaving me here all on my own, to forget, to let myself sink into oblivion and see nothing more, hear nothing more of the stories coming from the sitting room next door,

forget everything.

When she comes back from the shower room, Tana looks first at Tonino, Virginie and Gabriel. And now that she's coming back with the same clothes but without make-up, face bare, slightly reddened by the heat of the water, she looks more like that other Tana, the one I saw with us that afternoon. She sits down on the sofa, almost on the edge, with her hands on her knees.

As she moved past the door I saw her looking at the telephone. I remembered that when we came back and I saw the telephone, I'd thought I should phone my mother, too. I began to imagine how worried my mother might be if she had the slightest idea that I was here, something she doesn't know, since she knows almost nothing about me – even how much I hate the packet flans and chocolate rice pudding she stubbornly makes for me when I spend two days at home, in La Bassée. But in La Bassée there's this paradox that everyone's spying on everyone else and yet at the same time nobody knows anything about anyone else. Anyway. Why am I thinking about that?

Because of Tonino's voice just now, when he was on the blanket and I heard him calling for his mother, murmuring? When he's usually so quick to remember that he and his family . . . that his parents and he . . . So perhaps it's because of that, Tonino's voice lingering in my ears, when I look at him in that sky-blue shirt, with his hair neatly combed back, that I start thinking about La Bassée, my mother in her fleece-lined dressing-gown and the family 304 rotting away in our courtyard, beside privet hedges and piles of sand? As if I wanted to go home now. As if I wanted to go and sleep in my room, down in the basement.

I think I'm thinking about that because Tonino seems to have lost some of his confidence, that self-assurance I've always known, that way he has of holding his chin up high, that twinkle in his eye that seems to say: you're not going to get one over on me. And it's as if, with Gabriel's shirt, it's Tonino himself who has finally appeared, when for a while he seemed to be disguised, almost in disguise in that shirt, too smooth, too blue, too clean, too well-ironed. But very quickly it was as if that disguise revealed the true Tonino, unembellished, more real than he might have dared confess himself. Something emanating from him, his eyes lost far away in the greasy, blackish grooves of the table.

No, Tana doesn't want anything to eat. But Virginie insists, you must eat something, she says. It's true, Tana is so pale without her make-up. Tana's whiteness, the way she has of huddling up on the edge of the sofa, it all emphasises the narrowness of her shoulders, her fragility. And then there's the rest of us, incapable of doing anything to help her, except break this heavy silence and the state of shock from which she won't break free. And that's probably why Virginie gets up and goes towards the kitchen, from where we hear her voice talking loudly to say that there are slices of cheesecake, Couques de Dinant and Speculoos biscuits, if we want, with what's left of the coffee. But Tana doesn't want anything.

When Virginie comes back into the sitting room, Tana turns

towards her, her eyes steady, almost aggressive this time, and says again that she doesn't want anything. Her voice is loud, surprisingly loud. She says she still feels a bit like throwing up, because of the wine she's drunk and probably also because of her empty stomach. But it's better that way, she says, she couldn't keep anything down. And then she asks if she can open the window. Without waiting for a reply she gets up and heads towards it, opening it and then as she leans over the ledge we look at her, and the way she leans forwards to look outside, down on the pavement, as if waiting for someone to come. But no one's going to come. And now I'm suffocating, I can't stand it any longer. I say I want to go out and get a breath of air. Gabriel says that if we like we could sleep here, on the sofa-bed. I say I don't know, perhaps, and I look at Tonino, who looks back but doesn't say anything. Yes, why not. Why not? You want me to tell you why not? As if now he's lost the will to do anything, as if he's submerged in exhaustion. Whereas I don't want to stay here. I want to escape the awkwardness in everyone's eyes, that sense of waiting. Mutually incompatible kinds of awkwardness, that leave me even more alienated in this room, with them, with a Tonino now transformed into Gabriel but perhaps searching for a glance from Virginie as Gabriel might do – Gabriel who will end up transforming himself, so insistent is his gaze on Tonino. I decide to go and all of a sudden there she is, Tana turning round, her back to the window, standing very straight: let me come with you.

I see Tana as if I'd suddenly uttered the words she was waiting for, the words that would free her. Yes. If you want, shall I walk you back to your hotel? She nods, yes. Around me, Virginie and Gabriel look at each other in surprise. But we can't just sit there like that; everyone agrees, they all decide we've got to go outside, just because Tonino says he doesn't want to stay here and he wants to walk Tana back, too. Gabriel looks at Tonino, eyes bulging with anticipation. That redness on his cheeks, his teeth biting his lower lip – his lips are so thin that it looks as if they're about to disappear, beneath the teeth biting his lower lip – what does he want to say? What are the few words that are keeping him from tipping over completely, when is he finally going to unleash those insults that we feel are about to explode? Virginie can feel it too, and to make sure nothing happens she goes and picks up the jackets she'd thrown on the bed, rather than hanging them up on the coatstand by the front door. She immediately throws Gabriel's in front of him, on to his knees, and he barely has time to open his arms to grab his jacket, he isn't yet standing up and he's going to have to tie the lace of his left shoe, the one he's taken off and he's now putting his foot into, having been dangling it above the shoe from the moment we got here.

This time the night is cold. Its darkness enfolds the streets and the silence hums in our ears. We walk and the cobbled streets are so narrow that we hear nothing but our echoing footsteps, and none of the sounds of the city. Then, following Virginie and Gabriel, because we don't know where we're going – I vaguely remember a shop-front, some graffiti on a wall, but the really important thing to grasp is how the streets faded away in front of us, just before, as we were heading back to their flat – I'm thinking to myself that it's the alcohol making everything seem so strange and empty. We're walking more and more slowly. Gabriel and Virginie have both stopped talking now. But they're walking side by side, ahead of us, as we go down a little side-street. We're moving very slowly, and we don't immediately notice Tonino stopping to light a cigarette; I wait for him and, as I'm waiting, I light up too, letting Virginie and Gabriel get further ahead, leaving the three of us at the back, Tana with us, her hands in her jacket pockets.

We need to keep apart from Virginie and Gabriel; they don't want to talk and, even from behind, it's clear that the distance between them isn't the distance of the street, and that the metre of cobbles between them is really an enormous gulf. I look at Tonino who stays behind and, looking at him, I nod towards the couple in front of us, to suggest how embarrassed

I'm feeling; how to leave here and get back to the station, clear off, that's what we'd need to do, have done with it and jump on a train for Paris or the other end of the world, doesn't matter, just not to stay here. That's what I'd like, rather than seeing this couple walking ahead of me, where to, you might wonder, and how fast, suddenly quickening their step and starting to talk, his voice getting louder and more agitated, and she answering him without looking at him; head bowed she walks faster than he does, and then he tries to stop her by grabbing her arm. But she hasn't slowed down, she abruptly pulls back her arm; he starts talking too loudly, it's almost a yell to which she responds by coming to a sudden standstill. She stands and faces him, and now she's the one who's yelling, trying to leave while he tries to hold her back with his hands, bending over her, hands on her shoulders, fingers gripping her arms.

I barely have time to see Tonino running towards them, and Tana staying behind, with me. Her voice murmurs a barely perceptible *non è vero . . . non è vero . . .* her eyes are filled with tears, staring, terrified by the image of those two arguing over something, she doesn't know what. She can't understand, can't hear, she doesn't want the outrage of Gabriel's hands and fingers clutching Virginie's arms, and Tonino intervening; and she doesn't want to see Tonino run, stretch out his arms, unleashing his voice as he did before – when? so far away already, back when, and where, she can't even remember, she has no idea, just that she can't relive Tonino's voice filled with anger, Tonino's face filled with anger, his clutching hands, she comes to a dead stop,

I want to go back,

She doesn't wait; she walks in the void, all alone, and all she sees is a route that she doesn't know. She turns round and says she's going to the hotel. I want to hold her back, I tell her, wait, wait for me, and I barely have time to join Tonino to tell him, Tana's gone, I'm going with her. Tonino and the other two turn back towards me, there's this silence and my voice saying to Tonino, I'm going with Tana, we can't leave Tana on her own.

And I have to run to get her. She's gone down several streets, it's unbelievable, how could she have walked so quickly? Being so far from us when Tonino and I have only had time to exchange a few words, him telling me, yes, go and get her, go to Tana, I've got a couple of things to say to Gabriel.

9

I was going to say: my heart unsteady. But no, not just my heart. It's my whole body that's unsteady, ideas rattling around in the chaos of my head, when I decide to walk to see Elsie at her parents' house. I imagine my legs trembling and my bones creaking under my skin – the ideas that will go jostling around the feeling that everything's going too fast and that with the events of the last twenty-four hours, I won't have a way of turning back.

Then I'll go to Elsie's house to find answers to questions that I'll refuse to ask myself. As soon as I ring at the front door she'll come hurrying to open it. From the moment I hear her running footsteps, that way she has of sliding or scurrying in the hall, letting the heels of those patent-leather moccasins clatter on the tiles until she gets there and stopping at the door which she won't be able to open straight away, from that moment, then, when I'll have to hear beyond the sound of the bolt reverberating through the wood, Elsie's voice asking me not to get impatient, I'll know how worried she will be, how impatient to see me in front of her. I'll clear my throat and, for the first time since yesterday, I will smile. I'll want to relax just by smiling. Because it'll be for her. Almost because of her. Because of the mere fact of her presence behind the door.

We will throw our arms around each other even before we look at each other. We will kiss and for me it will be like a feeling of being at home, if you think that being at home means you don't have to be on your guard any more. I'll rest my fingers on Elsie's brow and then I'll stroke her smooth hair, deeply inhaling the sweet scent of the powder that she'll have on her cheeks, a light, pink dusting on her cheekbones. I'll kiss her neck and we'll stay like that, pressed together, my arms wrapped around her waist. And then we'll look at each other. And she, her eye already challenging – although in a nice way, for the moment – will start talking and asking why I didn't phone as I promised I would , and as I probably would have if, in one way or another, something hadn't stopped me. And to think how that thing would be bound, would be inevitably connected to the events of the match. That's what she'll be waiting for, already, from our first glance. Long enough for her impatience to subside and the feverishness to dwindle to nothing, in as long as it takes to smile, until it means she's waiting. Because at that moment she'll be waiting for something from me.

She won't want to look at me indulgently. Anything but that. Not her. That's not her way; she won't use a reassuring look on me, or a compassionate one, it won't be a look promising a cut-price redemption that I'll have done nothing to deserve. Because she'll probably think that what I'm looking for in her eyes is only the forgiveness that she can't grant me. As if I were coming to see her to find a place where I might be redeemed on the cheap, and nothing but that. And that's the very thing she won't want. Her eyes, her whole face, will say as much, not severely, not yet, but without a word when she brings me into the kitchen. She'll ask me if I want a beer, and when I've told her I don't, she'll ask me for a Benson's. As always she won't have any and, also as always, she'll have smoked the last one without thinking about it, and she won't have gone out to get some more. Because, as she often says, when you're on night duty, it's not so easy to go out during the day.

On the kitchen table, Arthur Rimbaud will stare from the middle of the fresh chives and the fat dried figs with their tails cut off. Elsie will tell me to make myself comfortable, without needing to point to the chair near the window and the sink, that's where I'll sit down and start looking at her, watching her smoke her cigarette and frowning from the smoke, as she bustles about near the table, and after putting the yolk-yellow apron around her waist, and going on setting out, one by one, the ingredients she's going to need. She will read from a photocopy a list of ingredients. Olive oil, mustard and sugar. Finally she'll tell me what she's making: mini-scones with stilton and figs for her brother's birthday, which she'll have to cook very quickly so that everything's ready at the right moment. I won't say anything. I might shrug vaguely, dubiously, with my chin and my eyebrows. And then I'll rest my forearm on the edge of the sink. The cigarette between my fingers will drop its ash on the enamel. I'll take a deep breath. She'll tell me that Toby's about to turn fourteen, can you imagine, she'll ask, fourteen already! And I won't say anything, getting more and more surprised, and I won't have anything to do but watch Elsie leaning into a cupboard to get one of those bowls, fake stoneware but genuine plastic, which she'll put on the table – one movement of the hand to push away Rimbaud and the photocopied recipe. She'll have to interrupt herself to tip off her ash and run the cigarette under the tap to put it out, then throw it in the bin before wiping her hands on her apron.

I couldn't phone.

The words will come like that, almost naked in my mouth. As if there were something indecent about saying them and disturbing the still air of the kitchen. But Elsie won't speak straight away. I'll watch her eyes staring at her hands, the attention she needs to sieve the flour and the yeast over the bowl. She won't have any of that impatience now, the heels clicking on the tiles as she came to answer the door as quickly as possible. Her voice will have lost that quaver that she seemed to have just now, as she opened the door. She'll be entirely engrossed in the motion of roughly cutting up a piece of butter and grating cheese into the flour. And completely absorbed in the act of amalgamating it all with her fingertips.

It seems to be a very English and fundamentally optimistic

belief that if you don't talk about terrible things, they have their own knack of fading and dissolving away through the fog. I'd love to see that. Because that's going to be one hell of a fog. We'll watch her fingers, sticky with flour and yeast – a damp sound of spit and chewing – and we'll stay like that for a moment, before Elsie turns round and runs her fingers under the tap-water and then, taking a knife, cuts the chives very fine. The *click*, *click*, *click* of the blade on the chopping-board won't cover her voice when she asks me what time I got to Liverpool. And before I can decide to reply, because I'll be busy watching the tip of my cigarette, which I'll crush between my index and my middle finger the better to see the yellowish stain, almost brown, haloing the woolly whiteness of the filter, a stain, in the image of a tobacco-charred, blackened lung, will conjure up for me the image that I myself am that brownish filth, in this kitchen where I'll still be amazed that Elsie isn't looking at me and doesn't expect a reply from me any more than she expects a wink from Arthur Rimbaud on his royal-blue book-jacket, I'll see her, paying attention only to the finely-chopped chives that she's about to combine with the rest of the mixture.

And I'll think to myself: because she doesn't have the same cast of mind as I do, thinking that my shoulders can't support anything, so I'll have to look at her and immediately hear the heavy, stubborn breathing that will grow increasingly impatient until I answer her question. My answer won't be detailed. I'll be incapable of throwing myself into the story of what's happened since the previous day. Because at that very moment I'll be able to imagine her alone in the void of the hospital, at night, suffocating with shame and horror at the sight of the devastated stadium. That vast weariness that she'll have felt as she reflected that nothing, no one will be able to change the rottenness that thrives in some people. And the vanity, no less vast and monstrous, of thinking that with me, listening to me as she has done every day, fussing over me and telling me home truths as often as necessary, she could have saved at least one of those people. And that this whole story will have to teach her a bit of modesty. Because you can't save people from themselves. And often it's more pretentious to try and lead them towards goodness than admit there's nothing you can do.

That's what I'll be thinking: the first sort of pain she feels about me will be a sense of her own failure. As if I were all the Liverpool supporters; as if the Liverpool supporters were all the England supporters; as if the whole dregs of humanity had met up in Brussels and I, sitting there in the same room as she, were living proof of humanity's irredeemable wickedness, but also, for Elsie, of her inability to change the world. That rage in me, all of a sudden, against those ideas that will come to me in gusts – and me . . . Elsie . . . who am I in all that? And if you think I love you so that I may become an offering of forgiveness, do you not think that what drives you through me might be your eagerness to help others, to help everyone else, so that you can feel complacent and exceptional? So that you can prove to yourself that you're a good person, and that everyone else, not being as generous as you, deserves to be left to die? And it's precisely because they don't deserve that help that you give it to them. Precisely because of the contempt that you feel for them. It makes you feel bigger. And she won't say a word as I look at her, I imagine her hands trembling slightly as she pours the milk in the bowl and looks for a fork to stir the mixture, with fresh, harsh doggedness, to turn it into big lumps of dough.

Why aren't you saying anything? It's not because of the phone call, is it? Did you watch it?

Of course I watched it, Geoff, why am I so sure that you were involved? And even if you weren't, why am I sure that you were? Why you agreed to go . . . That's what I don't understand.

And I know it won't really be because she doesn't understand that she'll want to show me how discontented she is, quite the contrary, because once more she'll have thought that everything in my behaviour is predictable and damaging, ludicrous even, that if she hadn't yet called that behaviour puerile and cowardly, she must have found it pathetic for ages, and she must have thought it was absurd of me to agree to go to a match on the continent, with my brothers, when I'd often complained to her that I never had anything to say to them, either of them, just as they hadn't – ever – had anything to say to me. Taking the train with them from Liverpool to Dover and the ferry and the bus and being willing to spend a night in this hotel room, with the three beds a bit like the ones in the Goldilocks story. Who could tell her that she was wrong to concentrate on all that was pitiful about this whole affair? Just for the illusion of strengthening a bond that had broken long ago, given that, in spite of the points of resemblance between the faces of the three brothers, nothing, neither hope nor expectation, nor taste, no gesture could leave the slightest chance of believing in any imaginable sign of recognition and *brotherhood* (because that's the word). But really, to end up with what? Nothing but the madness of recreating one's own past and stubbornly, blindly turning it into something quite different from what it really was.

The truth is that I'll know as I watch her, in spite of this silence and my surprise at seeing her movements – on a wooden board she will knead the thick and heavy ball of dough, and press it down with her hand into a big rectangle – that what she wants is for me to stop asking my brothers and my parents to be different from what they are, to stop asking life to change for me by abandoning its habits and its own reality, just so that I don't have to exhaust myself and break my heart complaining about it. At that moment, as she resumes kneading the dough, she'll think once again the same thing that she has thought of me ever since she's known me. Ever since we've been together. And I will even find myself thinking that it was that vision of me, even then, that drew her to me in the first place, and made it possible for us to meet. The very same thing that will repel her today, there, at her kitchen table, just as it did last night when she thought about it as she saw those images on television: that way I have of expecting other people to make my decisions for me, my way of being beyond redemption. And she'll be angry with me for forcing her to have horrible thoughts, she'll hold me responsible for what she thinks of me, that feeling of contempt that I'll inspire in her, and which will give her a bad image of herself.

I'll watch her work, I'll watch the care she devotes to it, and then I'll get up and go and stand behind her. And this time, resting my body against her, I'll lift her hair and kiss the back of her neck. The mixture of her smell and the apricot scent of her perfume will arouse me a little, I'll put my hands around her waist, but she won't say anything – I'll sense a faint sigh, hesitating between tenderness and weariness – her hands will bring the two ends of the rectangle to the middle and fold the dough in half, width-wise. We'll stay like that for a few minutes. For a few seconds her hands will be motionless above the dough; and then she'll ask me to get the pastry-cutter from a cupboard – no, not that one, the one on the left – and finally to take out the baking-tray and preheat the oven. Then, while I'm doing that, she'll ask me if I'd like to come to Toby's birthday party. I'll say that I would. That I'd love to. That that might change my mind about things. And then like that, with the same breath, I'll add: Doug was one of the first to charge.

And then, gently at first, and then more and more freely, shrugging her shoulders, rocking her head from side to side, she'll almost start sniggering, chuckling with that same contempt in her voice, irritation and condescension barely concealed in her laughter. Poor little Geoff. Hey, don't you know that your brothers are *real* fascists, as fascistic and stupid as anything you could ever find in England? Won't you acknowledge that even now?

And I'll take a deep breath as I sit down silently next to her, my hands gripping the pastry-cutter then plunging the metal into the dough and cutting little circles. I know she'll see my lips when they close as my jaw contracts – Elsie and me and, in the middle, like sleeping water beneath the whiteness of the water-lilies, that question of knowing whether I too am a fascist, like them? Elsie bringing together the off-cuts of dough to make a new ball which she'll flatten out just as she did the last one, while I will look at my hands and the little rounds of dough that Elsie will take one by one, placing them delicately on the baking tray, taking care to put them two or three centimetres apart. And in my head I'll say to myself, oh, Elsie, you would not doubt that I was a bastard, when you've desperately tried to imagine me so differently, yes, if you'd heard me with them as we came into the stadium yelling and singing. And the beers that I've drunk, Elsie, Elsie, would you want to see me again if you knew the truth? What I've seen. What I've done. Save me if you can . . . but what would you do, then, on your own behalf, to be sure you were helping an unfortunate rather than making yourself the accomplice of scum, like that piece of scum Doug, because I know what you think of him.

My fingers sticking to the dough. And then my hands under the lukewarm water from the tap that we'll both wash our hands under, side by side, perhaps in silence. Yes, definitely in silence. But knowing that all the words I've heard from Elsie over the years will be echoing between us, about the dangers of wanting to follow the kind of people you really don't want to hang out with and even, she said, all the more in that they're your brothers . . . And when she told me to give a thought to my parents, to be a bit less of a hard man then their other sons, to learn patience, to conceal my own violence and all the other things I might have wished to give vent to so that they could at least express their own, at home – they've worked, they've lived, they've suffered and they're suffering still, she told me. You'll have to learn to wait your turn. They have the right to be satisfied with at least one of their sons.

And I'll watch Elsie putting the port on to heat up, with the figs and the sugar in a pan. She'll look at the pan so she doesn't have to look at me. So that neither of us will start crying, there and then, right away, just to replace words exhausted in advance. She had told me time after time that it would all end badly . . . and unable to contradict her, I won't be able to say, no, we weren't involved. It will be so obvious to both of us that the Andrewson brothers were in there, with others, so many others, buried amongst the hooligans and the good family men, amongst people from here and elsewhere. It won't matter, then, because when I smell the port and figs simmering in the pan, I'll want to scream, Elsie, the things I don't understand are spinning too quickly around my head – if you'd seen the horror of what I've seen; I'm talking about the screams and the weeping, that woman covered with blood and dust; I'm talking about those people with their throats torn out by the fences; empty shoes on the concrete slabs; I'm talking about all that death; that moment when you see yourself running with the rest, when you hear your own voice above that seething mass that you are forming with the others; I'm talking about what you feel, what you see living inside you. You are living in the mob and you feel so strong, so protected as you attack that not one of your fears has hold of you; you can't die, that's it, for a few minutes you're sure of it, you can't die or know fear (death and fear are right at the bottom, slipping down on to the bodies that you hurl screaming to the bottom) and you think that this vertigo won't end.

Elsie who will still be trying to draw my attention to other things – OK, let's take out the figs, reduce the liquid. Elsie who will act as though nothing was the matter. She'll tell me to chop the figs roughly as soon as they're cold. And I'll see myself doing that, careful not to injure the flesh of the fruits as I cut them. I'll look at the colour and the sweetness of the figs, the wrinkled appearance of the skin and that reddish colour, the soft, pasty substance – what am I doing, isn't this too a kind of trickery, a lie? Hearing and seeing Elsie lowering her head so as not to look at me, as she washes the leeks and slices them in two (sometimes she'll lift her head towards the gas cooker, to check that the liquid's getting nice and syrupy). And I'll find it harder and harder to hold back my tears and then, never mind, I might take advantage of the fact that Elsie isn't looking at me to let my cheeks redden. And then feel the muscles tensing all over my face, tears blurring my vision, sobs issuing from my choked throat. My halting breath and trembling hands. I'll listen to Elsie, with her back to me, washing the bits of leek in the sink.

I'll hear all that, those meticulous movements, one by one, one stage after the other, and I will look at the splinters of fig in front of me. I'll find it all impossible. Sometimes I'll have to wipe my cheeks and eyelids with the palm of my hand. I'll wonder what's happening, I'll wonder what's the point of going on pretending – when it'll really just be a matter of going on, going on till all your blood has absolutely drained away, of never colluding. And Elsie won't be crying. She won't yield to tears. Because basically she'll be waiting for me to crack, to collapse there, at her feet, to tell her she's been right all along and that for everything to begin again I'll finally have to learn not to wait, not to hedge, to face the facts at last: I'll have to choose between my brothers and her. Acknowledge that they could have been used as illustrations of evil in old books. And as she acted out the part of the big-hearted, generous lady, dressed all in white in the uniform whose belt she will have tightened last night as she averted her head from the television to keep from seeing, to keep from hearing what was happening amongst those ant-like vermin, to keep from seeing the images of the tortured victims, as she arranged the mauve plastic carnations in their vase, she will have wished that a patient would ring so that she would be forced to leave the room and not see what was happening, and then she will have had doubts about her power, but not about her gentleness (she will have cried). And then, that's it. She'll have sat down saying, poor Geoff, I must keep him from falling, poor thing, he so needs to be told the truth.

She will wash the leek, drain it and then cook it in a different pan. At the same time, her voice will be gentle as she tells me it can't go on – she will have been so scared for me – and the time has come to choose. I'll go back and sit by the sink and the window (which I'll have opened to let the smoke out), and I'll light another cigarette as I listen. She will roughly chop the leek, mix it with the mustard, the wine, the oil and say to me, careful in her words and movements, that we're past the time of ambiguity, that the time has come to nail our colours to the mast. Loving your family is all very well, she'll tell me, but not when there are people like Doug in your family, not in contempt of intelligence. And I'll say, yes, I know, you're right. Except that I don't love Doug because he's my brother, I love him in spite of what he is – there's not much I can do about loving this bloke I have nothing in common with, this guy I've been frightened of since childhood, whom I hate for what he does, what he says, what he is, but whom I love unreasonably, irreducibly – there's a hard core that refuses to be subjugated by the idea that I shouldn't love him, him or Hughie, that good and evil are a simple opposition like want and don't want. I love my brother because I remember one day he lent me a catapult, because he taught me to skateboard and I used to like his Benny Hill impressions. And also, perhaps, because something in him scared me and the thing that worries me, and has done since childhood, seems more real, more fair than hands dividing the world into categories as they might cut ham into slices, or scones in half. Hands that tremble only when they're explaining how to think and who to love, hands that know and, calmly, with experience and certainty, lay a slice of ham on each lower half of scone and add a spoonful of leek mixture, and another spoonful of fig mixture. Then they replace the top part, proud of themselves, completely trusting and serene in the fullness of their gestures.

10

But that night, Francesco, that insurmountable night. The filterless Gauloise I'm smoking until my lips burn and the fingers
that hold it tightly pinched, crushed, while beside me Jeff is
talking about what happened yesterday, and I can't make it all
out because he's hacking up his story with a mechanical laugh,
apologising for talking to me incoherently about a ring and
some tickets; it's a story without rhyme or reason, which he
started telling me just to explain why Tonino didn't walk me
back, and also to make the situation easier, the two of us being
there, without Tonino, and without you or anyone else,

Francesco,

without you,

yes, you hear – without you, Francesco – I'm alone in the
street, in the middle of the night, with this guy who seems so
anxious because I must be scaring him too. That's what I think
to myself, that I must be scaring him with my silence and my
stubborn expression, my eyes trying to understand and find
something that must be in the order of things. But there is no
order of things. No meaning. Plenty of things, yes. But they're
all haphazard and they're spread out in front of me, cruel and
indifferent, and that's all. And the other guy who's still talking
a lot of hot air to explain his bafflement at seeing us there
together. And that tremulous voice of his, Jeff's. That laughter
quavering in his throat. And his embarrassment at making this
confession to me, when I'm inclined to imagine that his true
embarrassment is at having to walk me back and not knowing
what to do with the silence and that palpable tension between

us, everywhere, in the air, in the sky and the night. Perhaps I could make him forget if I talked to him about springtime at home, at my home, in the spring, I could, it would be enough, Jeff, to talk to you about the wisteria and the heavy rain that throws up the dust and crushes the corollas, the Hottentot figs, the petals of the red and yellow tulips and the powdery sun behind the fog in the sky, the mown grass in the morning, the shouts of the children and the sound of footballs knocking against the walls.

Francesco, tell me,

do you remember? the noise of the car horns when the cars formed terrible traffic jams throughout the whole of Italy in the evening, so that boys and girls could talk to each other from one car to another, like that evening when we met, you with your brother Gavino and his friends from the military, Ray-Bans over their eyes in the middle of the night, do you remember how much that made us laugh, Gina, Giovanna and me drinking red Martini in the little Austin I borrowed from my uncle,

Francesco,

talk to me,

But Jeff tells me we'll get lost if we don't look where we're going. Keep to the left, he says. Further down and further to the left. And in fact we probably are lost, because on the way there we hadn't walked so far, or so high up. Our tired legs and those unfamiliar images of the city, a boulevard we didn't cross on the way there, but it doesn't matter, we can see its name, it's the Boulevard du Jardin Botanique. We go on, and then soon we see half-demolished buildings, their interiors revealing sitting rooms and faded wallpaper, bathroom tiles; and then neon lights near the square we're approaching, a few lone men. And, on boardings, there are paintings and messages, and I'm laughing at myself for being lost because I'm certainly lost, Francesco, how strange it is, now, to think that last night I was in a stadium with you and afterwards I was alone in that hospital and then, later, during the night, amongst all these people;

I have a sore stomach, my hands hurt, but I feel as if it's all very far away, too far, so old, so tired; how tired they are, all the neon signs in the bars that are closing and spewing out their customers, who walk away quickly, hands in their pockets, slightly shifty expressions, lone men and silhouettes waiting lined up against the walls, cigarette-smoke beneath the neon, shop windows and filtered lights, the kind they say they have in the Northern cities, and in Amsterdam, too, girls in lamé and nylon in the shop windows where they wait, seated and languorous, mermaids scouring the streets for wide-eyed, slightly startled fish,

And you, Francesco,

Francesco, is it possible to imagine that for a very short time now your body has done nothing but plunge towards that cold so cold that soon the blood within it will be heavy and brittle as rock? And the pores of your skin, soon, and your eyes that will never open again as once you opened your arms so I could warm my fears and anxieties. All alone here, I'm thinking about Gavino and that story he told us about the old woman on the ground floor, surprised that she hadn't been seen or heard of until flies appeared outside the shutters half opened by the wind, and that the flies alerted him and then he risked a glance inside. The acrid stench had been so powerful, almost enough to make him faint, even more so than the body lying stretched out on the tiles. And the old woman's eyes, he said, it was as if her eyes had flowed down her cheeks and you Francesco,

oh, no, no, don't let me imagine your green eyes as viscous liquid on your cheeks, and that acrid stench around you, Francesco, is it possible to imagine your voice floating in the air, the sulphurous colour of pollen spreading and floating in puddles, lighter than water, on the bodywork of the cars, like grains of sand from Africa? That pollen and your voice – no – how do you expect me to believe such things ? If only I could stop imagining you feeling the cold on your back from that cold iron slab they laid you out on. And imagining, thinking that nothing means anything more to you now than the deep, deep silence, so deep that I'm putting off joining you, with Jeff saying that this time we really have got lost and we'll have to head back down the hill,

Francesco,

I need more forgetfulness than I can muster, so tired, my body aching. My painful breathing. That desire to smoke yet one more cigarette. Too bad about the pain in my stomach and that desire to vomit because of all those cigarettes and all those ideas knocking in my head, the blood thumping through my veins and arteries – how can I believe that you can't, that you will never again be able to laugh or breathe, or anything, never again open your eyes or your arms. Impossible to imagine, that word *never*. Your voice, what will become of your voice? We know each other too well for you to go and perform the great mystery of death and eternal silence by seriously going over, without an explosion of laughter, to the side of the dead since all eternity and for all eternity, the bothersome old dead; so no, no, you won't do that to me, you can't do that to me, not in this city, not like that, not here, you can't become as enigmatic and mysterious as that, Francesco, you can't leave me to wait for you to come back, as if you weren't going to come back, because you're going to come back, you must come back, you must, I want you to and for both of us,

Francesco,

I want a smoke, I'm out of cigarettes.

Francesco,

don't die,

I ask Jeff and he holds out his packet. We stop long enough for him to find the matches in his trouser pocket and try in vain to light my cigarette. I take the box from him and he says we'll have to go along the same street but in the other direction, and head back down the hill; after that we'll turn, and retracing our path we'll find the way to the hotel, to the room, the flowers on the old wallpaper, the plaster mouldings and the wooden arabesques on the feet of the bed, scary and threatening like the strange presence of the glass flowers of the bedside lamps. But I say nothing of this to Jeff. I can't say anything about the fear that's taking hold of me.

Oh yes, Francesco, I'm so tired. I wonder who will hold my hand to get through the door and the night that are both about to open up in front of me. I think of all those things, as if my whole life were being crushed against this night, surprised to find myself so empty and flat when a few hours ago I would have laughed at the very idea of unhappiness, so sure was I that everything had its reason and its place. And what reason, what place, here in this street where I can hear the sound of cars and Jeff's voice still talking about that theft of theirs. He says he's so sorry and that Tonino is sorry too, that they aren't thugs or bastards, we mustn't think that, we shouldn't think that; and I don't think anything at all, I tell him, I couldn't care less, Christ, you're taking a long time to come back, Francesco, Francesco,

suddenly that breath in my throat, too dry, the fury of fear, from thinking to myself that I've got to confront being alone in the room, no, do you think I'll just spill it all out the way women do, beating my breast in front of everyone? Fall and weep as my mother did every couple of mornings – when a canary died she would take it out of its cage, wrapping cotton wool around it she prayed and hoped so fervently that it would come back to life, that she would shut her eyes tight like a visionary. Once the bird did warm up and come back to life. Just once. And then, if you'd heard her laugh, that expansive, furious, terrifying explosion. And since then, every time a canary passed away she wouldn't lose her nerve, just roll it up in cotton wool, praying so fervently, fingers locking so tightly it looked as if the joints would burst, and I start telling that to Jeff, even though he isn't asking me anything, but just to break that silence and monotony that's setting in, as we head down the hill, because we're not far off now. I know that in a few minutes we'll be very close to the hotel. Yes, very close to the room. And I know I'm walking more slowly, I can't quite bear it, so, looking at Jeff, I go on talking and saying, yes, my mother always loved canaries because being alone in the house all day, the song of the canaries was like company for her, I swear, I never saw my mother as she was the day the last canary died. I thought she'd want to bury it and pray, but far from it: she rolled it up carefully in cotton wool, she stopped crying and she opened the lid of the bin, throwing in the white ball without a word.

We recognise the street, the one with the restaurant that Tonino leapt out of as I passed. And then in the distance, the façade of the hotel and its grey-green letters. Then, suddenly, the blood hammers so hard in my temples that I have to rub them and shut my eyes, and say once again, wait, wait, Jeff, why don't we sit on the pavement. Or outside the entrance to the jewellery shop opposite the restaurant where we were. Silence. The sound of breathing. The off-white swirls rising and dispersing, fading away with mad words dissolving away as they rise into our heads, dissolved in the images and shouts of grimacing Englishmen laughing in my face; and the bandannas, the shadow on the pitch and the players; I see the big wheel on the other side of the stadium turning slowly, heavily, clockwise direction. But it makes a rattling sound. It's the sound of the extractor fan in the shower room, with that particular whirring noise it makes like a piece of cardboard against a bicycle wheel, or the sound of the ivory marble dancing on a roulette wheel spinning at full speed in a casino – black, red,

lost,

Francesco in the night, lost, and you leave me alone with my dirty skirt and my scraped knees. My legs are cold. So, so who's going to hold my hand in this cul-de-sac in which there's nothing my life can do but huddle in the swirls that rise and disappear above my head, just to avoid going back to the hotel? I've gone mad, is that it? I hear Jeff's voice. He's talking, but . . . what's he saying, what could he be saying? Yes, that's what I'd like, I'd really like him to find some words. Because words are what is needed, well-chosen words, simple, true and gentle. Words that would hold out their hands to me to replace the men who have died. Because I refuse, you understand, to accept your absence without a murmur. And Jeff saying we have to go on, we can't stay here all night. So we get up. Then we go on. My heart. My heart bursting. I hear the night, because the night is that special silence, the slow breathing of sleeping humanity. I think of all those people in the houses and buildings around us, all those closed lids and you, your lids closed and behind them, no dream, nothing, nothing behind your eyelids?

We ring at the door of the hotel; inside, everything's dark. And then, soon, a little light comes on behind the front desk. An over-ornate little lamp and the pale pink light, then the figure of one of the twins. He presses a button and the glass door opens in front of us. We go in, I have to go in front. The man is there, one of the twins who looks at me with the blurred face of someone who's just woken up. He looks at me circumspectly, but perhaps it's because of the expression on my face? I don't know, I haven't time to ask him the number and already he's held out the key. And then, looking at us both, Jeff and me, he asks; will you be having breakfast?

Me, and Jeff behind me, completely flabbergasted by the question. I look at Jeff, saying to myself that the man hasn't seen anything, he hasn't understood anything because he's asleep on his feet. No, he can't have seen anything or understood anything, or it wouldn't be possible. He hasn't noticed the difference, and it's as if he'd erased everything by mistaking Jeff for you – as if anyone could mistake you for Jeff, with his shy, frail, young man's build, his unsettling, lanky look, his junkie walk, his hollow cheeks and dirty hair – how could anyone mistake him for you? And how can I make it bearable to myself when I thoughtlessly tell Jeff to follow me? We hear the sound of the wooden stairs and now our feet sinking into the plum-coloured carpet that leads to the room. The sounds are muffled and neither of us speaks. We walk, I'm holding back the tears that threaten to spill over my face with each stair I climb. And it's harder to fight against them, but, Francesco, I won't allow myself to be defeated, I'm going to leave, I'm thinking of my mother – the two gold wedding-rings and the portrait in the medallion around her neck – and this time I feel as if I understand her, but I'm going to live,

Francesco,

oh no, Francesco, you shouldn't have done what you did, saying she was right, agreeing with her about the unhappy lot of womankind when she bored on to me all through my teenage years about men dying like flies, and flies swirling around like balloons and pennants in stadiums, above men's heads. And I'll think of all those men there are to be loved, I'm scared, so scared, I won't do as she does, if you don't come back, I hear my rage against you rising, Francesco, I will be faithful only to life, you hear, you've gone, you're leaving me and I will never forgive you because it's to life that you must be true and not to a person, certainly not to the people we miss and who kill us too, you hear, no one can think themselves above the love we owe to life – or handsome enough, or strong enough to substitute for life. So too bad for you and for me, too bad, too bad, yes, that's it, too bad for us, too bad for love.

The first thing on entering the room is one of those big mirrors that you see in costume dramas, mounted on a pivot frame, so that you can set the mirror at an angle and see yourself full length. It's the first thing I see, even before I see the mosaic friezes along the tops of the walls, undulating flowers in green and blue. Yes, that's what I look at first of all, before I notice the ceiling and its white and yellow mouldings forming a kind of sun in the middle, where the chandelier is lit; three bulbs beneath the brass fittings, cherubs gazing into each corner of the room, wide-eyed, as if caught mid-flight. And us on the landing, with the same expression of surprise. Tana leaves her hand on the switch, long enough to look at the room and its chaos, an open suitcase and the tastelessness of a coarse wool bedspread, a patchwork quilt with a crudely imagined inter-locking sun and moon, staring with round, almost bovine eyes at the cherubs in the ceiling.

And us. And me, not daring to speak or move. I wonder now what I'm going to do, how I've come this far. Try as I might to understand and retrace my steps from the beginning, no, nothing comes, nothing to be done. We can't go back the way we came, not now that we've got here and Tana's shut the door behind us.

I look at the poster above the desk that stands against the wall, then say I'd like to have gone to the Musée des Beaux-Arts before we left because I like Magritte, OK, not all of Magritte, but anyway, most of his paintings are in Brussels – then I shut up, there's no point talking about painting. I think it's a bit strange to have put the poster of this particular painting in the room, it's a bit weird for a hotel bedroom. I ask her if she doesn't think it's a bit strange, too, and she, Tana, looks at me with the surprise that you sometimes get with someone you don't recognise, or someone who's suddenly said something completely irrelevant, and doesn't reply. Then I look at the poster again: two busts, a man and a woman kissing, their heads hidden by white sheets; and yet they're kissing, in spite of those sheets over their faces. I say I'm not going to go to the museum, I'm going to leave as early as possible, tomorrow morning, without telling anyone why I'm in such a hurry to get away.

I ask her if I can smoke in the room.

She'd rather not answer, but she says yes. And then that she'll have a cigarette too, when she's finished doing what she has to do – and in the meantime she bustles about and can't stay still; I see her hands. She turns round very quickly and walks from one end of the room to the other to pick up a sweater that she throws into the wardrobe, very quickly, looking very anxious about what she's doing. She picks up a polo shirt from a chair, puts it on another chair, near the desk, her face alert, her eyes rolling like marbles in their sockets, something tense and furious about them. Her hands roughly straighten the suitcase without looking at it. Tana is so white, and so stiff in her movements as she bends down to that pair of brown shoes – they're men's shoes – and it's then that I understand what she's doing, her fury and the energy she's exhibiting to do it, that mechanical compulsion to obey innocent resolutions, her clumsiness as she sets them to work – the suitcase clicks crisply shut, but a bit of sweater, perhaps a sleeve, is still sticking out, and she doesn't notice. I don't dare tell her.

I run my fingers through my hair, I look at the ashtray on the desk and the notepad with the name and address of the hotel, beside a gold plastic Manneken-Pis acting as a paperweight, and a box of matches. And now she's doing things very precisely, as quickly and nervously as before, but in a measured way, as if every second she were tallying each of her movements, each object that needed to be moved or straightened.

And then I see her, from behind, she opens the window without even taking the trouble to draw the curtains, just passing her arms between them. She has opened the window and the cool air struggles to enter the room; the curtains barely move, as though the air were filtering in only through the narrow gap between them. In silence, I watch the curtains move slightly as Tana's hands open the big wardrobe opposite the bed, into which she puts the shoes that she grips tightly without looking at them. She does it quickly, almost as if she's ashamed, as you might put away bits of underwear lying on a chair if you had an unexpected visitor, but without talking about anything or doing anything but inhabiting that movement and that decorum imposed upon her by my presence, to hold back her tears and her breathing, to keep, perhaps, from screaming or breaking everything, to keep from collapsing. But there's nothing. She has the strength to hold out. It involves extreme concentration. The application required to put shoes side by side in the wardrobe. And that's how I have the time to notice, suspended from hangers like floating shadows, black and grey clothes, a blue dress, her clothes and Francesco's. She quickly shuts the wardrobe door and turns back towards me, unsmiling, her forehead so furrowed that you could count, above her eyes, the wrinkles that she will have in time to come. She tries to smile and stands there with her neck absolutely rigid, her head held straight on her shoulders. She comes over to me to take the cigarette I've promised her.

The pack is on the desk. We're both standing, she tells me I can take my shoes off and relax, because it's so late now that we'll have to sleep here. She smokes and sits down at the desk. She looks at the Magritte poster, or, rather, she lets her eye drift across it, and repeats that movement that she had right at the beginning, when she came into the restaurant with Tonino: that movement of her hands over her forehead to push away some curls. But there are no stray curls, no, just her eyes straying and sliding across the walls, as though trying to settle on horizons other than the plants and the gilded arabesques of the flowers in the wallpaper; and then, all of a sudden, Tana pulls a face as she slips off her shoes – the cigarette is smoking in the ashtray – soon a sob that she stifles into a laugh, her voice softening suddenly to talk about the way hotel taps always leak, according to Francesco, because, she says, he often goes to hotels, that is, sometimes he does, when he doesn't sleep in the cabin of his lorry. Francesco drives to Germany to deliver washing-machine drums to a factory which sub-contracts and, sometimes, he goes to very basic hotels and brings back bars of soap the size of little matchboxes, tied up with ribbons and wrapped in aquamarine paper, shampoos and ballpoint pens with the name of the hotel written on them. As she says that, Tana looks at the desk to see if there's a biro. No. The bastards. They don't deserve their four stars. And then there's the Bible, apparently there's the Bible and the TV opposite the bed. She says she hasn't been to that many hotels. And then she starts talking again about how in the afternoon they'd gone through all their wedding presents, outside the entrance to the stadium, except this time she seems to be talking to herself, because her voice isn't pitched to be heard, or to capture anyone's attention. No, this time she repeats the same words in the monotone of a rattled-off prayer – stories about family and Francesco. She says her mother and sister really love her and they've always respected her, always, she says: since we lived at our uncle's, before the house in Montoggio.

Tana speaks almost shyly and, when she speaks, her face appears with that excessive whiteness, her skin is pale as a sheet, like the one in the Magritte poster; it looks as if her face has been covered with material and her voice is emerging from underneath it. Words, laughter that hiccups when she repeats three times in a row that the first thing that struck her since we came into the room was the lingering smell of Francesco. The smell of his after-shave. The pepperiness of it. But she remembers that the salesgirl had talked of a hint of chocolate which the two of them had never, try as they might, been able to smell or even get the slightest whiff of, in spite of the salesgirl's claims. And yet she'd had to accept her surprise when, just now, when she opened the door to the room, she had noticed the smell and, between pepper and wood, there was that discreet but suddenly obvious note of cocoa. And you can get rid of the idea that perfumes spread in thick layers like cigarette smoke, and seep into clothes and thoughts. She speaks, and I look at her in the big mirror beside the bed, near the window hidden from sight by the closed curtain. She had sat down, but she got up again straight away, she's standing behind me, and I've taken her place on the chair, near the desk. I can still hear the words she's saying about Francesco's after-shave before, feeling herself blush, she almost apologises for repeating the same stories she told earlier in the afternoon; she decides to go to the bathroom.

I stay like that, without moving, without thinking about anything apart from being here, wondering what Tonino might be getting up to (with the image of that well-ironed shirt on his back), what Gabriel might be saying, what Virginie dreads and then, at my house in La Bassée, what they'd say if they knew I was here, in a hotel room with a beautiful Italian girl – because there it is, out in the open, Tana is very beautiful. Something makes me find her very beautiful, in spite of everything that's happening, all of which makes me ashamed to think that I'm finding her beautiful, ashamed at being so unseemly, almost vulgar, the incongruity of thinking about her beauty when, well, when what? yes, what would they say? in La Bassée, to see me leaning over the chair, chest thrust forward, hands clasped together, forearms resting on my knees and looking, as I hear the sound of water running from the bathroom, shamelessly at Tana's shoes – the black leather torn from heel to tip, the shoe's crimson lining, the left one lying on its side, and the other one, whose sole I'm gazing at, and the talcum she must have put in it to make her foot more comfortable. The talcum, or white powder that looks like talcum, which leaves a fine film in the shoe. And here I am, looking at it, and needing to stand up and look at my face from the other side of the bed, in the big mirror, to find in it even more surprise and astonishment at being here than I would have imagined, when right now I'm aware of what my presence here means – my presence,

my presence?

And so, since Tana came out of the bathroom, without even paying attention, I ask her how long it is since her father died. Instead of a night-dress she's wearing a T-shirt that's too big for her, and reaches to the middle of her thigh. At first she doesn't answer. Her loose hair falls to her shoulders, and that hard look doesn't leave her face – her expression, more stubborn than sad, that all-devouring violence, her nose, her eyes, her forehead, neglecting nothing. Her amazement, when I ask my question, leaves a startled expression on her lips. She has to run her tongue over them to find the strength to answer, breaking through the dryness that covers her whole mouth. She walks around the bed and I see her, on the other side, facing me. I also notice her back in the full-length mirror, and hear her tiny, soft voice asking me how I could possibly know that her father is dead, how I can guess and say as much, because I don't know, she hasn't said anything, she never talks about him and even, sometimes, she forgets her father and the job he did; she was so young when the accident happened and that's why, as she lifts the bedspread, looking at the white sheet on the bed, she says she doesn't understand how I could have known. I reflect that I shouldn't have asked the question, but there you are, I know; I know that since the very first I'd understood what it was that she didn't want to say, that it was between us, that untenable, impossible death – the death of the father. I stir uneasily in my chair. I want to get up. No, not yet. But on the other hand, still smoking to have something to hold on to, a sustaining movement, something to look at, when it strikes me that, having asked the question, I will never again be able to look her in the eye. I strike the match and the sound of the striking-strip barely drowns my voice when I say: when people talk too much about their mother it's always the same old story, you talk about one when it's the other's absence that you want to rage about.

I'm so uncomfortable, please forgive me, I've had too much to drink, I don't know what I'm saying. I don't finish the cigarette, I stub it out, adding that I've been smoking too much. The cigarette breaks in two, I get up and, before going into the bathroom, I walk towards the door to turn out the chandelier. Tana switches on her bedside lamp and this time all that remains is that light and the one on the desk that I'd switched on before to look at the poster. In the bathroom I splash my face with water, a lot of water. I want to rinse my mouth out, but there's no mixing tap, just hot and cold. So under the cold tap I drink cold water and rinse out my mouth, too bad if my gums are sensitive to the cold and my gums are still bleeding slightly; when I spit the water out it's stained with pink blood in the basin. I want to rest, I say to myself that it would be good to sleep.

Tana is sitting up in bed, straight-backed. This time I know tears are running down her face and she looks apathetic, absent from herself, completely given over to her tears. She hasn't moved and yet she knows I've come back. She's fiddling with a handkerchief, sliding it from one joint of her finger to the next, staring at the square of fabric, her cheeks as crimson as those of a child ashamed of a couple of slaps she's been given in public, when her voice suddenly explodes with a hoarse and malicious laugh, very raw: she says the bedspread is really too ugly, with its ridiculous, silly patterns of the sun and moon with eyes, and she laughs a forced, brutal laugh as I turn out the lamp on the desk. The gloom, lit by nothing but Tana's bedside lamp, leaving me with just enough visibility to get undressed without having to fear the light too much. But I want to divert her attention. I don't want her to see my thin legs, or my knees, as knotty as big clenched fists when, as I take off my shirt and trousers, I take my socks off, and as I begin to lift the sheet on my side, the blanket and the bedspread, I burst out laughing in turn, good God, it really is ugly! with that dirty, coarse wool, and suddenly everything fits, it's all designed to fit, and we start talking without restraint, saying that the wallpaper is more rococo than Art Nouveau. We laugh, mocking the furniture and the chandelier with its chubby cherubs. But the truth is that at the moment we're still wary and we're averse to taking risks; our laughter, trembling fingers seeking comfort as they fiddle with the bedspread.

Now we're both lying down, breathless. We don't say a word, we just lie there with our eyes wide open, staring at the ceiling. We feel the blanket moving because we're breathing too hard. I'm thinking to myself that I wish I'd changed my T-shirt because of all the sweat, but it's too late now; I couldn't have predicted this, I lay down just as I was. The lamp on Tana's side is still switched on. I take off my watch and lay it on the bedside table next to me. My legs hurt. I'm going to relax. I'd like to relax a bit. I turn round and, on my side with my back to Tana, I hear her breathing and the sound of her biting her fingernails, chewing on them. When she stops, it's because she's waiting to decide to switch the light off. But first she'll have to take her pill. She's breathing so heavily. I hear the sobs in her throat, I listen to them, I listen out for the slightest sound of her panic, her terror. I want to calm her and I hear: before turning out the light she has to drink a mouthful of water and do without the sleeping tablet they gave her at the hospital, tell herself she doesn't need it, perhaps because I'm here. But we have to behave as before. As if nothing was wrong. As if everything was going to go on like that. Tana turns out the light. We're both alone, the two of us, with that breathing between us, so heavy, crushing, that thin space between us when either of us moves, the unexpected, dizzying rustle of the sheet, the sound we hear perhaps too clearly.

And that patience, yes, that boundless patience we need to stay like that trying to hold our breath and trembling, dazed and dumbfounded, that terror of making a sound; and the persistence of that silence between us like an echo of the sounds of the end of the world exploding inside our heads: Francesco and noises, screams, the rage in the stadium, all of it spreading and pouring between us. I search in vain for a strip of light under the bathroom door, I try lying on my back – she's on her back too – and minutes pass that last for hours. We don't say anything and I want to speak – we could hear our hearts beating in our chests – dry throats swallowing – breath brushing the sheet – eyes open in the night – I know she isn't asleep either.

Then I turn my head towards her, very gently, it's in the air, this vast fragility. I'm scared she'll hear me and interpret this movement as an attempt at a caress, a pass, when really it's just a rite of conjuration. But I'm scared of that movement, my eye resting on her – and what if she turns, too, and looks at me in the night? But no, I notice her profile and her wide-open eye, the glitter of an eye swollen with tears that have stopped flowing. Hours. Hours pass before Tana murmurs words I don't understand, words she has spoken to herself, perhaps even without being aware of it. There's that space between us and my hand out flat, my palm against the sheet. It's a long time, endless. And then slowly her hand moves and slides towards mine. It knows it's going to find my hand. I don't dare move. My heart is beating too fast, so fast, I have difficulty keeping my breath under control.

At first, hardly anything. Her fingertips, the flesh of her fingers on my nails. I don't move; I listen to the progression, I count millimetre by millimetre, the number of millimetres per second and the beats of a battered heart – we stay there, minute after minute, my hand out flat, her fingers barely resting on mine. It's very slow. It's a long time before my hand turns round, so that the palm is no longer facing the sheet and Tana's fingers can finally settle there.

And then that infinite slowness it takes her fingers to touch my palm. Her fingers advancing into my hand – my damp, hot palm. I feel as if I can't breathe, I shut my eyes. The whole of her hand rests on mine. But it isn't over, the movement that follows is very slow and gentle, infinitely precious, the movement of two hands clasping one another; fingers seeking through space to join and finally find one another. It's slow yet feverish, and there is urgency, in that clumsiness, that stumbling and acceleration, movements halted as soon as they are begun – her hand finally gripping mine – our hands clutching one another tightly, terribly tightly; we stay like that and, eyes open, breath quick, I look at the ceiling and see only the darkness of night.

Time doesn't exist, or else it's the opposite, there's a time that passes with extraordinary clarity, the seconds register, they mark themselves, they mark us, as though plunging their presence into my skin. And soon that sensation dissolves as I hear the movement and the rustle of the sheets – she turns towards me, head lowered, she lets go of my hand and her arms wrap around my neck. She says nothing, but I know she's probably crying; or maybe not; she moves towards me, her head seeks my chest and her chest heaves. This time she's pressed against me, her palms wet against my neck. My hands grip her tightly. I feel her breasts against my chest, she has a strong scent, her body seems so frail to me, so thin, that I'm scared to press her against me; she stays like that and sobs for a long time; I'd like to stroke her hair, I don't dare to, it's as if my heart has stopped beating. I wait – am I supposed to take her face in my hands, dry her tears or lick them around her eyes, gently, with infinite care, with the tip of my tongue? Is that what she wants? I don't know. What I do know is that we'll stay like that without moving, waiting for vague sleep to take hold of us, a drowsiness broken by the slightest sound, until our astonishment, in a few hours' time, at seeing the return of the greyish light of morning.

Geoffrey Andrewson. Andrewson, Geoffrey.

I will murmur my first name and my surname and I won't recognise them. In my mouth, the sonority of the syllables will burst like soap bubbles, in the evening over the city, and my trembling legs will have the strength to walk the streets of Liverpool. My legs, like bits of reed supporting me unsteadily. Stilts, too thin, too dry, almost twigs. But twigs still thick and solid enough to let me walk and hold me upright, straight enough to let me swell my ribcage and breathe as hard as possible (as though ideas circulated in the air, as though all it takes is a good deep breath to organise all the things in my head so that everything becomes clear, so that everything resumes the clear and natural order that people think it has).

Coming out of Elsie's house, I'll go to the Yellow Pub, Tim's; there'll be hardly anyone at the bar. On the right, just past the door, I'll see Terry, Jimmy, Stephen playing darts the way they do the same time every night and, behind the bar, at the back, Wendy and Linda. They'll wave to me to join them. Tim will smile that faint smile of his and, as he finishes changing the barrel, I'll ask for a bottle of special brew.

Haven't seen you for a while!

Yeah, a long time. Three months at least.

And I'll have to explain to Tim that I haven't had a lot of time, correspondence courses mean you have to keep regular hours. I'll just say that, and not how hard it is to work when it isn't really possible in my room, as cramped and low-ceilinged as all the other rooms, half of them used as store rooms for all the trinkets we don't need any more and which no one can quite get round to throwing away (those boxes stacked up in the hall, under an old nylon curtain with a pattern of red and orange flowers, have been joined by all kinds of other boxes that have started invading my bedroom, covering the whole of the left-hand wall to the ceiling). That wall where the poster was – it's still there but you can't see it – of the Beatles walking across the zebra crossing of a life-sized Abbey Road, there are now piles of tabloid newspapers, car magazines and the pile of *Penthouse* and *Razzle* that Hughie must have left here in response to a murderous glare from Faith, piles of comics that were the only taste that all three of us shared, my brothers and me, and whole cardboard boxes of motorcycle spare parts, a broken tape recorder which no one will throw away because all we would need to do, as they say, is sit down and fix it, some pre-recorded cassettes and a few vinyl records. And some fabrics. Some shoes too old to be worn, but not damaged enough to be thrown away. Waiting, like everything else.

Just as I will wait, there, in the Yellow Pub, not to be asked any more questions. Because, even if I had kept my silence over the past few months, and done a lot of work, being careful not to go out too much (and all my outings reserved for Elsie, because she wanted us to be on our own, and to leave the city, to go to Southport for the shady streets and the arcades on Lord Street, or its flower-beds and the tranquillity of the long, sandy beach), so that I could catch up on my geography studies, I still hadn't managed to finish all the work I'd accumulated. That fondness I have for geography. I could talk about maps, and say how much I'd like to design maps and globes. And the rest of the time I'll help out at the Chinese restaurant on the corner, Madame Kyon, making deliveries or even washing up a few times a week. Yes, not a lot of time for friends. No time for the pub. I'll have to talk about that, and say I don't get out much these days.

You're not being held prisoner, are you? Linda will ask with a laugh.

Oh, that's right, how's your girlfriend?

I'll be careful not to notice the irony with which Wendy asks her question, joining forces with Linda, trying to find out whether or not I'm being held prisoner. That's right, I don't see the people I used to see, because Elsie doesn't like it. She hasn't told me. She doesn't force me to do anything, but I do sense that she doesn't think much of my friends. Even if it has nothing to do with my family, even if it has nothing to do with her hatred for Doug and Hughie. But even so, you can sense these things.

David and John and I wanted to get a new-wave band together. Wendy might have been the singer, and I'd have been on bass. But we never did it, and we never will because that evening I'll go for a long walk after leaving the Yellow Pub, and I'll think for a long time and feel in my lungs that the air is impossible to breathe, oh, yes, all of a sudden, walking faster, listening to the cars leaving the city, walking towards them to stop feeling suffocated by the yellowing images that weighed so heavily on my heart, all my heaviness, that's it, the first time I made love it was with Wendy on her parents' sofa, my first joints were with John and David, our first concerts, our desire to get on the stage and write our own songs. But we waited too long, we waited years.

Did you see what happened?

What? Don't you know?

And I'll mumble that of course I know. Like everyone else. But not telling her I was there. Not having to say what I saw, what I was doing over there. But hearing everyone's stories. Gulping my beer down to drown the words and the confessions I won't be able to make, well aware that I can't cope with them. Blushing all the time, not knowing how to say that I wasn't in Liverpool, I was in Brussels, that I was in the stadium, feeling incapable, too cowardly to tell the truth, I'll look around for something to bind me to an idea, to something, but the bar and the glasses behind it, the yellow light above the dartboard, and even the voices and the laughter of the players, everything will seem hostile, unreal. I won't say anything, not a word, not a murmur. It'll be my way of lying.

They'll talk about their disgust and their sadness. They'll talk about it saying *us*, associating me with them, and I won't say a thing. Outside, just afterwards, as I resume my walk through the city, I'll be able to whisper to myself: from now on you'll have to run faster than your life and span all the years in one go, jettison everything that keeps you here, because you aren't here any more, you've left already, you're going, perhaps to London, to Amsterdam, perhaps to deliver pizzas and transport pork and beef carcasses to warehouses on the other side of the world, or throw sawdust on the oil and petrol stains in filling stations. Perhaps I'll look for my life as I look at the silty water of the Thames or the big white houses and the crowds in Carnaby Street, perhaps I'll try to understand, as I stare at the colonnaded porticos and the bronze-green, blood-red doors, chewing my spittle as I wonder how you get there, a desert right in the heart of London, or somewhere else, anywhere, when I'll have decided to let go and send my life wandering far in front of me – not far in space, but far, infinitely far in time, in front of me, where my memory will be able to free me from the grip of a Liverpool that I've barely known, the one of full employment and the smells of palm oil and coffee on Albert Dock, the taste of strawberry ice-creams that my mother bought us from a shop in Warwick Street; yes, to escape the memories of the fleas that nibbled our calves and our arms in the cinema, forget my brothers' voices and their encouragements, come on, go on, you can do it, and I'd learned to roller-skate, and ride a bike, and that evening will be the hardest, their childhood voices mingling with the screams in the stadium, and even before the street, in the pub, my throat will be blocked and my eyes will sting and redden – when I claim it's because of the smoke and Tim will climb on a stool to try and adjust the ventilator above the bar.

We'll go on talking to say that this time we could even find ourselves agreeing with Margaret Thatcher when she said that shame and disgrace had fallen upon our country. We'll almost be able to laugh as we hear ourselves saying we agreed with her, when we hate her so much. Agreeing with her as we say to ourselves that it would make you weep to agree with her. And now, defeated, bruised, saying we agree with her, it's quite right for the English clubs to pull out of the European competitions next year. And us agreeing with the woman for whom we were filled with hatred and disgust, such shame, as though we could have aged so quickly and, in an evening, gone over to the conservative side of the country which we've all hated, all of us here, for such a long time.

And I'll look at them, my friends drinking their beers, their faces closed and sad, to the sound of the music around us, which Tim will turn down. The sound of the darts hitting the cork board will drown out music and voices. I won't finish my beer. I'll take another cigarette and I'll have to go outside to avoid confronting my cowardice – shame and disgrace – or reflect that around me, now, it's the world I knew that has collapsed and that, even though I didn't do it all on my own, and even though I'll clearly be able to say to myself that I wasn't involved, because you can always hide behind the others, behind what we'll hear about unemployment and destiny, fate, poverty, or you might still be able to hide among reasons and excuses, statistics, I'll have to confess that my whole life will have been nothing but a lie that will lead me there, crimson-cheeked and short of breath, an accomplice of all that has happened, what I'll have joined in with in my own soft and luke-warm way, which is to say profoundly guilty, toxic, harmful to myself and others. That's what you'll have to have the courage to say to yourself, for once. Geoff. Andrewson. Geoffrey Andrewson. A little shadow in the picture.

And finally I'll wonder, fingers spread against the edge of the bar, if it's really because I love them and want to be close to them, or is it only because I'm a craven coward, that I won't admit what I know about my brothers, preferring to lie and deceive my friends, and the girl I love, to avoid acknowledging what they are? My brothers who will shamelessly and without scruple continue with what they have already started at my parents' house, abandoning themselves to it with utter lack of concern once they get home: starting where they left off two days earlier. They'll find their armchair in the sitting room. Then, both tired and enraged by what they've heard on television, they'll go and get a nice cold beer from the fridge. Then, even later, they'll turn out the light and go the bedroom to fuck their wives, as casual as dogs marking their territory.

Yes, that's what I'll think, incapable now of swallowing beer or spittle, making every effort to hold back tears as heavy as that inexpressible need to ask forgiveness and try to understand. But for that I'd have to take my time. I'd have to stop hearing, yet again, the lie I'll have told by nodding my head in a way that's puzzled and despondent rather than – who knows? – contrite and repentant. And then, pursing my lips knowingly, I may think to myself, what am I going to do afterwards? How will it be possible to look myself straight in the face, to look at myself, and look at my friends when they'll talk in front of me and with me, without suspecting that I've lied to them, just because they can't imagine that I was there (how could they, when I've never talked to them about my brothers and the family passion for football except to say the most terrible things about them?).

I'll look at my watch. The pub will be filling up soon, and Tim will have to turn up the music. The cigarette smoke will rise and cover the ceiling as I go to the toilet to splash water over my stinging eyes. And when I get back I'll say I've got to go, without waiting for the surprised reaction of Linda and Wendy,

Already?

And I won't reply, and I'll be thinking no, not already, you mean finally. I'm finally getting out of here. I won't be coming back to the people I've betrayed. I'll think about them, the ones I won't even take the time to say goodbye to. The air will be cool, almost cold, and it will slap my cheeks as though to wake me up. This time my cheeks won't be red with shame but red from the lash of the reviving air that will wake me up and finally let me understand everything that's happening. All that will be happening at that moment. My hands supporting my stomach as though it were about to fall out or explode from bloating and heartburn.

As I walk, my breath will quicken in my chest. Finally, everything will be clear and simple to me. My cheeks will be boiling, my lips dry and cracking, and my body in harmony with the racket thumping in my head. It'll be time to stop cheating, this time. Faces will surround me. My friends. My parents. Elsie. And then the city itself, which will want to spit me out like a cherry stone, a left-over, a lump of phlegm amongst the rest. And I'll know the city is right, because I will have harmed my city. I will keep on going and soon find myself over by Cavern Walks. So I'll still have time to hum 'Strawberry Fields Forever' when what I really want to do is scream, my voice swimming among the voices of the dead from over there, crossing the black waters of the Channel and climbing the white cliffs of Dover, devouring the whole of Great Britain until they reach the inside of my belly and my head. And then I'll think again of that girl with the black leather jacket and the ponytail, blood on her hands, that wild-eyed, crazy look on her face. And with me having seen some English supporters helping people on the ground – I could have helped, I needn't have stayed like that, rooted to the spot. I'll walk into the city and I'll wait, as I go back up Lime Street towards the station, to thinking of that girl I could have helped when she looked at me and I looked at her, when she was in front of me on the field and I was in front of her on the pitch. And I'll think of her face, her whiteness, her stunned expression, her mouth, while mine will express nothing but the void as I hold out my thumb and then pull open the door of the first car that stops. I'll only hear the engine turning. I won't see the silhouette of the driver leaning over to open the door from the other side, but I'll walk fast, fast, almost at a run, to grab the door, and dive as fast as possible into the car, waiting for what, dreaming of widening the gap still further,

nothing – just to take a great leap, desert my life and never return.

III

12

Three years and a few months.

It must have been a very long time for the families, waiting for the trial to begin, waiting for something to happen, for justice to be done, as they say. But we can't really talk about any of that. In La Bassée I saw the passing of those three years in a pocket handkerchief – a pocket that I could have emptied out on the kitchen table, and which would have held not years or keys or change or a handkerchief but six hundred thousand students protesting against educational reforms and the motorcycle units sent in against them, the suicide of the singer Dalida, the explosion of the space shuttle *Challenger* like an American echo of the thirty-two officially reported Chernobyl deaths; the death of Rock Hudson, but AIDS doesn't only kill film stars, Madonna's hot-pants were an icon for the end of the twentieth century, Fred Astaire, René Char, Rita Hayworth, Jean Genet, Simone de Beauvoir, but I could also have taken from my pockets my fear of understanding that we live exposed to the elements and that our skin isn't solid enough to protect us from scratches and bites, our skin is already our flesh, and like pearls or coins I would have rolled names across the table, songs and *Wings of Desire*, the arrival of Prozac and Super Mario Bros on Nintendo, our world emerging like a kick up the arse of our parents' dreams; the death at the hands of the police of the student Malik Oussekine and me and Tonino trying to understand as we worked, revising for our exams while selling burgers and chips as white as church candles, and in spite of the smell of frying and our caps on our heads, remembering at the same time the number of flutes on a Doric column and the golden age of classical architecture, reassuring ourselves by saying, OK, another ten credits and we'll have our degrees and then afterwards, afterwards,

afterwards I'm going to go often to La Bassée, to see my mother and my little brother – hi, bro, all right? – my mother who told me she saw the match on television without knowing I was there or that she might have spotted my silhouette among the ghosts and the ashen corpses in the wreckage. Three years and a few months, for a trial already finished before it had taken place. Italo Calvino is dead. Otto Preminger is dead, the stock-market crash and *Shoah* on television and Tonino wanting me to go with him, to go back to Brussels to be near the trial that I didn't want to see, when I dreamed only of having done with those landscapes of mud-spattered grass and rubble, those screams that woke me at night, months later, in my bedroom, even though it hadn't moved and I told myself time and again that nothing could happen in La Bassée.

Yes, I told myself, my room is the place where nothing moves, in this house where I still thought nothing could come out of its moth-balled stasis, apart from that strange world on television – and us, miraculously preserved from life and death, from unrest, in an unshifting universe, only disturbed from time to time by the doorbell and the flushed, chapped face of Bernard coming to see my mother and yelling at her that he loved her sister, that he wanted to see her sister, staggering around outside the fence, eyes glazed, clinging to the fence for a good ten minutes, mumbling and swearing. And then he would stagger off, his hair dusty and his eyes lost, disappointed and even more alone than he was before he started drinking. That was the event. The only one. The one that demanded we hide and turn off the lights, the television, just so we didn't have to escape the pathetic outpourings of a garrulous, lovelorn alcoholic. The only movement that called for us to hide a little, avoid a danger in this world that was without danger or risk because, basically, we didn't yet exist.

So, no, not the trial. I didn't want to go. Couldn't go . . . at least I told myself I couldn't go. I went to see Tonino at the Gare du Nord, in Paris, when he came back to Brussels, because he'd called me up to ask me to come, saying we could stay in Paris for a few days to walk around and take a bit of a break. And I thought, take a bit of a break? . . . let justice be done? . . . yes, yes, that's it, Tonino, we'll take a break, a breather, we'll rethink a few things . . . I'll certainly rethink a few things when I see you getting off that train and we find ourselves back in that station I haven't set foot in for three years, when we came back, the two of us, you still with your hair long and that gash in your eyebrow, your bomber jacket and *Chicago* in white letters, Gabriel's sky-blue shirt, telling me how your night ended, you and Gabriel in a bar where Virginie had left you on your own. And in the end you'd gone to sleep at theirs, because Gabriel had ended up saying he wouldn't be able to look himself in the face if he dared to go on with his jealousy, his *uncalled-for* jealousy as he called it himself: his *uncalled-for* rage and jealousy, worth nothing more than indifference, as if, during the night, after *that* night, he had worked out just how trivial it all was.

In the train, I had snoozed, and Tonino's voice had come back to me with the words he had spoken on the phone to say there's no point staying here, it's going to go on for months and I have nothing to do in Brussels . . . It's weird being here, to see the Grand-Place again . . . I have to speak to you, you have to know, the English, the trial. I have to talk to you about who I saw there.

His anxiety. Short hair, his beard, nearly red, a good week old. Tonino and that puffa jacket that made him look like the Michelin man, below an inscrutable face that right then, even though I'd seen him very recently, just a few weeks previously, I had felt I didn't completely recognise. But it wasn't because of the short hair or the beard, or even his tiredness and the puffa jacket that might have made his head look smaller than it really was. That way he had of not looking me in the face, lowering his eyes and smiling into the distance, talking about the cold and how nice it was for the two of us to meet up in Paris, was unfamiliar to me: a kind of awkwardness. Tonino, perhaps both relieved to see me and uneasy at having to justify his need for my presence, with a conversation that had only put off the time for us to leave the station and go towards the Rue de Dunkerque, jostled by the rush-hour crowd. Tonino, saved for another few minutes by the noise and the cold – a real, dry cold, this time I was sure of it – before finding a table at the back of the first brasserie we came to.

But why did I have to wait for revelations? Or even a special vision of things whose outcome I didn't really care about? A trial, photographers, television channels covering what three years had cleaned up anyway, covered with a layer of pointless information and swept aside by the next bit of information along – my pocket would have been stretched still further, at random across the brasserie table I'd have been able to throw the Red Baron's little plane landing in Red Square, the endless conversations about the *Rainbow Warrior* or the Channel Tunnel or whatever, when I was just wondering if Tonino would have anything to say other than what I already knew because I'd heard it repeated twenty times in the papers and on television, or even merely feared when he had wanted to go to Brussels, replying with a shrug when I told him he would only be reviving something that should be allowed to die out, that memory, the noise it made, which he thought would hurt him just by the fact of his being here – even from a distance, even just strolling through Brussels and approaching the Palace of Justice without ever going in – so that something would happen. For him, it was the desire to leap all at once over those three years in the hope of taking hold of them and making them his own, because this time there would be no surprise, there would be full knowledge of the case. That was what had brought him back to Brussels. Because, when he had gone back into the stadiums, it wasn't to see the matches there, but just to rediscover a tiny part of the pleasure that he would never know again. I knew almost by chance, in the course of a conversation with some friends on their way back from a match, from that banal and insignificant little phrase, cruel as phrases spoken innocently can sometimes be, when they pierce the heart so keenly precisely because they don't mean to: we saw your mate Tonino at the stadium just now. I can see myself hearing that phrase, and pretending not to see anything surprising about it (yes, I know, he likes going to games) when my head thronged with promises never to go near a stadium or a crowd ever again. Because that's what we'd sworn. We'd promised.

And then we'd never mentioned it again. I've often thought how surprised I was at not being able to – not wanting to – tell anyone I was there. As though it would have been vulgarly pretentious, like saying, I escaped that, so I was the strongest one, and I could tell stories and embellish them, present myself as a force of nature, when in fact that's impossible. Just as I didn't want to tell Tonino that I've never been able to sleep naked since then; yes, that need to cover myself, slip on a pair of pyjamas because I had this feeling that my skin was too fragile not to be covered by a pair of pyjamas and covered too by a silence heavier and more deafening than a shock-wave, isolating me and my ideas from everything and everyone, and from Tonino as much as anyone else; and while we had shared, although we didn't admit it, that need to return to a stadium, my skin was too fragile and porous. Not to say I was there. Not to acknowledge that everyone had had to lock himself away in his sense of being the only one unable to free himself from a memory placed in our lives like a block of granite in the middle of a field. Or rather like a hole in a field. A shell-hole. A devastation. An excavation to be covered over by lies and invented stories (handy, those, the stories we make up to avoid telling the ones that really haunt us), cover them over with a beard and a puffa jacket and silence and absences and projects you could carry out in your sleep because, yes, Tonino, you just have to let the world get on with its business and see how it covers everything, look, you see, it's covered already with a silky fog, hostages in the Lebanon or whatever it is the world talks about and our desire, so powerful, so dark, to slide across time. When we talked about Belgium, it was to talk about the beer and the girls in the cafés, the red flowers and the Musée des Beaux-Arts, which we didn't go to. Then as I walked towards the brasserie I thought, tell me, Tonino, did you go to the Musée des Beaux-Arts? What did you do that we weren't able to do when we were there? Will I have to lift my head and keep my hands pressed hard against my thighs to warm up a bit, on the seat in the brasserie? or will our conversation, right now, be enough to help us regain that trust, that friendship that's been weakened a little, calmly, almost as if it was pretending to do something else, and while the air around us had grown more and more rarefied over those three and a half years.

I should have asked you, Tonino, did you notice that I don't wear my father's watch any more? No one noticed that. And yet it's one of the first things I did when I came back from Brussels. I went into my mother's room – she was out – and opened the wardrobe with the mirror on it. In there, hanging up on their hangers, I saw my father's suit and his blue parka, almost grey, his only tie. I opened the drawer. There I recognised his broken glasses, his cufflink box, his fireman's insignia and a medallion: I put his wristwatch back amongst all his things; I took one more look at his fireman's uniform and cap. I shut the wardrobe door, and it was as if I was closing it on my past.

I ordered a beer saying, OK, shit, Tonino, do you know that in all that time, we're, look, do you realise that it's changed us both? You see, a change, a shift that's occurred on the quiet, really, like the continental plates, you know, did you notice? Would it have happened anyway? Was there no other solution than that subsidence, that need to see each other less, even if I know that it's normal to see each other less, to tell each other less, because friendships change like everything else. Tonino looked at me, smoking, and I went on, my voice rising, my hands already trying to attack the beer-mat. And as I began to break it, to fold it first in four, then in eight, eyes fixed, nailed, screwed on my fingers, feverishly fiddling with the cardboard square, Tonino spoke. He began to talk about the fear and the diffuse sensations that he had always known, but which he thought had taken a new turn, imperceptible at first, but constantly weighing on him a little more, encircling him when he failed to understand, he said, why he was short of breath in the street, in the open air, when his eyes opened at night because of the pressure he thought he could feel against him. Pressure from hands, arms. And you see, Jeff, Tonino said to me, I thought about all that when I was on my way there, and the fact that the more life moves forward the more I have to put a lid on it and speak of nothing, nothing now, I can't share anything.

OK. Let's start over. It all means nothing. Nothing at all. We know that. We said it then, in the brasserie. We're alive, we're fine, everything's fine. And his trembling fingers and his heavy intonation, the vibration in his voice . . . What have we done in the course of three years that's so different from what we did before? Nothing special, nothing in particular. Nothing. The same days and the same nights. The games of pinball in the back room of the Longchamp, on the illuminated box from which the lubricious smiles of two big blondes in blue bikinis and a super-confident James Bond welcomed us each morning, and the games of table football with a baker's apprentice and a hard-rock guitarist that we liked. Girls were born beneath our fingertips as springtime came, like leaves and birds in the trees, on the Île Simon where we always drank the same bottles of Jenlain. What, then? I don't know. We wanted to go on talking and had another beer to tell ourselves that we couldn't understand, that it wasn't a lack of friendship so much as a truth like the need to return to oneself, to regain a part of oneself, an idea of oneself; the sense of something forgotten, like a piece of clothing left in the stadium, whose absence we were reminded of every day, every minute, demanding that total silence be imposed upon it, a withdrawal, a silent glance unwitnessed, merely seeking what was missing, to feel its lack, its need. Then it's true, Tonino said, I feel this need to go to stadiums to think.

He also talked of the strange shyness he had felt from the first day, when he arrived at Brussels-Midi early one rainy morning. He said he had planned how he would spend the day. But also that he hadn't done anything as planned.

At the station, he had bought a map of the city, because as he arrived he realised he had only been there once before. That had been his first surprise: his astonishment at forgetting that he didn't know the city, because it was as if Brussels had been with him in France for those last three years, with its chocolate and its Manneken-Pis, its four-lane roads obliterating an old city scarred and run down by time. The city was inside him, and he couldn't understand how he could disembark there as ignorant as any other stranger. No. Impossible. And he understood just how impatient he was to get back there. He chose to take a taxi to the stadium. To see the entrance to the stadium. A stadium soon, no doubt, to be renamed rebuilt. But Tonino, in the taxi that took him there (Tonino would have said *took him back* there), he had thought that changing names or rebuilding façades, transforming, remodelling, disguising, was like leaving or travelling for people who want to escape the shadow that's snapping at their feet, without understanding that it's actually their own, or rather desperately trying to ignore it, to pretend not to recognise it as part of themselves. Remaking, breaking, changing everything, the walls, the architecture, the name. If the very building had been demolished, if all that was left had been a hole on the edge of the city, then its crevasse would have sullied and polluted the air in the same way for all the people whose lives had been broken there.

He saw the taxi turning round in the car park and stayed there like that, in the rain – a fine rain, almost drizzle – waiting to decide what to do. He walked and then he turned round to look at Avenue Houba-de-Strooper. He hadn't remembered such a big and imposing avenue, the amount of traffic. And the oily black of the soft tarmac, gleaming like the skin of a seal. He hadn't remembered that, the church on the corner past the stadium, or the bushes . . . He decided not to stay there, why stay rooted to the ground like that, what was the point? The images recalled by his memory didn't superimpose themselves over what he had before his eyes: the sun of a spring afternoon, dust, the crowd by the ticket-desks and the policemen, the voices – nothing, it didn't work, that attempt to do what he had done in childhood with sticker-books, sticking them in to a picture to complete the scene, that was what Tonino wanted to do, standing there motionless in the rain, trying to roll a cigarette with fingers that tried to keep the calm he needed to pull himself together and find an image that wouldn't return, which didn't fit the frame he had in front of him, and yet that's it, it's here, it's here, he said to himself, and yet it was never here; beneath this rain, at this very moment, there was nothing but the void, but the desert of a setting drained of substance, barely enriched by a configuration, a possible space, yes, there was a faint resemblance from a distance, a vague sense of déjà-vu, perhaps, but denied by the grey of the sky, and then by the people on the pavements, walking too slowly, too calmly, indifferent and busy with thoughts other than his.

And that void surrounding Tonino when he decided to walk around the stadium, slowly, trying to fetch back something more distant than his presence here, but with a certainty that he was not alone, walking in the void but not being alone, or only seeming to be on that rainy day, in October, in 1988, but plagued by visions more than three years old, by the heat and impatience before entering the stadium. And even when he gave up walking around the stadium and, coming back to

Avenue Houba-de-Strooper, sat down in a restaurant to have lunch, he couldn't help remembering the meat-balls and tomato sauce – it was all there, images, sensations, returning memories, or rather they found their place there by embracing old habits; although perhaps that wasn't the same thing. Like being alone in the streets and the metro, coming back towards the city centre, had been even stranger, because of the presence of the orange seats that he remembered very clearly. But the metro was almost empty that day. And this time he was going in the opposite direction, and there was no one on the seats opposite him. The echoes of Francesco and Tana's voices were barely capable of reaching him, while the voices and faces were erased by the metallic clatter of the train and for a long time now Tonino knew that he had forgotten both of them, Francesco and Tana.

He put his things down on the edge of the basin, his gap-toothed comb, his toothbrush, a deodorant. He had forgotten his razor so, too bad, he wouldn't shave as long as he was here. That was what he thought immediately, before reflecting that he would only have had to go downstairs and leave the hotel to buy blades and foam. But no. He had bought *Le Soir* and hadn't opened it, just as he hadn't opened his street-map. On the edge of this single bed, in this room with its walls a pink so faint you could hardly see it, he had stayed sitting almost all afternoon eating oranges and boiled eggs that he had prepared before setting off. Then he had lain on the bed without knowing what to do or what to expect from his trip.

In the brasserie on Rue de Dunkerque, he spoke and didn't wait for me to answer, to tell him what I thought. His voice advanced unwavering, seeking calm, avoiding gaps and anything that might have brought his story to an end. It wasn't cold that day. He looked at the newspapers in the kiosks; they talked of the historic trial, the twenty-six hooligans who would be there, in the defendants' box, as the victims and their representatives would be, too. It was only then that he opened up the street-map to look for the court. Page 7, box 18, a petrol-blue shape with an orange surround, black letters above it: *Palais de Justice/Justitiepaleis*. He had to go back down, perhaps take the metro. But Tonino preferred to walk. He rolled a few cigarettes and put them in his tin. He looked at his map, the names of the streets around the Palace of Justice. He walked slowly but got lost because, in spite of the map, he couldn't find it; he had seen on the map the long Rue de la Régence, which leads straight from the Place Royale to the Place Polaert but, no, he got lost again, wandered as far as the Rue Haute, then the Rue du Temple. He became irritated and got angry with himself; he stopped looking at the map and spat away the flabby, stained cigarette-butt that hung between his lips.

When he saw the law court he went on walking. He took one of the cigarettes that he had rolled before. He brought it to his mouth and didn't light it, not straight away. As he entered the street, the Palace of Justice became enormous and, surrounding the cupola of its dome, griffons and statues seated a hundred metres above him seemed to beckon him over with a dubious look, vaguely bored and blasé from seeing so much coming and going around the court – cars, vans, cameras, photographers, not to mention the ceaseless ballet of the magistrates' robes when they brushed the cobbles like ball-gowns; a dance, yes, the sad dance of the twenty-six heads of the hooligans that might soon be about to fall, which Tonino would try to spot to recognise through the shaved heads and the fat faces, the massive necks stuck on heavy clumsy bodies, bomber jackets and jeans, Doc Martens, animals that live in a pack and kill in a pack, just because none of them are worth a thing on his own. And Tonino recognising the hatred rising up within him at the idea of those twenty-six faces that he would try to see, knowing that it would be so easy to hate them on behalf of the others, all the ones who should have been there in the defendants' box, but who will have stayed at home, good family men, respectable youths. But it would be even worse to see the journalists and onlookers amongst the crowd approaching the court, and to know that there, in a courtroom, they would talk, deliver their testimonies, bring together the evidence and the files and then wait for what, in fact? No, then. Tonino didn't want to get any closer. He stopped about fifty metres away from the palace, and stayed there for about twenty minutes, standing on the pavement, smoking as he looked straight ahead of him to work out what had to be done, saying to himself that he wouldn't be able to bear that today.

It was a Monday, the first day of a sickly-sweet trial that would go on for ages. Tonino smiled as he told me about that first afternoon when he had gone to see *Baron Munchhausen* at the cinema. Yes, he had laughed that afternoon, as he had laughed the following day, too, when he saw *A Fish Called Wanda*, from the first shot, a breathless laugh that would relax him after that Monday afternoon when, coming back from the Grand-Place, his attention had been caught by a demonstration outside a brasserie. It was the same brasserie we went to that morning, do you remember? he asked me. And then he wanted to be quiet for a while, take a break. But this time – and only this time – in the brasserie on Rue de Dunkerque, he raised his eyes towards me and stared at me.

You'll never guess.

His voice, choked with barely contained rage and fury as he repeated those words to me.

You'll never guess.

On the Grand-Place, around the brasserie terrace, he could hear the clicking of cameras, the din of overlapping voices. Tonino murmuring with astonishment at the sight of the television interviewing a group of people, men smiling like film stars. He had slipped among the crowd clustered behind the camera and the photographers; it was opposite the brasserie terrace, and Tonino kept on walking without really asking himself any questions, because he didn't understand what was going on, not yet; he didn't understand straight away, not until he heard the English voices and questions about the fear of punishment; the punishment that was already falling upon Tonino and all those who waited, hoped, believed that,

You'll never guess.

There they were, sipping on beers, and talking and replying without concern, smoking and sniggering, exuding a sense of impunity; they have shopping bags, yes, some of them have been shopping! – one of them might have bought some perfume for his wife, another some chocolates for his children – leaving Tonino to carry the ghosts of skinheads that he would never see again except in his nightmares, because they were there in front of him and none of them had a shaved head, none of them, not even the one with the blankest, most unsmiling face, had a face more terrifying or threatening than the average man in the street. They all sat there looking astonished to be the object of such attention, amused as a child at Christmas, waiting for what? A reward? A gift? As if it weren't already too great a gift to train cameras and microphones on them. But none of it matters to them. Nothing, because they're in the street, they're still together, never isolated or separated from one another, and here too it's as a whole that they have existence, those faces belonging to conformist, indifferent young men. And what was it that allowed them to look so remote from what they were accused of? Their ties? Their smart suits, making them look like teenagers dressed up for a village wedding? Seeming to say, with a chuckle, you see, nothing happened, we're not animals, we're not killers, we're just like you because our clothes are like your clothes, and our wives are like your wives, our habits are like yours – do you like chocolate? – we're like you, exactly like you, and now we want to go home because we've got homes, too, and families waiting for us there.

Oh, yes, that simmering rage and the tears that would have flowed if it hadn't been for that numbness that kept Tonino frozen there, staring at the seven or eight boys around the table. And that agitation, the attention being paid to the guys with sports bags at their feet, Tonino could see, because nothing would happen to them and most of them would be going home that evening. He listened to the voice of the young man answering the questions with a serious air, the half-ashamed, half-worried look of someone who doesn't know what he's being accused of, what he could have done. He must be twenty-three or twenty-four, he's a plasterer and lives in Upminster, and he says he doesn't remember very clearly, he witnessed the first charge but not the second, and he turned round and went the other way. He really doesn't remember what happened, back there. He says again that if he can't remember it's because there was nothing he could do, because, he claims, there would be hell to pay and he wouldn't be able to forgive himself. And because he can and there's nothing to make him feel guilty, he says it's because he didn't do anything. That's what Tonino understands. That there are other people around him, too, understanding and listening. They'll have to settle for that. In spite of the desire to plunge into the crowd. In spite of that desire to yell and throw himself on that guy or one of the others, saying to himself that if he had a gun he would shoot; yes they know, this time, they know; at that moment Tonino feels that he would shoot if he had a gun in his hands. Others would shoot, too. And it was then that Tonino decided to take a few steps back, not to stay there and honour these *animals* with an audience, because now that was what he would call them, both for himself and to pretend to cleanse humanity of their presence – but suddenly there's that voice behind him, excuse me, I'm sorry, excuse me,

Tonino?

Gabriel hadn't changed much. A fine blond moustache. Hair shorter than Tonino remembered. Same sky-blue shirt. But a slightly ill-fitting tie round his neck. He was wearing a suit in which he seemed to float, the same pale grey jacket as the Englishmen on the terrace, and shoulder-pads that made him look like an American football player.

Tonino was very disconcerted by how pleased Gabriel seemed to be to see him. He insisted that Tonino come for dinner at his place that evening, and he could even sleep there if he wanted, rather than staying at the hotel where, Gabriel said, you always spend too much money. But Tonino refused to sleep at his place, although he did accept his invitation to dinner. Gabriel was working in a travel agency not far from the Grand-Place, which meant that every evening he came home this way, the journey long enough to clear his head of his work worries.

He parked his green 205 convertible outside his block. Along the way he'd told Tonino the whole history of Ixelles, where he had now chosen to live: its artists and the students at the Free University of Brussels, its middle class and its immigrants, the night-life near the cemetery, the little shops, the cafés, a real beating heart, he said, as Tonino, swallowing down his hatred and disgust for what he had seen at the brasserie terrace, enraged by the voice of a singer he didn't know and whose miaowings spewed from the car radio, tried to listen to what Gabriel was saying. He didn't mention the trial, not a word, not even that scene he had witnessed in the distance, on the Grand-Place, as if the whole business had no hold on either of them, no more existence than a news bulletin that you turn down so that you can go on talking. And Gabriel went on talking about his district, Avenue Louise and Place Stéphanie, you should see the town-houses! On Sunday we go walking in the Bois-de-la-Cambre . . . We like to go there with our little boy, over by the stables and the jetty; we stay by the water as long as the weather allows.

Tonino tried to smile as he heard there was a child in Gabriel's life – a child! – and yet he had been immediately horrified by Gabriel's oddly excitable air as he got home, dropping his keys on the coffee-table in the sitting room. He had assumed a honeyed voice, its sweetness apparently demonstrative because of the presence of his guest, asking Darling? Are you there? Before adding, ah . . . no . . . sorry . . . not with our little boy, no smoking, I'm afraid. And since Viviane gave up we decided it was better for us.

Tonino stayed like that, open-mouthed, almost pleased that the cigarette he wouldn't be smoking was an opportunity to learn the name of Viviane, charming Viviane who has just come in from the bathroom, smartly-dressed and pink, bony, eyes wide and smiling. Yes. Hello. And Gabriel nagging them both, Tonino and Viviane, swearing on all the gods that if they didn't recognise each other, they'd still seen each other once, more than three years before. Over dinner they had both tried to remember the evening before the match . . . She remembered dancing in the bar, as she often did, because she liked dancing. Well, Tonino! Viviane was there . . . She's never been very far away . . . And then, you see, we've all met up again. We've been married for two years now, the little one was born last summer.

In the car, as Gabriel drove him to the hotel, Tonino barely spoke. He would have liked to talk about the trial, about how he hadn't felt he could go to the court, or even how surprised he had been as they crossed the Grand-Place, past the cinema. Over dinner they'd talked about anything and everything, mostly about work, the changes a child brings to your life, etc. But they'd said nothing about the trial. When the hotel had swung into view, Gabriel stopped the car, but left the engine running, vaguely embarrassed, OK, well, there we are, we're there. And it was then that Tonino had to reply, perhaps in the same tone, thanks and goodbye, adding a word about Viviane, yes, Viviane's very nice.

Yes, she is, Gabriel replied. She's also not as pretty as Virginie. But Virginie . . . She left a few weeks after what happened. That's the way it is . . . But OK, sorry, it's late; I've got to go, I've got an early start tomorrow.

13

It was our honeymoon and the grains of rice like fireflies flying around you, falling on you, on your inert body – and that tiled wall at the morgue in the military hospital, the cafeteria where I thought I waited for hours; at the end of the long corridor, I can still hear my echoing footsteps, and the trolleys, Francesco, all the trolleys, your name like bits of glass shattering in my throat, and the number hanging from your toe, Francesco, your clothes; your shirt; your shoes. That shoelace you'd told me the previous day you'd have to change before it broke, and which held in spite of everything; all those images imprinted within me that I brought home when we landed at the airport.

Gavino was at the funeral, in Brussels. And Adriana, Roberta, they were there, and they saw the coffins lined up in that vast military hangar. It was near Brussels, I remember wreaths of flowers and the organ playing 'Ce n'est qu'un au revoir' as I looked at the concrete and my shoes and sometimes my mother and my sister, they were there too, around me; my sister was biting her nails and I could hear her breathing, her sobs, stop moving, stop it, she was constantly fidgeting, her left foot on its side, and her pulling it inwards and making the sole click and I remember my voice squeaking, stop fidgeting, and she stopped for a minute and then without realising she started up again, to break the silence, to silence her sobs and her voice, she looked at my mother and leaned in front of me, we couldn't make out a word, my mother was crushing my fingers, I said stop, my hands still hurt, but she didn't hear and took my hands and her fingers slipped between mine and then she folded them saying I'm here, I'm here. My heart beat so hard at the sight of the flags on the coffins. And to think that our loved ones were lying in all those coffins. It just can't be that in those boxes, those brown boxes, you were there with the rest, lying so far from me in the darkness of a closed box, so tightly confined while we were in such a big hangar; there were all the people, and that ceremony lasted at least two hours, such a long time. I was tired, I thought I was going to collapse, and it was then, not when he arrived with your parents and Roberta, and with his wife Adriana, at the embassy, when they came towards me in the waiting room, but at that moment, in the hangar, while the organ was playing or the speeches were being delivered, that I saw for the first time how much Gavino looked like you.

And that violence in his tears and his impenetrable face, that great breach that no one could heal – and he, usually so straight, so strong, was trembling and didn't know what to do or what to say, when I saw for the first time how cruel and unbearable the resemblance between two brothers can be; your expression in his eyes, your smile in his mouth, and I wanted to tell Gavino to give you his eyes and your mouth, your startled expression. But actually, no,

no, no,

I'm completely wrong,

I'm just saying the first thing that comes into my head, it's not the worst, the most scandalous thing about this resemblance that struck me suddenly and made me tense up and look towards him to see something of you, no, the violence and the horror weren't in his resemblance to you, on the contrary, it's precisely because that resemblance wasn't perfect, because it was repulsive: how can I see you almost there, in front of me, with almost your eyes and almost your mouth, with almost the shape of your face because in that 'almost' what leapt out at me was the realisation that I would never see you before me again. And I looked at your brother, waiting for the differences to disappear, I wished he had been your twin at

230

least to have the pleasure of believing you were a bit more there, even though I knew it wasn't so. I would have accepted that illusion, a mask just to soothe me, to calm me a little through the illusion of your image; then I could have basked in the idea of looking at you, even in the knowledge that it wasn't you, talking to you knowing that you couldn't hear me, I would have done that as I looked at your brother, but I saw only that it wasn't you, like a failed copy, poor Gavino, what malicious thoughts I directed at him, and all of them, and even at you.

Yes, something has freed me from you, my rage against them; they took you back from me, by taking me in their arms they tore me from yours; they all did that and they did it deliberately, I know, covering me in kisses, stroking my hair, crumpling grandfather Gianni's blue-and-white checked cotton handkerchiefs. And then that silence that barely covered the sound of the engine of the plane that brought us home, it roared in my ears as soon as we began the descent, my eardrums pressing in on my head as I said to myself, today we should be in Amsterdam holding each other's hands in the street, and instead I see the blue-and-white checked handkerchief between my fingers, and the bandages on my fingers, Italy, Roberta and Adriana's faces, the crowd in the square and the scratches on my hands.

Oh Francesco, if you knew how much I blessed that roaring in my ears, deafening me. The others chewed chewing-gum and sweets, forced themselves to yawn to unblock their ears while I shut my mouth as hard as I could and in the plane I refused their chewing-gum and their lemon sweets because I wanted that roar to hide me inside it, not to hear the fury in the streets, when we climbed the streets of the village with your remains, when the bells rang and we had to see our neighbours' eyes, their rage, and that mass where they spoke of forgiveness and love, rage and pride, saying we must be strong enough not to seek revenge; but you beneath the flowers and the wreaths you stayed as well-behaved as the wooden Christ above you, before you: he looked at you from the top of his cross with wooden eyes, round and bulging, like the eyes of the goldfish in the pet section of the supermarket, turning round and round in their bowl; they turn round and never get bored because they don't have the memory that pierces the heart of those who can't forget. And I can't forget those days or the roaring in my ears stifling the voices and the rage around me, yes, Francesco, that rage that rose as exhaustion fell around us. And I was able to keep my silence. They didn't need me now. I wanted to escape the whole business and say nothing more, watching and listening as people wept and threatened English journalists, shouting during the ceremony in Belgium: we will always be there to remind you what you did.

I spent hours at your parents' house, in the sitting room, with Gavino who couldn't sit still and your parents around the big smoked-glass table, with the newspaper open in the middle and the photograph of Princess Paola, you can see that she's weeping, she wears dark glasses but under the grey newsprint you know there are tears. Everyone noticed the princess's tears, and your mother, moving around the table, murmured that all those tears were perfectly normal, the tears of a Roman woman, a Roman woman crying, your mother said, lowering her eyes over the table where she looked at the photograph of Paola in the paper. Your father said nothing and just sat there, and sometimes he went off to do something, who knows what, but so slowly, with such caution in his movements that one would have thought he was about to break or crumble into dust.

But no. We held our breath so that nothing would move in the dining room, apart from the pages of the newspaper that your mother wanted to turn and turn again as though she might learn something else from them apart from the death of her son. When you read the news you say that the news is sad, but when the news tells you that this time you're the news, it's your turn to be the dead whose names are figures and numbers, waiting for the next day's paper, waiting for worse, well, it isn't the same, your chest is torn apart while even yesterday the same news and the same number of dead disgusted you so you just went and brushed your teeth and washed your face. But not this time. You sit around the table, you take another coffee, an infusion, you play with your wedding ring, you massage the back of your neck with your fingers and then you say to yourself that this time because the paper says it's true it must be false, absolutely false, it happened to someone else because it's in the paper, you say to yourself: nothing ever happens to me so it can't happen to me, simple as that,

and yet Francesco,

it's your name, it's you, it's that day, and I still remember the gold cross separating the flowers and the flags of the different countries on the coffins in Brussels, the speeches in four languages and that boredom that gripped me because I couldn't keep going. I thought about Amsterdam and the canals and the museums, our hotel in Brussels, and even Tonino and Jeff, then those hours of waiting, my footsteps in the corridor, all those voices, all those people who kept me going when all I could see was the night and the flashing blue lights of the ambulances, whose sirens broke my eardrums and my heart. So that's what I thought about during the ceremony, my longing to make love with you, to hear your voice, and then, too, the photographs of you on your mother's sideboard. They can say what they like, I'll never be at peace and I'll never want to be at peace, or at night, drinking, singing, weeping but never the way I wanted peace before, when I believed in it as simply as saying to myself, the future is just smiling at someone.

They can all go to hell.

I can't go on.

I finally realised I couldn't go on at the precise moment when they joined me in Brussels, the next day and the day after that, when they opened their arms to me and said those sickly words to me that I couldn't hear. They tore me from you, they came with their ashen faces and their perfumes, their clothes as black as the grime I felt within me, saying nothing when they wanted to do everything, hear everything, bring everything back to zero, at the embassy. They wanted to hide from me the fact that all the bodies had been autopsied – that's what they said to defend themselves, afterwards, the next day, when I knew the bodies had been autopsied and the knife had sliced your skin as well. So unimaginable is that horror that on the contrary you desperately try to imagine it and see it in your mind: it takes hours, all night, in spite of all the tranquillisers, it's not diluted by sleeping pills or tears. I'd slept all day and no one asked me anything, no permission, it must have been your mother and father who talked to them, and it was only afterwards that they shared my rage, when they opened the coffins; but I was already mad and furious.

Do you understand? Do you hear? Do you see? The first thing they wanted to do was to start coming between us again and imposing upon us ideas that would never have occurred either to you or to me. They reached the embassy, all together, my mother and my sister Grazia beside your brother Gavino and his wife. Adriana and Roberta, the eldest, and your mother and your father, he in his black Sunday suit and she in a black dress, her features so drawn, her face so white that the wrinkles had faded in a single night; it was like a smooth, white ball, split by hollow eyes, red from crying since the previous day, in the middle of the night – and how did they find out? Their eyes were lost amongst the millions and millions of eyes watching the television. They said: four hundred million pairs of eyes. Imagine that four hundred million people saw and we were what they saw. They had finished their dinner, perhaps sitting calmly in their armchairs, and the television yelling at top volume while they, my parents and yours, were enjoying themselves and stamping their feet impatiently to see the match on television, to be with us a little on our honeymoon, almost beside us, through the television, and they must have thought again of your face and mine as we received from their hands the two grey tickets printed with the letter Z. I'll never know what I went through there, that day. And they can say, that's how things happened: it was 7.22 pm, the first charge, etc., etc., and then an England supporter provoked a policeman until the policeman struck him with a truncheon and he bled, until his face was nothing more than the red of the Liverpool Reds before joining his mates with his arms raised in a sign of victory; they can tell me about the corpses and the casualties carried on metal barriers while they waited for the stretchers, and millions of eyes floating over all that, millions of people, the whole of Europe dumbfounded by games and blood, television, radio, death and games for everyone and us at the mercy of our own eyes and the newspapers, the big wheel still turning behind the stadium, is it possible?

Is it true? Probably, because it seems fake, it's obscene, people can explain and say whatever they like and get the sociologists and the psychiatrists and God knows who else to explain, what, your body, your hand, your absence, life going off the rails and the derailment that life recovers in photographs and newspapers and the television, while we are nothing now, little lost heaps, nothing, grains of nothing in the sand needed to make the machine turn,

and it turns,

it turns,

And all the things they'll use to try and get a bit of logic into this crazy head of mine, oh, yes, I was mad, completely mad for the first few evenings, the first few days, the hours spent lying in your sister's room. The patterns on the wallpaper and the Doors poster danced in front of my eyes, floated with my tears, the condensation in my eyes – but I did nothing, I let my hands lie on either side of my hips, and that's all. Nothing but wait until the night came to free me from the day and the day to free me from the night, come on, come on, make it go faster,

and in my room, at your parents' house, there was a roaring in my ears for three days; such a loud whistling noise that I was left in a distant, deafened world where I had hot drinks made for me and where people rang at the door at all hours, and your mother begged them to make less noise so that I could sleep. Sleep a little bit more. But it was impossible. It was more than I could bear when I heard your father crying, the only time, because of the autopsy: they opened up your shoulders to the small of your back and didn't even bother to sew it back up again. Fine, you died of *asphyxia resulting from a mechanical compression of the ribcage*, that's it, pointless, Francesco,

how can everything deviate from its trajectory like that? How is it possible, tell me? Oh, yes, because there is no trajectory. No direction. Nothing. We're thrown like that at full speed and you have to tell yourself that with a bit of luck you won't fall until much later, far away, but not immediately, not too close, and there was no point crying that it was unfair, or wanting the death of the English whether from Liverpool or anywhere else. What could it matter to me when from your sister's room I looked at the portrait of Jim Morrison and sang 'This is the End' so afraid was I of hearing more people coming and knocking at the door, my friends, my sister, my colleagues coming to give their support to the family and the family spreading out in puddles of words and gestures, fists aloft, such rage, that sadness everywhere, on the radio and the television, in the street. It was everywhere and I wanted to hear a bit more silence in my head to pull myself together. You have to pull yourself together, that was what I said to myself. And then Grazia came to see me and with her I got up, I went with her and walked a little and asked her why my mother didn't come and see me, why she shut herself away at home,

I got no reply.

I looked at the rabbit hutches, the embroidered carnations on the curtains and your mother's petrol-blue apron – she came over to me and took me in her arms. Then she looked at my hands, yes, that's better, that's better she said, and then she hugged me saying poor baby, poor child. I couldn't believe that, why your mother wasn't yelling as I was sure she would, repeating: you wouldn't get married in church and now it's the church that has claimed you back. That's what I expected her to shout, her face filled with hatred. But her face was smooth and white, almost waxy, so pale that the wrinkles had disappeared; you see, Francesco, imagine your mother forcing me to sit down on the laundry basket in the shower room: she stands and looks at my hands, then rubs them slowly with eau de Cologne, not saying a word to me, you hear, not saying anything at all, not a word of complaint, nothing, no anger, not a thing, her gaze concentrated in her gestures, the slowness of her movements, sometimes suppressing a sob, she blushes, she puts a curl back behind her ear, she tries to smile and perhaps the effort causes her pain but she says nothing, and we both hear your father sanding planks and banging away like a madman with a hammer to finish a piece of furniture or a shelf – he still has to polish the wood – and he perseveres and goes on doing that without replying when little Leandra hovers around and around him; she wants to have her poems read to her, or be told why you won't come back, why she hasn't had any postcards as you promised her so that she could complete her collection of cards of the cities of Europe, why there were no foreign coins, why I look so sad and empty, and why the whole of Italy seems unable to hold itself upright, clinging to the handles of a trophy it isn't sure it still wants,

Oh Francesco, if only you knew, everyone's rage reassured me. It gave me strength, it lifted me up somewhere, to a place I didn't know of and then, without warning, I plunged even lower and knew that the world had ceased to exist, that in the end I would be left alone with nothing on my hands but my abandonment and your memory. I will be a widow at twenty-three with the loose trouser-hems of a husband who is dead somewhere. So I decided to take them in anyway, and I got the trousers and the sewing box from the cupboard where your mother kept it. She watched me doing it, when I came and sat down in the sitting room and slipped the thread through the eye of the needle. I redid the hems of your trousers, I didn't speak, then I washed your clothes so that you could use them. No one said anything to me. Your mother was amazed and then she looked at Gavino who wanted me to stop, even though he didn't say so I saw it very clearly, I understood his awkwardness, his horror, because he got up a few times to drink and rinse the glass of water from which he drank again every time he finished rinsing it, and clicked his tongue as if to say to me, won't she stop? won't she stop stubbornly denying the evidence as she's doing, with such cool, such calm? The needle did its slaloming and the hems were nearly finished. I had never done any needlework, certainly not hems. Gavino knew it, and that must have been what exasperated him even more, I'm sure. But after a moment, it was your mother who nodded to him, and he did nothing more and put down his glass then came back towards us. He sat down. He understood that he mustn't stop me. Then they saw me getting your things and going towards the shower room. They heard the lid of the washing-machine opening, then the click of the button when I set the programme, the water running, then the first turns of the machine, and the door of the shower room as I shut it behind me before I went to back lie down again. I hadn't put your striped sweater among the washing. I left it to one side. I smelt your smell through the fabric, so at the last moment I chose not to wash the striped sweater and took it with me, to bring it into the bedroom; I slept with it.

I woke with a start, at about two in the morning, because we'd forgotten to cancel the reservation for two nights on the houseboat in Amsterdam. And it was at night that I thought about all the others, all the other men and women who must have been lying there, eyes open, in the middle of the night, astonished that they were still breathing, knowing the miracle of not being dead *of asphyxia resulting from a mechanical compression of the ribcage.* It's so precious, and suddenly so painful, to feel your carcass getting up again and doing what it knows how to do without asking anything else than to do it again, always, it goes on so stupidly that day breaks to leave you amorphous and defeated, yet more exhausted than the previous day. It's something so hard to perceive, when you feel it without having identified it: that shame that leaks in, slips inside you and obstructs your breathing, almost to the point of suffocation but not that far, almost to the point of unconsciousness but not that far, almost to the point of death but never that: nothing will free you. Not even the letters that come in from everywhere to tell you that you have to keep going.

People tell you about themselves and tell you that you can do it, you must, you can't give up. Letters whose handwriting you don't recognise, or the name of the person writing with as much care, as much delicacy as they can muster, emphasising anecdotes, I'm Giuliana and we were at school together, perhaps you remember me? As I read, I imagined I remembered and invented faces for these people I'd forgotten or never known, it didn't matter, they talked of a life that had died twice, dead with my childhood and dead with you. I would have liked to reply, and I'd asked for some paper and something to write with, some envelopes; but I didn't reply. I began a few words of thanks, but I was too bad at lying to thank them. I didn't want to thank them, I didn't want to be supported the way you support a dead weight, a body, an object, and I would have liked to write, no Giuliana, I don't know who you are, I don't remember a girl whose brother used to come and pick her up on his motorbike wearing an apple-green jumpsuit, and I don't remember your brace, and anyway I don't give a damn about you, the memories, the boys in apple-green jumpsuits and the years before Francesco or all the ones to come. So no, Francesco, in the church, I might have heard as I looked at your coffin, that we have to be able to forgive and not forget – but anyway, how would I forget, eh, do you know, Francesco? What could I have done to jettison such a mess, such madness and your absence like an air pocket that surrounds me in space, that has become the whole of the space around me? So what could I have done to speak of forgiveness and love, rage and pride, how could I have kept going as the priest said we had to, we had to do it in honour of the victims and he repeated that you have to be able not to seek revenge, you have to be able to forgive and not forget, and without that nothing will ever be possible, you hear? I remember that in the church the words came and slipped towards me and bounced off the flowers and the wreaths, on the goldfish-eyed Christ with his arms held out in a cross-shape, split along their whole length, and his patience in his eyes, all the dead passing beneath his round, bulging eyes for how long, how many centuries?

I chose instead to go to your parents', Francesco, because they said to me, come on, we'll be together, we're already together because you're like our daughter now. They were weeks that lasted who knows how, suspended in the void, waiting for something to come and calm the noise and the rage that could be seen all around, heard all around. There were newspapers and the television. Journalists behind every door and microphones as threatening as flags, cameras, men with notebooks; what did they want, what did they want to know, when they knew more than anyone, when they spoke and commented; they wrote articles, provoked debates, launched polemics, and the newspapers abounded with slogans and ideas, protests, dismay and figures, while the others, the rest of us, had nothing but choking for words, waiting for cries, trembling hands for decision. They can go to hell, all those people who wanted to support us by having a good place in the photograph and the others, the ones with things to say, they have things to say about everything, always have done, since the beginning and till the end of time there will always have been some fool clever enough to explain why there's no one so clever as he in a world reduced to ashes, and he will explain it to the corpses and the stones, pointing a threatening finger at them, shrugging his shoulders at the ignorance of the clouds, the dead rabbits, the dry rivers, he will despise them and we have been despised – that was what I felt. The husbands, the wives, the children, you, and you, then you, and the mothers, the fathers, the colleagues, the friends, all of those people have the right to weep and their tears are given away, not sold.

Yes, Francesco, they aren't sold, but everything has been sold and scorned by the gaze focused upon us. And the presses turned so quickly, so hard, harder than the big wheel in Brussels and faster than our lives parted from the trajectory we had planned for it, the two of us together. We want to be silent, but people don't seem to know. There was that rage against everyone, against the English and the Belgians. We wanted scapegoats, trophies for our fury. There was talk of trials, shame, humiliation. And I heard those words lost in the distance like the gabbling of children in a school playground, the peeping of birds fighting in the magnolia bushes, shaking the leaves and the corollas of the white flowers; Adriana and Gavino were more shocked than anyone else, and it was they, not me, who agreed to take part in the trial, to lay claim to their rage and despair; and at bottom I envied them, because I'd have liked to know how to take my rage and turn all my rancour and violence into a genuine desire for justice. But I couldn't do it. I gave in. I dreaded the moment when I'd have to go back to the apartment we'd rented – do you remember – and I found the canary at your mother's, she was going to look after it while we were on honeymoon, but it's going to stay at hers. It was Gavino and Adriana and Roberta who came and brought all our things in cardboard boxes and big bin-bags for the clothes. They came and left it all at your parents', and gave the keys to the owners, and I never went back, not once. I couldn't have. I tell myself that I should perhaps have done just that to understand that you and I were finished. You haven't left me; I haven't left you either: and yet it's over before it even began.

Do you realise? In the little back room, behind your father's workbench and on the shelves, there were the boxes from our move, with meaningless words written in fat black marker pen: *crockery, fragile, books, records, clothes, papers, knick-knacks, miscellaneous crap*. And then there's that law of probability that means we couldn't have been there, we couldn't have been there, when I'd never seen a football match in my life, I was only a last-minute supporter and you loved it, it was impossible, impossible. And yet we arrived in Brussels, we took the metro and we met Tonino and Jeff, we went into the stadium and we took our places and what happened happened: how I would have loved to believe in God to know the pleasure of stripping the capital letter from his name and stamp on it so that he too would stumble and die of asphyxia through compression of the ribcage. But I don't believe in him and I would have nothing to curse but chance and its indifference, which doesn't leave the same taste in the mouth.

I didn't want to go to the flat where for three weeks we repainted every room and the ceilings, because I could never have afforded to live there alone. I had no wages and no desire to breathe in the smell of fresh paint in a flat that was already too old for me, for us, with the memory of that bed right in the middle of the sitting room, and the windows open on to the street, moonlight falling in the middle of the room and rising to us in the bed, with that pale grey light of summer nights. Because there were already nights like the ones we will never know together, but which had reached us at the end of March and the beginning of April, on the open bed where we made love right in the middle of the sitting room, surrounded by pots of paint and sheets of newspaper to protect the tiled floor, not to mention our strange, childish joy when we discovered the noises that happened at night – I remember we spotted them, but I've forgotten them all.

And all of a sudden I think of it, moving in together meant getting away and inventing a life that the others couldn't manage, and we'd send them postcards,

perhaps,

postcards that Leandra will never receive, that Gina and Giovanna will no longer wait to receive, like the confidences the three of us used to pass on to each other about the men we saw in the evening, after lectures, squeezing out of one secrets told by the other, pleading that they wouldn't be repeated, and of course in the end each of us knew everything about the other two; they waited for me to talk about you, how you made love and how considerate you were. But honestly, seriously, can you really say what you expect from a tablecloth? You think you expect nothing from objects, on the quiet you try to convince yourself that you don't attach any kind of symbolism to them, oh yes, what a farce, expecting the whiteness of a tablecloth to be like a promise or a clear, cloudless, stainless sky! You'd have to be stupid to be gulled by that, weeping for fear you might sink: you won't sink, we're already at the bottom and now,

now you're the one who's dead and the world has turned upside-down completely: your mother is there and she doesn't say a word, she doesn't cry and she stays upright in her pain, she holds back her tears, saving them for later, when they'll belong only to her, and she holds out her hand to me as my mother didn't do, because all of a sudden that's quite clear to me, my mother said nothing not out of respect but out of contempt, she waited for the fall, sniggering, saying poor innocent children, poor fool, my daughter, what do you think you're doing with your little flat all done up nicely and your hearts so full of love and the smells of acrylic paint, all those clean smells and your hearts full of love? She didn't come. Not once.

But your friends, your neighbours, journalists too, and then the mayor and the politicians, the priest and others I didn't see, they did come. From the bedroom I heard words and phrases reaching me, dulled by the roaring in my ears, or by the softness of the sleep in which I sometimes found refuge, between two terrors and two mouthfuls of water, because my mouth was so dry that my lips cracked and almost bled. My tongue was swollen, I had trouble breathing and that's why I woke up; I was lulled by voices I heard coming from the kitchen, or by the silence, by the television that little Leandra was watching, by the sander or the hammer in your father's workshop, the jigsaw, and the birds – oh, yes, that's true, it was still spring – and I had regular visits from Gina and Giovanna, my two friends from university. They came to your place often, and I can see your mother coming to get me in the bedroom the first time they came: your mother puts first her hand, then her face into the frame of the door to tell me that my friends are there. I remember how startled I was, that moment of uncertainty when I forgot who they were, Gina and Giovanna, oh, yes, my friends, my studies, real life and me not moving, not hearing, I got up and I saw the two of them, at the end of the corridor, almost as hesitant as I was, as if for them too I no longer existed, or I didn't exist, or only in a dream the two of them had dreamed at the same time, without being sure that we'd ever meet up again. They walked towards me very slowly at first, then faster and faster, as if each step brought us closer together, until finally the fog dispersed and we'd finally recognised each other and seen each other as before, it's you, it's you, yes, perhaps it's me, it must be me,

it must be me.

Gina and Giovanna, so very real and present and yet, when I saw them in front of me, I found them wearing an unfamiliar expression, as if their faces were younger than mine, or as if I understood how young they were, the two of them, just as I must be, but with a youthfulness that had fled from my mirror never to return, as if your mother had erased her wrinkles so that her skin could be white, just by smoothing her cheeks and her forehead with the flesh of her fingers, and collected the wrinkles in the hollow of her hand, like twigs or hairs, and blown them into my face – no, it wasn't aggressive or malicious, but gentle and protective, she gave me her story as a part of her son, and I accepted it. So fully did I accept it that I accepted her hands, and hers alone, on my hair, when she stroked it so that she didn't have to speak or say the usual nonsense, all the nonsense and regrets that people should keep to themselves but which they come out with, expecting you to be moved. As if we had nothing else to do but accept the fate that is made for us.

But in the end those few weeks were very short, bathed in a vast vagueness. And yet, one day, you understand that something is over: the morning has passed without a visitor, without a single phone call. No one suggested you go anywhere with them, no one offered to do your shopping for you, and it even seemed as if the newspapers and the television had assumed their familiar face, the one we knew from before, stamped at once with indifference and empathy, confusion and details. That returning life like a strange and violent reminder of the fact that several weeks had passed, that it was time to regain possession of a pain that no longer meant anything to anyone else; in the streets you no longer turn back, you don't talk about what happened, you have to go on, you have to go on, they tell you, and I said to myself, OK, fine, let's go on, let's rush on in silence, stubbornly and precisely, without turning round. And everything resumes as before.

I wore the same dresses, the oleanders are the same, the canary sings the same, and I swear, the same sun heats the same roofs and the children run the same and laugh the same as they did when you were there, the same, everyone, everything. And the journalists who wanted to know everything have deserted the streets, I have found myself alone in my surprise at surviving the apocalypse, and returning to find that the apocalypse was just an invisible, odourless flaw that doesn't say anything or hurt anyone. Everything is calm and peaceful once more. I saw your mother starting to sit down, one day tears spilled from her eyes. Her cheeks were suddenly less smooth, less white. I saw that she had become the woman she was before, then even more so, then it couldn't stop, her cheeks, her forehead, her chin, her hands, everything was covered with wide, deep wrinkles. Her eyes were red, narrowed to slits. I saw her weeping so hard, not saying a word, not moving, with no other expression than that steady flow of tears. I worked out that it was time for everyone to discover what was his, and return to the site of his pain, but this time each one for himself. I went towards her and this time it was I who took her shoulders in my arms, I who stroked her hair thinking poor baby, poor child. I let her weep as we heard your father's footsteps in his workshop. I said now I think things can't go on like this, I'm not your daughter, I never will be, I've got to go home.

I left that same day. I took a few clothes and my sponge-bag, I never even phoned to say I was coming back. I walked along the road leading towards my house, and turned the door-handle. As I entered, I smelt the cool air and the smell of boiled potato. There was no sound in the house, just the ventilator spinning in the window above the sink. Finally I heard the sound of flip-flops, dragging footsteps on the tiles. My mother appeared in the door, holding a handkerchief; we stayed like that, saying nothing at first, and I waited for her to understand why I was there. Then I said hello, as if I were coming home after having done something fantastically stupid, as though my voice were asking forgiveness. All she said by way of reply was: your room is ready, I've had the windows open all day, Grazia changed the sheets yesterday.

From the first few weeks of moving back into the house, when I came back to the room I'd left a few months earlier to go and live with Francesco, I said straight away that I wouldn't shut myself away, waiting until it was time for the market or mass, that I would never be the sort of widow you thought one had to be. I said immediately that I rejected all that. I said I didn't want to live like that, I told you, I'm twenty-three and I don't want to live like an old lady waiting patiently to lose heart and the courage to breathe, to join in his grave a man she had no plans to survive, in slow motion, as though hibernating, before being freed by death and at long last being able to rot away as she smiles at her husband.

I thought, no, never; but you, mother, you hated me for not wanting to stay and mourn a dead man who will never die for me, you tried to tell me, Tana, Tana, we can go to the cemetery together today *anyway*. And there was I pretending not to hear when that obsequious, cooing tone in your voice stirred my determination all the more, my resolution sharpened still further by those words, *anyway, in spite of everything*, which I read in your tone, without too much ambiguity, hardly more hidden than a face behind a window by the fog of its breath.

Behind that *anyway* I heard the rest of the words that came afterwards, all the rest, that scandal that you were able to repress into that simple *anyway*, when I'd rather have heard you pouring it all out, all at once, and revealing your innermost thoughts by saying, come on, Tana, you could come with me to the cemetery at least once, you could make an effort, we never see you here and you come back early in the morning blind drunk and your eyes even blacker than your hair, dyed with that black dye, too black, *anyway*, you had to mess around with your lovely blonde hair with that blue-black, crow-black dye, that make-up around your eyes, and that unfeminine black jacket, my daughter, Tana, you could come to the cemetery, *anyway*, you thought, Mamma.

And when you just said *anyway*, I lit a cigarette, and, if I sometimes turned back towards you it was just to blow my smoke in the direction of your face, to see your features and your expression dissolving and softening as they became blurred and grey, to warm you up a little, or for your hardness to soften in the bluish grey of the smoke; your face, your skin, your expression of hatred suppressed just as you suppressed your breathing so as not to smell or inhale the smoke – you were so afraid of being poisoned when here, yes, it's true, we were suffocating on air that was sticky and dangerous in a different way, air poisoned by our looks and our silences, with poor Grazia, all of fifteen, passing between us to restore bonds that no longer existed, about which she alone still believed, or tried to believe, that there was something still to be done, when in fact it had been rotten for ages – we both knew it – for just over three years.

Because Francesco, all my life will be yours, I know that well enough not to have to act out eternal mourning, Mamma, as you would have wished, as you immediately hoped, from the first few days when I accepted that we would go walking together every morning and every evening, arm in arm, along the Via Rebora to the sound of barking dogs, walking slowly as we waited to reach the campsite where the road descended, where we always acknowledged the same sense of both arriving in the middle of a forest, just as we reached the short avenue of lime trees, outside the cemetery with its little car park and its grey gate, the three black crosses facing us, one on each side of the gate, and the last one above it, crowning the grille and our courage, the two of us, mother and daughter dressed all in mourning and piety – do you see that? – how can you imagine anything so arrogant, so comical? without suspecting that you would want us to perform those gestures every day, for ever, with that pleasure you already felt at the thought that I too would assume the calm habit of coming with you along the gravel path, in that calm, welcoming setting: the row of fir trees on the left, the grass between the graves and, on the hillside, the mausoleums on the other side of the path on the right, and then at the end the largest mausoleums, with the wall bordering and framing the cemetery with its tiered graves. We see the rows of plaques. There they are, one after the other with surnames and Christian names, dates and that hyphen that represents a life squashed between birth and death, as though the life itself were the accident. There they are, words stuck on or engraved or inlaid in black or gold inside the plaque. I saw that so often with you, those names, Papa and Francesco's among them.

So, no question . . .

because in Brussels I worked out that things keep upright only by chance and accident; it's chaos that's the norm, not the reverse. And there's nothing that all your rituals and timetables can do about it, not your preciousness, your endless concern for cleanliness and all the minutes of your life and ours nicely ordered between the hands of the clock, your obsession with doing everything at the right time, to the minute; I saw how stubborn you were, wanting to make yourself believe that if you could struggle like that, rather than yielding to the desire to scream and hit the first person that comes along; that powerful desire whose greed spoke to me from all your features, a little more each time, even if you stayed calm and didn't shout as often as before, like when Grazia and I were little, railing against our uncle and the noises from the garage, or the disgusting smell of hot oil, which you said you wouldn't survive and which you did survive until we got here, to Montoggio, all three of us nice and peaceful in your husband's parents' little house, which we inherited on Grandfather's death, like mountains around us to stifle your rage and your rancour against the whole world.

Ah, yes, and as for you, since we got here you imposed a system upon everything so that the sense of the void, the sense of chaos, would never take possession of you ever again, would never leave you as helpless as you had been in Genoa, when Papa died. But poor Mamma, why do you stand so stiffly, and why does your mouth form that unbearable rictus, as though you had won something that no one but you had ever noticed. You think you have conquered grief. You think you have nothing more to wait for, you think you have to be true to what was expected of you, as if obeying some ancient order. But you're not fooling anyone but yourself, because all you're doing to me is driving me mad and making me furious with you, you never do anything, and furious with your pretension, too. Because basically it is pretentious, all that, that way of clinging to the idea of a truth to which one must glue every hour of one's life and one's every desire – if you only knew, on the other hand, what you gain from ceasing to believe in anything that lasts, anything solid, if you know, you can't imagine, I'm sure you don't even imagine, so successful have you been at erecting barricades around you to protect yourself and your fear, to assert immutable laws, securely framed in a life devoted solely to the observation of those laws. But, Mamma, why do you really think that plastic and fabric flowers, yellow lilies, roses, wild flowers and carnations, sunflowers or those washed-out red or sun-bleached yellow tulips, are a reflection of eternity? Don't you see that even flowers made to last for ever show signs of weakness? Like the flames in those little red night-lights that flicker gently by the names and the flowers; and even the little electric lights will go out in the end. Nature will eat away at the graves from all directions; some people who chose to plant shrubs and lavender rather than flowers, or to surround the graves with pine cones, let the grass grow, they're right, because the plants will win, the slabs will crack, the concrete will finally crumble between our fingers; that's why we shouldn't waste too much time with illusions of duration and permanence, no, there's no point in that, there never has been, and you knew that, but you preferred to persevere as though you would be right in the end just by being the only one to persist; and you could always curse and complain when I lingered behind you, far behind you, since the first days when the two of us came, each to her husband's grave.

You thought: men die like flies, and you fight flies by putting up mosquito nets over the windows. And dragging my feet as I refused to take your arm, I lit my first cigarette before we'd even left the cemetery. Since those first days I have let bitterness mingle with sadness, when, as we left the house, we had to accept the barking of the dogs answering one another from one house to the next, a garland of barking to open up the road ahead for me, and subject myself to the ludicrous experience of the voices from a television set turned up full, or the no less ridiculous spectacle, on a balcony, of a yellow dog sniffing a budgerigar in its cage, while a plaster Snow White and Seven Dwarfs hail us with idiotic gestures and depressing smiles: yes, I had to bear all that, saying to myself, nothing matters.

We were in mourning, but you wanted to become mourning personified. You wear mourning within yourself, gently, like a pain you like to study when you're alone, in the evening, but not in front of others, not to live like that, as you wanted me to do and as you saw I wouldn't. And your hatred for me, your desolation when you saw that I was rearing up and resisting, I wanted music and the windows wide open, I wanted to go out and when I had to resume my studies and rediscover Genoa and Gina and Giovanna, you said nothing, you envied me a little, I know – I know now – I saw how your hatred of me had doubled, because you had to struggle against your desire to scream at me that you, when your husband died, had resigned yourself as women have always resigned themselves, as far back as your memory would go.

Here, you'll always be in the shadow of the mountains and the photographs of the tribe of the dead, with the strange shock produced by colour photographs, the ones whose colours seem suddenly so bright, so sharp compared to black and white, sepia and the vague outlines from which head-scarfed grandmothers smiled, and moustachioed old men with clear, clear eyes and wrinkles deep as scars. You hated me as if I had deprived you of your rebellion, as though I were telling you you'd been wrong and that it was your life itself that I was judging, and you, you that I was rejecting. But it's true, I haven't got a child of my own. It's true, I have only myself for the future, no part to play out for a child, but . . . Mamma . . . will you ever manage to forgive your daughters for keeping you from being a woman? Because I hear it, there, that wonderful excuse, that you couldn't rebuild your life because you had children to bring up.

It might have been possible, I could have agreed to live like you, to share more than the facial resemblance between a daughter and her mother, when you saw that wasn't going to happen, that things were escaping your control, that was when everything blew apart, because your immediate reproach to me wasn't my black hair or my torn jeans, not the loud-coloured tights, the make-up, or even the heavily ringed eyes in the morning, or even all the rest of the crap, my breath stinking of alcohol and dark tobacco, the Havanas that men smoke in discotheque backrooms, the men's heavy after-shave, not even the men, not that smell of sex that I trailed around the kitchen all morning, or rather, yes, all the very things you'd taken care to keep away; and you were furious because I rejected the heroism of not yielding to life – no, I should say: to *your* life – I wasn't faithful, and I even dispossessed you of what you'd managed not to do. Because you hadn't yielded, no one should yield. Ever. That's what made you most furious: precisely the fact that I'd jumped in feet first to the place where you lay at night biting your lip for not having gone. Mamma, didn't you miss men so much at night that you were constantly getting out of bed? And that way you had of criticising and despising them, the stubbornness with which you ran them down, taking as a personal attack the slightest smile, the merest invitation to dinner or a party, as if they were going to devour your daughters and devour you, too, so suspicious and contemptuous when I introduced you to Francesco, as you will inevitably despise Grazia when she appears in the doorway with a man on her arm.

Was it,

was it to hide your dissatisfaction that you got up at night? Did you at least know how to appease your body by touching your breasts and your belly, sighing as you brought your fingers down to touch yourself? Or were you so self-punishing that you were able not to listen to that terrible lack to which you subjected yourself so severely? Was it enough, one day, to throw a canary in the bin to have nothing else to expect, and say to yourself, all right, that's it, I'm free of everything, everything leaves me cold but the respect I owe to the memory of my husband? And the doggedness, rigid and ridiculous, of a little soldier standing at attention, never opening up to any kind of open discussion, or laughing, as you had been able to do when I was small. I was a child and I remember our laughter as if it was yesterday, or, tell me, without blushing, without lying, am I inventing that laughter?

Perhaps.

You wanted me to rot quietly with you, you wanted our wrinkles to protect us from life and from ourselves, from the yearnings of sleepless nights that we might have had after drinking too much, in the evening, too much fortified wine or sweet peach liqueur, the kind women are supposed to like. But I don't like fortified wine or sweet liqueurs. I like strong spirits and hands on my hips. You envied me that, to the point of disgust, of shame. You were jealous of me as an animal is jealous of its young, thoughtlessly; you were just bitter and stubborn to the point of stupidity, without saying a word, just narrowing your eyes, scratching underneath your bra-strap, so that I wouldn't leave the house; and the rest of the time you envied

253

me the fact that I'd gone out anyway, in spite of you. You envied me and even admired me for looking down on you and not respecting you. But you also envied me when you stayed there stunned, without a murmur, dumbfounded, outraged, because I'd spent the night in Genoa and hadn't come home until the small hours, without a sound, always waking you none the less, as I opened my bedroom door.

First of all I saw the chink of light under the door, a golden, almost orange strip, then I heard the springs of your bed; and then I imagined you struggling to get up, to get off your soft mattress, disentangle yourself from a jungle of big, loose blankets. I had barely time to lie down and already I could hear your footsteps in the corridor, with that way you had of dragging them, sniffing very loudly to show your anger and disapproval. A widow probably doesn't do that, no, go on with her studies in Genoa or anywhere else, she mustn't follow her friends to bars and discos in the evening. She doesn't go to the cinema or put on her make-up without risking criticism, mocking laughter or salacious comments; yes, Mamma, it's perfectly clear, your daughter was a whore as you say whores are: vulgar and sophisticated, rebellious and submissive, fake, thieving, cheating, and women in spite of themselves, in spite of all they do to harm the women they are; they are still women, and they live by plundering their own bodies; they are women dressed up, disguised, they live under masks and you thought, that's it, my daughter isn't a whore yet, but she might as well be, because she's dyed her hair crow-black and disfigured her face, not just her features and her expression, but her whole face, making it look more aggressive and brittle, plaster-pale under thick, dense black. And she puts on make-up. She emphasises the black line of her eyes. She goes out a lot. She gets home late, so white, almost deathly pale. And all the water of the Scrivia slips between the mountains and under all the bridges to say what she does when she's drunk those Negronis that get her so drunk so quickly. They make her laugh, yes, they do that. She laughs with her friends Gina and Giovanna, even if her friends think she's going too far, far too far when she offers herself to men who offer her drinks in bars and discotheques – she's stripped naked in a car, a Jaguar or a Bentley, a man poured champagne between her breasts and all the way down to her belly-button, then between her pubic hairs and her labia; and after he licked her body and she did nothing but lie there lazily, laughing. She liked it so much she could have wept. She came very quickly. She liked the man's tongue, with that smell, a mixture of her cunt and the taste of champagne when he kissed her, all things that she told her friends the next day, Gina and Giovanna, and the noise of the leather car-seats, not to mention the eyes, and the cocks of the men masturbating on the other side of the car windows by the roadside.

You see, I'm still modest enough to say she when I talk about your daughter.

Even my friends fled, both of them, Gina and Giovanna, when they began to understand that I wasn't getting over it, and they wished I would get over it – and there's a stupid expression if ever there was one, *getting over it*, over what? the void? when I'd been living in the shadow of a man whose wife I never had the chance to be? That's it . . . That's it . . . except it wasn't just that I didn't want to get over it, quite the opposite, I wanted to get *under* it, creeping like the pebbles that slip along the bed of the Scrivia, like the dirt under my fingernails or the feeling that was gnawing away at me, that I was throwing my life away, out of pique, for nothing, just to trouble still further the water in which my life was stagnating and even, in a sense, to act as you did: to flunk everything and have nothing more to expect from my life, to put it beyond repair, because I can tell you one thing, that you're beyond repair once you've let go of the hand of the one who told you,

run! run, Tana!

Tana, you've got to run and get to the field,

that you feel completely beyond repair when four hundred million people have seen your life stamped on, and thousands upon thousands of words have been written, even more afterwards

255

than before, by newspapers and by regret and remorse and questions, and then gradually by the silence that follows, from above, to cover the noise and make even more of a deafening racket than the noise itself. You're left all alone and you're stamped on once again, trampled all over because you were told there would be a before and after, that things would never be the same, except that for you, afterwards, there's nothing, everything's normal except that the one who said

run! run, Tana!

will never come back, never ever, and your life is irrecoverable, and you understand that you haven't been trampled on by history, only by the present day, and the present day has no time for you, no time for those who die slowly, on a low heat, in front of the television and their dog's multicoloured biscuits, going back and forth to the cemetery, or those who fight back, preferring violent deaths, slow and violent, as I did, running, losing myself, falling into arms that didn't say

run! run, Tana!

but the ones I ran and fell into, just to forget Francesco's voice and to forget you, too, Mamma, because your way of dying didn't fit with mine. I chose instead to forget myself in arms that were second-rate, with men who I will never love but who are the only ones who don't die too quickly, we don't know why, perhaps because they know how to hide and come out at the right moment? In any case, it doesn't matter, they smell of garlic and hair cream, they talk quickly and thrust out their chests, inside which their ribcages inhale putrid air that they offer to women like me when they renounce, once and for all, the idea of survival.

Something in me no longer wanted to hear or understand. There was that astonishment at not being able to hear a word, a sound, because not one of those history classes could interest me or grasp so much as a part of me, resonate with my intelligence or such mind as I still had left. Nothing. That had struck me immediately, as soon as I'd walked into the first lecture theatre: I'll never be able to come back, I'll never be able to take lecture notes or pretend to blacken exercise books with words to write up later. And yet for months I did try. I desperately tried to believe it would be possible to rediscover the pleasure of study, which I had known in the past. I forced myself, telling myself it would come back, and I opened exercise books, text books, I took the lids off ballpoint pens and pricked up my ears, like an eager little schoolgirl at the start of term.

And then nothing. In my exercise books: nothing. A few vague scribbles and some drawings of leaves and trees; then creepers and scratches, stripes, and finally spheres whose volume I attempted to indicate by drawing in the areas of shade with an application to match my boredom and confusion at finding myself there, in a lecture theatre, unable to believe it and drawing in the margins of the exercise books, dogs' faces and screaming faces, an outstretched hand, wide-open eyes. There were also pages torn out as my heart visibly expanded, and swelled so heavily that I thought my chest was going to burst open to throw out my heart, round and heavy as a red-hot iron ball, on the lecturer's desk, and I wouldn't even have been surprised, simply said to myself, my heart has just left me, it was bound to happen sooner or later.

And then there was that morning in Milan. That morning I will always remember, because every day I dreaded its arrival. I had gone down to buy some cigarettes and, on the corner of the street, I found myself facing him; and he – he and I – we were both frozen with surprise for a few seconds, absolutely silent, as though time had stopped and he'd hesitated between two possible directions he could take, one that would have allowed him to go on fleeing still further, without stopping to think, and the other, more dangerous, stronger, which ordered him to stop for a moment and let the past rise up again, in waves, flowing from a distance less great than one might have wished, in spite of every attempt to repel and rebuff it, knowing it would be in vain, realising then that the three years behind us had given us nothing, in spite of all our struggles to refuse to stop and stroke the photographs or the pink marble plaques, those years spent rejecting regret and the hours spent cultivating the scenarios of those aborted lives, with their trips every summer and their children who will never be born, those houses and holidays. We stood there face to face, Gavino and I, and he was the first to speak. Not that I couldn't have spoken, or that I was any more startled than he, because I know what he must have thought when he saw me, during that long moment when I had to digest his image with my memory, and decode his features, still battling against the horror of seeing him suddenly appear like that, all of a sudden, on the corner of a street whose name I didn't even know, in a city that wasn't mine, and where I had only ever gone to get drunk and fuck in dodgy hotels with the first Angelo who came along. Yes, assuming that you'll suddenly see on a street corner, just before the kiosk where I went to buy my Marlboros and stop a while to look at the newspaper headlines and the magazine covers (just to be alone a little longer, rather than go straight back upstairs to join an Angelo who was probably still snoring, or getting impatient for me to come back with his cigarettes), all those faces hidden in the middle of the face, still so recognisable, of Gavino; from his mother's forehead to his father's eyes, perhaps, and then to that indiscernible resemblance and that gap, that bond and that insurmountable difference from Francesco.

He spoke first. He was the one, although I knew that for him too, meeting me there must have been the same astonishment, the same leap back three years in time and, unfolding in that single movement, Gavino must have seen all the years to which the memory of his brother must inevitably have sent him back; Gavino had fallen upon me. And through me, he had fallen upon Francesco, and through him, he had fallen into his own childhood and adolescence. Yes, he had fallen upon me, and now he was falling towards a constantly receding ground, he stood in front of me open-mouthed, the time passing in front of his eyes the few weeks I spent at his parents' house. The time of his brother's funeral and the ceremony in Brussels, and the time of the wedding and then further back in his memory he must have felt like a slap his games of table football with his brother, secrets and revelations must have floated to the surface, all of a sudden, depths so buried he had thought they would never float back up to him, or cause him any pain. And yet he saw me on this street corner. And both of us had to grasp that porosity, those subterranean tectonic plates waiting only for a signal to destroy everything above them, and lay waste to the garden and the enclosing walls we'd spent so much time striving to make presentable.

Oh, Tana!

That's all he said before smiling and hugging me. I think I blushed a little, and I was ashamed too, like that, without really knowing why – and I thought he must think me ugly with my hollow cheeks and my dirty black hair falling on my shoulders and my old Perfecto, that he must be surprised by my T-shirt with its picture of a junkie Mickey Mouse apparently exploding and sticking out his tongue, my red mini skirt and my tights, red too, and my breasts, he must have seen that I wasn't wearing a bra, and I was embarrassed by that, by the idea that he might see my nipples hardened by the cool morning air. Yes, at that moment I knew I was ashamed of the way I dressed. Or rather, no, that I would just have preferred him not to see me like that, so he could tell his mother, Tana is fine, she's looking well, I'd say she's happy. And instead, Gavino looked at me for a moment with his hands on my arms, until I finally suggested he walk me to the kiosk. We walked side by side, looking at each other and smiling; I asked him about his family, and he asked about mine.

He talked about the birthday of Adriana, his wife, and he said he'd come here, to Milan, from Genoa to buy her a dress or some jewellery. His voice as he spoke was gentle and almost shy, like mine, oh, yes, I said, and Leandra how old is Leandra? He said she was thirteen now and I nodded and didn't say anything else. We had reached the kiosk and the customer in front of us had just moved away, so I stepped forward to get some cigarettes. I remember my hands shivering as I took the two or three packs and held out my money. I remember my hands searching through the pockets of my jacket and the desire burning in mouth to say to Gavino, please, you've got to understand, I have nothing against you or anyone in your family, you've got to tell your mother I think of her and Leandra all the time, that even in my sleep I hear the jigsaw in your father's workshop, and that shrill sound echoes like a scream in my head, a kind of entreaty, you've really got to tell them all that I've forgotten no one, no one, that I think of them all the time but I haven't the strength to go to your place, I haven't the strength to see that house where you all took me in like a daughter or a sister, I'm not ungrateful, I can't, I'd like to but I can't, the idea of your faces is too painful and I'm too fragile, my arms would break, yes, it's true, I know, my face is a bit dirty at the moment, they say I'm drinking too much and going out with the wrong sort of guy, but it won't last, it can't last, I miss Francesco so much, and going to see you, you see, would be like bumping into you by chance in the street like this, like going back over frozen time, over there, too far away, and I'd risk breaking down and weeping without being able to stop, what's the point, what's the point, Gavino?

And we both smiled at my embarrassment as I tried to put away my change and my three packs of cigarettes. Yes, I've got two in one hand, the other must be in the other hand, and if I've got three in one it means there's nothing in the other, the change is in my pocket, is one of the packs in my pocket? I don't know, I'm not going to try. And we smiled again. I said, I'm really not that clever, and I've got to go now (I can still hear my quavering voice saying: I'm staying in a hotel with a friend, as if I had to justify myself to Gavino, as if he'd caught me here in this city with a lover, and could threaten to tell Francesco). But Gavino said barely another word. He looked at his watch and, in his turn, apologised and said he had to be going.

15

It was Grazia who picked up the phone to him. She said he'd
introduced himself as a friend of mine, and said he wanted to
talk to me. But Grazia must have told him I wasn't there and
she didn't know when I was getting back, it could be a few
hours or a few days. There had been a long silence, which he
had broken by saying it didn't matter. She must have thought
he would be disappointed, but he'd just said he'd call back
later when he reached Casella. He'd said we hadn't seen each
other for more than three and a half years, but without saying
where or under what circumstances we had met.

He just said his name was Tonino.

That name, when she repeated it to me, got no reaction from
Grazia. But for a second I was disappointed that she couldn't
hear it as I heard it when she said it. I had thought that she
would remember, too, that as soon as she heard it she'd
remember all the things I'd talked to her about, just as I
remembered all the things I'd told her at Francesco's parents'
house, those words, three and a half years previously. I see
myself in the bedroom of one of Francesco's sisters and, on the
wall opposite me, there was that Jim Morrison poster that I
looked at as I told the story to Grazia. It was hot and she wasn't
wearing a blouse, but that little peach cotton top that revealed
her neck and her shoulders; and around her neck I saw the
gold chain she'd been given for first communion, with her
medallion of the Virgin floating above our hands, because
she'd put her hands on mine – and I repeated that story again,
the one I'd already repeated endlessly since the ceremony in

Brussels, in the plane on the way back, at the funeral, with every passing second and even with my eyes shut, in my sleep, in the endless loop of a constantly recommencing present. And I had so exhausted my words by repeating them that perhaps, when I had come to tell them to Grazia, they were like fabrics with faded colours and worn-out fibres, perhaps they were so pale that they hadn't stayed in her mind? I don't know. So it could be that once again, telling the story out loud for Grazia, it was really for me that I was mumbling that same old refrain, to run before my eyes the same images and the same moments, and not so that Grazia would hear, not so that she would understand. I must have murmured my gibberish while she wept just to see me in that bed, face numb, hands still scratched and blue, and she hadn't retained the names or the details of what I had said because basically I myself no longer recognised the words I invented as I used them. But I had said: Tonino and Jeff. I had repeated their names several times, and described the characters of each, their faces, their appearance, I had spoken of their friendship and the complicity that exist-ed between them, I thought I'd talked about it at length . . . But perhaps not, perhaps I'd hardly mentioned their names, no more than those of Gabriel and Virginie . . . And yet I thought I'd told Grazia everything.

That's why I was surprised that she didn't react when she said: someone called Tonino rang to speak to you. She thought it was an old lover coming back from who knows where, another of those men, young and not so young, who were known as Tana's lovers – one of your lovers? she asked. I wanted to say no, but I said nothing. I hesitated for a few sec-onds, long enough to repeat Tonino's name to myself and won-der, is it possible that Tonino remembers me and wants to see me, why would he want to see me? I could no longer hear Grazia's voice even though she was still walking around me, as she always had done, champing with impatience for me to tell her a secret or explain conversations, stories she had heard only in scraps, only grasping their importance because they were shrouded in secrets, whispers (and it was always to me that she addressed her questions and looks, when she tried to understand what it would be like to be a woman, later on, but also at what age that would happen, when she would be capable of having lovers and wanting to come home late at night, so late, unafraid of the dark? She asked how such a thing was possible, and I always told her it wasn't possible, you're just as scared as before but you learn not to run or scream beneath the stars, you support yourself on men or banisters, you cling to bottles of gin or prestigious qualifications, that's just about all you need to know) – a lover? she said again. I stopped listening and, still not listening to the question, perhaps just with the hint of a smile lingering on my lips, I went to the bathroom. In there, I turned on the cold water and drank from the tap, then washed my hands.

I left them under the water for a long time, not hearing the running water, then dried my hands, taking endless time and care, without ever really looking at my movements, my eyes floating straight ahead. Then at last I sat down on the toilet seat. I lit a cigarette and smoked it without really paying attention. I looked at the growing ash and said to myself that when the time came I would curve my hand into the shape of a shell, and the ash would fall into it. I took my time, not listening to my mother's footsteps in the kitchen, the cupboard noises, yes, it's that late, it'll be dinner time in an hour, nor the unbearable music that Grazia was listening to in her room, the pop and easy listening with Madonna's voice recurring most often, or, at that precise moment, Michael Jackson's voice yelling his wretched *I'm bad, I'm bad*, while I kept my eyes fixed on the tip of the cigarette that I was barely smoking.

I stayed there without moving, nibbling at my dead skin every two seconds, hastily bringing my hand up underneath my cigarette, my heart beating so fast that I felt an inrush of blood to my fingertips – and that was probably what would make the ash fall into the hollow of my hand – saying to myself that Tonino's name had been like a thunderclap over my head,

when I remembered no more of him than I did of Jeff, not their faces or their voices. I had so stubbornly set about forgetting and denying them, so that I wouldn't know where they were, just passing people I'd dispatched to nothingness, the nothingness of their existence before I met them. And now Tonino had taken it into his head to see me again, when for three years he hadn't had the idea, or the desire, or the strength, unless he'd suddenly found himself able to come back once in three years and spend a few days in Casella? I looked at the ash in my hand and, blowing on it, rolled it about in my palm and no,
    no,
perhaps Tonino won't want to talk about the trial either, or about three years ago, or pretend to ask me what I would have done with all that time and perhaps he'll choose to be clever enough to realise that he's on holiday and that the only past that should interest him in Italy is that of his old father and all of his family, the erotic memories of a cousin who asked him the time in the kitchen very late one night or, I don't know, a teacher uncle trying to foist a Red Brigade revolutionary bible on him? And otherwise, too bad if he has to pretend to talk about the trial, I'll be strong enough to talk to him about it the way you talk about the rain and the fine weather, I won't admit to him how I refused to take part in it, refused to accept the very idea of possible compensation, I didn't want it, not for me, for Gavino, for Francesco's parents and for all the others, yes, but for myself I wanted only to forget. To forget and not talk about anything any more because I just wanted to find sleep in the night without screams or pennants, without yellow or red and gold flags; I wanted nights without grains of cement rolling under my hands, without numb faces, covered with dust and blood; but to be a twenty-three-year-old girl who's just got married and thinks she has a life ahead of her and her husband to give her children, perhaps, even if deep down she isn't sure she wants children, but anyway, that at least it's a possibility, that the world is possible, open to her, that it expands and doesn't shrink as it has shrunk for her, with voices

and judgements, shouts and fury, forgiveness and love seeking so deep within her that she herself comes back in rags, scrawny the way a herd of cattle is skin and bones after crossing a desert, having come all that way to stop grazing on sand. So, yes, a trail to find peace, that's what some people wanted, what they needed was nights when you can sleep, when you stop wandering between the gates and the entrance to a stadium that you should never have walked towards.

So, no, I didn't want to talk about a trial. Tipping the ash from my palm into the basin, after turning on a thin stream of lukewarm water, watching the grey water running towards the plughole, I thought to myself, hang on, Tonino hasn't phoned until now. When for a few months I'd vaguely hoped, vaguely waited for him to call, and he hadn't rung until I'd stopped waiting. And I had to make a considerable effort not to hear the murmur of voices on the radio and television talking about the trial – just as I'd refused to hear people being amazed that I never knew what was going on, or very little, when I told them I knew only what was being said in the papers and on TV. I avoided people's eyes. I dreaded questions and opinions; all around me, anger had risen up again. One morning the whole of Italy rediscovered its rage of three and a half years before, because everyone said, yes, the *animals* are going to be acquitted. And I said, maybe, maybe not. I was just amazed that I didn't feel more hatred for the people we'd seen charging along the terraces, who we still saw, this time the images put everything back in its context, you remember, three years ago. So, sometimes my mother put on her most horrified face for me, because she saw a void in my eyes in which she and her rage and her desire for justice had just been lost and drowned so completely that she was breathless and silent, drying her hands, picking up the carrot peelings that made her fingers orange, to go and throw them in the bin, shrugging and breathing hard so that I would hear just how much she didn't understand me and how ashamed of me she was, of what she saw as my indifference, refusing to allow herself to reproach me openly, but, always, letting that idea hang in the air as she shrugged her shoulders, murmuring, you could still have called Francesco's parents.

At that moment I was silent, and my own trial and my own war, each morning, was that I had to think of getting up and getting dressed before I dared look at myself in the mirror, in spite of the camouflage of the black hair that I allowed to fall on my shoulders or crimped like a superannuated Siouxsie. But I liked doing that. And I liked listening to music all day on my headphones, so that I would hear nothing but the songs of the Stooges or Nick Cave – the one thing I still had of Francesco, the one thing I couldn't have broken with, and which had, over time, assumed an ever greater place in my life. I listened only to them, and to the coldwave bands that had meanwhile disappeared into some musical limbo. I dragged that era out a few years beyond its natural lifespan, yes, I listened to Francesco's records and cassettes – the only box I ever opened – without knowing why, because a chorus had come into my head, like that; and I listened to the records more and more often, until they became mine, until now I listen to them and love them for themselves.

So, the trial, no, never, apart from that one time, when it was over and in April I got a letter from Francesco's mother. My mother had left the envelope on the table, against the water-jug. First of all I'd seen my name and our address, the stamp. The letter was heavy, the envelope was thick, a long letter that I'd opened after sitting down, without even taking off my Perfecto. The words began with an improvised capital letter, which could barely conceal the fact it was only the visible part of compact blocks of thought that planed and moulded phrases, words, streams, because when Francesco's mother had written that letter it was because it was the end of the trial as far as she was concerned, she wanted to tell me how testing it had been for them all, and perhaps even more for Gavino, who had gone to Brussels with Adriana. One of the first things she had written, the first injustice she wanted to speak about, was that after the death of one of her sons, she had to see the other one coming back as worn and pale as if he himself had returned from death, after too long a battle. She said I might have been right not to want to confront, as he had done, the faces of the *murderers*, those twenty-four *murderers*. She said the twenty-four *murderers* and in her letter the word *murderers* appeared without nuance, without any concern to say that they must be judged and condemned on the evidence before the court. That was the word she had found, anxious to throw it in and repeat it, the word that rang out as it must have rung out in the minds of the families in Brussels, watching the people who weren't yet murderers, just defendants, twenty-year-old kids or men of about thirty-five, in their Sunday best for the occasion, hidden behind moustaches or beards. She told everything in the present tense. She wrote. And as I read, I felt what it was that stirred her hand when she wrote, they wait, they chew, they move a lot and shift about, the judge has to tell them to sit down properly; beneath her fingers words described what she had not seen, what she would only ever see in her imagination. She told how Gavino and the others were lost in the big hearing room of the appeal court, on the first floor of the Palace of Justice,

and I,

I was alone in the kitchen and I had looked at the black ink and the compressed handwriting beneath my fingers, the short strokes of the letters, too short, the crossings-out, the corrections and repetitions; and always the word *murderers* returning to punctuate the letter, like her only certainty, the stumbling-block for all the descriptions she attempted when she tried to tell me about faces she hadn't seen, which she had imagined as she tried to transcribe what Gavino had told her. I saw the faces and the apprehension of those waiting for the twenty-six accused to enter the hearing room, except that when they came in there were only twenty-four. Everyone turned to look at them, some with tears in their eyes, all with rage in their hearts. Gavino was one of them. Gavino with that face that was almost Francesco's, his voice that was almost his brother's and yes, his heart, almost his heart, which I imagine in shreds at that moment, like his fingers gripped in Adriana's fingers. She taps his hand and smiles to say it'll be OK. Perhaps he thought of me when he saw the lawyers and the public prosecutors, the hundreds of journalists – he'll have thought everybody's here and Tana didn't come, she's scared, we're all scared. And they're scared too, that's why we're the same today, in spite of their Sunday-best appearance and that arrogant look they're wearing, the smirks they're giving each other.

She described all that, word for word, minute after minute, all that Gavino had seen and endured, the fear that he had finally seen in the *murderers*; they were frightened, finally, and Gavino still wasn't overjoyed. He felt nothing but disgust, seeing them in front of him, concentrating to avoid, at all costs, his eyes or the eyes of the others. Because they don't want to be seen. They give each other winks of encouragement and consolation, they stand bolt upright and lean into their interpreters to understand a discussion that's taking place in French; they take advantage of this to avoid looking at the victims' parents, they shift in their seats, they're pale as death and there's a strong desire in the courtroom to wash their faces of the arrogance or the smiles stamped on them, but it's impossible. And soon they forget about their interpreters, no point, they're not speaking Scouse here, they're talking untranslatable legal jargon. And in the end, how can anyone say they're responsible for a wave in which each was merely a tiny droplet? how can you say that a blow from a fist or a hurled stone could have killed nearly forty people? They'll just shrug; in Liverpool a chucked stone wouldn't even mean an hour down the nick. What else has happened? Nothing. And time has passed, people have got married, they've matured, they've quietened down. And also you can see in the pictures, that guy isn't hitting anyone, he's dancing. They've got this specialist interpreter of aerial images, they can zoom into the pictures and get closer and closer and you can see them in close-up and all of a sudden there's no more evidence, none at all, the guy who was seen grabbing an iron bar to hit someone is only clinging on to it, the one accused of striking three times has three different faces; the truth crumbles, the truth doesn't exist, it's a fact told by the pictures, indifferent to the women in black and the sombre faces listening and watching the ten acquitted men leaving as they look at the others, the ones who have been sentenced, the fourteen *animals* who can't get over the fact that they're free, too, they've served their time on remand and can't be held for much longer. They walk free. They congratulate one another. They laugh with the others and talk about going for a beer, and the others are there, the mothers and wives dressed in the same black as the barristers who try to explain and soothe the rage, try to stifle the cries, the hatred that rises up and Gavino's face, his hand clutched tightly in Adriana's, and then the journalists and the photographers, the world hanging on that truth: the *animals* are free and I,

I,

reading the letter from Francesco's mother, for the first time in my life I know what it feels like to want to kill.

There's also the fact that my whole life was tensed with the fear of meeting Francesco's mother. I would have been afraid of anyone in his family, but especially her, because she had taken me in as she did, and I felt indebted to her, at least for the words she had given me. You're like our daughter, she had said, and I was still stunned that she could have said something like that, so convinced was I that she hated me for taking her son away, when she had so disliked the idea of a wedding from which she had been excluded, so certain that you don't get married as we had done, and who thought she knew better than her son what was best for him, better than me what was the right and appropriate thing to do; she who had treated me with such suspicion that I'd ended up practically laughing at her, I found it so ridiculous to be locked into that old mother-in-law-daughter-in-law hatred! But no, it's all been quite different. Everything has been swept aside, even the things I thought I knew about her, or about my mother, and in a way even about me, it's all been pulverised, and soon all that was left was her kindness and her presence, sweet, gentle phrases whose bitter aftertaste wouldn't leave me: now you're like our daughter. That was also what she said in the letters she sent me, the three, no, the four letters, five, I can't remember, sent at ever more irregular intervals. I received the first two a few weeks apart. Then another, nearly a year later. And then others. I didn't reply to any of them. I immediately threw them away after receiving and opening them. She wished me well, hoped I would remake my life, hoped my studies would be successful. And then she added that they were all very well, Leandra was good at school, they'd love to see me, especially her, she said, and when they came to the cemetery, she'd often thought of coming to see me. She looked at the fresh flowers to imagine the last time I'd visited the grave. She would have liked to come and see me because basically, she said to me, we didn't know each other very well, not *as one woman to another*, and she would have liked to know what I was like as a woman, as a person. But without having heard from me, she confessed that she didn't dare press the point.

I remember how quickly I threw her letters away, and how, just as quickly, driven by the same urgency, I fled our house for the darkness of bars and clubs in Genoa or Milan, not to suffocate at home, not to yield to tears, but instead to shut myself away in my room like a belated adolescent girl worrying because her nose is too long or her hips too wide, spending hours lying on her bed, headphones over her ears, background music, singing as she weeps for the image of the person she'd like to be, without which nothing seems possible. And sometimes I would spend hours and hours lying on my bed. I listened to music and I smoked, my eyes lost in the distance, expecting nothing but the dissipation and oblivion of the words I had read. And from that I emerged exhausted and furious. I knew that then I would use my lack of cigarettes as an excuse to go out and not come back before the next day, as had happened a few months before I came back, after the phone rang and Gavino told me he was going to pop by that same day to drop off *our* things.

He had said our things, meaning the boxes they'd been storing at their place. But the things were just mine, and he'd stuck to his guns when I'd refused to take them back, saying that we'd never have enough room at home to store boxes and souvenirs. I had said I would never open those boxes. And he had come anyway, as he'd said he would. Except that I wasn't there, all of a sudden the air had seemed impossible to breathe, and I had dashed towards the bathroom, my mother coming after me when she'd seen that I was getting ready to go out; behind me I heard her voice saying, you're not going to go out when Gavino's on his way, you can't go; and I didn't reply, I looked at my rings and my bracelets, already cursing Grazia for having taken, or rummaged, or searched through my chaos for pencils or a bracelet that belonged to me, and I poked around in my pile of clothes, hands trembling, ignoring my mother's voice; I took everything I needed to go out and not come back before the following day. My mother knew, she could see it, she watched me putting on my lipstick and, as always, she repeated, you didn't put on so much lipstick before. I must have shrugged, thinking, yeah, that was before, and nothing will be like before. I didn't reply and started working faster and faster, taking care not to look at her behind me, in the door-frame reflected in the mirror, with her looking at me bug-eyed, murmuring once and then repeating, raising her eyes to the sky, what am I going to say to Gavino if you aren't there? What am I going to make up to explain why you're not here? He's your brother-in-law, he's still your brother-in-law, after all, and where am I going to put all your things? she yelled, when I'd have liked to burn them or throw them away, and my past with them, never to see them again, because I was so afraid of seeing Gavino and finding myself exposed and stupid in the face of some simple boxes.

And I was angry with my mother, because she refused to

understand how scared I was and instead she said, you wanted to get married, well it's done, and now you're bolting like a rabbit when your in-laws show up, and once again it's going to be your mother who sorts out your things! Don't say a word, don't reply: I didn't want to reply, and I can see myself picking up my Perfecto from the back of one of the chairs in the kitchen, saying, leave me alone, all you have to do is chuck it all and leave me alone,

And I see myself tearing down the stairs as fast as I can without hearing my mother's voice on my heels, shouting at me to wait and the more she shouted the less I heard her voice which disappeared among the barking dogs and the birdsong while my heart thumped to remind me how scared I had been of bumping into Gavino in the street, seeing him coming, perhaps with his wife, his sisters, his mother, and how long would I spend rooted to the spot if I bumped into them; I still hadn't taken the great stride that would bring me away from them. Yes, the idea of seeing them again was unbearable. As had been the idea, coming home the next morning, of seeing my mother squatting in the middle of cardboard boxes, scrabbling among them to take out the new things, one by one, and arrange them on the shelves or in the sitting-room sideboard, in the shoe cupboard. She had anticipated everything, and was clutching a feather duster. She dusted the boxes and then each object, one by one – so I couldn't help recognising, in spite of my hangover and my sweat mingled with the smell of tobacco and the bitter morning coffee, the black letters written by me and Francesco, *crockery, fragile, books, records, clothes, papers, knickknacks, miscellaneous crap.* How long ago was it? Ten years? Twenty? And perhaps a thousand years that had squeezed into a handful of months, of weeks, and yet, watching my mother busying herself with them, before even seeing the objects, just the open cardboard boxes and the big marker-pen letters, I saw the word *fragile* in capitals, firmly underlined twice and the box of knickknacks and the one of miscellaneous crap, the ones containing all the tiny objects I thought I'd been attached to for years, when they'd been holding me prisoner for months. What am I going to do with those ridiculous objects? A pack of cards. A loaded dice. A snuff box. Old bracelets and stones taken from beaches since my childhood; things as stupid and tiny as the terror they inspired in me was profound and violent.

But I didn't want to say anything, try to do anything that might display that fear, so I looked at my mother and told her not to unpack anything, just to arrange the boxes like that, without opening them, because we weren't to use the things. But she, squatting by the shoe cupboard, had begun to arrange things and start sorting them out; the little souvenirs wouldn't leave their boxes, fine, but the new sheets and that lovely white embroidered tablecloth, at least that, and she had decided to wash and iron the sheets, to fold them; she had decided to put the service of crystal glasses with her own, those glasses with the white lines forming vine-leaves and arabesques, in the glass sideboard in the sitting room; the silver cutlery with the four-leaf clover on the handle – what would I have wanted with silver cutlery – fine, then, they'll be OK in the bottom of the sideboard, in the drawer where she too had put her silver cutlery which we never used, only ever for the occasional Sunday lunch, when guests came from a long way away (but not for my uncle, who was too much a part of the family to deserve special treatment). I remember that day I had the feeling, once again, that it was me she was undressing, particularly when she said there were things we could sell. We needed money, I was expensive to keep and didn't bring much in, she had said. And I see myself in the middle of the hall, with my eyes on her. I'd have liked to show up later, when everything was finished, when she'd put everything away or sold it, and I muttered, yeah, you sell what you can sell, it doesn't matter, we could give Francesco's things to the Red Cross, that's it, do that, don't tell me, I don't want to know, and now,

now:

three years after Gavino brought the boxes, after my mother put everything away, and managed to make a little money out of some trinkets that wouldn't be any use to anyone, at least not straight away, not yet, as if it were obvious to my mother and everyone else that I would be spending the whole of my life in Montoggio, in her house, that I would never leave to live anywhere else, whether alone or with someone, perhaps with an Angelo to make up for not being loved and cared for, calm seemed almost to have returned; a semblance of calm in which I could find myself a place to move and stretch out and breathe with no fear of going back, almost forgetting, sometimes, to wake up haunted by the smells of dust and blood. Yes, everything had almost calmed down at least and daily life had slowly resumed, gently, peacefully, as it does for convalescents and old people, astonished to relearn movements they had thought they would never make again. And it was now that I stopped seeing Gina and Giovanna completely, that I abandoned my studies once and for all and earned a little cash by giving French lessons or doing a bit of secretarial work for a knitwear shop in Genoa city centre, now that I was being taken care of by Angelo, on and off, that I learned to smile, that I regained the pleasure of smiling, of walking and, well, inevitably, it was at that very time that I'd bumped into Gavino one September morning in Milan, and then there was a trial I would rather have known nothing about and about which I had to know everything, from the first minute to the last. And it was now, in June, that is, when the trial had been over for two months, that Tonino had decided to call my mother's house.

16

It was the day I went to meet him at the Gare du Nord and, on the Rue de Dunkerque, he'd told me about seeing Gabriel, about the few days he'd spent in Brussels, wandering about on the edges of a trial he'd finally given up on. It was that day that Tonino said to me: Jeff, I think I'm going to go to Italy this summer, I haven't been to Casella for a long time . . . I think this time I'm going to call Tana and go and see her.

Will you come with me?

I hesitated for a moment, keeping from replying without really knowing why, because deep inside I'd already said yes. I must have answered with a smile, thinking or even saying that it was a very good idea and we should have thought of it a long time before, a long time ago, that it was good that we could finally make our minds up to do that – as though just now, through the simple idea of seeing Tana again, there was the chance that we might regain a power that until then we had merely been subjected to, that strength, that persistence of memory, or rather of images and memories that acted upon us, because with them there had been that sense of repeating an unfinished story, rather the way a severed limb jerks about as it waits to die completely; the desperation with which we, Tonino and me, acted as if nothing was up, as if we'd had to hold our breath and breathe sparingly as we waited for refreshing sleep to come. It had taken the cold of that brasserie on the Rue de Dunkerque, that afternoon, and Tonino coming back, his meeting with Gabriel, the sight of the English in the Grand-Place, before the two of us could talk and say what we wanted to say: to confess our desire to see Tana again, to talk to her and know who she was today, to have done with that image in which our memory kept her prisoner (I had even said to myself – not daring to share the idea with Tonino – that we'd taken too long already and that, perhaps because of us, because we'd waited three and a half years to break the spell in which I imagined her trapped, Tana had stayed as we had left her all that time ago; I even told myself that by resuming contact with her we would free ourselves from our image of her from back then, and free her from that time as well, from the terror on her face and that numb, ashen look she had when we left her).

But equally, it might be the opposite. Perhaps we would only be closing a circuit, or even reversing it to take it back to its starting-point? And rather than freeing us it might shut us away even more securely? We would have liked to think, yes, Tana is here, in Italy, and the past is far behind us, there's nothing more to fear now, the past is a perception, nothing more, a shadow fixed on the walls as I've been told the shadows were fixed in Hiroshima, because of the intense light and the radioactivity, and even though I've never been able to imagine that being possible, the fixed shadow surviving irradiated bodies after the bodies themselves had vanished, I was able to tell myself that when we saw each other again, the three of us, even far from Brussels in time and space, it would be like a backward surge, the return of a nightmare so intimate that it had ended up as a story, a myth for use as personal as our first love affairs and our little teenage secrets. I wondered what would happen if Tana awakened or, instead, dissolved our memories. I said to myself, we won't have to talk about anything, and then the past will disappear.

When summer came and we set off for Casella, Tonino and I didn't say a thing to each other, we barely even mentioned Tana. The summer was there, lying stretched out before us like the illusion that summers bring, of a new, possible life, amorous encounters and evening conversations over glasses of rosé. We had set off by car, in that old white crate of a Golf belonging to Tonino's mother (a car on which you could have written *wash me* with your finger on the back window, or on the wings, or on the boot, or on the bonnet), and I remember the terrible racket of the engine and the glass shivering in the doors, that car radio that couldn't pick up a single channel, and in which the only available cassette was the Bee Gees, who made us laugh when they repeated *Staying alive, staying alive, oh, oh, oh, oh, staying alive*, stretching out the last *alive* for ever; we sang along, imitating them as we smoked out the car (the windows opened, but it was so hard to shut them again that we were never daft enough to touch them), looking at the people overtaking us, and the drivers glanced at us as they overtook us (were they outraged by how slowly we were driving, or worried about the curtain of white smoke inside the car, or surprised by our improvised gestures as we sang?).

We set off in early summer, and it was the first time in my life that I saw the blue water of the Mediterranean and dipped my feet in it; that water so blue and so calm that it seemed to have been invented for painters and the very rich, so much so that I had a sense of breaking a rule just by approaching its shores, when all I knew of the sea was the ocean and the beach at Noirmoutier on family holidays, the same every summer, in the same blue and orange canvas tent, on the same campsite, two hundred metres from the sea and yes, in fact, it wasn't all that bad, the pines, the sandy beach, the waves and the grey water of the Vendée, and then nothing; nothing to see or do but wait to grow up so that one day I could finally see whether the Mediterranean really is that TV-screen, postcard blue that would turn swimming-pool water green with envy.

So, when we reached Marseille I sat in silence and looked out the window, and suddenly I saw the sea below, with its sparkling light. And it was then that I felt, coming from a long way away, that strange melancholy, almost sadness, at the sight of the sea and that presence that sent me back to the water of Noirmoutier where the seaweed swam, already trying to imagine what the depths of the Mediterranean might be like, when the depths of the ocean opened up before me to reveal the Gois Causeway and the figure of my father, his shorts and his thin, tanned back, a smile on his face, buckets and nets for shells, bubbles escaping from the thick mud. What lies beneath the water of the Mediterranean? That was what I wondered then, when I saw that lovely, fascinating, flat surface I'd dreamt of as a child, promising me unparalleled wonder when the time came for me to dip my feet in it, the blue water that I imagined lukewarm and voluptuous as a caress, without the jolting waves coming in and rolling me over on the sand of Noirmoutier, making me spit salt water – not a chance! said Tonino, the water here is just as treacherous as it is anywhere else!

We spent the night in Marseille. The next day we set off quite early. I didn't dare say how much I would have liked to stop on a beach, dip my feet in the water straight away and send a message to the boy I had been ten years before, in reply to the ones he had sent me then, messages in which he begged me not to forget all the things that were close to his heart, the things I had to do, like breaking the infernal cycle that brought us to Noirmoutier every summer, cutting us off from the possibility of the South. And I would have said, OK, there you are, it's done. But Christ it's cold! And I'm not even talking about the pebbles! But no, I said nothing to that old child asleep in my head, and we set off again.

I sensed that Tonino was in a hurry to cross the border and get to Casella. We barely spoke in the car, and we'd even stopped listening to the Bee Gees some time ago; I saw the vast glass roofs on the coast at San Remo and the reflections of a cloudy sky on the glass panels before it rained – a summer rain that left nothing but the smell of lifted dust, and that road with hardly anyone on it but us and our silence, Tonino impatient to get to the family home, to see his uncle, his aunt, and perhaps already worried by the phone call he was going to have to make to Tana, which had been my only real worry since we left. Suddenly, in front of me, there were orange lights in the tunnels, olive trees and the sea shrouded in fog, the laurels between the carriageways, pink or white laurels, thick and round, the concrete tanks and the pistachio-green buildings, then vines on the slopes, and suddenly that dizziness, that gravity that told me we were getting close to Tana, that we were approaching her and that day when, face to face with her, we would probably be as keen to leave as we were happy to have come, yes, happy without a doubt and worried at the sight of that face, which had come back to haunt us so many times, distorted by that numbness, that violence. And what would we see? Who would she be? That was what I was wondering as my lips grew dry and I tried to reassure myself, telling myself over and over that what scared me was driving across that void rather than seeing Tana again. Below me the blue of the sea emerged sometimes from the mist; I looked at the glass roofs on the hillsides, houses, a dry river bed far below and sometimes, when we came out of a tunnel, the sun appeared, as blinding as a flashbulb at dead of night; down below I saw the houses clustered around the sea, as if they had come in a flock to drink; I needed to smoke and stretch my back. I felt my heart beating fast and Tonino's anxiety, asking him every two minutes if he was OK, when he replied impatiently, yes, yes, how far is it now? So I looked at the map on my knees, it took me ages to find the road even though my finger hadn't left it, then I looked up and replied, glancing up at the twisted black branches of bony olive trees on the hillsides, disappearing quickly in our wake. Then, looking at the towns below us, I wondered, is Casella going to be like that? Are the houses in Tonino's village like these, and what's Tana's village like? It's funny, I have no idea of the place where she lives, or what her life is like. Why look, reality will come soon enough, always more imaginative than I am, more definite and resolved not to be changed: once I have it in front of me, there's no question of expecting it to be otherwise.

I saw the green shutters and those high-rises appearing

behind the roofs of the houses, surrounded by vegetation as diverse as the blossoming houses and flyovers, and the juniper-bush and the hills with the corpses of trees with whitened trunks in a dry, almost russet soil, the colour of the tiles that stand out against the blue-grey of the sea. I thought, we'll be there in less than an hour. The factories of Savona displayed huge green tanks, red and white chimneys that imitated the cypress trees on the hillsides, then dirty buildings and cranes, a cemetery flanked by flyovers against the void, carried only con-crete columns thin as the legs of pink flamingos, cement grooves, fields of burnt grass beneath metal pylons, while scaf-folding encased buildings under renovation, like skeletons or armour. As I lit a cigarette I saw the flyover just below the one we were driving on, and I felt vertigo, the beginnings of vertigo, images, Tana's shoes beside the bed in a supposedly Art Nouveau hotel in the heart of Brussels, I heard her voice, we were driving amidst factories, the blue of the sky and the blue of a Tamoil filling-station, surrounded by television aerials aimed at the sky like the parasol pines, rusty rails and a balcony as crammed with shrubs as my head was crammed with projec-tions of what would happen when we were face to face with her, Tana, already imagining myself hiding behind Tonino to avoid having to confront her eyes or the few words of French she would doubtless address to me, but to ask what? to make me talk to her about what? when in the car, not very far away now, I wondered if it wasn't stupid to want to see her again, if it wasn't going to take us straight to the place from which we wouldn't be able to get away, the image of that enormous bumble-bee I had once seen trapped in a spider's web, fighting so hard, exhausting itself for so long that it had completely wrecked the web while the web, like a compact, grey parcel, had buried the insect beneath its own ruin, keeping it from leaving and doom-ing it to a certain death if I hadn't intervened.

I remembered that and, in front of me, Italy opened its gates beneath a flood of objects, high-rise buildings with orange or green blinds, a cable car with rusty carriages, suspended high above us, the tunnel entrances like Tom-and-Jerry mouse-holes, derelict buildings and suburban trains, ivy devouring the flyovers and rust trying hard to do the same; the passing sounds on the viaducts were like the sounds of the trains on the rails. Tana's ponytail in the metro, that dancing ponytail, its tick-tock, metronomic rhythm, and the mixture of concrete and rock, concrete and mineral, her smile and her tears, the pallor of her face in the night, beneath the neon lights of Brussels, and sometimes, too, at intervals, depleted pines, balconies and shutters. All that reality welcomed us, familiar to Tonino, who saw each bit as a part of himself and his history.

And pretty soon we reached Casella. A house by the roadside, three storeys, the top one belonging to Tonino's father. The uncle, the aunt and their three children lived on the first floor and the ground floor. The children didn't live there any more, the last one having left over a year and a half ago. The uncle and aunt didn't complain about being alone, but they didn't hide their joy at seeing us arrive, inviting us to share their meals every day. Tonino's aunt had made up the beds on the second floor, which she had opened up wide so that the fresh air could blow away the persistent damp that had incrusted itself even in the very folds of the blankets and bedcovers, even though they were safe in the shelter of cupboards and wardrobes. We went to Genoa and Milan. Tonino showed me the cities and the countryside, the landscapes and places where he knew people, with a gravity and application very much his own, very proud and probably very touched to relive, as in a museum, the places where part of his life had been not only lived but also constructed and invented. And then, in Milan, we were looking at the cathedral when Tonino took a piece of paper from his pocket, a small, white piece, folded in four. He just said, OK, then, I'm going to call her.

That was it, nothing more. Not even who he wanted to call. Not even why he wanted to do it now, because the silence between us hadn't been silence, it had been an all-sufficient word, a word containing all the others. We headed towards a telephone box. Tonino took out some change, then pulled open the glass door. I heard his voice. He spoke slowly, smiling very broadly, perhaps too broadly – as though calling were the most natural thing in the world, because he had spoken to Tana's sister a few weeks earlier, it was perfectly normal and ordinary for him to call back now, and not as strange and incongruous as the first time, a few weeks earlier. This time, no one would say it was strange to phone an almost total stranger, someone no sooner met than lost once more from sight. It was as simple as Tonino coming back out of the cabin smiling, folding up the paper on which he had written the number. Through the glass, I had seen him concentrating on the piece of paper, folding and unfolding it, head bent forward but never looking at me, smiling into the distance and then speaking only for a few minutes. He had agreed with Tana that we'd go and see her for lunch the following Sunday, in two days' time.

And two days later we set off for Montoggio; it was late morning, and already hot. Montoggio is on a hillside, the streets are narrow and steep. Gardens, a lot of rose bushes. Tonino told me he had gone there a few times in his childhood, but he couldn't remember why, it was just for an outing or visiting somebody. It didn't matter. He was just talking for the sake of it. Yes, that's it, you have to be able to talk for the sake of it, to say nothing and not listen to what's thundering away inside you and frightening you that the whole world might come to an end it's banging away so loudly in your head. So you've got to talk to keep from hearing anything, you've got to talk to be silent. Tonino was talking as I thought I'd never heard him talk before, about everything and nothing, childhood memories, oh, yes, I clearly remember the church where we went on walks that lasted for hours and I hated that, he said, one day along a path we were stopped by a pack of dogs and I remember we turned right round with a yell, the dogs had appeared suddenly, just like that, and lined up in a row in front of us, threatening us, and without further ado we'd fled, my brothers and me, he said.

As he was talking we walked through Montoggio, looking at the rose bushes and the little kitchen gardens, the trellised balconies. We followed the directions that Tana had given Tonino, without saying a word or commenting on what we saw, the cherry trees and peach trees in the gardens. But we smiled a few times, at the sight of some strange, kitsch objects, bronze dogs on top of a pair of gateposts, the fake mouldings and crenellated tower of a brick-coloured villa. There was a smell of herbs or of leaves being burned somewhere. We began to climb a flight of concrete steps. The closer we got, the more the silence assumed its place, a place destined to open up and expand still further, to become more and more wide and threatening, to engulf us both or open up beneath our feet. We went on walking and our steps grew slower; to distract our-selves we looked far across the hills, seeing a few sheep on either side, the river that divided the village, walnut trees, pumpkins, dogs barking and replying or threatening sparrows, it doesn't matter, but still what mattered to us was getting clos-er and closer to us. And then there we were and we saw, as Tana had said we would, the red shutters, the big light over the garage door, lyre-shaped, to light the paved courtyard, and someone in the window, a woman's face watching us. Waiting for us.

I tossed aside my half-smoked cigarette and followed Tonino when the gate opened. Tana was there, looking down at us from her vantage-point a few metres above the courtyard. She watched us coming towards her, climbing the few concrete steps.

Tana.

That girl who was Tana and not Tana, at least not as I thought I remembered her. Her hair was raven-black, but I saw very quickly that the roots of her hair were lighter, almost tawny blond; her hair wasn't tied up, and fell on bony shoul-ders. We could see her collar-bones through her grey T-shirt. I hadn't remembered her so thin. I did seem to remember a slim girl, almost thin, yes, but not as thin as that, at least not as she appeared to me at that moment, when we reached her place and we saw each other, each one of us noting what had changed in the others or what had not, what had survived in spite of time and misrememberings, imagination and that way it has of redesigning everything to make it match models that it follows, or patterns that it invents without regard for how true they are to reality, or what reality might have been. Because for Tana too, in all likelihood, what she wanted to do was rediscover expressions and features in Tonino and me, when we couldn't have had an inkling whether we really resembled them or not, or whether, like her, we had been changed, renewed, as I knew that Tonino had changed, and how he had changed, not just because of what Tana had noticed immediately, such as the fact that he no longer wore his hair long, but very short, and that his clothes were different, too. I couldn't tell whether she thought I looked myself or not, or at least, whether I looked like the image of me that she had kept, or reconstructed, just as I, when I kissed her, had recognised her eyes and her features. But not her. It seemed to me that it was Tana's face, but it wasn't her. I remembered her so clearly that I could have said, no, it's not you, you're not who you say you are, I know, you can't pull the wool over my eyes. And yet, she was there. I recognised her voice, but her voice struck me as different, too, not exactly the same as the one I thought I remembered just by hearing it again, when in fact I'd forgotten it very quickly, because sounds and words are retained as easily as images and words. And yet now I did remember. So clearly, in fact, so precisely, that I could have said, yes, that voice probably is Tana's, but something in it has changed, it's cracked, it's flawed, or else it's more serious; a lower voice, a heavier breath.

And a few weeks later I'll still be busy trying to understand, hear and rediscover Tana's voice without beginning to reinvent it in a form closer to my wishes. I'll have the whole of the rest of the summer in La Bassée, in the improvised bedroom in the basement – the only room that stays cool – telling myself stories that are already false, already distorted. And nothing will do any good, certainly not my reading of *Don Quixote* or *Lord Jim*, nothing, not even my obsession with jotting down in notebooks all the insignificant details I'd sworn to store in my memory like secrets my life depended on; I'll still have a month of summer left, and I'll use it to try and understand what I experienced during the first month, since that day, that Sunday when we found ourselves sitting round the table, Tonino and me, with Tana, her mother and her little sister Grazia, who had, I remember thinking, exactly the same Venetian fair hair that I had remembered Tana as having. But her hair was thicker. Grazia's wavy hair fell to her shoulders, held back by butterfly slides, and her face was completely unlike her sister's. She had a round face and quite thick eyebrows, a little mouth which was always laughing, and which opened on to white teeth that she hid with her fingers, doubtless to show off her polished nails and her bracelets, identical to the ones that Tana wore. And Tana didn't look like the girl I'd met on the metro in Brussels, or the one we'd turned up with outside the stadium, the one we'd laughed with, Tonino and me, as we ate tubs of over-salted chips and let ketchup or mustard run down our fingers, but the other one, the other Tana, the one who had appeared afterwards.

And how long will it take me, down there in my room, elbows on my desk, concentrating on doing nothing, or getting up to look through the little window that opened at ground level, at the lawn and the cherry tree, the washing on the line, Monsieur Arnand's house and, further off in the background, the railway line and the old signalman's house where Nimbus and his sister lived, to understand that Tana hadn't got over that night (I wondered: how many millions of women spend their whole lives by the wayside where life has spat them out, indifferent to their fates and too anxious to continue along their life's trajectory?).

That was what I saw, that was what had shocked me and

not, as I had thought at first, her thinness and her badly dyed hair, tired and broken, and nor was it her make-up, although it did overemphasise her eyes and make her cheekbones stand out even more than they did already; her eyes shone, and I remember that several times during the meal I had to avert my eyes to avoid meeting hers. Her mother got up every two minutes to fetch things we didn't need or want. When she was away, Tana had been able to confide that it was her mother who had been keen to meet us and to have us for lunch. Tana had said that for her part she'd rather have been somewhere else, maybe Genoa? We had talked about Genoa and Montoggio, the winter here, and then about Casella and Tonino's uncle and aunt's house.

And it was he and Tana's mother who did most of the talking, at least at first. You'd have to acknowledge that Tonino displayed a formidable, even unexpected talent, gliding elegantly over all the clichés that arose, picking them up with an offhand ease that was disconcerting, at least for me, knowing how repellent and difficult he found it to play a social game in a setting that was far from elegant. I'm not joking. And he pretended not to have been struck to find so many rosaries twisted around the branches of the little wooden crucifixes on the walls, and he talked to fill the void, oh, yes, the number of hours it takes to get here from France! And he talked without a break, he told anecdotes, and our glasses were constantly refilled, first with a very cold sparkling white wine that we drank with pretzels and tiny tapenade toasts, then a light, cool red wine. We drank, I said nothing because I was still camouflaged by my ignorance of Italian, and Tonino quite the contrary, finding in the wine the strength to speak to say nothing and protect himself behind inoffensive words, unmoved by the portrait of John Paul II in its aluminium frame above the sideboard, without reflecting that Tana's mother wore an expression of infinite sadness that was almost grotesque, so strongly did she resemble the image one might expect of the *mamma*, the granite brow, the proud and shadowy Italy of cheap novels, religious and obscurantist, obstinate, and a mother I knew you would find copies of wherever people had been convinced that misfortune adds value to life and human emotions.

But no. No value added. Nothing to be gained, the loser doesn't win, the victim doesn't win, and in any case, what would be won? And what would we have gained by bringing up the subject of how we had met up with Tana? On the sideboard there were photographs, and I dreaded spotting a picture of Francesco, and seeing his face again, even if the photograph was bad and blurred, the face of the one who wasn't here but existed in the gap between each mouthful of chewed bread, each word, each gesture – Yes, Grazia, go and get your encyclopaedia! It must be in her encyclopaedia, what's it called, the place you come from? Grazia had done as her mother asked and got up to go to her room; she had come back with an enormous blue book, had looked and then found, read out the relevant passage and assumed an air of confidence that would remain with her from that moment onwards. She had started laughing at everything, saying she would like to go to *Parigi* and buy some perfume, that she'd like to take a trip in a bateau-mouche, but to do that you'd have to be a bit older than fifteen, that annoying age that kept her trapped at home beneath her mother's watchful eye. And her mother listened to Grazia without laughing, her eyes wide, as if she had been surprised to hear her daughter speaking so openly in front of her, and even more so in front of two boys, two young men who, it was increasingly clear, did not daunt her in the slightest.

Grazia had stayed standing between Tonino and her mother, the encyclopaedia open on the table. I said nothing and looked at them, as Tana looked at them sometimes, then glancing towards the table or, more precisely, the tablecloth. I see her putting her hand down, her palm flat and her fingers spread; she opens her right hand like that and gently rubs the tablecloth, or could it be that her hand is floating above it and she doesn't touch it? I don't know. Tana performs that motion without suspecting that I'm watching her, that I can see how hard her face is; her attention darkens when she lights a cigarette and dives into her glass of wine. She seems to be emerging from strange, slightly frightening thoughts, and suddenly I dread disaster, seeing the ghosts of the Brussels stadium joining us at the table – but now, things crowd in, there's the sound of laughter and I laugh too even though I don't understand what's been said. Tana smiles at me and translates when I shrug to say, I didn't get a word! Do something! And she starts laughing and coming back among us, never leaving us for very long. Grazia starts talking about summer and the holidays, yes, she says, Tana and I go to see our uncle every summer, he lives in Sardinia, do you know Sardinia?

Tana stares at the cutlery, looking more and more surprised – no, that's not quite right, her face can't be captured in a single word, it would take several, to convey a sequence of variations, because her face has passed from one state to another in a movement that is imperceptible at first, surprise, perhaps, then increasingly marked, until it becomes that look of disgust and incomprehension, almost panic. She blanches and fills her glass to pull herself together, to keep from yielding to her revulsion, but she doesn't touch her plate.

You don't know Sardinia? That's where our uncle bought his house! He's retired and lives there now, he has nothing to do with cars now, or only for fun with his friends, but we go there for the sea and the *dolce far niente*, don't we, Tana?

Tana increasingly deaf to what is happening around her; I'm sure she doesn't hear her sister or Tonino translating what Grazia is saying with a laugh, nervous, pointless and happy, and proud to be allowed to talk, even if her mother tries to tell her, my darling, please, leave your uncle where he is . . . I don't know if you're going this year, don't you know that Tana doesn't like going down there any more? And Grazia immediately replying, oh, yes, yes, Mamma, of course we're going, just ask Tana!

Tana, Tana? Do you hear me?

And Tana turning to her sister with a start. I see how she's drinking and how, in a single movement, she draws back before Grazia asks her question, a gesture of defiance – I'm not sure, but it's gradually becoming clear, as she looks at her glass – of defiance about her glass. She stares numbly at the glass as though something had shattered inside her, just clutching the glass in her hand and looking not at the redness of the wine through the crystal, but perhaps at the figures, the white lines forming vine-leaves and arabesques. Then suddenly she puts the glass down, with a movement so abrupt that it's as if she's just been poisoned, but not by the wine, not by what she might have heard, but rather by the glass itself. A simple wine glass. one of those crystal glasses that can be made to sing by running a damp finger along the rim, as people sometimes do to surprise children at family parties, or as musicians do, or circus clowns. She puts down her glass so quickly that in the end, just as it's about to touch the table, she has to slow her hand to avoid snapping the stem. She tries something like that, but now her face betrays a confusion which I don't understand, and which no one seems to see.

At Santa Catarina Pitturini there are hardly any seagulls but the sea is calm and blue and peaceful, there are pink flamingos in the South, and in the South the water is so clear that you can see your feet and you can't even have a pee without being seen! Grazia blushes as she says that, while Tonino translates for me. He laughs as he does so, and Tana's mother laughs, too, a little out of embarrassment and out of shame at what her daughter has said, and a little because basically she must find it quite funny and cheerfully improper, a childish joke, when her daughter was trying to charm us with a frankness that she doubtless thought more suited to an adolescent than a little girl. She tries to make us laugh and we laugh, but Tana doesn't laugh. She just smiles and smokes – her body moves as if she were rocking back and forth, her feet moving under the table. She looks completely absent and I'm worried that we'll finally notice her distress, in which she is entirely alone – aren't Grazia's voice and Tonino's ending up by isolating her still further? Is she able to protect herself while she remains certain that she's not drawing attention to herself, or quite the reverse, isn't it more that she's isolated because she has no words to hook on to the ones she can hear, words to hook on to the others and let herself be pulled out of her isolation? But no. It isn't that at all.

Something that began with the hand brushing the tablecloth. As a blind man recognises the path he must walk along every day; that's it, she was walking like a blind person, but she was walking none the less, and getting faster and faster. After the tablecloth it was the knives and the forks, Tana staring with insane concentration at their handles, shaped like four-leafed clovers, with such application that one might have wondered whether she had ever seen knives and forks before in her life. And then there had been that glass that she had set down with that gesture of rejection, a violence so powerful that she had had to take a deep breath, perhaps thinking, fuck don't scream, don't scream, as though we could hear her begging behind her forehead and her eyes not to scream yet, to wait, first reply to Grazia with a kind of smile that she'd dragged up from within herself after searching for ages through the detritus and the thoughts of rage that she must have been forcing herself to ignore.

She doesn't reply to Grazia. Or rather, she replies indirectly, speaking to her mother. Tana sits up straight, stretches her back, lifts her head to relax her neck for a moment, and then the words come almost as easily as Grazia's, of course, Mamma . . . Why not? We'll go to Sardinia, Uncle will enjoy it and we'll enjoy it too, won't we, Grazia? And they both start laughing and complimenting one another, communicating with smiles and movements that they alone understand, which their mother imagines she's capable of absorbing as she laughs louder than they do, calling across to us, Tonino and me, along the lines of oh! My poor friends! You see what they're like! They are naughty! I love them and I do everything for them and they both laugh, how funny and gorgeous they are, lively and funny, my darlings, how they worry me, such anxiety they give me, how they exasperate and tyrannise me, my two vipers, my little bitch puppies waiting only for the dogs to come and sniff them and take them, they're poking fun because you're here, otherwise they don't laugh together that often, believe me! They wouldn't dare! I'll teach them to make fun of me, to make a mockery of me! And I'm going to fuss over you even more than they would, especially the little French boy, he doesn't speak a word of Italian and he's so thin, so ugly, so pale! His thinness would put the wind up death itself, he's even worse than Tana! I'm going to fuss over you even more than Tana and Grazia put together and then, then, my lambs, you will leave never to come back, never again, because you won't have the slightest interest in my daughters ever again.

That isn't what she said, I don't know what she *really* says to keep her daughters quiet, not to keep them really quiet, that is, but rather to hide and soften what she senses between them, that thing that makes her feel so excluded that she has to take her turn to speak and talk to us, Tonino and me, as if we were the sole object of her attention, when it's not so, we can all see it's not so. Even me, without understanding what she says, even I understand what she thinks, what she's going through and why she's struggling like that, smiling at us, cooing words in our ears in a way that betrays her need to turn us into objects, which she could then throw between her two daughters to silence them, so that they would finally stop ganging up against her as they are doing. That's what she is thinking and what she so much wants to hide that she shows it even more clearly to us, and to Tana and Grazia.

So, yes. Yes. We're going to go to Sardinia. Uncle will be pleased to see us. Tana insists, talking loudly, staring at her mother. In a loud, almost angry voice she says she'll go to Sardinia this year because it's so long since she's been there, depriving Grazia of those holidays she yearned for every year. So this year they'll go. And then she talks to Tonino. He doesn't translate what she says. By way of reply, he just looks at me

with a shrug, smiling and indicating with a twitch of his eyebrows that he's a bit surprised, as if to say, why not? or, what
do you think? I barely have time to think and say, OK, when I
know what's being said to me I'll be able to say what I think
about it, but I see Grazia's wide-eyed stare, she's waiting for an
answer, holding her breath and blushing. Tana has started
drinking again; she looks steadily at Tonino – or rather, steadily isn't what I mean, because if a gaze is so (how should I put
it?) *keen*? so intense, so *fiery*? it still doesn't mean it's steady, it
turns quickly, it moves quickly, that gaze, and soon I see that
it's switching from Tonino to Tana's mother and back again.

Her mother sits there in silence, until she decides to get to
her feet and pretend, perhaps, to take the heat out of the situation, not to be taken hostage by a reply that we might give
without taking into account what it might mean for her, something she didn't want. Not for anything in the world does she
want to hear Tonino say it's OK, we'll go with them to
Sardinia for a few days. Why not? Tonino asks in French. Why
not? Why not *what*? Ah? Go to Sardinia? To their uncle's
place, well, if the uncle hasn't got a problem with it, then why
not? And then I add: your rotten old banger is just about capable of getting us there! We'll just have to sort out the crossing.
Yes, why not. Tana says it's a good idea. She looks at her mother firmly, without a hint of a smile, and I think she's suggested
our going with them – with her and her sister – just because her
mother won't be able to say no in front of us. I reflect that for
Tana it's a kind of trap and, in fact, her mother won't put up
much of a fight. Her mother tries to suggest that perhaps their
uncle wouldn't want to be disturbed, that they should ask him
first, and what about Angelo, do you think Angelo will be
happy for you to go away like that, with some friends of yours
that he doesn't even know? She says that almost carelessly,
going to the kitchen and coming back again, clearing the plates
and making coffee, helped by Grazia who has stopped hiding
her delight and kissed Tana (who didn't move when her sister
threw her arms around her, but merely shrugged and smiled a

smile without any real joy in it, but rather a kind of weariness, or perhaps relief).

And we'll have to wait until we meet up on the boat that will take us to Sardinia a few days later, before we really understand what happened that Sunday. It was at sunset, and all four of us had already visited the ferry. We were on the upper deck. Grazia and Tonino had strolled over to that huge black circle with a capital H in the middle, in white. The balustrades were yellow on that side, and white where Tana and I were standing. I remember the soot and the black smoke. We saw people bringing their dogs out on deck, where there was a kennel. Tana and I looked at the sea, and already we couldn't see the city. Our last image was of the red and black tugs and a container ship, huge blue cranes and then Genoa disappearing, plunging into the fog. It's that long tracking shot in which the sea wall seems to be never-ending, then finally disappearing, dissolving in the wine-dark water of dusk. When the moon appears, it's almost red and lends its colour to the sea.

It's at that precise moment that Tana chooses to ask me if I had any idea why she had wanted us to go with her to Sardinia, a place that she herself didn't have any great desire to revisit. Yes, she really didn't want to come. But it's true, she'd reacted very quickly. She'd wanted to provoke her mother, to hurt her, she'd wanted to wound her as much as she possibly could, by doing the one thing her mother would have wanted her not to do. And she even, get this, Tana said, told me that poor Angelo might make a scene because I'm going away with two friends! What do I care about Angelo, if you knew, pfft! Angelo! And my mother is well aware that I couldn't give a toss about Angelo – and neither could she! – what she really wanted was for us not to go, much less with you; but I didn't want to leave her in peace, you know, what she did, she claimed it was because you were my guests and that's why she did it, just because you were my guests, and you'd come to see me. She said, it's up to you to welcome them, they're your friends, that's why, when I would rather we'd seen each other somewhere else, in Genoa, for example. But she was the one who insisted that you come and have lunch at our house, she was adamant, it was unusual, so I agreed because often I think I'm too hard on her, I never give her a break, I never talk to her, we never say anything to each other, I don't want anything that comes from her, I'm just waiting to get out, it'll be soon, soon I'll have saved enough to get out, but right then, you see, I agreed, I said OK and you came to the house as she wanted. So why she did that unless it was out of spite, that's all, it's just that, she wants to hurt me and that's why I pounced on the opportunity to hurt her back, just because Grazia talked about Sardinia. It was the best way of hitting back at her for welcoming you. I wasn't paying attention, I didn't see when she laid the table in the sitting room, that was my fault, I should have taken more care and done it myself. I should have put out the cutlery and the tablecloth, rather than letting her do it, since she insists on doing everything, as always, she wants to do everything and tell everybody else off for not helping her, that's what she's like, and I will never forgive her for what she's done, that cutlery should never have been used, or those glasses, I should have thrown them away rather than let her put them with hers, I should have refused when Gavino wanted me to take them,

I should have,

And her voice had frozen like that above the water, its colour slipping towards blackness, you could hardly see the sparkle of the foam. There was the sound of turbines and the wind was cold now, cigarettes burned away all by themselves above the void.

Not like the ones I'll be smoking until the end of the summer, in my basement bedroom in La Bassée, watching the swirls colliding softly against the white ceiling. Then I'll have all the time in the world to think again about that night on the boat, and the time to try and understand why I agreed, on the way back from Sardinia, to let her give me that white tablecloth that I didn't want and she didn't want to keep. It's a present for you, it's very important, I don't want to keep these things, and you're the only one who knows why.

In the end I'd accepted the tablecloth, which she had put in a plastic bag, and I'd gone off with it. Then I'll have all the time in the world to wonder why she'd been so keen for me to take it, and when I'd held that tablecloth in my hands almost with regret, as if Tana had given me something that humiliated me and wounded me all the more because it didn't mean to. I don't know why, but I'd rather she hadn't given me that bit of fabric, I don't like relics, it was too white, too embroidered, and too simple and too beautiful all at the same time; it was too bitter a gift, a sign of failure – a failure? But what had I hoped for, what had I expected of our little trip to Sardinia, Tonino, Tana and her sister, when we'd been welcomed by the girls' uncle? Oh, yes, that famous uncle. His Ferrari cap clamped on his head. The Pirelli calendars on the walls. And everywhere, in every room, beside each chair, ashtrays bearing car trademarks and half-naked girls to make them look attractive (unless it's the other way round?)

He was the one who fed us, every day. A few friends, and particularly his cocker spaniels, which he had called Zeus and Apollo like the dogs in *Magnum*, because Magnum drives a Ferrari and has a moustache, like the girls' uncle. He was delighted to have us there, to talk to his nieces and to us, more than happy to do the cooking. In the evening we ate outside and sat for hours talking and drinking red wine. He had a radio-cassette player and, from one evening to the next, we had to listen to the same Italian songs, the same looped easy-listening music, as the midges and mosquitoes whirled above us, and the moths crashed noisily against the glass of the lantern above the table.

We spent three weeks down there. It's both a long and a short time, long enough to start picking up habits and losing them as soon as you've got them. Tana and Grazia reacquired the ones they'd had in their uncle's house before, while we made up our own without deliberately inventing them. Tonino and I slept in the same room, on a mattress on the floor. The two girls each had their own room, and their uncle lived on the ground floor, where he waited for us every morning, on the terrace, having made coffee and toast, all accompanied by the radio and the Italian songs (but turned down low, because he thought he'd worked out that Tana wasn't exactly a fan of the local music).

Every time we took the car during those three weeks, we saw the same dry vegetation along the roadside, the arid ground and prickly pears as high as walls, their flaps all facing in different directions until they collapsed in on themselves. The fig trees and the stems of the high grass, frail as matches and the same colour; a smell of aniseed ran through our stay, and the smell of mud just before Cabras, yes, that's it, all those smells and all that distance in the car, with Grazia constantly wanting to hear the Bee Gees, come on! Again! Put on the other side! And Tonino looking in the rear-view mirror and finding Grazia's eyes, telling her he was going to stop in the road and chuck her out along with that bloody cassette that we'd been laughing at since the Auvergne at least, so no, not now, no way, too bad for Grazia if she missed the party, but by now we weren't laughing that much at *staying alive, staying alive*, and if we wanted to stay alive too, it would have to stop, we'd had enough, quite enough; she laughed to hear Tonino swearing that he was going to strangle her with the cassette tape or hang her up by her feet with it, turn her into a mummy, make her eat the whole tape in a Bolognese sauce. Meanwhile the car drove on, Grazia rested her elbows on the two front seats and ended up talking to Tonino or Tana. And sitting on the back seat next to Grazia, I withdrew and looked at the passing landscape without saying a word. I snoozed, surprised to see Tana's face in the rear-view mirror when I sometimes looked out of her open window rather than mine – where the tracking shot had just filled my eyes with those images that would come with me all the way to La Bassée, and which I would think about for a long time, sitting on the little wall in the garden, watching the washing dry and especially, because it'll be windy that day and the wind will strike the embroidered fabric hard enough, that tablecloth stretched on the line, which will dance – not for very long – in the afternoon, long enough to dry in the sun and dazzle my eyes with its whiteness and its incongruous presence.

And again I will wonder why I'd accepted such a strange gift, one of those gifts that are rarely given but perhaps even more seldom refused, because Tana had shrugged as she gave it to me, suggesting that she'd already decided to give me that tablecloth when she'd arrived. I'd taken it as a kind of almost ironic compliment, as if I were worthy of her, or no, not of her, perhaps not worthy of her, but at least worthy to share her wedding presents, just as I had shared a bed with her one night on her honeymoon, in nearly the same way, wordlessly shared, which had made me take the handle of the plastic bag (I remember on the bag there was a picture of a ball of wool and a pair of scissors, the name of a shop and an address in Genoa), telling myself the same story about myself, over and over, poor you, poor Jeff, and then disgusting myself with my self-pity for my life and all the things I'll never understand. So I had taken the bag and kept it in my hand, not even trying to put it in my rucksack when we left Genoa.

Because there's that too, that I came back to La Bassée on the train, because Tonino had decided to stay down there for a few more weeks. And that image of the tablecloth from Italy floating in the blue of the sky, with the noise of the lorries crossing the rails in the background, a shake in the lorry tow-rope, then that metallic noise that wakes anyone having a siesta in La Bassée, Lecossard and Sanchez, old Lucas, and Rouard, and me too, in my own way, crushing my umpteenth cigarette beneath a furious foot. Why did I accept that tablecloth? Yes, why did I have to remember sharing a night of a honeymoon that death had just embraced, and receiving, as though it were perfectly natural, as though I were the sole possible trustee, that white embroidered tablecloth, beautiful perhaps, but so strange that I couldn't understand why Tana had given it to me, saying that I was the only one who could understand. But understand what? Oh, yes, I said to myself, why did I have to be the one that Tana chose to give that present to, when by doing so she kept me from thinking that I was closer to her than the boundary that she was setting, by appointing me guardian of the temple, and guardian, too, of the time the two of us had shared.

Looking at the outstretched tablecloth, I considered its whiteness but also its embroidered pattern, and it was as if, superimposed upon it, I saw a procession of all the images I had seen in Sardinia, through the car window: that car on fire we had seen on the road to Cagliari, the frescos on the village walls, the lack of pavements, the Piaggio delivery tricycles and the Cagliari refineries, or that pig in the middle of the road, or a white cow, eyes ringed with brown; all those images that I will suddenly remember again in the evening, when I'm reading, because other memories will come into my head, like the ones of the beach we went to every day.

Yes, we went there in the morning, all four of us together, or else we met up there. Grazia was first, without fail, and Tana was last, equally without fail. In the morning there weren't many people on the beach. You could hear the lapping of the water against the rocks, almost the only sound. Because in the morning we barely talked to each other. Grazia went swimming, soon joined by Tonino. Tana and I stayed on the beach, and it was a long time before I made up my mind to join the other two in the water, although I never quite reached them, because it took me an impossible amount of time to bear the coldness of the water, to immerse myself up to the neck, my body shivering, looking for support to keep from slipping, constantly wondering by what miracle it was that some people enjoyed moving about in water, when I had to use a whole strategy to combine breathing and stability, trying to smile and not to slip, whoops, yes, no, the first one to splash me gets my fist in their face, yes, yes, and I saw Grazia and Tonino getting

298

dangerously close; and then I got out more quickly than anticipated, because people definitely don't take you seriously when
you threaten them with a smile. But OK. Doesn't matter. Tana
watched us from the shore.

For the first week she'll have stayed like that, smoking cigarettes or reading, wearing her jacket and jeans in spite of the
heat, her grey T-shirt and a pair of jeans, trainers that she won't
take off until several days have passed, one morning when she'll
finally look up at us and start smiling, first at Grazia and
Tonino, and finally at me, or rather the poor puppet version of
me, emerging from the water with his hair plastered over his
face, followed by the other two, both dying with laughter at the
sight of me so furious, splashing, striking the surface of the
water with my palm, spitting out the water I'd gulped and
yelling at Grazia that I cursed her for cheating me, when she'd
thrown herself on top of me to make me swallow seawater. Oh
fuck, shit, bollocks and the whole dictionary of available
insults, the lot, accompanied by big waving gestures, arms in
the air to look like a moron, to turn my fear to my advantage
and make everyone laugh. And in fact it's one of the first times
we've all laughed – although I didn't really, it took me a while,
long enough to show off and pretend I'm enjoying myself, and
perhaps long enough to see and hear, through sea-blurred eyes
and blocked ears, that Tana was standing facing us, that she
had got to her feet and this time she was laughing with us.

And that laugh had left me dumbfounded. For a few seconds
I'd stayed in the water, up to my thighs, without saying anything, without moving, just seeing how Tana had taken off her
jacket and risen to her feet. She had picked up a towel and
approached the water to hold it out to me, smiling half in
mockery, half in sympathy, but most importantly she was present, really with us, as though this time she had decided to join
us, to give us the gift of her presence and her laughter, not the
way she was able to laugh over dinner in the evening, because
with her uncle laughter was an easy matter that slipped
between the wine glasses and the pasta or the tomato salad,

but simply without the resistance that she had put up between herself and us, in such a subtle, barely perceptible way that I will never, ever know how wrong I might have been to imagine I saw in her that inhibition, that resistance that wasn't in her smile, or in her gait, or even in her way of suggesting, or not suggesting, that we go to a particular place (because she was happy to suggest showing us Sardinia, and, in the evening, she liked to laugh with her uncle and involve us completely in everything that made her laugh, that made her live). So why did I have that feeling? Why, until that day, had I sensed in her a kind of mistrust of us? As though, until that moment, she had dreaded that one of us would start talking about how we met, or about Francesco, or the trial, or that sense of injustice that still hovered and would continue to hover when she opened the newspaper and plunged her eyes into those of some poor unfortunate exposed by the newspaper photographs, body covered by a rescue blanket, wild-eyed and bloody-browed, barely happy to have survived what? An explosion? An accident? A natural disaster? But extending the sequence of an endless story in which it is nothing but an illustration, which will be driven away by another illustration, leaving him more empty and isolated than if he'd simply been left alone.

So perhaps Tana was held back by her fear of hearing us, one evening, in the middle of a conversation about nothing, sport, love, marriage, football, television, travel, Belgium, causing a landslide that would carry us all away and destroy us on the spot, making it impossible for us to stay together, forcing us suddenly to lower our eyes, to be silent, to leave the next morning claiming it was an emergency and we had to go home. But we talked about nothing. Not even Tonino and me. When the two of us met up, in the room where we slept, neither Tonino nor I had mentioned wanting to talk about Tana, or the trial, or even what she might have been through during those three and a half years. For myself, I didn't want to do it any more, I felt nothing, no desire to talk about it. All I wanted was to see the collapse of the resistance that Tana put up, perhaps without even realising, but which she had shown every day, since the morning on the beach, in that way she had of sitting watching us walk towards the sea, still dressed, dark glasses covering eyes lost in the distance, towards the horizon, towards a few sailing-boats hesitating to lose themselves in the blue of the sea or the sky, or very close to us, where choughs had replaced gulls, when she sat and watched them cawing into the void and pecking at each other above the cliff.

Every morning, two women met at the top of the cliff. Each came with her dog, and Tana looked at them for a long time; the two dogs, one a setter and the other a yappy little black and white dog, surprised to see the other one, bigger and more nervous – the one that Tana was looking at as well – coming down the cliff, sniffing the earth and the stones and plunging its muzzle into the cracks, where there were holes and thick clumps of grass. It ran like a mad thing, like that, every morning. Tana watched it frolicking about as it came down that limestone cliff, so white and steep that it looked as if it would fall; the women at the top went on talking, unworried; the cliff was almost sheer, almost a vertical drop to the water, and the dog looked for the nests of the choughs that whirled around it, trying to keep it from poking its long muzzle into the cracks that riddled the cliff.

For a very long time I will see Tana on the beach again: it's from there that she's watching the dog. Every morning. She gets to her feet and leans back to see it more clearly. The dog could slip on the gravel but it isn't concerned about the danger, and neither are the women. It could fall, and if it did it might not fall into the sea but be crushed on the rocks. Tana worries about it every morning, but she says nothing about how she watches and worries, saying nothing to anyone, not wanting to show anything. From the top of the cliff, the other dog looks down. It doesn't move, and stays close to the two women who go on talking calmly, indifferent to what's going on, only distracted, from time to time, by the beauty of the sea that they have come to survey.

Sometimes Tana stays there motionless, looking at the other side of the cove, a plunging cliff where the rock has crumbled and shattered in the sea. There are huge pieces of stone, the colour of bread-crust, almost red; she also looks at the limestone peak that sticks out into the sea: it is white and porous, it looks like the head of a bird, its beak is very long, perhaps a Venetian mask, no, a white whale, no one has ever been seen there, even though there's said to be a path. In the evening, that's where the moon rises. Tana likes this place, we can tell although we don't say so, ever, for fear of disturbing her calm and her need for privacy. And then there's that morning when all of a sudden she's there, in front of me, with a towel in her hands. I'm getting out of the water, furious because Grazia and Tonino are still enjoying splashing me, and I notice that Tana has taken off her trainers. She's barefoot, she's taken off her denim jacket, which is rolled up in a ball next to our things. I can still hear Grazia and Tonino's voices. I can hear their legs moving in the water. They are walking towards us, both laughing at my bad mood, but I'm not in a bad mood any more, I'm there, I come out of the water and I've taken the towel that Tana has held out to me – and it's at that very moment that I notice the thing that I hadn't seen before, or hadn't wanted to notice, when I doubtless could have done, except no, perhaps not, perhaps it was impossible to guess its presence because of the denim jacket or the bracelets, with all those bracelets that cover her wrist with a rattle that you quickly get used to and learn to ignore. But I know: I wipe my face. I hear the movements of the water behind me and breathe so hard, my ears are blocked, and the sounds that reach me are muffled and distant, but her face is very close, and for the first time I become aware of total trust. She has kept on her sunglasses, but I know she's completely with us now, and her skin is already less white, the freckles have begun to reawaken her face, still very gently, a few beneath her eyes, her nose, that's all. I have time to see that she's tied up her hair, that she's made a ponytail. Is that why I sense that she's coming back towards us? I don't dare to think *towards me*, I don't think it's me she's coming back to. So I use the towel to hide my collar-bones, too thin, too white. I smile with a forced smile, long and embarrassed, which I camouflage still further by drying my hair because, when I see her, I'm worried that Tana will catch my eye, that she will guess what I've seen. And that's partly why I laugh and turn back towards Grazia and Tonino, to hide the fact that this time I've seen it – even if it's fine and white and yet wide enough to be unmistakable – that L-shaped swelling at the base of her wrist: the scar that runs up to her forearm.

And immediately it's nothing, it doesn't matter, I start running in the water like a lunatic, splashing the two others and yelling, and they both run towards the beach. Tana has time to get back, but she gets splashed in turn, and all four of us laugh. Soon it'll be time to go for lunch, to go back to the uncle's house, on foot, as we do every day, enjoying walking barefoot on the concrete slabs, and leaving the afternoon to heat and the sun, then to children, whole families and young people who turn up in gangs. Late every afternoon we look at the same women who come with their children and spend their time talking to each other. We meet up with that young couple that we recognise immediately because he has his arm in plaster and she takes advantage of the fact to drench him as soon as he puts his camping seat too close to the water. Everyone here seems to know each other. I'm a bit surprised that neither Tana nor Grazia knows anyone, when they've often been here before, but I don't dare ask any questions. I could, I sense that I could, but instead I hold back. However, Tana isn't wearing her denim jacket any more, she's in a T-shirt, sometimes she wears a bathing costume. She has her hair in a ponytail, and her freckles have gained ground on her face. She keeps her sunglasses on and I often catch her looking at children on the sand, playfully throwing handfuls of wet sand at one another; they use a rock as an improvised diving-board, call to each other and shout a lot. Their mothers are there, and perhaps Tana is looking at them too, they're almost the same age as she but they already look much older. There's something heavy abut their limbs, their pale thighs, their soft bellies.

But she's too white, too, her skin almost pink, not white like mine, but the kind of whiteness on which freckles quickly appear, a few, which will never hide her thinness, which I will think about again on the train, on my way back to La Bassée, when I have to agree to go back while Tonino extends his stay in Casella, and it'll be time for me to allow the thoughts that I've kept muzzled until then to ebb away, even before I get rid of that tablecloth – it's the plastic bag that I'll keep for longest, for years, under the pretext that I don't know which object to keep, not the object, in fact, long since forgotten, but the plastic bag that's supposed to keep it protected against the outside world – so before reflecting that I won't be able to keep that tablecloth and going to get it from the washing line where it will have stopped drying, before ironing it and folding it, before even deciding to give it to the first person who comes to see us – and that person will come the following day, Marthe, who lives on the other side of the street, and whom my mother will have met at the market.

That's what will happen when I get back, because I won't be able to keep the tablecloth, it'll be impossible, there will be too many questions already, too many ideas, words held back or mumbled so as not to be forced to get rid of the tablecloth – yes, give it to a neighbour, someone who will like it, because for me it would always have that weight, that bitterness, bound to that presence behind the story of that poor bit of fabric. And still, I'll also have to wonder how Tana could have imagined that I would accept her gift *with pleasure*. Couldn't she guess, couldn't she understand what that meant, accepting a gift like that, while on returning to Montoggio the first thing she did was throw away all those old cardboard boxes squatting amidst the furniture, and the cutlery we'd had our lunch with, after throwing away the glasses before her mother's outraged glare, but without asking any questions, without saying anything, just hesitating about the tablecloth and giving it to

304

me a few days later, when I left, at Genoa railway station. And when she tells us she threw away a pile of old things, saying only that she couldn't bring herself to throw away that table-cloth and that she'd like me to keep it in memory of her, yes, I understood what it was that she'd thrown away, and Tonino understood as well.

But in the train, and then later, in La Bassée, whether in my basement room or outside, sitting in front of the house, between the plum tree and the acacia, even though I may stop reading to think, to go back to the kitchen to pour a *menthe à l'eau* and drink it on the balcony, smoke on the concrete steps, even though I'll have managed to give the tablecloth to a neighbour, well, anyway, my heart will still tremble at the idea of that scar, the glimpse I had of that scar and the fear that Tana might see my glance, my surprise, that she might ask me, vaguely embarrassed, oh . . . that? And at first I'll wonder, of course, why she had done that, that movement, why she had done it, why she had had to think of doing it? But most impor-tantly, the real question that will arise is about knowing when it was from, because it'll take time to convince me that that scar happened before Francesco's death and not after. Because in the end, it could all have happened before, there was a life before, and what did that life consist of? And then, if it had happened before, everything would be different for me, includ-ing the reason why she'd given me the tablecloth, the thing I was supposed to understand, the thing she said I alone could understand; I'll have to think that it wasn't what had hap-pened in Brussels, it was something that united the two of us secretly, but at a greater distance, from deeper down and longer ago, as old as a father going off to get some cigarettes and never coming back,

but no, my thoughts will stumble over that idea. Not an idea, a flaw. Impossible. I won't let it. Everything else. Just as for months I'll have to see her smile fading more and more each day, metamorphosing and leaving Tana looking more like herself each day than she ever did before. Rejecting, I've rejected everything. Just like the day after my father's death when I decided to write down everything about him, to make a book about him, his life, his death, and the feeling of shame with the notebook only just opened, the impossibility of shame, shame and the obligation to do what is forbidden, and resolve not to do it and be consumed by the imperative to resign oneself, but another day, another time,

and I will think of that, looking at the tablecloth in its plastic bag, then I will try to stop thinking about it and, each night, I will think again of Tana and why she had such a special tenderness for me, that look on her face as she handed me the plastic bag and then kissed me – and my shame at having seen something else in that expression, or having waited for it when I should have known it all straight away, or at least since the second week of the holidays: yes, they're both there, the two sisters. And now there's a sort of game between them, they laugh often. I'm not enjoying the water so much any more, I stay on the beach.

And now, gently, it's Tana who steps towards the water, her outline is so slender, so white, it looks fragile but it isn't. On the contrary, her body is lithe and muscular; she likes the water, you can tell she likes swimming. The pleasure doesn't return to her straight away. First of all she walks in the water for quite a long time, then stays like that, the water is up to her hips, she looks at me and laughs, she says it's a bit cold. Her arms spread from her body, her hands flat on the water. She steps forwards and walks towards Grazia and Tonino, who are already quite far away. I'm reading *Don Quixote*, but my eyes keep slipping back to Tana, watching her plunge into the water and disappear completely. She slipped without a sound, barely stirring the water. Having slipped beneath, she reappears a few metres off. Her hair sticks to her face, soon she's nothing to me but a silhouette. When she gets back, she'll say she hadn't been swimming for years. Yes. Perhaps three years. Maybe more? I wonder. The days follow one another like that, with the feeling of a knot finally being untied, the original suspicion making way for trust, deep, fluid relaxation, like the unreflective, unhampered breathing of someone asleep.

I've learned a few words of Italian and in the evening, when we've had a couple of drinks, I start talking to everyone, whether it's the uncle or Grazia, Tana and Tonino, in Italian, and understand it as well as if it were my own language, a nimble language that tells me that all people can understand each other when they're slightly drunk. We laugh easily, at nothing, I don't even know what we're talking about. Tonight Tana's uncle turned up the radio and asked her to dance. She danced with him, with her uncle. They're on the balcony. It's night, and the night is surprisingly mild; the moon is white, the night is pale and glowing. Grazia wants me to dance with her, she insists. A waltz or a slow dance to an Italian pop song, a *ti amo* that Grazia hums, taking me by the arm, OK, then. We dance, the two of us, Grazia and me, while Tonino watches us and pours himself some more of the red wine we've already drunk too much of, apart from Grazia, whose uncle is keeping an eye on her to make sure she doesn't drink too much. But he's had a bit to drink himself, although less than Tonino and me, and certainly less than Tana, who is drinking a lot, and quickly. She likes to drink till she's exhausted. Wine doesn't make her say things she would regret. On the contrary. She talks less, she watches with a smile, then her eyes close, her strength leaves her. But not tonight.

Tonight I'm dancing with Grazia. The wine makes her head spin, even if she hasn't drunk very much and, in spite of Grazia's laughter and her youthful way of making herself unbearable, touching, yes, sometimes unbearable but still touching, I can't help wondering whether she knows that pressing yourself against a boy is a game that can degenerate quite seriously, or how aware she is that the shapes of her body have already left far behind the childhood in which her age still holds her trapped. But OK. Let's not get annoyed. Of course she knows. She laughs with all her heart, she wants to rest her head on my shoulder and whispers a *ti amo* with a seriousness and sincerity that send a cold shiver down my spine – hey, steady on, not quite ready for that, thank you, that's all I need.

And then the night wears on, and the girls' uncle goes to bed.

For the first time, it's Tana who decides to go to the beach. The night is wearing on, what time can it be? Take a midnight dip, straight away? why not? we haven't done that yet; so, OK. Grazia is the first to say yes, she looks at me and says we can go to the beach, it would be fun to swim at night. You don't want to? No, I don't want to, but I pick up the bottle of grappa from the table, right, then, let's go. The beach is deserted. At the end, the beak shape, or whale shape, hangs over the water and seems to dive into it – it's almost black, and above it the sky is a milky blue, a day-for-night sort of blue, too pale beneath a tiny, white moon that falls upon the water very far out, where the sailing-boats will disappear into the morning when I look at them from here, on the sand. And this time the sand is packed, damp and a little bit cold. I'm the only one who doesn't go in; I look at the three of them, they're only a few metres away from me and they're laughing so loudly that the echo of their voices seems to resonate around the cove. I see their clothes where they've dropped them in front of me, like old skins that they don't need any more. Laughing, they plunge into the water, Grazia tries to draw attention to herself, splashing the two others; but they round on her and both of them, Tana and Tonino, run at her, splashing as they do so. From the beach I can see their silhouettes, the glittering spray of water like shards of golden light on the surface of the sea; and then Grazia stops shouting and laughing, she comes out of the water and joins me. She's cold. She wraps herself up in a towel and, sitting beside me, she wants to take my hand. I smile at her and tell her she mustn't – I'm speaking French but she understands what I'm saying – we're not the same age, she has to understand that; I vaguely want to touch her, stroke her breasts, but no, I know what complications that would lead to. I push her away and she moans playfully, complaining, telling

308

me I'm not being nice, and perhaps for fun, too. And then she gets to her feet and says goodbye to me with a shrug. I watch her walk away, thinking that perhaps, for her, the moment means something that I don't fully understand, but I don't care. I watch her in her one-piece swimsuit, she climbs back up to her uncle's house, wrapped in her towel, her clothes under her arms; she doesn't turn round.

Now I want to have another drink. The grappa burns the back of my throat, but never mind, I have to go on drinking because I know, even though I can't see them, that Tana and Tonino have swum as far as the strip of stone in the distance, and that perhaps they've even swum back close to where I am. I know it isn't the alcohol or smoking too much that is blurring my ideas and giving the sound of the water against the rocks that gentleness, that calm in the night – perhaps because the night is bright – and enwraps the world to protect it; there's nothing to understand, nothing to wait for, just listen to that long night walking, surprised to find us there, all three of us, so old already, and so tired. And when I hear Tana and Tonino laughing, I grasp rather than see that Tana is lying down, she's on her back, trying to float on her back. Tonino is beside her, he wants to help her, but she's arguing and saying she can't do it, it's a thing she can't do. I haven't got up, the world has re-entered me, and all of a sudden it feels as if I know that sensation, that intoxication that comes from witnessing the world, keeping myself on the margin, feet straight, breath bated, nearly falling into an unknown precipice. As though I were there among the shadows, and they were watching them with me, Tonino and Tana, themselves silhouettes in the darkness; but the night is wakeful, it embraces them as Tonino is now embracing Tana. It bends over them and kisses them as Tonino kisses Tana, dissolving the world around them, slaughtering it with happiness and indifference, as if the shadows on the shore were incredulously clinging to one another, breath bated, waiting for the dizziness to stop.